PAT

THE ULTIMATE CYBERPUNK

PAT CADIGAN, acclaimed by the *London Guardian* as "the Queen of Cyberpunk," is the author of four novels—*Mind-players, Synners, Fools*, and *Tea from an Empty Cup*—and three short story collections: *Patterns, Home by the Sea*, and *Dirty Work*. Some of her short stories have also appeared in *Letters from Home*, alongside work by Karen Joy Fowler and Pat Murphy. Pat continues to publish short fiction, with recent stories in *New Worlds, Dark Terrors 3, Disco 2000*, and the Christmas 2001 issue of *Interzone*. Born in Schenectady, New York, she grew up in Fitchburg, Massachusetts, where she attended the University of Massachusetts on a scholarship, eventually transferring to the University of Kansas, where she received her degree. Pat was an editor and writer for Hallmark Cards in Kansas City for ten years before embarking on her career as a fiction writer in 1987. Since that time her Hugo and Nebula Award-nominated short stories have appeared in such magazines as *Omni, The Magazine of Fantasy and Science Fiction*, and *Isaac Asimov's Science Fiction Magazine*, as well as numerous anthologies. Her first collection, Patterns, was honored with the Locus Award in 1990. She moved to England in 1996, and now lives in North London with her husband, Chris Fowler, and their cat, Calgary.

THE ULTIMATE CYBERPUNK

PAT CADIGAN

Editor

ibooks
new york
www.ibooks.net

DISTRIBUTED BY SIMON & SCHUSTER, INC

contents

CONTENTS

NOT A MANIFESTO

BY PAT CADIGAN

Excerpt from the Cadigan FAQ:
Q. Isn't cyberpunk dead?
A. If it were, you wouldn't be asking me that question.

It's been roughly two decades since the writing that was specifically identified as cyberpunk started making waves. The key phrase in the previous sentence is *specifically identified*.

Countless novels, stories, movies, analyses, deconstructions, and controversies after the fact, the only thing most people would probably agree on is that cyberpunk has left its mark not just on the genre known as science fiction, but on popular culture in general.

Now, I know somebody somewhere will take issue with that last statement, mostly out of some kind of pique. But that's the way life is, especially in the field of science fiction—no matter what you say, there's always someone somewhere ready to get in your face about it. That's actually one of the things I like most about the field. It's not that I'm always spoiling for a fight; it's knowing that I'd better have substantial thought behind whatever I say, because someone will call me on it. I find this sort of thing far preferable to cozy group-think.

Of course, this doesn't necessarily mean I'll end up being swayed. I might not even react politely. But I try not to make a rude noise before hearing anyone out.

The first thing many people might take issue with is the title on the cover of this book.

The prime mover behind this anthology has put the rather grandiose word "ultimate" in the title. To tell the truth, I don't concur, but this is publishing and publishing has never been an easy business. The struggle to survive affects people in various ways; the tendency to hyperbole is one of the more innocuous, in that it's free, legal, and doesn't require lengthy stays in expensive rehab facilities. So just deal with it, OK?

Now, where was I?

I'm not going to attempt a definitive history of cyberpunk, science fiction, or popular culture. I'm only an end-user—I just work here. My career as a professional writer began at roughly the same time that cyberpunk started to make its presence felt in the area of literature I chose to work in. I'd call it a coincidence, except for the fact that I use Chad Mulligan's definition of that word: "You weren't paying attention to the first half of what was going on." Synchronicity is really more like it. John Shirley called cyberpunk tribal, which is probably the most accurate description—the writers associated with it were of the same generation and prone to similar cultural influences, ranging from their politics to their preferences in music. And, of course, they were all science fiction writers.

Many people only marginally involved with SF—i.e., casual readers as opposed to those active in the subculture called "fandom"—have asked me why cyberpunk was so controversial, why it seemed to arouse such a degree of hostility from some quarters.

Not being an anthropologist or a behavioral psychologist, I can't come up with an expert, plausible theory, let alone a definitive answer. As someone who was there, of course, I naturally have my own opinions, but opinions are like, uh, well, you know—everybody's got one. For that matter, opinions are even more like nostrils, in that everybody usually has two.

At the end of the day, however, this is a completely unimportant question unless you *are* an anthropologist or a behavioral psychologist. If the hostility in question had had any real effect on cyberpunk—if a *fatwah* had been issued on one or more of the writers, if they had been jailed, censored, or killed, we'd be talking about something serious.

But nobody died. Nobody even took a hit in a bar fight. There were a few articles and reviews that got more personal and/or nasty than they should have been—not exactly unprecedented in the history of the written word. The original Gutenberg Bible probably had at least one review that was actually a whetstone for some ax-grinding.

But, as I said, nobody died. The would-be hostility didn't stop the books and the stories and the commentaries and, eventually, inevitably, the movies. That last is a subject for some other treatise, written by someone far more knowledgeable than I am.

Why was there so much hostility to cyberpunk? Jeez, I don't know—put it down to human nature. People are funny.

Not all of the questions or challenges put to the concept of cyberpunk were trivial displays of hostility, nor should they be regarded that way. Alert and thoughtful readers, familiar with science fiction from its pulp beginnings through the

New Wave all the way up to what's coming out tomorrow, have pointed out that cyberpunk itself is hardly brand-new, totally original and never-before-seen. Alfred Bester did it, they say, and Samuel Delany; Cordwainer Smith, Norman Spinrad, Harlan-for-chrissakes-Ellison.

True enough, no argument here. In fact, William Gibson has acknowledged Samuel Delany's influence on his work, and Delany has acknowledged Bester's. I acknowledge them as well, along with J.G. Ballard, the aforementioned Cordwainer Smith, and the almost never mentioned James Tiptree, Jr./Alice Sheldon.

To this end, I have included a few of these root stories. Many will argue with my choices; argue away. I tried to choose work that would be representative but by no means exclusive. Constraints of time and space—mostly space—have meant this cannot be a definitive selection of cyberpunk's forebears. Just deal with it, OK?

Now, where was I?

So if cyberpunk is not original, why didn't it happen with Delany or Bester? What was so special about William Gibson, et al?

Timing, of course. It's all in the timing.

Popular culture in general is a reflection, warts and all, of what's going on in its society. That goes double for science fiction; maybe even triple.

We—i.e., the science fiction field—had the concept of cyberspace long before we had the word itself. But we didn't have the word until we had cyberspace itself for real. William Gibson gave us the term along with the observation that "The street finds its own uses for things." Once we had cyberspace in the form of the desktop computer, the technological trinity was complete: the telephone, the television, and the personal computer. These items have since merged into one unit with three functions.

Cordwainer Smith and Alfred Bester most certainly did not grow up watching television as the cyberpunk writers did; I doubt it played as much a part in Samuel Delany's background as it did in ours.

To see the Vietnam War live on television as an adult is one kind of life experience; to see it at the age of thirteen is something else entirely.

Of course, we already have a generation of adults who grew up without seeing the Vietnam War on TV and don't remember not having a personal computer in the house. Time marches on, and it will make of future writers what it will. Time, and timing.

A limited number of pages also meant that the selection of recognized original cyberpunk authors as well as those whose careers began later is not definitive. Elsewhere you will find Bruce Sterling's reading list, which I cribbed off the net so that you can expand your horizons. It's certainly a good place to start any serious reading.

In any case, many of the more well-known and/or familiar stories won't be here. There is no point, after all, in simply reprinting most of *Mirrorshades*. Of course, *Mirrorshades* does get it right (and of course, I'm biased), but *Mirrorshades* is not all there is.

Not any more.

One more question from the Cadigan FAQ that I've been asked possibly more often than any other has to do with women writers, or rather, the lack of them. I was the only female writer in *Mirrorshades;* two decades later, things have changed . . . but not much.

In the past, science fiction itself was not just male-dominated but male-oriented, so much so that the female author usually used her initials and surname—e.g., "C.L. Moore"—for the sake of, well, not alienating the male readership. Younger readers will find it hard to get their minds around this one. My sixteen-year-old son even accused me of making this up. I'm not going to go into a history of sex roles in western civilization—you've heard it, I've heard it, and I feel a deeper obligation to the future than to the past. But I will note for the record that American women have had the legal right to vote for fewer than one hundred years, and that as late as 1977, my own health insurance would not cover out-of-wedlock pregnancy, or the birth of a child in wedlock whose conception obviously occurred before the legal marriage.

As I said earlier, people are funny.

So how does this account for the continuing dearth of women cyberpunk writers? Is the field that sexist? Does the relative scarcity of women in cyberpunk prove that it's somehow completely invalid?

Actually, all it proves is that sometimes, gender is a red herring. Sometimes, evaluating an area of the arts by counting the number of men or women active in it is to miss the point entirely. I hesitate to use the term *political correctness*, mostly because it's a charge that has often been unfairly made against people who haven't stopped questioning the *status quo*. On the other hand, one size does *not* fit all, and one standard does not measure all; looks can be deceiving and sometimes a cigar is just a cigar.

I think it's safe to say that if someone were to identify a movement of writers composed almost entirely of women, it would not be immediately dismissed as fake or unacceptable. It wouldn't go uncriticized, of course—are you kidding?!—but the biology of the writers could not be the sole consideration for *all* criticism, favorable and unfavorable.

Cyberpunk was never concerned with the biology of the writers involved, regardless of what anyone might think. To force the issue of how many men vs. how many women there are is simply another way to begin from an improper assumption—i.e., like asking someone, "So when did you *stop* beating your children?" Or perhaps, "So, Pat Cadigan, sole woman cyberpunk—how is it you write like a man?" Or my favorite: "Isn't it amazing how all those cyberpunk guys write like a woman?"

Bottom line: *I don't know why there aren't more women SF writers whose work could be identified as cyberpunk.*

Did I mention people are funny?

Well, I can't and won't presume to speak for other writers of any sexual persuasion. I will only tell you this: most of the time, I don't identify myself as anything but a science fiction writer—which is to say, I don't add a gender-specific qualifier.

I say most of the time because I do allow (or compel) my publishers to use the blurb "the Queen of Cyberpunk," bestowed on me by the *London Guardian* back in the mid-1990s. I like it; it makes me feel good. It's what they called me—they used the word "queen" because they noticed I was female. Believe me, if they'd said "King of Cyberpunk," I'd be using that one with equal relish. Likewise, "Supreme Deity of Cyberpunk," or even "The Ultimate Cyberpunk."

Did I mention publishing is a tough business?

So, that's about all I have to say. If you're disappointed not to find a detailed history of cyberpunk here, well, sorry about that. But that's something you can find in any number of places, although I would recommend consulting *The Encyclopedia of Science Fiction*, edited by John Clute and Peter

Nicholls, for information on cyberpunk or anything else having to do with science fiction.

The original *Mirrorshades* is still The Daddy, as it were. Many readers will find it valuable historically, but it is remains a damned fine anthology of fiction. When I re-read it, I don't feel nostalgic—instead, I'm reminded of how important it is to stay alert to the milieu, to keep asking what Theodore Sturgeon called The Next Question.

Cyberpunk—a term I'll continue to use until someone comes up with a better one—has never shied away from asking The Next Question. That's why it still works. After two decades, the new may have worn off and there's as much grey hair as there is chrome, but the energy is still there.

FONDLY
FAHRENHEIT

ALFRED BESTER

He doesn't know which of us I am these days, but they know one truth. You must own nothing but yourself. You must make your own life, live your own life and die your own death... or else you will die another's.

The rice fields on Paragon III stretch for hundreds of miles like checkerboard tundras, a blue and brown mosaic under a burning sky of orange. In the evening, clouds whip like smoke, and the paddies rustle and murmur.

A long line of men marched across the paddies the evening we escaped from Paragon III. They were silent, armed, intent; a long rank of silhouetted statues looming against the smoking sky. Each man carried a gun. Each man wore a walkie-talkie belt pack, the speaker button in his ear, the microphone bug clipped to his throat, the glowing viewscreen strapped to his wrist like a green-eyed watch. The multitude of screens showed nothing but a multitude of individual paths through the paddies. The annunciators uttered no sound but the rustle and splash of steps. The men spoke infrequently, in heavy grunts, all speaking to all.

"Nothing here."

"Where's here?"

"Jenson's fields."

"You're drifting too far west."

"Close in the line there."

"Anybody covered the Grimson paddy?"

"Yeah. Nothing."

"She couldn't have walked this far."

"Could have been carried."

"Think she's alive?"

"Why should she be dead?"

The slow refrain swept up and down the long line of beaters advancing toward the smoky sunset. The line of beaters wavered like a writhing snake, but never ceased its remorseless advance. One hundred men spaced fifty feet apart. Five thousand feet of ominous search. One mile of angry determination stretching from east to west across a compass of heat. Evening fell. Each man lit his search lamp. The writhing snake was transformed into a necklace of wavering diamonds.

"Clear here. Nothing."

"Nothing here."

"Nothing."

"What about the Allen paddies?"

"Covering them now."

"Think we missed her?"

"Maybe."

"We'll beat back and check."

"This'll be an all-night job."

"Allen paddies clear."

"God damn! We've got to find her!"

"We'll find her."

"Here she is. Sector seven. Tune in."

The line stopped. The diamonds froze in the heat. There

was silence. Each man gazed into the glowing screen on his wrist, tuning to sector seven. All tuned to one. All showed a small nude figure awash in the muddy water of a paddy. Alongside the figure an owner's stake of bronze read: VAN-DALEUR. The end of the line converged toward the Vandaleur field. The necklace turned into a cluster of stars. One hundred men gathered around a small nude body, a child dead in a rice paddy. There was no water in her mouth. There were fingermarks on her throat. Her innocent face was battered. Her body was torn. Clotted blood on her skin was crusted and hard.

"Dead three-four hours at least."

"Her mouth is dry."

"She wasn't drowned. Beaten to death."

In the dark evening heat the men swore softly. They picked up the body. One stopped the others and pointed to the child's fingernails. She had fought her murderer. Under the nails were particles of flesh and bright drops of scarlet blood, still liquid, still uncoagulated.

"That blood ought to be clotted, too."

"Funny."

"Not so funny. What kind of blood don't clot?"

"Android."

"Looks like she was killed by one."

"Vandaleur owns an android."

"She couldn't be killed by an android."

"That's android blood under her nails."

"The police better check."

"The police'll prove I'm right."

"But andys can't kill."

"That's android blood, ain't it?"

"Androids can't kill. They're made that way."

"Looks like one android was made wrong."

"Jesus!"

And the thermometer that day registered 92.9° gloriously Fahrenheit.

So there we were aboard the *Paragon Queen* enroute for Megaster V, James Vandaleur and his android. James Vandaleur counted his money and wept. In the second-class cabin with him was his android, a magnificent synthetic creature with classic features and wide blue eyes. Raised on its forehead in a cameo of flesh were the letters MA, indicating that this was one of the rare multiple-aptitude androids, worth $57,000 on the current exchange. There we were, weeping and counting and calmly watching.

"Twelve, fourteen, sixteen. Sixteen hundred dollars," Vandaleur wept. "That's all. Sixteen hundred dollars. My house was worth ten thousand. The land was worth five. There was furniture, cars, my paintings, etchings, my plane, my—And nothing to show for everything but sixteen hundred dollars. Christ!"

I leaped up from the table and turned on the android. I pulled a strap from one of the leather bags and beat the android. It didn't move.

"I must remind you," the android said, "that I am worth fifty-seven thousand dollars on the current exchange. I must warn you that you are endangering valuable property."

"You damned crazy machine," Vandaleur shouted.

"I am not a machine," the android answered. "The robot is a machine. The android is a chemical creation of synthetic tissue."

"What got into you?" Vandaleur cried, "Why did you do it? Damn you!" He beat the android savagely.

"I must remind you that I cannot be punished," I said. "The pleasure-pain syndrome is not incorporated in the android synthesis."

"Then why did you kill her?" Vandaleur shouted. "If it wasn't for kicks, why did you—"

"I must remind you," the android said, "that the second-class cabins in these ships are not soundproofed."

Vandaleur dropped the strap and stood panting, staring at the creature he owned.

"Why did you do it? Why did you kill her?" I asked.

"I don't know;" I answered.

"First it was malicious mischief. Small things. Petty destruction. I should have known there was something wrong with you then. Androids can't destroy. They can't harm. They—"

"There is no pleasure-pain syndrome incorporated in the android synthesis."

"Then it got to arson. Then serious destruction. Then assault . . . that engineer on Rigel. Each time worse. Each time we had to get out faster. Now it's murder. Christ! What's the matter with you? What's happened?"

"There are no self-check relays incorporated in the android brain."

"Each time we had to get out it was a step downhill. Look at me. In a second-class cabin. Me. James Paleologue Vandaleur. There was a time when my father was the wealthiest—Now, sixteen hundred dollars in the world. That's all I've got. And you. Christ damn you!"

Vandaleur raised the strap to beat the android again, then dropped it and collapsed on a berth, sobbing. At last he pulled himself together.

"Instructions," he said.

The multiple android responded at once. It arose and awaited orders.

"My name is now Valentine. James Valentine. I stopped off on Paragon III for only one day to transfer to this ship for Megaster V. My occupation: Agent for one privately owned MA android which is for hire. Purpose of visit: To settle on Megaster V. Fix the papers."

The android removed Vandaleur's passport and papers from a bag, got pen and ink and sat down at the table. With an accurate, flawless hand—an accomplished hand that could draw, write, paint, carve, engrave, etch, photograph, design, create, and build—it meticulously forged new credentials for Vandaleur. Its owner watched me miserably.

"Create and build," I muttered. "And now destroy. Oh God! What am I going to do? Christ! If I could only get rid of you. If I didn't have to live off you. God! If only I'd inherited some guts instead of you."

Dallas Brady was Megaster's leading jewelry designer. She was short, stocky, amoral and a nymphomaniac. She hired Vandaleur's multiple-aptitude android and put me to work in her shop. She seduced Vandaleur. In her bed one night, she asked abruptly, "Your name's Vandaleur, isn't it?"

"Yes," I murmured. Then: "No! It's Valentine. James Valentine."

"What happened on Paragon?" Dallas Brady asked. "I thought androids couldn't kill or destroy property. Prime Directives and Inhibitions set up for them when they're synthesized. Every company guarantees they can't."

"Valentine!" Vandaleur insisted.

"Oh come off it," Dallas Brady said. "I've known for a week. I haven't hollered copper, have I?"

"The name is Valentine."

"You want to prove it? You want I should call the cops?" Dallas reached out and picked up the phone.

"For God's sake, Dallas!" Vandaleur leaped up and struggled to take the phone from her. She fended him off, laughing at him, until he collapsed and wept in shame and helplessness.

"How did you find out?" he asked at last.

"The papers are full of it. And Valentine was a little too close to Vandaleur. That wasn't smart, was it?"

"I guess not. I'm not very smart."

"Your android's got quite a record, hasn't it? Assault. Arson. Destruction. What happened on Paragon?"

"It kidnapped a child. Took her out into the rice fields and murdered her."

"Raped her?"

"I don't know."

"They're going to catch up with you."

"Don't I know it? Christ! We've been running for two years now. Seven planets in two years. I must have abandoned fifty thousand dollars' worth of property in two years."

"You better find out what's wrong with it."

"How can I? Can I walk into a repair clinic and ask for an overhaul? What am I going to say? 'My android's just turned killer. Fix it.' They'd call the police right off." I began to shake. "They'd have that android dismantled inside one day. I'd probably be booked as accessory to murder."

"Why didn't you have it repaired before it got to murder?"

"I couldn't take the chance," Vandaleur explained angrily. "If they started fooling around with lobotomies and body chemistry and endocrine surgery, they might have destroyed its aptitudes. What would I have left to hire out? How would I live?"

"You could work yourself. People do."

"Work at what? You know I'm good for nothing. How could I compete with specialist androids and robots? Who can, unless he's got a terrific talent for a particular job?"

"Yeah. That's true."

"I lived off my old man all my life. Damn him! He had

to go bust just before he died. Left me the android and that's all. The only way I can get along is living off what it earns."

"You better sell it before the cops catch up with you. You can live off fifty grand. Invest it."

"At three percent? Fifteen hundred a year? When the android returns fifteen percent on its value? Eight thousand a year. That's what it earns. No, Dallas, I've got to go along with it."

"What are you going to do about its violence kick?"

"I can't do anything . . . except watch it and pray. What are you going to do about it?"

"Nothing. It's none of my business. Only one thing. . . . I ought to get something for keeping my mouth shut."

"What?"

"The android works for me for free. Let somebody else pay you, but I get it for free."

The multiple-aptitude android worked. Vandaleur collected its fees. His expenses were taken care of. His savings began to mount. As the warm spring of Megaster V turned to hot summer, I began investigating farms and properties. It would be possible, within a year or two, for us to settle down permanently, provided Dallas Brady's demands did not become rapacious.

On the first hot day of summer, the android began singing in Dallas Brady's workshop. It hovered over the electric furnace which, along with the weather, was broiling the shop, and sang an ancient tune that had been popular half a century before.

Oh, it's no feat to beat the heat.
All reet! All reet!
So jeet your seat
Be fleet be fleet

Cool and discreet
Honey . . .

It sang in a strange, halting voice, and its accomplished fingers were clasped behind its back, writhing in a strange rumba all their own. Dallas Brady was surprised.

"You happy or something?" she asked.

"I must remind you that the pleasure-pain syndrome is not incorporated in the android synthesis," I answered. "All reet! All reet! Be fleet be fleet, cool and discreet, honey . . ."

Its fingers stopped their writhing and picked up a heavy pair of iron tongs. The android poked them into the glowing heart of the furnace, leaning far forward to peer into the lovely heat.

"Be careful, you damned fool!" Dallas Brady exclaimed. "You want to fall in?"

"I must remind you that I am worth fifty-seven thousand dollars on the current exchange," I said. "It is forbidden to endanger valuable property. All reet! All reet! Honey . . ."

It withdrew a crucible of glowing gold from the electric furnace, turned, capered hideously, sang crazily, and splashed a sluggish gobbet of molten gold over Dallas Brady's head. She screamed and collapsed, her hair and clothes flaming, her skin crackling. The android poured again while it capered and sang.

"Be fleet be fleet, cool and discreet, honey . . ." It sang and slowly poured and poured the molten gold. Then I left the workshop and rejoined James Vandaleur in his hotel suite. The android's charred clothes and squirming fingers warned its owner that something was very much wrong.

Vandaleur rushed to Dallas Brady's workshop, stared once, vomited and fled. I had enough time to pack one bag and raise nine hundred dollars on portable assets. He took a third-class cabin on the *Megaster Queen*, which left that morning for Lyra Alpha. He took me with him. He wept and counted his money and I beat the android again.

And the thermometer in Dallas Brady's workshop registered 98.1° beautifully Fahrenheit.

On Lyra Alpha we holed up in a small hotel near the university. There, Vandaleur carefully bruised my forehead until the letters MA were obliterated by the swelling and the discoloration The letters would reappear again, but not for several months, and in the meantime Vandaleur hoped the hue and cry for an MA android would be forgotten. The android was hired out as a common laborer in the university power plant. Vandaleur, as James Venice, eked out life on the android's small earnings.

I wasn't too unhappy. Most of the other residents in the hotel were university students, equally hard-up, but delightfully young and enthusiastic. There was one charming girl with sharp eyes and a quick mind. Her name was Wanda, and she and her beau, Jed Stark, took a tremendous interest in the killing android which was being mentioned in every paper in the galaxy.

"We've been studying the case," she and Jed said at one of the casual student parties which happened to be held this night in Vandaleur's room. "We think we know what's causing it. We're going to do a paper." They were in a high state of excitement.

"Causing what?" somebody wanted to know.

"The android rampage."

"Obviously out of adjustment, isn't it? Body chemistry gone haywire. Maybe a kind of synthetic cancer, yes?"

"No," Wanda gave Jed a look of suppressed triumph.

"Well, what is it?"

"Something specific."

"What?"

"That would be telling."

"Oh, come on."

"Nothing doing."

"Won't you tell us?" I asked intently. "I . . . We're very much interested in what could go wrong with an android."

"No, Mr. Venice," Wanda said. "It's a unique idea and we've got to protect it. One thesis like this and we'll be set up for life. We can't take the chance of somebody stealing it."

"Can't you give us a hint?"

"No. Not a hint. Don't say a word, Jed. But I'll tell you this much, Mr. Venice. I'd hate to be the man who owns that android."

"You mean the police?" I asked.

"I mean projection, Mr. Venice. Projection! That's the danger . . . and I won't say any more. I've said too much as it is."

I heard steps outside, and a hoarse voice singing softly: "Be fleet be fleet, cool and discreet, honey . . ." My android entered the room, home from its tour of duty at the university power plant. It was not introduced. I motioned to it and I immediately responded to the command and went to the beer keg and took over Vandaleur's job of serving the guests. Its accomplished fingers writhed in a private rhumba of their own. Gradually they stopped their squirming, and the strange humming ended.

Androids were not unusual at the university. The wealthier students owned them along with cars and planes. Vandaleur's android provoked no comment, but young Wanda was sharp-eyed and quick-witted. She noted my bruised forehead and she was intent on the history-making thesis she and Jed Stark were going to write. After the party broke up, she consulted with Jed walking upstairs to her room.

"Jed, why'd that android have a bruised forehead?"

"Probably hurt itself, Wanda. It's working in the power plant. They fling a lot of heavy stuff around."

"That all?"

"What else?"

"It could be a convenient bruise."

"Convenient for what?"

"Hiding what's stamped on its forehead."

"No point to that, Wanda. You don't have to see marks on a forehead to recognise an android. You don't have to see a trademark on a car to know it's a car."

"I don't mean it's trying to pass as a human. I mean it's trying to pass as a lower grade android."

"Why?"

"Suppose it had 'MA' on its forehead."

"Multiple aptitude? Then why in hell would Venice waste it stoking furnaces if it could earn more—Oh. Oh! You mean it's—?"

Wanda nodded.

"Jesus!" Stark pursed his lips. "What do we do? Call the police?"

"No. We don't know if it's an MA for a fact. If it turns out to be an MA and the killing android, our paper comes first anyway. This is our big chance, Jed. If it's *that* android we can run a series of controlled tests and—"

"How do we find out for sure?"

"Easy. Infrared film. That'll show what's under the bruise. Borrow a camera. Buy some film. We'll sneak down to the power plant tomorrow afternoon and take some pictures. Then we'll know."

They stole down into the university power plant the following afternoon. It was a vast cellar, deep under the earth.

It was dark, shadowy, luminous with burning light from the furnace doors. Above the roar of the fires they could hear a strange voice shouting and chanting in the echoing vault: "All reet! All reet! So jeet your seat. Be fleet be fleet, cool and discreet, honey ..." And they could see a capering figure dancing a lunatic rumba in time to the music it shouted. The legs twisted. The arms waved. The fingers writhed.

Jed Stark raised the camera and began shooting his spool of infrared film, aiming the camera sights at that bobbing head. Then Wanda shrieked, for I saw them and came charging down on them, brandishing a polished steel shovel. It smashed the camera. It felled the girl and then the boy. Jed fought me for a desperate hissing moment before he was bludgeoned into helplessness. Then the android dragged them to the furnace and fed them to the flames, slowly, hideously. It capered and sang. Then it returned to my hotel.

The thermometer in the power plant registered 100.9° murderously Fahrenheit. All reet! All reet!

We bought steerage on the *Lyra Queen*, and Vandaleur and the android did odd jobs for their meals. During the night watches, Vandaleur would sit alone in the steerage head with a cardboard portfolio on his lap, puzzling over its contents. That portfolio was all he had managed to bring with him from Lyra Alpha. He had stolen it from Wanda's room. It was labeled ANDROID. It contained the secret of my sickness.

And it contained nothing but newspapers. Scores of newspapers from all over the galaxy, printed, microfilmed, engraved, etched, offset, photostated ... Rigel *Star-Banner* ... Paragon *Picayune* ... Megaster *Times-Leader* ... Lalande *Herald* ... Lacaille *Journal* ... Indi *Intelligencer* ... Eridani *Telegram-News*. All reet! All reet!

Nothing but newspapers. Each paper contained an account of one crime in the android's ghastly career. Each paper also contained news, domestic and foreign, sports, society, weather, shipping news, stock exchange quotations, human interest stories, features, contests, puzzles. Somewhere in that mass of uncollated facts was the secret Wanda and Jed Stark had discovered. Vandaleur pored over the papers helplessly. It was beyond him. So jeet your seat!

"I'll sell you," I told the android. "Damn you. When we land on Terra, I'll sell you. I'll settle for three percent on whatever you're worth."

"I am worth fifty-seven thousand dollars on the current exchange," I told him.

"If I can't sell you, I'll turn you in to the police," I said.

"I am valuable property," I answered. "It is forbidden to endanger valuable property. You won't have me destroyed."

"Christ damn you!" Vandaleur cried. "What? Are you arrogant? Do you know you can trust me to protect you? Is that the secret?"

The multiple-aptitude android regarded him with calm accomplished eyes. "Sometimes," it said, "it is a good thing to be property."

It was three below zero when the *Lyra Queen* dropped at Croydon Field. A mixture of ice and snow swept across the field, fizzing and exploding into steam under the *Queen*'s tail jets. The passengers trotted numbly across the blackened concrete to customs inspection, and thence to the airport bus that was to take them to London. Vandaleur and the android were broke. They walked.

By midnight they reached Piccadilly Circus. The December ice storm had not slackened, and the statue of Eros was encrusted with ice. They turned right, walked down to Trafalgar Square and then along the Strand shaking with cold and wet. Just above Fleet Street, Vandaleur saw a solitary figure coming from the direction of St. Paul's. He drew the android into an alley.

"We've got to have money," he whispered. He pointed at the approaching figure. "He has money. Take it from him."

"The order cannot be obeyed," the android said.

"Take it from him," Vandaleur repeated. "By force. Do you understand? We're desperate."

"It is contrary to my prime directive," I said. "I cannot endanger life or property. The order cannot be obeyed."

"For God's sake!" Vandaleur burst out. "You've attacked, destroyed, murdered. Don't gibber about prime directives. You haven't any left. Get his money. Kill him if you have to. I tell you, we're desperate!"

"It is contrary to my prime directive," I said. "I cannot endanger life or property. The order cannot be obeyed."

I thrust the android back and leaped out at the stranger. He was tall, austere, competent. He had an air of hope curdled by cynicism. He carried a cane. I saw he was blind.

"Yes?" he said. "I hear you near me. What is it?"

"Sir . . ." Vandaleur hesitated. "I'm desperate."

"We all are desperate," the stranger replied. "Quietly desperate."

"Sir . . . I've got to have some money."

"Are you begging or stealing?" The sightless eyes passed over Vandaleur and the android.

"I'm prepared for either."

"Ah. So are we all. It is the history of our race." The stranger motioned over his shoulder. "I have been begging at St. Paul's, my friend. What I desire cannot be stolen. What is it you desire that you are lucky enough to be able to steal?"

"Money," Vandaleur said.

"Money for what? Come, my friend, let us exchange

confidences. I will tell you why I beg, if you will tell me why you steal. My name is Blenheim."

"My name is . . . Vole."

"I was not begging for sight at St. Paul's, Mr. Vole. I was begging for a number."

"A number?"

"Ah, yes. Numbers rational, numbers irrational, numbers imaginary. Positive integers. Negative integers. Fractions, positive and negative. Eh? You have never heard of Blenheim's immortal treatise on Twenty Zeros, or The Differences in Absence of Quantity?" Blenheim smiled bitterly. "I am the wizard of the Theory of Number, Mr. Vole, and I have exhausted the charm of number for myself. After fifty years of wizardry, senility approaches and the appetite vanishes. I have been praying in St. Paul's for inspiration. Dear God, I prayed, if You exist, send me a number."

Vandaleur slowly lifted the cardboard portfolio and touched Blenheim's hand with it. "In here," he said, "is a number. A hidden number. A secret number. The number of a crime. Shall we exchange, Mr. Blenheim? Shelter for a number?"

"Neither begging nor stealing, eh?" Blenheim said. "But a bargain. So all life reduces itself to the banal." The sightless eyes again passed over Vandaleur and the android. "Perhaps the All-Mighty is not God but a merchant. Come home with me."

On the top floor of Blenheim's house we shared a room—two beds, two closets, two washstands, one bathroom. Vandaleur bruised my forehead again and sent me out to find work, and while the android worked, I consulted with Blenheim and read him the papers from the portfolio, one by one. All reet! All reet!

Vandaleur told him so much and no more. He was a

student, I said, attempting a thesis on the murdering android. In these papers which he had collected were the facts that would explain the crimes of which Blenheim had heard nothing. There must be a correlation, a number, a statistic, something which would account for my derangement, I explained, and Blenheim was piqued by the mystery, the detective story, the human interest of number.

We examined the papers. As I read them aloud, he listed them and their contents in his blind, meticulous writing. And then I read his notes to him. He listed the papers by type, by typeface, by fact, by fancy, by article, spelling, words, theme, advertising, pictures, subject, politics, prejudices. He analyzed. He studied. He meditated. And we lived together in that top floor, always a little cold, always a little terrified, always a little closer ... brought together by our fear of it, our hatred between us. Like a wedge driven into a living tree and splitting the trunk, only to be forever incorporated into the scar tissue, we grew together. Vandaleur and the android. Be fleet be fleet!

And one afternoon Blenheim called Vandaleur into his study and displayed his notes. "I think I've found it," he said, "but I can't understand it."

Vandaleur's heart leaped.

"Here are the correlations," Blenheim continued. "In fifty papers there are accounts of the criminal android. What is there, outside the depredations, that is also in fifty papers?"

"I don't know, Mr. Blenheim."

"It was a rhetorical question. Here is the answer. The weather."

"What?"

"The weather." Blenheim nodded. "Each crime was committed on a day when the temperature was above ninety degrees Fahrenheit."

"But that's impossible," Vandaleur exclaimed. "It was cool on Lyra Alpha."

"We have no record of any crime committed on Lyra Alpha. There is no paper."

"No. That's right, I—" Vandaleur was confused. Suddenly he exclaimed. "No. You're right. The furnace room. It was hot there. Hot! Of course. My God, yes! That's the answer. Dallas Brady's electric furnace . . . The rice deltas on Paragon. So jeet your seat. Yes. But why? Why? My God, why?"

I came into the house at that moment, and passing the study, saw Vandaleur and Blenheim. I entered, awaiting commands, my multiple aptitudes devoted to service.

"That's the android, eh?" Blenheim said after a long moment.

"Yes," Vandaleur answered, still confused by the discovery. "And that explains why it refused to attack you that night on the Strand. It wasn't hot enough to break the prime directive. Only in the heat . . . The heat, all reet!" He looked at the android. A silent lunatic command passed from man to android. I refused. It is forbidden to endanger life. Vandaleur gestured furiously, then seized Blenheim's shoulders and yanked him back out of his desk chair to the floor. Blenheim shouted once. Vandaleur leaped on him like a tiger, pinning him to the floor and sealing his mouth with one hand.

"Find a weapon," he called to the android.

"It is forbidden to endanger life."

"This is a fight for self-preservation. Bring me a weapon!" He held the squirming mathematician with all his weight. I went at once to a cupboard where I knew a revolver was kept. I checked it. It was loaded with five cartridges. I handed it to Vandaleur. I took it, rammed the barrel against Blenheim's head and pulled the trigger. He shuddered once.

We had three hours before the cook returned from her day off. We looted the house. We took Blenheim's money and jewels. We packed a bag with clothes. We took Blenheim's notes, destroyed the newspapers; and we left, carefully locking the door behind us. In Blenheim's study we left a pile of crumpled papers under a half inch of burning candle. And we soaked the rug around it with kerosene. No, I did all that. The android refused. I am forbidden to endanger life or property.

All reet!

They took the tubes to Leicester Square, changed trains, and rode to the British Museum. There they got off and went to a small Georgian house just off Russell Square. A shingle in the window read: NAN WEBB, PSYCHOMETRIC CONSULTANT. Vandaleur had made a note of the address some weeks earlier. They went into the house. The android waited in the foyer with the bag. Vandaleur entered Nan Webb's office.

She was a tall woman with gray shingled hair, very fine English complexion, and very bad English legs. Her features were blunt, her expression acute. She nodded to Vandaleur, finished a letter, sealed it and looked up.

"My name," I said, "is Vanderbilt. James Vanderbilt."

"Quite."

"I'm an exchange student at London University."

"Quite."

"I've been researching on the killing android, and I think I've discovered something very interesting. I'd like your advice on it. What is your fee?"

"What is your college at the University?"

"Why?"

"There is a discount for students."

"Merton College."

"That will be two pounds, please."

Vandaleur placed two pounds on the desk and added to the fee Blenheim's notes. "There is a correlation," he said, "between the crimes of the android and the weather. You will note that each crime was committed when the temperature rose above ninety degrees Fahrenheit. Is there a psychometric answer for this?"

Nan Webb nodded, studied the notes for a moment, put down the sheets of paper, and said: "Synesthesia, obviously."

"What?"

"Synesthesia," she repeated. "When a sensation, Mr. Vanderbilt, is interpreted immediately in terms of a sensation from a different sense organ from the one stimulated, it is called synesthesia. For example: A sound stimulus gives rise to a simultaneous sensation of definite color. Or color gives rise to a sensation of taste. Or a light stimulus gives rise to a sensation of sound. There can be confusion or short circuiting of any sensation of taste, smell, pain, pressure, temperature and so on. D'you understand?"

"I think so."

"Your research has uncovered the fact that the android most probably reacts to temperature stimulus above the ninety-degree level synesthetically. Most probably there is an endocrine response. Probably a temperature linkage with the android adrenal surrogate. High temperature brings about a response of fear, anger, excitement, and violent physical activity . . . all within the province of the adrenal gland."

"Yes. I see. Then if the android were to be kept in cold climates . . ."

"There would be neither stimulus nor response. There would be no crimes. Quite."

"I see. What is projection?"

"How do you mean?"

"Is there any danger of projection with regard to the owner of the android?"

"Very interesting. Projection is a throwing forward. It is the process of throwing out upon another the ideas or impulses that belong to oneself. The paranoid, for example; projects upon others his conflicts and disturbances in order to externalize them. He accuses, directly or by implication, other men of having the very sicknesses with which he is struggling himself."

"And the danger of projection?"

"It is the danger of believing what is implied. If you live with a psychotic who projects his sickness upon you, there is a danger of falling into his psychotic pattern and becoming virtually psychotic yourself. As, no doubt, is happening to you, Mr. Vandaleur."

Vandaleur leaped to his feet.

"You are an ass," Nan Webb went on crisply. She waved the sheets of notes. "This is no exchange student's writing. It's the unique cursive of the famous Blenheim. Every scholar in England knows this blind writing. There is no Merton College at London University. That was a miserable guess. Merton is one of the Oxford Colleges. And you, Mr. Vandaleur, are so obviously infected by association with your deranged android ... by projection, if you will ... that I hesitate between calling the Metropolitan Police and the Hospital for the Criminally Insane."

I took out the gun and shot her.

Reet!

"Antares II, Alpha Aurigae, Acrux IV, Pollux IX, Rigel Centaurus," Vandaleur said. "They're all cold. Cold as a witch's kiss. Mean temperatures of forty degrees Fahrenheit. Never gets hotter than seventy. We're in business again. Watch that curve."

The multiple-aptitude android swung the wheel with its accomplished hands. The car took the curve sweetly and sped on through the northern marshes, the reeds stretching for miles, brown and dry, under the cold English sky. The sun was sinking swiftly. Overhead, a lone flight of bustards flapped clumsily eastward. High above the flight, a lone helicopter drifted toward home and warmth.

"No more warmth for us," I said. "No more heat. We're safe when we're cold. We'll hole up in Scotland, make a little money, get across to Norway, build a bankroll, and then ship out. We'll settle on Pollux. We're safe. We've licked it. We can live again."

There was a startling *bleep* from overhead, and then a ragged roar: "ATTENTION JAMES VANDALEUR AND ANDROID. ATTENTION, JAMES VANDALEUR AND ANDROID!"

Vandaleur started and looked up. The lone helicopter was floating above them. From its belly came amplified commands: "YOU ARE SURROUNDED. THE ROAD IS BLOCKED. YOU ARE TO STOP YOUR CAR AT ONCE AND SUBMIT TO ARREST. STOP AT ONCE!"

I looked at Vandaleur for orders.

"Keep driving," Vandaleur snapped.

The helicopter dropped lower: "ATTENTION ANDROID. YOU ARE IN CONTROL OF THE VEHICLE. YOU ARE TO STOP AT ONCE. THIS IS A STATE DIRECTIVE SUPERSEDING ALL PRIVATE COMMANDS."

"What the hell are you doing?" I shouted.

"A state directive supersedes all private commands," the android answered. "I must point out to you that—"

"Get the hell away from the wheel," Vandaleur ordered. I clubbed the android, yanked him sideways, and squirmed over him to the wheel. The car veered off the road in that

22

moment and went churning through the frozen mud and dry reeds. Vandaleur regained control and continued westward through the marshes toward a parallel highway five miles distant.

"We'll beat their goddamned block," he grunted.

The car pounded and surged. The helicopter dropped even lower. A searchlight blazed from the belly of the plane.

"ATTENTION JAMES VANDALEUR AND ANDROID. SUBMIT TO ARREST. THIS IS A STATE DIRECTIVE SUPERSEDING ALL PRIVATE COMMANDS."

"He can't submit," Vandaleur shouted wildly. "There's no one to submit to. He can't and I won't."

"Christ!" I muttered. "We'll beat them yet. We'll beat the block. We'll beat the heat. We'll—"

"I must point out to you," I said, "that I am required by my prime directive to obey state directives which supersede all private commands. I must submit to arrest."

"Who says it's a state directive?" Vandaleur said. "Them? Up in that plane? They've got to show credentials. They've got to prove it's state authority before you submit. How d'you know they're not crooks trying to trick us?"

Holding the wheel with one arm, he reached into his side pocket to make sure the gun was still in place. The car skidded. The tires squealed on frost and reeds. The wheel was wrenched from his grasp and the car yawed up a small hillock and overturned. The motor roared and the wheels screamed. Vandaleur crawled out and dragged the android with him. For the moment we were outside the circle of light boring down from the helicopter. We blundered off into the marsh, into the blackness, into concealment ... Vandaleur running with a pounding heart, hauling the android along.

The helicopter circled and soared over the wrecked car, searchlight peering, loudspeaker braying. On the highway we had left, lights appeared as the pursuing and blocking

23

parties gathered and followed radio directions from the plane. Vandaleur and the android continued deeper and deeper into the marsh, working their way toward the parallel road and safety. It was night by now. The sky was a black matte. Not a star showed. The temperature was dropping. A southeast night wind knifed us to the bone.

Far behind there was a dull concussion. Vandaleur turned, gasping. The car's fuel had exploded. A geyser of flame shot up like a lurid fountain. It subsided into a low crater of burning reeds. Whipped by the wind, the distant hem of flame fanned up into a wall, ten feet high. The wall began marching down on us, crackling fiercely. Above it, a pall of oily smoke surged forward. Behind it, Vandaleur could make out the figures of men...a mass of beaters searching the marsh.

"Christ!" I cried and searched desperately for safety. He ran, dragging me with him, until their feet crunched through the surface ice of a pool. He trampled the ice furiously, then flung himself down in the numbing water, pulling the android with us.

The wall of flame approached. I could hear the crackle and feel the heat. He could see the searchers clearly. Vandaleur reached into his side pocket for the gun. The pocket was torn. The gun was gone. He groaned and shook with cold and terror. The light from the marsh fire was blinding. Overhead, the helicopter floated helplessly to one side, unable to fly through the smoke and flames and aid the searchers who were beating far to the right of us.

"They'll miss us," Vandaleur whispered. "Keep quiet. That's an order. They'll miss us. We'll beat them. We'll beat the fire. We'll—"

Three distinct shots sounded less than a hundred feet from the fugitives. *Blam! Blam! Blam!* They came from the last three cartridges in my gun as the marsh fire reached it where it had dropped, and exploded the shells. The searchers turned toward the sound and began working directly toward us. Vandaleur cursed hysterically and tried to submerge even deeper to escape the intolerable heat of the fire. The android began to twitch.

The wall of flame surged up to them. Vandaleur took a deep breath and prepared to submerge until the flame passed over them. The android shuddered and burst into an earsplitting scream.

"All reet! All reet!" it shouted. "Be fleet be fleet!"

"Damn you!" I shouted. I tried to drown it.

"Damn you!" I cursed him. I smashed his face.

The android battered Vandaleur, who fought it off until it exploded out of the mud and staggered upright. Before I could return to the attack, the live flames captured it hypnotically. It danced and capered in a lunatic rhumba before the wall of fire. Its legs twisted. Its arms waved. The fingers writhed in a private rumba of their own. It shrieked and sang and ran in a crooked waltz before the embrace of the heat, a muddy monster silhouetted against the brilliant sparkling flare.

The searchers shouted. There were shots. The android spun around twice and then continued its horrid dance before the face of the flames. There was a rising gust of wind. The fire swept around the capering figure and enveloped it for a roaring moment. Then the fire swept on, leaving behind it a sobbing mass of synthetic flesh oozing scarlet blood that would never coagulate.

The thermometer would have registered 1200° wondrously Fahrenheit.

Vandaleur didn't die. I got away. They missed him while they watched the android caper and die. But I don't know which of us he is these days. Projection, Wanda warned me. Projection, Nan Webb told him. If you live with a crazy man or a crazy machine long enough, I become crazy too Reet!

But we know one truth. We know they were wrong. The new robot and Vandaleur know that because the new robot's started twitching too. Reet! Here on cold Pollux, the robot is twitching and singing. No heat, but my fingers writhe. No heat, but it's taken the little Talley girl off for a solitary walk. A cheap labor robot. A servomechanism . . . all I could afford . . . but it's twitching and humming and walking alone with the child somewhere and I can't find them. Christ! Vandaleur can't find me before it's too late. Cool and discreet, honey, in the dancing frost while the thermometer registers 10° fondly Fahrenheit.

THE GAME OF RAT AND DRAGON

CORDWAINER SMITH

THE TABLE

Pinlighting is a hell of a way to earn a living. Underhill was furious as he closed the door behind himself. It didn't make much sense to wear a uniform and look like a soldier if people didn't appreciate what you did.

He sat down in his chair, laid his head back in the head-rest, and pulled the helmet down over his forehead.

As he waited for the pin-set to warm up, he remembered the girl in the outer corridor. She had looked at it, then looked at him scornfully.

"Meow." That was all she had said. Yet it had cut him like a knife.

What did she think he was—a fool, a loafer, a uniformed nonentity? Didn't she know that for every half hour of pinlighting, he got a minimum of two months' recuperation in the hospital?

By now the set was warm. He felt the squares of space around him, sensed himself at the middle of an immense

27

grid, a cubic grid, full of nothing. Out in that nothingness, he could sense the hollow aching horror of space itself and could feel the terrible anxiety which his mind encountered whenever it met the faintest trace of inert dust.

As he relaxed, the comforting solidity of the Sun, the clockwork of the familiar planets and the Moon rang in on him. Our own solar system was as charming and as simple as an ancient cuckoo clock filled with familiar ticking and with reassuring noises. The odd little moons of Mars swung around their planet like frantic mice, yet their regularity was itself an assurance that all was well. Far above the plane of the ecliptic, he could feel half a ton of dust more or less drifting outside the lanes of human travel.

Here there was nothing to fight, nothing to challenge the mind, to tear the living soul out of a body with its roots dripping in effluvium as tangible as blood.

Nothing ever moved in on the Solar System. He could wear the pin-set forever and be nothing more than a sort of telepathic astronomer, a man who could feel the hot, warm protection of the Sun throbbing and burning against his living mind.

Woodley came in.

"Same old ticking world," said Underhill. "Nothing to report. No wonder they didn't develop the pin-set until they began to planoform. Down here with the hot Sun around us, it feels so good and so quiet. You can feel everything spinning and turning. It's nice and sharp and compact. It's sort of like sitting around home."

Woodley grunted. He was not much given to flights of fantasy.

Undeterred, Underhill went on, "It must have been pretty good to have been an Ancient Man. I wonder why they burned up their world with war. They didn't have to planoform. They didn't have to go out to earn their livings among the stars. They didn't have to dodge the Rats or play the Game. They couldn't have invented pinlighting because they didn't have any need of it, did they, Woodley?"

Woodley grunted, "Uh-huh." Woodley was twenty-six years old and due to retire in one more year. He already had a farm picked out. He had gotten through ten years of hard work pinlighting with the best of them. He had kept his sanity by not thinking very much about his job, meeting the strains of the task whenever he had to meet them and thinking nothing more about his duties until the next emergency arose.

Woodley never made a point of getting popular among the Partners. None of the Partners liked him very much. Some of them even resented him. He was suspected of thinking ugly thoughts of the Partners on occasion, but since none of the Partners ever thought a complaint in articulate form, the other pinlighters and the Chiefs of the Instrumentality left him alone.

Underhill was still full of the wonder of their job. Happily he babbled on, "What does happen to us when we planoform? Do you think it's sort of like dying? Did you ever see anybody who had his soul pulled out?"

"Pulling souls is just a way of talking about it," said Woodley. "After all these years, nobody knows whether we have souls or not."

"But I saw one once. I saw what Dogwood looked like when he came apart. There was something funny. It looked wet and sort of sticky as if it were bleeding and it went out of him—and you know what they did to Dogwood? They took him away, up in that part of the hospital where you and I never go—way up at the top part where the others are, where the others always have to go if they are alive after the Rats of the Up-and-Out have gotten them."

Woodley sat down and lit an ancient pipe. He was burning something called tobacco in it. It was a dirty sort of habit, but it made him look very dashing and adventurous.

"Look here, youngster. You don't have to worry about that stuff. Pinlighting is getting better all the time. The Partners are getting better. I've seen them pinlight two Rats forty-six million miles apart in one and a half milliseconds. As long as people had to try to work the pin-sets themselves, there was always the chance that with a minimum of four hundred milliseconds for the human mind to set a pinlight, we wouldn't light the Rats up fast enough to protect our planoforming ships. The Partners have changed all that. Once they get going, they're faster than Rats. And they always will be. I know it's not easy, letting a Partner share your mind—"

"It's not easy for them, either," said Underhill.

"Don't worry about them. They're not human. Let them take care of themselves. I've seen more pinlighters go crazy from monkeying around with Partners than I have ever seen caught by the Rats. How many of them do you actually know of that got grabbed by Rats?"

Underhill looked down at his fingers, which shone green and purple in the vivid light thrown by the tuned-in pin-set, and counted ships. The thumb for the *Andromeda*, lost with crew and passengers, the index finger and the middle finger for *Release Ships 43* and *56*, found with their pin-sets burned out and every man, woman, and child on board dead or insane. The ring finger, the little finger, and the thumb of the other hand were the first three battleships to be lost to the Rats—lost as people realized that there was something out there *underneath space itself* which was alive, capricious, and malevolent.

Planoforming was sort of funny. It felt like—

Like nothing much.

Like the twinge of a mild electric shock.

Like the ache of a sore tooth bitten on for the first time. Like a slightly painful flash of light against the eyes.

Yet in that time, a forty-thousand-ton ship lifting free above Earth disappeared somehow or other into two dimensions and appeared half a light-year or fifty light-years off.

At one moment, he would be sitting in the Fighting Room, the pin-set ready and the familiar Solar System ticking around inside his head. For a second or a year (he could never tell how long it really was, subjectively), the funny little flash went through him and then he was loose in the Up-and-Out, the terrible open spaces between the stars, where the stars themselves felt like pimples on his telepathic mind and the planets were too far away to be sensed or read.

Somewhere in this outer space, a gruesome death awaited, death and horror of a kind which Man had never encountered until he reached out for interstellar space itself. Apparently the light of the suns kept the Dragons away.

Dragons. That was what people called them. To ordinary people, there was nothing, nothing except the shiver of planoforming and the hammer blow of sudden death or the dark spastic note of lunacy descending into their minds.

But to the telepaths, they were Dragons.

In the fraction of a second between the telepaths' awareness of a hostile something out in the black, hollow nothingness of space and the impact of a ferocious, ruinous psychic blow against all living things within the ship, the telepaths had sensed entities something like the Dragons of ancient human lore, beasts more clever than beasts, demons more tangible than demons, hungry vortices of aliveness and hate compounded by unknown means out of the thin tenuous matter between the stars.

It took a surviving ship to bring back the news—a ship in which, by sheer chance, a telepath had a light beam ready, turning it out at the innocent dust so that, within the panorama of his mind, the Dragon dissolved into nothing at all and the other passengers, themselves non-telepathic, went about their way not realizing that their own immediate deaths had been averted.

From then on, it was easy—almost.

Planoforming ships always carried telepaths. Telepaths had their sensitiveness enlarged to an immense range by the pin-sets, which were telepathic amplifiers adapted to the mammal mind. The pin-sets in turn were electronically geared into small dirigible light bombs. Light did it.

Light broke up the Dragons, allowed the ships to reform three-dimensionally, skip, skip, skip, as they moved from star to star.

The odds suddenly moved down from a hundred to one against mankind to sixty to forty in mankind's favor.

This was not enough. The telepaths were trained to become ultrasensitive, trained to become aware of the Dragons in less than a millisecond.

But it was found that the Dragons could move a million miles in just under two milliseconds and that this was not enough for the human mind to activate the light beams.

Attempts had been made to sheath the ships in light at all times.

This defense wore out.

As mankind learned about the Dragons, so too, apparently, the Dragons learned about mankind. Somehow they flattened their own bulk and came in on extremely flat trajectories very quickly.

Intense light was needed, light of sunlike intensity. This could be provided only by light bombs. Pinlighting came into existence.

Pinlighting consisted of the detonation of ultra-vivid miniature photonuclear bombs, which converted a few ounces of a magnesium isotope into pure visible radiance.

The odds kept coming down in mankind's favor, yet ships were being lost.

It became so bad that people didn't even want to find the ships because the rescuers knew what they would see. It was sad to bring back to Earth three hundred bodies ready for burial and two hundred or three hundred lunatics, damaged beyond repair, to be wakened, and fed, and cleaned, and put to sleep, wakened and fed again until their lives were ended.

Telepaths tried to reach into the minds of the psychotics who had been damaged by the Dragons, but they found nothing there beyond vivid spouting columns of fiery terror bursting from the primordial id itself, the volcanic source of life.

Then came the Partners.

Man and Partner could do together what Man could not do alone. Men had the intellect. Partners had the speed.

The Partners rode their tiny craft, no larger than footballs, outside the spaceships. They planoformed with the ships. They rode beside them in their six-pound craft ready to attack.

The tiny ships of the Partners were swift. Each carried a dozen pinlights, bombs no bigger than thimbles.

The pinlighters threw the Partners—quite literally threw—by means of mind-to-firing relays direct at the Dragons.

What seemed to be Dragons to the human mind appeared in the form of gigantic Rats in the minds of the Partners.

Out in the pitiless nothingness of space, the Partners' minds responded to an instinct as old as life. The Partners attacked, striking with a speed faster than Man's, going from attack to attack until the Rats or themselves were destroyed.

Almost all the time it was the Partners who won.

With the safety of the interstellar skip, skip, skip of the ships, commerce increased immensely, the population of all the colonies went up, and the demand for trained Partners increased.

Underhill and Woodley were a part of the third generation of pinlighters and yet, to them, it seemed as though their craft had endured forever.

Gearing space into minds by means of the pin-set, adding the Partners to those minds, keying up the mind for the tension of a fight on which all depended—this was more than human synapses could stand for long. Underhill needed his two months' rest after half an hour of fighting. Woodley needed his retirement after ten years of service. They were young. They were good. But they had limitations.

So much depended on the choice of Partners, so much on the sheer luck of who drew whom.

THE SHUFFLE

Father Moontree and the little girl named West entered the room. They were the other two pinlighters. The human complement of the Fighting Room was now complete.

Father Moontree was a red-faced man of forty-five who had lived the peaceful life of a farmer until he reached his fortieth year. Only then, belatedly, did the authorities find he was telepathic and agree to let him late in life enter upon the career of pinlighter. He did well at it, but he was fantastically old for this kind of business.

Father Moontree looked at the glum Woodley and the musing Underhill. "How're the youngsters today? Ready for a good fight?"

"Father always wants a fight," giggled the little girl named West. She was such a little little girl. Her giggle was high and childish. She looked like the last person in the world one would expect to find in the rough, sharp dueling of pinlighting.

Underhill had been amused one time when he found one of the most sluggish of the Partners coming away happy from contact with the mind of the girl named West.

Usually the Partners didn't care much about the human minds with which they were paired for the journey. The Partners seemed to take the attitude that human minds were complex and fouled up beyond belief, anyhow. No Partner ever questioned the superiority of the human mind, though very few of the Partners were much impressed by that superiority.

The Partners liked people. They were willing to fight with them. They were even willing to die for them. But when a Partner liked an individual the way, for example, that Captain Wow or the Lady May liked Underhill, the liking had nothing to do with intellect. It was a matter of temperament, of feel.

Underhill knew perfectly well that Captain Wow regarded his, Underhill's, brains as silly. What Captain Wow liked was Underhill's friendly emotional structure, the cheerfulness and glint of wicked amusement that shot through Underhill's unconscious thought patterns, and the gaiety with which Underhill faced danger. The words, the history books, the ideas, the science—Underhill could sense all that in his own mind, reflected back from Captain Wow's mind, as so much rubbish.

Miss West looked at Underhill. "I bet you've put stickum on the stones."

"I did not!"

Underhill felt his ears grow red with embarrassment. During his novitiate, he had tried to cheat in the lottery because he got particularly fond of a special Partner, a lovely young mother named Murr. It was so much easier to operate with Murr and she was so affectionate toward him that he forgot pinlighting was hard work and that he was not instructed to have a good time with his Partner. They were both designed and prepared to go into deadly battle together.

One cheating had been enough. They had found him out and he had been laughed at for years.

Father Moontree picked up the imitation-leather cup and shook the stone dice which assigned them their Partners for the trip. By senior rights he took first draw.

He grimaced. He had drawn a greedy old character, a tough old male whose mind was full of slobbering thoughts of food, veritable oceans full of half-spoiled fish. Father Moontree had once said that he burped cod liver oil for weeks after drawing that particular glutton, so strongly had the telepathic image of fish impressed itself upon his mind. Yet the glutton was a glutton for danger as well as for fish. He had killed sixty-three Dragons, more than any other Partner in the service, and was quite literally worth his weight in gold.

The little girl West came next. She drew Captain Wow. When she saw who it was, she smiled.

"I *like* him," she said. "He's such fun to fight with. He feels so nice and cuddly in my mind."

"Cuddly, hell," said Woodley. "I've been in his mind, too. It's the most leering mind in this ship, bar none."

"Nasty man," said the little girl. She said it declaratively, without reproach.

Underhill, looking at her, shivered.

He didn't see how she could take Captain Wow so calmly. Captain Wow's mind *did* leer. When Captain Wow got excited in the middle of a battle, confused images of Dragons, deadly Rats, luscious beds, the smell of fish, and the shock of space all scrambled together in his mind as he and Captain Wow, their consciousnesses linked together through the pin-set, became a fantastic composite of human being and Persian cat.

That's the trouble with working with cats, thought Underhill. It's a pity that nothing else anywhere will serve as Partner. Cats were all right once you got in touch with them telepathically. They were smart enough to meet the needs of the fight, but their motives and desires were certainly different from those of humans.

They were companionable enough as long as you thought tangible images at them, but their minds just closed up and went to sleep when you recited Shakespeare or Colegrove, or if you tried to tell them what space was.

It was sort of funny realizing that the Partners who were so grim and mature out here in space were the same cute little animals that people had used as pets for thousands of years back on Earth. He had embarrassed himself more than once while on the ground saluting perfectly ordinary non-telepathic cats because he had forgotten for the moment that they were not Partners.

He picked up the cup and shook out his stone dice.

He was lucky—he drew the Lady May.

The Lady May was the most thoughtful Partner he had ever met. In her, the finely bred pedigree mind of a Persian cat had reached one of its highest peaks of development. She was more complex than any human woman, but the complexity was all one of emotions, memory, hope, and discriminated experience—experience sorted through without benefit of words.

When he had first come into contact with her mind, he was astonished at its clarity. With her he remembered her kittenhood. He remembered every mating experience she had ever had. He saw in a half-recognizable gallery all the other pinlighters himself with whom she had been paired for the fight. And he saw himself radiant, cheerful, and desirable.

He even thought he caught the edge of a longing—

A very flattering and yearning thought: *What a pity he is not a cat.*

Woodley picked up the last stone. He drew what he deserved—a sullen, scarred old tomcat with none of the verve of Captain Wow. Woodley's Partner was the most animal of all the cats on the ship, a low, brutish type with a dull mind. Even telepathy had not refined his character. His ears were half chewed off from the first fights in which he had engaged.

He was a serviceable fighter, nothing more.

Woodley grunted.

Underhill glanced at him oddly. Didn't Woodley ever do anything but grunt?

Father Moontree looked at the other three. "You might as well get your Partners now. I'll let the Scanner know we're ready to go into the Up-and-Out."

THE DEAL

Underhill spun the combination lock on the Lady May's cage. He woke her gently and took her into his arms. She humped her back luxuriously, stretched her claws, started to purr, thought better of it, and licked him on the wrist instead. He did not have the pin-set on, so their minds were closed to each other, but in the angle of her mustache and in the movement of her ears, he caught some sense of the gratification she experienced in finding him as her Partner.

He talked to her in human speech, even though speech meant nothing to a cat when the pin-set was not on.

"It's a damn shame, sending a sweet little thing like you

whirling around in the coldness of nothing to hunt for Rats that are bigger and deadlier than all of us put together. You didn't ask for this kind of fight, did you?"

For answer, she licked his hand, purred, tickled his cheek with her long fluffy tail, turned around and faced him, golden eyes shining.

For a moment, they stared at each other, man squatting, cat standing erect on her hind legs, front claws digging into his knee. Human eyes and cat eyes looked across an immensity which no words could meet, but which affection spanned in a single glance.

"Time to get in," he said.

She walked docilely into her spheroid carrier. She climbed in. He saw to it that her miniature pin-set rested firmly and comfortably against the base of her brain. He made sure that her claws were padded so that she could not tear herself in the excitement of battle.

Softly he said to her, "Ready?"

For answer, she preened her back as much as her harness would permit and purred softly within the confines of the frame that held her.

He slapped down the lid and watched the sealant ooze around the seam. For a few hours, she was welded into her projectile until a workman with a short cutting arc would remove her after she had done her duty.

He picked up the entire projectile and slipped it into the ejection tube. He closed the door of the tube, spun the lock, seated himself in his chair, and put his own pin-set on.

Once again he flung the switch.

He sat in a small room, *small, small, warm, warm*, the bodies of the other three people moving close around him, the tangible lights in the ceiling bright and heavy against his closed eyelids.

As the pin-set warmed, the room fell away. The other

people ceased to be people and became small glowing heaps of fire, embers, dark red fire, with the consciousness of life burning like old red coals in a country fireplace.

As the pin-set warmed a little more, he felt Earth just below him, felt the ship slipping away, felt the turning Moon as it swung on the far side of the world, felt the planets and the hot, clear goodness of the Sun which kept the Dragons so far from mankind's native ground.

Finally, he reached complete awareness.

He was telepathically alive to a range of millions of miles. He felt the dust which he had noticed earlier high above the ecliptic. With a thrill of warmth and tenderness, he felt the consciousness of the Lady May pouring over into his own. Her consciousness was as gentle and clear and yet sharp to the taste of his mind as if it were scented oil. It felt relaxing and reassuring. He could sense her welcome of him. It was scarcely a thought, just a raw emotion of greeting.

At last they were one again.

In a tiny remote corner of his mind, as tiny as the small-est toy he had ever seen in his childhood, he was still aware of the room and the ship, and of Father Moontree picking up a telephone and speaking to a Scanner captain in charge of the ship.

His telepathic mind caught the idea long before his ears could frame the words. The actual sound followed the idea the way that thunder on an ocean beach follows the light-ning inward from far out over the seas.

"The Fighting Room is ready. Clear to planoform, sir."

THE PLAY

Underhill was always a little exasperated the way that Lady May experienced things before he did.

He was braced for the quick vinegar thrill of planoforming, but he caught her report of it before his own nerves could register what happened.

Earth had fallen so far away that he groped for several milliseconds before he found the Sun in the upper rear right-hand corner of his telepathic mind.

That was a good jump, he thought. This way we'll get there in four or five skips.

A few hundred miles outside the ship, the Lady May thought back at him, "O warm, O generous, O gigantic man! O brave, O friendly, O tender and huge Partner! O wonderful with you, with you so good, good, good, warm, warm, now to fight, now to go, good with you . . ."

He knew that she was not thinking words, that his mind took the clear amiable babble of her cat intellect and translated it into images which his own thinking could record and understand.

Neither one of them was absorbed in the game of mutual greetings. He reached out far beyond her range of perception to see if there was anything near the ship. It was funny how it was possible to do two things at once. He could scan space with his pin-set mind and yet at the same time catch a vagrant thought of hers, a lovely, affectionate thought about a son who had had a golden face and a chest covered with soft, incredibly downy white fur.

While he was still searching, he caught the warning from her.

We jump again!

And so they had. The ship had moved to a second planoform. The stars were different. The Sun was immeasurably far behind. Even the nearest stars were barely in contact. This was good Dragon country, this open, nasty, hollow kind of space. He reached farther, faster, sensing and looking for danger, ready to fling the Lady May at danger wherever he found it.

Terror blazed up in his mind, so sharp, so clear, that it came through as a physical wrench.

The little girl named West had found something—something immense, long, black, sharp, greedy, horrific. She flung Captain Wow at it.

Underhill tried to keep his own mind clear. "Watch out!" he shouted telepathically at the others, trying to move the Lady May around.

At one corner of the battle, he felt the lustful rage of Captain Wow as the big Persian tomcat detonated lights while he approached the streak of dust which threatened the ship and the people within.

The lights scored near misses.

The dust flattened itself, changing from the shape of a sting ray into the shape of a spear.

Not three milliseconds had elapsed.

Father Moontree was talking human words and was saying in a voice that moved like cold molasses out of a heavy jar, "C-a-p-t-a-i-n." Underhill knew that the sentence was going to be "Captain, move fast!"

The battle would be fought and finished before Father Moontree got through talking.

Now, factions of a millisecond later, the Lady May was directly in line.

Here was where the skill and speed of the Partners came in. She could react faster than he. She could see the threat as an immense Rat coming direct at her.

She could fire the light-bombs with a discrimination which he might miss.

He was connected with her mind, but he could not follow it.

His consciousness absorbed the tearing wound inflicted by the alien enemy. It was like no wound on Earth—raw, crazy pain which started like a burn at his navel. He began to writhe in his chair.

Actually he had not yet had time to move a muscle when the Lady May struck back at their enemy.

Five evenly spaced photonuclear bombs blazed out across a hundred thousand miles.

The pain in his mind and body vanished.

He felt a moment of fierce, terrible, feral elation running through the mind of the Lady May as she finished her kill. It was always disappointing to the cats to find out that their enemies whom they sensed as gigantic space Rats disappeared at the moment of destruction.

Then he felt her hurt, the pain and the fear that swept over both of them as the battle, quicker than the movement of an eyelid, had come and gone. In the same instant there came the sharp and acid twinge of planoform.

Once more the ship went skip.

He could hear Woodley thinking at him. "You don't have to bother much. This old son-of-a-gun and I will take over for a while."

Twice again the twinge, the skip.

He had no idea where he was until the lights of the Caledonia space board shone below.

With a weariness that lay almost beyond the limits of thought, he threw his mind back into rapport with the pinset, fixing the Lady May's projectile gently and neatly in its launching tube.

She was half dead with fatigue, but he could feel the beat of her heart, could listen to her panting, and he grasped the grateful edge of a "Thanks" reaching from her mind to his.

THE SCORE

They put him in the hospital at Caledonia.

The doctor was friendly but firm. "You actually got touched by that Dragon. That's as close a shave as I've ever seen. It's all so quick that it'll be a long time before we know what happened scientifically, but I suppose you'd be ready for the insane asylum now if the contact had lasted several tenths of a millisecond longer. What kind of cat did you have out in front of you?"

Underhill felt the words coming out of him slowly. Words were such a lot of trouble compared with the speed and the joy of thinking, fast and sharp and clear, mind to mind! But words were all that could reach ordinary people like this doctor.

His mouth moved heavily as he articulated words, "Don't call our Partners cats. The right thing to call them is Partners. They fight for us in a team. You ought to know we call them Partners, not cats. How is mine?"

"I don't know," said the doctor contritely. "We'll find out for you. Meanwhile, old man, take it easy. There's nothing but rest that can help you. Can you make yourself sleep, or would you like us to give you some kind of sedative?"

"I can sleep," said Underhill. "I just want to know about the Lady May."

The nurse joined in. She was a little antagonistic. "Don't you want to know about the other people?"

"They're okay," said Underhill. "I knew that before I came in here."

He stretched his arms and sighed and grinned at them. He could see they were relaxing and were beginning to treat him as a person instead of a patient.

"I'm all right," he said. "Just let me know when I can go see my Partner."

A new thought struck him. He looked wildly at the doctor. "They didn't send her off with the ship, did they?"

"I'll find out right away," said the doctor. He gave Underhill a reassuring squeeze of the shoulder and left the room.

The nurse took a napkin off a goblet of chilled fruit juice.

Underhill tried to smile at her. There seemed to be something wrong with the girl. He wished she would go away. First she had started to be friendly and now she was distant again. It's a nuisance being telepathic, he thought. You keep trying to reach even when you are not making contact.

Suddenly she swung around on him.

"You pinlighters! You and your damn cats!"

Just as she stamped out, he burst into her mind. He saw himself a radiant hero, clad in his smooth suede uniform, the pin-set crown shining like ancient royal jewels around his head. He saw his own face, handsome and masculine, shining out of her mind. He saw himself very far away and he saw himself as she hated him.

She hated him in the secrecy of her own mind. She hated him because he was—she thought—proud and strange and rich, better and more beautiful than people like her.

He cut off the sight of her mind and, as he buried his face in the pillow, he caught an image of the Lady May.

"She *is* a cat," he thought. "That's all she is—a *cat!*"

But that was not how his mind saw her—quick beyond all dreams of speed, sharp, clever, unbelievably graceful, beautiful, wordless and undemanding.

Where would he ever find a woman who could compare with her?

WE CAN REMEMBER IT FOR YOU WHOLESALE

PHILIP K. DICK

He awoke—and wanted Mars. The valleys, he thought. What would it be like to trudge among them? Great and greater yet: the dream grew as he became fully conscious, the dream and the yearning. He could almost feel the enveloping presence of the other world, which only Government agents and high officials had seen. A clerk like himself? Not likely.

"Are you getting up or not?" his wife Kirsten asked drowsily, with her usual hint of fierce crossness. "If you are, push the hot coffee button on the darn stove."

"Okay," Douglas Quail said, and made his way barefoot from the bedroom of their conapt to the kitchen. There, having dutifully pressed the hot coffee button, he seated himself at the kitchen table, brought out a yellow, small tin of fine Dean Swift snuff. He inhaled briskly, and the Beau Nash mixture stung his nose, burned the roof of his mouth.

But still he inhaled; it woke him up and allowed his dreams, his nocturnal desires and random wishes, to condense into a semblance of rationality.

I will go, he said to himself. *Before I die I'll see Mars.*

It was, of course, impossible, and he knew this even as he dreamed. But the daylight, the mundane noise of his wife now brushing her hair before the bedroom mirror—everything conspired to remind him of what he was. A *miserable little salaried employee*, he said to himself with bitterness. Kirsten reminded him of this at least once a day and he did not blame her; it was a wife's job to bring her husband down to Earth. *Down to Earth*, he thought, and laughed. The figure of speech in this was literally apt.

"What are you sniggering about?" his wife asked as she swept into the kitchen, her long busy-pink robe wagging after her. "A dream, I bet. You're always full of them."

"Yes," he said, and gazed out the kitchen window at the hovercars and traffic runnels, and all the little energetic people hurrying to work. In a little while he would be among them. As always.

"I'll bet it has to do with some woman," Kirsten said witheringly.

"No," he said. "A god. The god of war. He has wonderful craters with every kind of plant-life growing deep down in them."

"Listen." Kirsten crouched down beside him and spoke earnestly, the harsh quality momentarily gone from her voice. "The bottom of the ocean—*our* ocean is much more, an infinity of times more beautiful. You know that; everyone knows that. Rent an artificial gill-outfit for both of us, take a week off from work, and we can descend and live down there at one of those year-round acquatic resorts. And in addition—" She broke off. "You're not listening. You should be. Here is something a lot better than that compulsion, that obsession you have about Mars, and you don't even listen!" Her voice rose piercingly. "God in heaven, you're doomed, Doug! What's going to become of you?"

"I'm going to work," he said, rising to his feet, his breakfast forgotten. "That's what's going to become of me."

She eyed him. "You're getting worse. More fanatical every day. Where's it going to lead?"

"To Mars," he said, and opened the door to the closet to get down a fresh shirt to wear to work.

Having descended from the taxi, Douglas Quail slowly walked across three densely-populated foot runnels and to the modern, attractively inviting doorway. There he halted, impeding mid-morning traffic, and with caution read the shifting-color neon sign. He had, in the past, scrutinized this sign before ... but never had he come so close. This was very different; what he did now was something else. Something which sooner or later had to happen.

REKAL, INCORPORATED

Was this the answer? After all, an illusion, no matter how convincing, remained nothing more than an illusion. At least objectively. But subjectively—quite the opposite entirely.

And anyhow he had an appointment. Within the next five minutes.

Taking a deep breath of mildly smog-infested Chicago air, he walked through the dazzling polychromatic shimmer of the doorway and up to the receptionist's counter.

The nicely-articulated blonde at the counter, barebosomed and tidy, said pleasantly, "Good morning, Mr. Quail."

"Yes," he said. "I'm here to see about a Rekal course. As I guess you know."

"Not 'rekal' but *re*call," the receptionist corrected him. She picked up the receiver of the vidphone by her smooth elbow and said into it, "Mr. Douglas Quail is here, Mr. McClane. May he come inside, now? Or is it too soon?"

"Giz wetwa wum-wum wamp," the phone mumbled.

"Yes, Mr. Quail," she said. "You may go in; Mr. McClane is expecting you." As he started off uncertainly she called after him, "Room D, Mr. Quail. To your right."

After a frustrating but brief moment of being lost he found the proper room. The door hung open and inside, at a big genuine walnut desk, sat a genial-looking man, middle-aged, wearing the latest Martian frog-pelt gray suit; his attire alone would have told Quail that he had come to the right person.

"Sit down, Douglas," McClane said, waving his plump hand toward a chair which faced the desk. "So you want to have gone to Mars. Very good."

Quail seated himself, feeling tense. "I'm not so sure this is worth the fee," he said. "It costs a lot and as far as I can see I really get nothing," *Costs almost as much as going*, he thought.

"You get tangible proof of your trip," McClane disagreed emphatically. "All the proof you'll need. Here; I'll show you." He dug within a drawer of his impressive desk. "Ticket stub." Reaching into a manila folder, he produced a small square of embossed cardboard. "It proves you went—and returned. Postcards." He laid out four franked picture 3-D full-color postcards in a neatly-arranged row on the desk for Quail to see. "Film. Shots you took of local sights on Mars with a rented moving camera." To Quail he displayed those, too. "Plus the names of people you met, two hundred poscreds worth of souvenirs, which will arrive—from Mars—

49

within the following month. And passport, certificates list-
ing the shots you received. And more." He glanced up
keenly at Quail. "You'll know you went, all right," he said.
"You won't remember us, won't remember me or ever
having been here. It'll be a real trip in your mind; we guarantee that. A full two weeks of recall; every last piddling
detail. Remember this: if at any time you doubt that you
really took an extensive trip to Mars you can return here
and get a full refund. You see?"

"But I didn't go," Quail said. "I won't have gone, no
matter what proofs you provide me with." He took a deep,
unsteady breath. "And I never was a secret agent with Interplan." It seemed impossible to him that Rekal, Incorporated's extra-factual memory implant would do its job—
despite what he had heard people say.

"Mr. Quail," McClane said patiently. "As you explained
in your letter to us, you have no chance, no possibility in
the slightest, of ever actually getting to Mars; you can't
afford it, and what is much more important, you could never
qualify as an undercover agent for Interplan or anybody
else. This is the only way you can achieve your, ahem, life-
long dream; am I not correct, sir? You can't be this; you
can't actually do this." He chuckled. "But you can *have been*
and *have done*. We see to that. And our fee is reasonable;
no hidden charges." He smiled encouragingly.

"Is an extra-factual memory that convincing?" Quail
asked.

"More than the real thing, sir. Had you really gone to
Mars as an Interplan agent, you would by now have forgotten a great deal; our analysis of true-mem systems—authentic recollections of major events in a person's life—
shows that a variety of details are very quickly lost to the
person. Forever. Part of the package we offer you is such
deep implantation of recall that nothing is forgotten. The

packet which is fed to you while you're comatose is the creation of trained experts, men who have spent years on Mars; in every case we verify details down to the last iota. And you've picked a rather easy extra-factual system; had you picked Pluto or wanted to be Emperor of the Inner Planet Alliance we'd have much more difficulty ... and the charges would be considerably greater."

Reaching into his coat for his wallet, Quail said, "Okay. It's been my life-long ambition and so I see I'll never really do it. So I guess I'll have to settle for this."

"Don't think of it that way," McClane said severely. "You're not accepting second-best. The actual memory, with all its vagueness, omissions and ellipses, not to say distortions—that's second-best. He accepted the money and pressed a button on his desk. "All right, Mr. Quail," he said, as the door of his office opened and two burly men swiftly entered. "You're on your way to Mars as a secret agent." He rose, came over to shake Quail's nervous, moist hand. "Or rather, you have been on your way. This afternoon at four-thirty you will, um, arrive back here on Terra; a cab will leave you off at your conapt and as I say you will never remember seeing me or coming here; you won't, in fact, even remember having heard of our existence."

His mouth dry with nervousness, Quail followed the two technicians from the office; what happened next depended on them.

Will I actually believe I've been on Mars? he wondered. *That I managed to fulfill my lifetime ambition?* He had a strange, lingering intuition that something would go wrong. But just what—he did not know.

He would have to wait to find out.

The intercom on McClane's desk, which connected him with the work-area of the firm, buzzed and a voice said, "Mr.

Quail is under sedation now, sir. Do you want to supervise this one, or shall we go ahead?"

"It's routine," McClane observed. "You may go ahead, Lowe; I don't think you'll run into any trouble." Programming an artificial memory of a trip to another planet—with or without the added fillip of being a secret agent—showed up on the firm's work-schedule with monotonous regularity. *In one month;* he calculated wryly, *we must do twenty of these . . . erstaz interplanetary travel has become our bread and butter.*

"Whatever you say, Mr. McClane," Lowe's voice came, and thereupon the intercom shut off.

Going to the vault section in the chamber behind his office, McClane searched about for a Three packet—trip to Mars—and a Sixty-two packet: secret Interplan spy. Finding the two packets, he returned with them to his desk, seated himself comfortably, poured out the contents—merchandise which would be planted in Quail's conapt while the lab technicians busied themselves installing false memory.

A one-poscred sneaky-pete side arm, McClane reflected; *that's the largest item. Sets us back financially the most.* Then a pellet-sized transmitter, which could be swallowed if the agent were caught. Code book that astonishingly resembled the real thing . . . the firm's models were highly accurate: based, whenever possible, on actual U.S. military issue. Odd bits which made no intrinsic sense but which would be woven into the warp and woof of Quail's imaginary trip, would coincide with his memory: half an ancient silver fifty cent piece, several quotations from John Donne's sermons written incorrectly, each on a separate piece of transparent tissue-thin paper, several match folders from bars on Mars, a stainless steel spoon engraved PROPERTY OF DOME-MARS INTERNATIONAL KIBBUZIM, a wire tapping coil which—

The intercom buzzed. "Mr. McClane, I'm sorry to bother you but something rather ominous has come up. Maybe it would be better if you were in here after all. Quail is already under sedation; he reacted well to the narkidrine; he's completely unconscious and receptive. But—"

"I'll be in." Sensing trouble, McClane left his office; a moment later he emerged in the work area.

On a hygienic bed lay Douglas Quail, breathing slowly and regularly, his eyes virtually shut; he seemed dimly—but only dimly—aware of the two technicians and now McClane himself.

"There's no space to insert false memory-patterns?" McClane felt irritation. "Merely drop out two work weeks; he's employed as a clerk at the West Coast Emigration Bureau, which is a government agency, so he undoubtedly has or had two weeks vacation within the last year. That ought to do it." Petty details annoyed him. And always would.

"Our problem," Lowe said sharply, "is something quite different." He bent over the bed, said to Quail, "Tell Mr. McClane what you told us." To McClane he said, "Listen closely."

The gray-green eyes of the man lying supine in the bed focused on McClane's face. The eyes, he observed uneasily, had become hard; they had a polished, inorganic quality, like semi-precious tumbled stones. He was not sure that he liked what he saw; the brilliance was too cold. "What do you want now?" Quail said harshly. "You've broken my cover. Get out of here before I take you all apart." He studied McClane. "Especially you," he continued. "You're in charge of this counter-operation."

Lowe said, "How long were you on Mars?"

"One month," Quail said gratingly.

"And your purpose there?" Lowe demanded.

The meager lips twisted; Quail eyed him and did not

speak. At last, drawling the words out so that they dripped with hostility, he said, "Agent for Interplan. As I already told you. Don't you record everything that's said? Play your vid-aud tape back for your boss and leave me alone." He shut his eyes, then; the hard brilliance ceased. McClane felt, instantly, a rushing splurge of relief.

Lowe said quietly, "This is a tough man, Mr. McClane."

"He won't be," McClane said, "after we arrange for him to lose his memory-chain again. He'll be as meek as before." To Quail he said, "So *this* is why you wanted to go to Mars so terribly bad."

Without opening his eyes Quail said, "I never wanted to go to Mars. I was assigned it—they handed it to me and there I was: stuck. Oh yeah, I admit I was curious about it; who wouldn't be?" Again he opened his eyes and surveyed the three of them, McClane in particular. "Quite a truth drug you've got here; it brought up things I had absolutely no memory of." He pondered. "I wonder about Kirsten," he said, half to himself. "Could she be in on it? An Interplan contact keeping an eye on me . . . to be certain I didn't regain my memory? No wonder she's been so derisive about my wanting to go there." Faintly, he smiled; the smile—one of understanding—disappeared almost at once.

McClane said, "Please believe me, Mr. Quail; we stumbled onto this entirely by accident. In the work we do—"

"I believe you," Quail said. He seemed tired, now; the drug was continuing to pull him under, deeper and deeper. "Where did I say I'd been?" he murmured. "Mars? Hard to remember—I know I'd like to see it; so would everybody else. But me—" His voice trailed off. "Just a clerk, a nothing clerk."

Straightening up, Lowe said to his superior, "He wants a false memory implanted that corresponds to a trip he actually took. And a false reason which is the real reason. He's telling the truth; he's a long way down in the narkidrine. The trip is very vivid in his mind—at least under sedation. But apparently he doesn't recall it otherwise. Someone, probably at a government military-sciences lab, erased his conscious memories; all he knew was that going to Mars meant something special to him, and so did being a secret agent. They couldn't erase that; it's not a memory but a desire, undoubtedly the same one that motivated him to volunteer for the assignment in the first place."

The other technician, Keeler, said to McClane, "What do we do? Graft a false memory-pattern over the real memory? There's no telling what the results would be; he might remember some of the genuine trip, and the confusion might bring on a psychotic interlude. He'd have to hold two opposite premises in his mind simultaneously: that he went to Mars and that he didn't. That he's a genuine agent for Interplan and he's not, that it's spurious. I think we ought to revive him without any false memory implantation and send him out of here; this is hot."

"Agreed," McClane said. A thought came to him. "Can you predict what he'll remember when he comes out of sedation?"

"Impossible to tell," Lowe said. "He probably will have some dim, diffuse memory of his actual trip, now. And he'd probably be in grave doubt as to its validity; he'd probably decide our programming slipped a gear-tooth. And he'd remember coming here; that wouldn't be erased—unless you want it erased."

"The less we mess with this man," McClane said, "the better I like it. This is nothing for us to fool around with; we've been foolish enough to—or unlucky enough to—uncover a genuine Interplan spy who has a cover so perfect that up to now even he didn't know what he was—or rather is." The sooner they washed their hands of the man calling himself Douglas Quail the better.

"Are you going to plant packets Three and Sixty-two in his conapt?" Lowe said.

"No," McClane said. "And we're going to return half his fee."

" 'Half'! Why half?"

McClane said lamely, "It seems to be a good compromise."

As the cab carried him back to his conapt at the residential end of Chicago, Douglas Quail said to himself, *It's sure good to be back on Terra.*

Already the month-long period on Mars had begun to waver in his memory; he had only an image of profound gaping craters, an ever-present ancient erosion of hills, of vitality, of motion itself. A world of dust where little happened, where a good part of the day was spent checking and rechecking one's portable oxygen source. And then the life-forms, the unassuming and modest gray-brown cacti and maw-worms.

As a matter of fact he had brought back several moribund examples of Martian fauna; he had smuggled them through customs. After all, they posed no menace; they couldn't survive in Earth's heavy atmosphere.

Reaching into his coat pocket, he rummaged for the container of Martian maw-worms—

And found an envelope instead.

Lifting it out, he discovered, to his perplexity, that it contained five hundred and seventy poscreds, in cred bills of low denomination.

Where'd I get this? he asked himself. *Didn't I spend every 'cred I had on my trip?*

With the money came a slip of paper marked: *One-half*

fee ret'd. By McClane. And then the date. Today's date.

"Recall," he said aloud.

"Recall what, sir or madam?" the robot driver of the cab inquired respectfully.

"Do you have a phone book?" Quail demanded.

"Certainly, sir or madam." A slot opened; from it slid a microtape phone book for Cook County.

"It's spelled oddly," Quail said as he leafed through the pages of the yellow section. He felt fear, then; abiding fear. "Here it is," he said. "Take me there, to Rekal, Incorporated. I've changed my mind; I don't want to go home."

"Yes sir, or madam, as the case may be," the driver said. A moment later the cab was zipping back in the opposite direction.

"May I make use of your phone?" he asked.

"Be my guest," the robot driver said. And presented a shiny new emperor 3-D color phone to him.

He dialed his own conapt. And after a pause found himself confronted by a miniature but chillingly realistic image of Kirsten on the small screen. "I've been to Mars," he said to her.

"You're drunk." Her lips writhed scornfully. "Or worse."

" 'S god's truth."

"When?" she demanded.

"I don't know." He felt confused. "A simulated trip, I think. By means of one of those artificial or extra-factual or whatever it is memory places. It didn't take."

Kirsten said witheringly, "You *are* drunk." And broke the connection at her end. He hung up, then, feeling his face flush. *Always the same tone*, he said hotly to himself. *Always the retort, as if she knows everything and I know nothing. What a marriage. Keerist*, he thought dismally.

A moment later the cab stopped at the curb before a modern, very attractive little pink building, over which a shifting polychromatic neon sign read: REKAL, INCORPORATED.

The receptionist, chic and bare from the waist up, started in surprise, then gained masterful control of herself. "Oh, hello, Mr. Quail," she said nervously. "H-how are you? Did you forget something?"

"The rest of my fee back," he said.

More composed now, the receptionist said, "Fee? I think you are mistaken, Mr. Quail. You were here discussing the feasibility of an extra-factual trip for you, but–" She shrugged her smooth pale shoulders. "As I understand it, no trip was taken."

Quail said, "I remember everything, miss. My letter to Rekal, Incorporated, which started this whole business off. I remember my arrival here, my visit with Mr. McClane. Then the two lab technicians taking me in two and administering a drug to put me out." No wonder the firm had returned half his fee. The false memory of his "trip to Mars" hadn't taken–at least not entirely, not as he had been assured.

"Mr. Quail," the girl said, "although you are a minor clerk you are a good-looking man and it spoils your features to become angry. If it would make you feel any better, I might, ahem, let you take me out ..."

He felt furious, then. "I remember you," he said savagely. "For instance the fact that your breasts are sprayed blue; that stuck in my mind. And I remember Mr. McClane's promise that if I remembered my visit to Rekal, Incorporated I'd receive my money back in full. Where is Mr. McClane?"

After a delay–probably as long as they could manage–he found himself once more seated facing the imposing walnut desk, exactly as he had been an hour or so earlier in the day.

"Some technique you have," Quail said sardonically. His disappointment–and resentment–was enormous, by now.

"My so-called 'memory' of a trip to Mars as an undercover agent for Interplan is hazy and vague and shot full of contradictions. And I clearly remember my dealings here with you people. I ought to take this to the Better Business Bureau." He was burning angry, at this point; his sense of being cheated had overwhelmed him, had destroyed his customary aversion to participating in a public squabble.

Looking morose, as well as cautious, McClane said, "We capitulate, Quail. We'll refund the balance of your fee. I fully concede the fact that we did absolutely nothing for you." His tone was resigned.

Quail said accusingly, "You didn't even provide me with the various artifacts that you claimed would 'prove' to me I had been on Mars. All that song-and-dance you went into—it hasn't materialized into a damn thing. Not even a ticket stub. Nor postcards. Nor passport. Nor proof of immunization shots. Nor—"

"Listen, Quail," McClane said. "Suppose I told you—" He broke off. "Let it go." He pressed a button on his intercom. "Shirley, will you disburse five hundred and seventy more 'creds in the form of a cashier's check made out to Douglas Quail? Thank you." He released the button, then glared at Quail.

Presently the check appeared; the receptionist placed it before McClane and once more vanished out of sight, leaving the two men alone, still facing each other across the surface of the massive walnut desk.

"Let me give you a word of advice," McClane said as he signed the check and passed it over. "Don't discuss your, ahem, recent trip to Mars with anyone."

"What trip?"

"Well, that's the thing." Doggedly, McClane said, "The trip you partially remember. Act as if you don't remember; pretend it never took place. Don't ask me why; just take my advice: it'll be better for all of us." He had begun to perspire. Freely. "Now, Mr. Quail, I have other business, other clients to see." He rose, showed Quail to the door.

Quail said, as he opened the door, "A firm that turns out such bad work shouldn't have any clients at all." He shut the door behind him.

On the way home in the cab Quail pondered the wording of his letter of complaint to the Better Business Bureau, Terra Division. As soon as he could get to his typewriter he'd get started; it was clearly his duty to warn other people away from Rekal, Incorporated.

When he got back to his conapt he seated himself before his Hermes Rocket portable, opened the drawers and rummaged for carbon paper—and noticed a small, familiar box. A box which he had carefully filled on Mars with Martian fauna and later smuggled through customs.

Opening the box he saw, to his disbelief, six dead maw-worms and several varieties of the unicellular life on which the Martian worms fed. The protozoa were dried-up, dusty, but he recognized them; it had taken him an entire day picking among the vast dark alien boulders to find them. A wonderful, illuminated journey of discovery.

But I didn't go to Mars, he realized.

Yet on the other hand—

Kirsten appeared at the doorway to the room, an armload of pale brown groceries gripped. "Why are you home in the middle of the day?" Her voice, in an eternity of sameness, was accusing.

"Did I go to Mars?" he asked her. "You would know."

"No, of course, you didn't go to Mars; *you* would know that, I would think. Aren't you always bleating about going?"

He said, "By God, I think I went." After a pause he added, "And simultaneously I think I didn't go."

"Make up your mind."

"How can I?" He gestured. "I have both memory-tracks grafted inside my head; one is real and one isn't but I can't tell which is which. Why can't I rely on you? They haven't tinkered with you." She could do this much for him at least—even if she never did anything else.

Kirsten said in a level, controlled voice, "Doug, if you don't pull yourself together, we're through. I'm going to leave you."

"I'm in trouble." His voice came out husky and coarse. And shaking. "Probably I'm heading into a psychotic episode; I hope not, but—maybe that's it. It would explain everything, anyhow."

Setting down the bag of groceries, Kirsten stalked to the closet. "I was not kidding," she said to him quietly. She brought out a coat, got it on, walked back to the door of the conapt. "I'll phone you one of those days soon," she said tonelessly. "This is goodbye, Doug. I hope you pull out of this eventually; I really pray you do. For your sake."

"Wait," he said desperately. "Just tell me and make it absolute; I did go or I didn't—tell me which one." *But they may have altered your memory-track also*, he realized.

The door closed. His wife had left. Finally!

A voice behind him said, "Well, that's that. Now put up your hands, Quail. And also please turn around and face this way."

He turned, instinctively, without raising his hands.

The man who faced him wore the plum uniform of the Interplan Police Agency, and his gun appeared to be UN issue. And, for some odd reason, he seemed familiar to Quail; familiar in a blurred, distorted fashion which he could not pin down. So, jerkily, he raised his hands.

"You remember," the policeman said, "your trip to Mars. We know all your actions today and all your thoughts—in particular your very important thoughts on the trip home from Rekal, Incorporated." He explained, "We have a telep-transmitter wired within your skull; it keeps us constantly informed."

A telepathic transmitter; use of a living plasma that had been discovered on Luna. He shuddered with self-aversion. The thing lived inside him, within his own brain, feeding, listening, feeding. But the Interplan police used them; that had come out even in the homeopapes. So this was probably true, dismal as it was.

"Why me?" Quail said huskily. What had he done—or thought? And what did this have to do with Rekal, Incorporated?

"Fundamentally," the Interplan cop said, "this has nothing to do with Rekal; it's between you and us." He tapped his right ear. "I'm still picking up your mentational processes by way of your cephalic transmitter." In the man's ear Quail saw a white-plastic plug. "So I have to warn you: anything you think may be held against you." He smiled. "Not that it matters now; you've already thought and spoken yourself into oblivion. What's annoying is the fact that under narkidrine at Rekal, Incorporated you told them, their technicians and the owner, Mr. McClane, about your trip—where you went, for whom, some of what you did. They're very frightened. They wish they had never laid eyes on you." He added reflectively, "They're right."

Quail said, "I never made any trip. It's a false memory-chain improperly planted in me by McClane's technicians." But then he thought of the box, in his desk drawer, containing the Martian life-forms. And the trouble and hardship he had gathering them. The memory seemed real. And the box of life forms; that certainly was real. Unless McClane had planted it. Perhaps this was one of the "proofs" which McClane had talked glibly about.

The memory of my trip to Mars, he thought, *doesn't convince me—but unfortunately it has convinced the Interplan Police Agency. They think I really went to Mars and they think I at least partially realize it.*

"We not only know you went to Mars," the Interplan cop agreed, in answer to his thoughts, "but we know that you now remember enough to be difficult for us. And there's no use expunging your conscious memory of all this, because if we do you'll simply show up at Rekal, Incorporated again and start over. And we can't do anything about McClane and his operation because we have no jurisdiction over anyone except our own people. Anyhow, McClane hasn't committed any crime." He eyed Quail. "Nor, technically, have you. You didn't go to Rekal, Incorporated with the idea of regaining your memory; you went, as we realize, for the usual reason people go there—a love by plain, dull people for adventure." He added, "Unfortunately you're not plain, not dull, and you've already had too much excitement; the last thing in the universe you needed was a course from Rekal, Incorporated. Nothing could have been more lethal for you or for us. And, for that matter, for McClane."

Quail said, "Why is it 'difficult' for you if I remember my trip—my alleged trip—and what I did there?"

"Because," the Interplan harness bull said, "what you did is not in accord with our great white all-protecting father public image. You did, for us, what we never do. As you'll presently remember—thanks to narkidrine. That box of dead worms and algae has been sitting in your desk drawer for six months, ever since you got back. And at no time have you shown the slightest curiosity about it. We didn't even know you had it until you remembered it on your way home from Rekal; then we came here on the double to look for it." He added, unnecessarily, "Without any luck; there wasn't enough time."

A second Interplan cop joined the first one; the two briefly conferred. Meanwhile, Quail thought rapidly. He did remember more, now; the cop had been right about narkidrine. They—Interplan—probably used it themselves. Probably? He knew darn well they did; he had seen them putting a prisoner on it. Where would *that* be? Somewhere on Terra? More likely Luna, he decided, viewing the image rising from his highly defective—but rapidly less so—memory.

And he remembered something else. Their reason for sending him to Mars; the job he had done.

No wonder they had expunged his memory.

"Oh god," the first of the two Interplan cops said, breaking off his conversation with his companion. Obviously, he had picked up Quail's thoughts. "Well, this is a far worse problem, now; as bad as it can get." He walked toward Quail, again covering him with his gun. "We've got to kill you," he said. "And right away."

Nervously, his fellow officer said, "Why right away? Can't we simply cart him off to Interplan New York and let them—"

"*He* knows why it has to be right away," the first cop said; he too looked nervous, now, but Quail realized that it was for an entirely different reason. His memory had been brought back almost entirely, now. And he fully understood the officer's tension.

"On Mars," Quail said hoarsely, "I killed a man. After getting past fifteen bodyguards. Some armed with sneakypete guns, the way you are." He had been trained, by Interplan, over a five year period to be an assassin. A professional killer. He knew ways to take out armed adversaries . . . such as these two officers; and the one with the ear-receiver knew it, too.

If he moved swiftly enough—

The gun fired. But he had already moved to one side,

and at the same time he chopped down the gun-carrying officer. In an instant he had possession of the gun and was covering the other, confused, officer.

"Picked my thoughts up," Quail said, panting for breath. "He knew what I was going to do, but I did it anyhow."

Half sitting up, the injured officer grated, "He won't use that gun on you, Sam; I pick that up, too. He knows he's finished, and he knows we know it, too. Come on, Quail." Laboriously, grunting with pain, he got shakily to his feet. He held out his hand. "The gun," he said to Quail. "You can't use it, and if you turn it over to me I'll guarantee not to kill you; you'll be given a hearing, and someone higher up in Interplan will decide, not me. Maybe they can erase your memory once more; I don't know. But you know the thing I was going to kill you for; I couldn't keep you from remembering it. So my reason for wanting to kill you is in a sense past."

Quail, clutching the gun, bolted from the conapt, sprinted for the elevator. *If you follow me*, he thought. *I'll kill you. So don't.* He jabbed at the elevator button and, a moment later, the doors slid back.

The police hadn't followed him. Obviously they had picked up his terse, tense thoughts and had decided not to take the chance.

With him inside the elevator descended. He had gotten away—for a time. But what next? Where could he go?

The elevator reached the ground floor; a moment later Quail had joined the mob of peds hurrying along the runnels. His head ached and he felt sick. But at least he had evaded death; they had come very close to shooting him on the spot, back in his own conapt.

And they probably will again, he decided. *When they find me. And with this transmitter inside me, that won't take too long.*

Ironically, he had gotten exactly what he had asked Rekal, Incorporated for. Adventure, peril, Interplan police at work, a secret and dangerous trip to Mars in which his life was at stake—everything he had wanted as a false memory.

The advantages of it being a memory—and nothing more—could now be appreciated.

On a park bench, alone, he sat dully watching a flock of perts: a semi-bird imported from Mars' two moons, capable of soaring flight, even against Earth's huge gravity.

Maybe I can find my way back to Mars, he pondered. But then what? It would be worse on Mars; the political organization whose leader he had assassinated would spot him the moment he stepped from the ship; he would have Interplan and *them* after him, there.

Can you hear me thinking? he wondered. Easy avenue to paranoia; sitting here alone he felt them tuning in on him, monitoring, recording, discussing . . . He shivered, rose to his feet, walked aimlessly, his hands deep in his pockets. *No matter where I go*, he realized, *you'll always be with me. As long as I have this device inside my head.*

I'll make a deal with you, he thought to himself—and to them. *Can you imprint a false-memory template on me again, as you did before, that I lived an average, routine life, never went to Mars? Never saw an Interplan uniform up close and never handled a gun?*

A voice inside his brain answered, "As has been carefully explained to you: that would not be enough."

Astonished, he halted.

"We formerly communicated with you in this manner," the voice continued. "When you were operating in the field, on Mars. It's been months since we've done it; we assumed in fact, that we'd never have to do so again. Where are you?"

"Walking," Quail said, "to my death." *By your officers; guns*, he added as an afterthought. "How can you be sure it wouldn't be enough?" he demanded. "Don't the Rekal techniques work?"

"As we said. If you're given a set of standard, average memories you get—restless. You'd inevitably seek out Rekal or one of its competitors again. We can't go through this a second time."

"Suppose," Quail said, "once my authentic memories have been canceled, something more vital than standard memories are implanted. Something which would act to satisfy my craving," he said. "That's been proved; that's probably why you initially hired me. But you ought to be able to come up with something else—something equal. I was the richest man on Terra but I finally gave all my money to educational foundations. Or I was a famous deep-space explorer. Anything of that sort; wouldn't one of those do?"

Silence.

"Try it," he said desperately. "Get some of your topnotch military psychiatrists; explore my mind. Find out what my most expansive daydream is." He tried to think. "Women," he said. "Thousands of them, like Don Juan had. An interplanetary playboy—a mistress in every city on Earth, Luna and Mars. Only I gave that up, out of exhaustion. Please," he begged. "Try it."

"You'd voluntarily surrender, then?" the voice inside his head asked. "If we agreed to arrange such a solution? *If* it's possible?"

After an interval of hesitation he said, "Yes." *I'll take the risk*, he said to himself, *that you don't simply kill me*.

"You make the first move," the voice said presently. "Turn yourself over to us. And we'll investigate that line of possibility. If we can't do it, however, if your authentic memories begin to crop up again as they've done at this time, then—" There was silence and then the voice finished, "We'll have to destroy you. As you must understand. Well, Quail, you still want to try?"

"Yes," he said. Because the alternative was death now—and for certain. At least this way he had a chance, slim as it was.

"You present yourself at our main barracks in New York," the voice of the Interplan cop resumed. "At 580 Fifth Avenue, floor twelve. Once you've surrendered yourself we'll have our psychiatrists begin on you; we'll have personality-profile tests made. We'll attempt to determine your absolute, ultimate fantasy wish—then we'll bring you back to Rekal, Incorporated, here; get them in on it, fulfilling that wish in vicarious surrogate retrospection. And—good luck. We do owe you something; you acted as a capable instrument for us." The voice lacked malice; if anything, they—the organization—felt sympathy toward him.

"Thanks," Quail said. And began searching for a robot cab.

"Mr. Quail," the stern-faced, elderly Interplan psychiatrist said, "you possess a most interesting wish-fulfillment dream fantasy. Probably nothing such as you consciously entertain or suppose. This is commonly the way; I hope it won't upset you too much to hear about it."

The senior ranking Interplan officer present said briskly, "He better not be too much upset to hear about it, not if he expects not to get shot."

"Unlike the fantasy of wanting to be an Interplan undercover agent," the psychiatrist continued, "which, being relatively speaking a product of maturity, had a certain plausibility to it, this production is a grotesque dream of your childhood; it is no wonder you fail to recall it. Your fantasy is this: you are nine years old, walking alone down a rustic lane. An unfamiliar variety of space vessel from another star system lands directly in front of you. No one on Earth but you, Mr. Quail, sees it. The creatures within are very small and helpless, somewhat on the order of field mice, although they are attempting to invade Earth; tens of thousands of other such ships will soon be on their way, when this advance party gives the go-ahead signal."

"And I suppose I stop them," Quail said, experiencing a mixture of amusement and disgust. "Single-handed—I wipe them out! Probably by stepping on them with my foot."

"No,' the psychiatrist said patiently. "You halt the invasion, but not by destroying them. Instead, you show them kindness and mercy, even though by telepathy—their mode of communication—you know why they have come. They have never seen such humane traits exhibited by any sentient organism, and to show their appreciation they make a covenant with you."

Quail said, "They won't invade Earth as long as I'm alive."

"Exactly." To the Interplan officer the psychiatrist said. "You can see it does fit his personality, despite his feigned scorn."

"So by merely existing," Quail said, feeling a growing pleasure, "by simply being alive, I keep Earth safe from alien rule. I'm in effect, then, the most important person on Terra. Without lifting a finger."

"Yes, indeed, sir," the psychiatrist said. "And this is bedrock in your psyche; this is a life-long childhood fantasy. Which, without depth and drug therapy, you never would have recalled. But it has always existed in you; it went underneath, but never ceased."

To McClane, who sat intently listening, the senior police official said, "Can you implant an extra-factual memory pattern that extreme in him?"

"We get handed every possible type of wish-fantasy there is," McClane said. "Frankly, I've heard a lot worse than this. Certainly we can handle it. Twenty-four hours from now he won't just *wish* he'd saved Earth; he'll devoutly believe it really happened."

The senior police official said, "You can start the job, then. In preparation we've already once again erased the memory in him of his trip to Mars."

Quail said, "What trip to Mars?"

No one answered him, so reluctantly, he shelved the question. And anyhow a police vehicle had now put in its appearance; he, McClane and the senior police officer crowded into it, and presently they were on their way to Chicago and Rekal, Incorporated.

"You had better make no errors this time," the police officer said to heavyset, nervous-looking McClane.

"I can't see what could go wrong," McClane mumbled, perspiring. "This has nothing to do with Mars or Interplan. Single-handedly stopping an invasion of Earth from another star-system." He shook his head at that. "Wow, what a kid dreams up. And by pious virtue, too; not by force. It's sort of quaint." He dabbed at his forehead with a large linen pocket handkerchief.

Nobody said anything.

"In fact," McClane said, "it's touching."

"But arrogant," the police official said starkly. "Inasmuch as when he dies the invasion will resume. No wonder he doesn't recall it; it's the most grandiose fantasy I ever ran across." He eyed Quail with disapproval. "And to think we put this man on our payroll."

When they reached Rekal, Incorporated the receptionist, Shirley, met them breathlessly in the outer office. "Welcome back, Mr. Quail," she fluttered, her melon-shaped breasts—today painted an incandescent orange—bobbing with agitation. "I'm sorry everything worked out so badly before; I'm sure this time it'll go better."

Still repeatedly dabbing at his shiny forehead with his neatly-folded Irish linen handkerchief, McClane said, "It better." Moving with rapidity he rounded up Lowe and Keeler, escorted them and Douglas Quail to the work area, and then, with Shirley and the senior police officer, returned to his familiar office. To wait.

"Do we have a packet made up for this, Mr. McClane?" Shirley asked, bumping against him in her agitation, then coloring modestly.

"I think we do." He tried to recall, then gave up and consulted the formal chart. "A combination," he decided aloud, "of packets Eighty-one, Twenty, and Six." From the vault section of the chamber behind his desk he fished out the appropriate packets, carried them to his desk for inspection. "From Eighty-one," he explained, "a magic healing rod given him—the client in question, this time Mr. Quail— by the race of beings from another system. A token of their gratitude."

"Does it work?" the police officer asked curiously.

"It did once," McClane explained. "But he, ahem, you see, used it up years ago, healing right and left. Now it's only a memento. But he remembers it working spectacularly." He chuckled, then opened packet Twenty. "Document from the UN Secretary General thanking him for saving Earth; this isn't precisely appropriate, because part of Quail's fantasy is that no one knows of the invasion except himself, but for the sake of verisimilitude we'll throw it in." He inspected packet Six, then. What came from this? He couldn't recall; frowning, he dug into the plastic bag as Shirley and the Interplan police officer watched intently.

"Writing," Shirley said. "In a funny language."

"This tells who they were," McClane said, "and where

they came from. Including a detailed star map logging their flight here and the system of origin. Of course it's in *their* script, so he can't read it. But he remembers them reading it to him in his own tongue." He placed the three artifacts in the center of the desk. "These should be taken to Quail's conapt," he said to the police officer. "So that when he gets home he'll find them. And it'll confirm his fantasy. SOP—standard operating procedure." He chuckled apprehensively, wondering how matters were going with Lowe and Keeler.

The intercom buzzed. "Mr. McClane, I'm sorry to bother you." It was Lowe's voice; he froze as he recognized it, froze and became mute. "But something's come up. Maybe it would be better if you came in here and supervised. Like before, Quail reacted well to the narkidrine; he's unconscious, relaxed and receptive. But—"

McClane sprinted for the work area.

On a hygienic bed Douglas Quail lay breathing slowly and regularly, eyes half-shut, dimly conscious of those around him.

"We started interrogating him," Lowe said, white-faced. "To find out exactly when to place the fantasy-memory of him single-handedly having saved earth. And strangely enough—"

"They told me not to tell," Douglas Quail mumbled in a dull drug-saturated voice. "That was the agreement. I wasn't even supposed to remember. But how could I forget an event like that?"

I guess it would be hard, McClane reflected. *But you did—until now.*

"They even gave me a scroll," Quail mumbled, "of gratitude. I have it hidden in my conapt; I'll show it to you.

To the Interplan officer who had followed after him, McClane said, "Well, I offer the suggestion that you better not kill him. If you do they'll return."

"They also gave me a magic invisible destroying rod," Quail mumbled, eyes totally shut now. "That's how I killed that man on Mars you sent me to take out. It's in my drawer along with the box of Martian maw-worms and dried-up plant life."

Wordlessly, the Interplan officer turned and stalked from the work area.

I might as well put those packets of proof-artifacts away, McClane said to himself resignedly. He walked, step by step, back to his office. *Including the citation from the UN Secretary General. After all—*

The real one probably would not be long in coming.

THE GIRL WHO WAS PLUGGED IN

JAMES TIPTREE, JR.

Listen, zombie. Believe me. What I could tell you—you with your silly hands leaking sweat on your growth-stocks portfolio. One-ten lousy hacks of AT&T on twenty-percent margin and you think you're Evel Knievel. AT&T . . . You doubleknit dummy, how I'd love to show you something.

Look, dead daddy, I'd say. See for instance that rotten girl?

In the crowd over there, that one gaping at her gods. One rotten girl in the city of the future. (That's what I said.) Watch.

She's jammed among bodies, craning and peering with her soul yearning out of her eyeballs. Love! Oo-ooh, love them! Her gods are coming out of a store called Body East. Three youngbloods, larking along loverly. Dressed like simple streetpeople but . . . smashing. See their great eyes swivel above their nose-filters, their hands lift shyly, their inhumanly tender lips melt? The crowd moans. Love! This whole boiling megacity, this whole fun future world loves its gods.

You don't believe gods, dad? Wait. Whatever turns you on, there's a god in the future for you, custom-made. Listen to this mob. "I touched his foot! Ow-oow, I TOUCHED Him!"

Even the people in the GTX tower up there love the gods—in their own way and for their own reasons.

The funky girl on the street, she just loves. Grooving on their beautiful lives, their mysterioso problems. No one ever told her about mortals who love a god and end up as a tree or a sighing sound. In a million years it'd never occur to her that her gods might love her back.

She's squashed against the wall now as the godlings come by. They move in a clear space. A holocam bobs above but its shadow never, falls on them. The store display screens are magically clear of bodies as the gods glance in and a beggar underfoot is suddenly alone. They give him a token. "Aaaaah!" goes the crowd.

Now one of them flashes some wild new kind of timer and they all trot to catch a shuttle, just like people. The shuttle stops for them—more magic. The crowd sighs, closing back. The gods are gone.

(In a room far from—but not unconnected to—the GTX tower a molecular flipflop closes too, and three account tapes spin.)

Our girl is still stuck by the wall while guards and holocam equipment pull away. The adoration's fading from her face. That's good, because now you can see she's the ugly of the world. A tall monument to pituitary dystrophy. No surgeon would touch her. When she smiles, her jaw—it's half purple—almost bites her left eye out. She's also quite young, but who could care?

The crowd is pushing her along now, treating you to glimpses of her jumbled torso, her mismatched legs. At the corner she strains to send one last fond spasm after the godlings' shuttle. Then her face reverts to its usual expression of dim pain and she lurches onto the moving walkway, stumbling into people. The walkway junctions with another. She crosses, trips and collides with the casualty rail. Finally she comes out into a little place called a park. The sportshow is working, a basketball game in 3-di is going on right overhead. But all she does is squeeze onto a bench and huddle there while a ghostly free-throw goes by her ear.

After that nothing at all happens except a few furtive hand-mouth gestures which don't even interest her benchmates.

But you're curious about the city? So ordinary after all, in the FUTURE?

Ah, there's plenty to swing with here—and it's not all that *far* in the future, dad. But pass up the sci-fi stuff for now, like for instance the holovision technology that's put TV and radio in museums. Or the worldwide carrier field bouncing down from satellites, controlling communication and transport systems all over the globe. That was a spin-off from asteroid mining, pass it by. We're watching that girl.

I'll give you just one goodie. Maybe you noticed on the sportshow or the streets? No commercials. No ads.

That's right. NO ADS. An eyeballer for you.

Look around. Not a billboard, sign, slogan, jingle, skywrite, blurb, sublim-flash in this whole fun world. Brand names? Only in those ticky little peep-screens on the stores and you could hardly call that advertising. How does that finger you?

Think about it. That girl is still sitting there.

She's parked right under the base of the GTX tower as a matter of fact. Look up and you can see the sparkles from the bubble on top, up there among the domes of godland. Inside that bubble is a boardroom. Neat bronze shield on the door: Global Transmissions Corporation—not that that means anything.

I happen to know there's six people in that room. Five of them technically male, and the sixth isn't easily thought of as a mother. *They are absolutely unremarkable.* Those faces were seen once at their nuptials and will show again in their obituaries and impress nobody either time. If you're looking for the secret Big Blue Meanies of the world, forget it. I know. Zen, do I know! Flesh? Power? Glory? You'd horrify them.

What they do like up there is to have things orderly, especially their communications. You could say they've dedicated their lives to that, to freeing the world from garble. Their nightmares are about hemorrhages of information: channels screwed up, plans misimplemented, garble creeping in. Their vast wealth only worries them, it keeps opening new vistas of disorder. Luxury? They wear what their tailors put on them, eat what their cooks serve them. See that old boy there—his name is Isham—he's sipping water and frowning as he listens to a databall. The water was prescribed by his medistaff. It tastes awful. The databall also contains a disquieting message about his son, Paul.

But it's time to go back down, far below to our girl. Look!

She's toppled over sprawling on the ground.

A tepid commotion ensues among the bystanders. The consensus is she's dead, which she disproves by bubbling a little. And presently she's taken away by one of the superb ambulances of the future, which are a real improvement over ours when one happens to be around.

At the local bellevue the usual things are done by the usual team of clowns aided by a saintly mop-pusher. Our girl revives enough to answer the questionnaire without which you can't die, even in the future. Finally she's cast up, a pumped-out hulk on a cot in the long, dim ward.

Again nothing happens for a while except that her eyes leak a little from the understandable disappointment of finding herself still alive.

But somewhere one GTX computer has been tickling another, and toward midnight something does happen. First comes an attendant who pulls screens around her. Then a man in a business doublet comes daintily down the ward. He motions the attendant to strip off the sheet and go.

The groggy girl-brute heaves up, big hands clutching at bodyparts you'd pay not to see.

"Burke? P. Burke, is that your name?"

"Y-yes." Croak. "Are you . . . policeman?"

"No. They'll be along shortly, I expect. Public suicide's a felony."

". . . I'm sorry."

He has a 'corder in his hand. "No family, right?"

"No."

"You're seventeen. One year city college. What did you study?"

"La-languages."

"H'm. Say something."

Unintelligible rasp.

He studies her. Seen close, he's not so elegant. Errand-boy type.

"Why did you try to kill yourself?"

She stares at him with dead-rat dignity, hauling up the gray sheet. Give him a point, he doesn't ask twice.

"Tell me, did you see Breath this afternoon?"

Dead as she nearly is, that ghastly love-look wells up. Breath is the three young gods, a loser's cult. Give the man another point, he interprets her expression.

"How would you like to meet them?"

The girl's eyes bug out unequally.

"I have a job for someone like you. It's hard work. If you did well you'd be meeting Breath and stars like that all the time."

Is he insane? She's deciding she really did die.

"But it means you never see anybody you know again. Never, *ever*. You will be legally dead. Even the police won't know. Do you want to try?"

It all has to be repeated while her great jaw slowly sets. *Show me the fire I walk through.* Finally P. Burke's prints are in his 'corder, the man holding up the rancid girl-body without a sign of distaste. It makes you wonder what else he does.

And then—THE MAGIC. Sudden silent trot of litterbearers tucking P. Burke into something quite different from a bellevue stretcher, the oiled slide into the daddy of all luxury ambulances—real flowers in that holder!—and the long jarless rush to nowhere. Nowhere is warm and gleaming and kind with nurses. (Where did you hear that money can't buy genuine kindness?) And clean clouds folding P. Burke into bewildered sleep.

... Sleep which merges into feedings and washings and more sleeps, into drowsy moments of afternoon where midnight should be, and gentle businesslike voices and friendly (but very few) faces, and endless painless hyposprays and peculiar numbnesses ... and later comes the steadying rhythm of days and nights, and a quickening which P. Burke doesn't identify as health, but only knows that the fungus place in her armpit is gone ... and then she's up and following those few new faces with growing trust, first tottering, then walking strongly, all better now—clumping down the short hall to the tests, tests, tests, and the other things.

And here is our girl, looking—

If possible, worse than before. (You thought this was Cinderella transistorized?)

The disimprovement in her looks comes from the electrode jacks peeping out of her sparse hair, and there are other meldings of flesh and metal. On the other hand, that collar and spinal plate are really an asset; you won't miss seeing that neck.

P. Burke is ready for training in her new job.

The training takes place in her suite, and is exactly what you'd call a charm course. How to walk, sit, eat, speak, blow her nose, how to stumble, to urinate, to hiccup—DELICIOUSLY. How to make each nose-blow or shrug delightfully, subtly different from any ever spooled before. As the man said, it's hard work.

But P. Burke proves apt. Somewhere in that horrible body is a gazelle, a houri who would have been buried forever without this crazy chance. See the ugly duckling go!

Only it isn't precisely P. Burke who's stepping, laughing, shaking out her shining hair. How could it be? P. Burke is doing it all right, but she's doing it through something. The something is to all appearances a live girl. (You were warned, this is the FUTURE.)

When they first open the big cryocase and show her her new body she says just one word. Staring, gulping, "How?"

Simple, really. Watch P. Burke in her sack and scuffs stump down the hall beside Joe, the man who supervises the technical part of her training. Joe doesn't mind P. Burke's looks, he hasn't noticed them. To Joe system matrices are beautiful.

They go into a dim room containing a huge cabinet like a one-man sauna and a console for Joe. The room has a glass wall that's all dark now. And just for your information, the whole shebang is five hundred feet underground near what used to be Carbondale, Pa.

Joe opens the sauna-cabinet like a big clamshell standing on end with a lot of funny business inside. Our girl shucks her shift and walks into it bare, totally unembarrassed. *Eager.* She settles in face-forward, butting jacks into sockets. Joe closes it carefully onto her humpback. Clunk. She can't see in there or hear or move. She hates this minute. But how she loves what comes next!

Joe's at his console and the lights on the other side of the glass wall come up. A room is on the other side, all fluff and kicky bits, a girly bedroom. In the bed is a small mound of silk with a rope of yellow hair hanging out.

The sheet stirs and gets whammed back flat.

Sitting up in the bed is the darlingest girl child you've EVER seen. She quivers—porno for angels. She sticks both her little arms straight up, flips her hair, looks around full of sleepy pazazz. Then she can't resist rubbing her hands down over her minibreasts and belly. Because, you see, it's the godawful P. Burke who is sitting there hugging her perfect girl-body, looking at you out of delighted eyes.

Then the kitten hops out of bed and crashes flat on the floor.

From the sauna in the dim room comes a strangled noise. P. Burke, trying to rub her wired-up elbow, is suddenly smothered in *two* bodies, electrodes jerking in her flesh. Joe juggles inputs, crooning into his mike. The flurry passes; it's all right.

In the lighted room the elf gets up, casts a cute glare at the glass wall and goes into a transparent cubicle. A bathroom, what else? She's a live girl, and live girls have to go to the bathroom after a night's sleep even if their brains are in a sauna cabinet in the next room. And P. Burke isn't in that cabinet, she's in the bathroom. Perfectly simple, if you have the glue for that closed training circuit that's letting her run her neural system by remote control.

Now let's get one thing clear. P. Burke does not *feel* her brain is in the next room, she feels it's in that sweet little body. When you wash your hands, do you feel the water is running on your brain? Of course not. You feel the water on your hand, although the "feeling" is actually a potential-pattern flickering over the electrochemical jelly between your ears. And it's delivered there via the long circuits from your hands. Just so, P. Burke's brain in the cabinet feels the water on her hands in the bathroom. The fact that the signals have jumped across space on the way in makes no difference at all. If you want the jargon, it's known as eccentric projection or sensory reference and you've done it all your life. Clear?

Time to leave the honey-pot to her toilet training—she's made a booboo with the toothbrush, because P. Burke can't get used to what she sees in the mirror—

But wait, you say. Where did that girl-body come from?

P. Burke asks that too, dragging out the words.

"They grow 'em," Joe tells her. He couldn't care less about the flesh department. "PDs. Placental decanters. Modified embryos, see? Fit the control implants in later. Without a Remote Operator it's just a vegetable. Look at the feet—no callus at all." (He knows because they told him.)

"Oh . . . oh, she's incredible . . ."

"Yeah, a neat job. Want to try walking-talking mode today? You're coming on fast."

And she is. Joe's reports and the reports from the nurse and the doctor and style man go to a bushy man upstairs who is some kind of medical cybertech but mostly a project administrator. His reports in turn go—to the GTX boardroom? Certainly not, did you think this is a *big* thing? His reports just go up. The point is, they're green, very green. P. Burke promises well.

So the bushy man—Doctor Tesla—has procedures to initiate. The little kitten's dossier in the Central Data Bank, for instance. Purely routine. And the phase-in schedule which will put her on the scene. This is simple: a small exposure in an off-network holoshow.

Next he has to line out the event which will fund and target her. That takes budget meetings, clearances, coordinations. The Burke project begins to recruit and grow. And there's the messy business of the name, which always gives Doctor Tesla an acute pain in the bush.

The name comes out weird, when it's suddenly discovered that Burke's "P." stands for *Philadelphia*. Philadelphia? The astrologer grooves on it. Joe thinks it would help identification. The semantics girl references *brotherly love, Liberty-Bell, main-line, low teratogenesis*, blah-blah. Nicknames—Philly? Pala? Pooty? Delphi? Is it good, bad? Finally *Delphi* is gingerly declared goodo. ("Burke" is replaced by something nobody remembers.)

Coming along now. We're at the official checkout down in the underground suite, which is as far as the training circuits reach. The bushy Doctor Tesla is there, braced by two budgetary types and a quiet fatherly man whom he handles like hot plasma.

Joe swings the door wide and she steps shyly in.

Their little Delphi, fifteen and flawless.

Tesla introduces her around. She's child-solemn, a beautiful baby to whom something so wonderful has happened you can feel the tingles. She doesn't smile, she ... brims. That brimming joy is all that shows of P. Burke, the forgotten hulk in the sauna next door. But P. Burke doesn't know she's alive—it's Delphi who lives, every warm inch of her.

One of the budget types lets go a libidinous snuffle and freezes. The fatherly man, whose name is Mr. Cantle, clears his throat.

"Well, young lady, are you ready to go to work?"

"Yes sir," gravely from the elf.

"We'll see. Has anybody told you what you're going to do for us?"

"No, sir." Joe and Tesla exhale quietly.

"Good." He eyes her, probing for the blind brain in the room next door.

"Do you know what *advertising* is?"

He's talking dirty, hitting to shock. Delphi's eyes widen and her little chin goes up. Joe is in ecstasy at the complex expressions P. Burke is getting through. Mr. Cantle waits.

"It's well, it's when they used to tell people to buy things." She swallows. "It's not allowed."

"That's right." Mr. Cantle leans back, grave. "Advertising as it used to be is against the law. *A display other than the legitimate use of the product, intended to promote its sale.* In former times every manufacturer was free to tout his wares any way, place, or time he could afford. All the media and most of the landscape was taken up with extravagant competing displays. The thing became uneconomic. The public rebelled. Since the so-called Huckster Act, sellers have been restrained to, I quote, 'displays in or on the product itself, visible during its legitimate use or in on-premise sales.' " Mr. Cantle leans forward. "Now tell me, Delphi, why do people buy one product rather than another?"

"Well . . ." Enchanting puzzlement from Delphi. "They, um, they see them and like them, or they hear about them from somebody?" (Touch of P. Burke there; she didn't say, from a friend.)

"Partly. Why did *you* buy your particular body-lift?"

"I never had a body-lift, sir."

Mr. Cantle frowns; what gutters did they drag for these Remotes?

"Well, what brand of water do you drink?"

"Just what was in the faucet, sir," says Delphi humbly. "I—I did try to boil it—"

"Good God." He scowls; Tesla stiffens. "Well, what did you boil it in? A cooker?"

The shining yellow head nods.

"What *brand* of cooker did you buy?"

"I didn't buy it, sir," says frightened P. Burke through Delphi's lips. "But—I know the best kind! Ananga has a Burnbabi, I saw the name when she—"

"Exactly!" Cantle's fatherly beam comes back strong; the Burnbabi account is a strong one, too. "You saw Ananga using one so you thought it must be good, eh? And it is good or a great human being like Ananga wouldn't be using it. Absolutely right. And now, Delphi, you know what you're going to be doing for us. You're going to show some products. Doesn't sound very hard, does it?"

"Oh, no, sir . . ." Baffled child's stare; Joe gloats.

"And you must never, *never* tell anyone what you're doing." Cantle's eyes bore for the brain behind this seductive child.

"You're wondering why we ask you to do this, naturally. There's a very serious reason. All those products people use, foods and health aids and cookers and cleaners and clothes and car—they're all made by *people*. Somebody put in years of hard work designing and making them. A man comes up with a fine new idea for a better product. He has to get a factory and machinery, and hire workmen. Now. What happens if people have no way of hearing about his product? Word-of-mouth is far too slow and unreliable. Nobody might ever stumble onto his new product or find out how good it was, right? And then he and all the people who worked for him—they'd go bankrupt, right? So, Delphi, there has to be *some way* that large numbers of people can get a look at a good new product, right? How? By letting people see you using it. You're *giving that man a chance.*"

Delphi's little head is nodding in happy relief.

"Yes, sir, I do see now—but sir, it seems so sensible, why don't they let you—"

Cantle smiles sadly.

"It's an overreaction, my dear. History goes by swings. People overreact and pass harsh unrealistic laws which attempt to stamp out an essential social process. When this happens, the people who understand have to carry on as best they can until the pendulum swings back. He sighs. "The Huckster Laws are bad, inhuman laws, Delphi, despite their good intent. If they were strictly observed they would wreak havoc. Our economy, our society would be cruelly destroyed. We'd be back in caves!" (His inner fire is showing; if the Huckster Laws were strictly enforced he'd be back punching a databank.)

"It's our duty, Delphi. Our solemn social duty. Nor are we breaking the law. You will be using the product. But people wouldn't understand, if they knew. They would become upset, just as you did. So you must be very, very careful not to mention any of this to anybody."

(And somebody will be very, very carefully monitoring Delphi's speech circuits.)

"Now we're all straight, aren't we? Little Delphi here"—he is speaking to the invisible creature next door—"Little Delphi is going to live a wonderful, exciting life. She's going to be a girl people watch. And she's going to be using fine products people will be glad to know about and helping the good people who make them. Yours will be a genuine social contribution." He keys up his pitch; the creature in there must be older.

Delphi digests this with ravishing gravity.

"But sir, how do I—?"

"Don't worry about a thing. You'll have people behind

you whose job it is to select the most worthy products for you to use. Your job is just to do as they say. They'll show you what outfits to wear to parties, what suncars and viewers to buy and so on. That's all you have to do."

Parties—clothes—suncars! Delphi's pink mouth opens. In P. Burke's starved seventeen-year-old head the ethics of product sponsorship float far away.

"Now tell me in your own words what your job is, Delphi."

"Yes sir. I—I'm to go to parties and buy things and use them as they tell me, to help the people who work in factories."

"And what did I say was so important?"

"Oh—I shouldn't let anybody know, about the things."

"Right." Mr. Cantle has another paragraph he uses when the subject shows, well, immaturity. But he can sense only eagerness here. Good. He doesn't really enjoy the other speech.

"It's a lucky girl who can have all the fun she wants while doing good for others, isn't it?" He beams around. There's a prompt shuffling of chairs. Clearly this one is go.

Joe leads her out, grinning. The poor fool thinks they're admiring her coordination.

It's out into the world for Delphi now, and at this point the up-channels get used. On the administrative side account schedules are opened, subprojects activated. On the technical side the reserved bandwidth is cleared. (That carrier field, remember?) A new name is waiting for Delphi, a name she'll never hear. It's a long string of binaries which have been quietly cycling in a GTX tank ever since a certain Beautiful Person didn't wake up.

The name winks out of cycle, dances from pulses into modulations of modulations, whizzes through phasing, and shoots into a giga-band beam racing up to a synchronous satellite poised over Guatemala. From there the beam pours twenty thousand miles back to earth again, forming an all-pervasive field of structured energics supplying tuned demand-points all over the CanAm quadrant.

With that field, if you have the right credit rating you can sit at a GTX console and operate a tuned ore-extractor in Brazil. Or—if you have some simple credentials like being able to walk on water—you could shoot a spool into the network holocam shows running day and night in every home and dorm. Or you could create a continentwide traffic jam. Is it any wonder GTX guards those inputs like a sacred trust?

Delphi's "name" appears as a tiny analyzable nonredundancy in the flux, and she'd be very proud if she knew about it. It would strike P. Burke as magic; P. Burke never even understood robotcars. But Delphi is in no sense a robot. Call her a waldo if you must. The fact is she's just a girl, a real live girl with her brain in an unusual place. A simple real-time on-line system with plenty of bit-rate—even as you and you.

The point of all this hardware, which isn't very much hardware in this society, is so Delphi can walk out of that underground suite, a mobile demand-point draining an omnipresent fieldform. And she does—eighty-nine pounds of tender girl flesh and blood with a few metallic components, stepping out into the sunlight to be taken to her new life. A girl with everything going for her including a meditech escort. Walking lovely, stopping to widen her eyes at the big antennae system overhead.

The mere fact that something called P. Burke is left behind down underground has no bearing at all. P. Burke is totally un-self-aware and happy as a clam in its shell. (Her bed has been moved into the waldo cabinet room now.) And P. Burke isn't in the cabinet; P. Burke is climbing out of an airvan in a fabulous Colorado beef preserve and her name is Delphi. Delphi is looking at live Charlais steers and live cottonwoods and aspens gold against the blue smog and stepping over live grass to be welcomed by the reserve super's wife.

The super's wife is looking forward to a visit from Delphi and her friends and by a happy coincidence there's a holocam outfit here doing a piece for the nature nuts.

You could write the script yourself now while Delphi learns a few rules about structural interferences and how to handle the tiny time lag which results from the new forty-thousand-mile parenthesis in her nervous system. That's right—the people with the leased holocam rig naturally find the gold aspen shadows look a lot better on Delphi's flank than they do on a steer. And Delphi's face improves the mountains too, when you can see them. But the nature freaks aren't quite as joyful as you'd expect.

"See you in Barcelona, kitten," the head man says sourly as they pack up.

"Barcelona?" echoes Delphi with that charming little subliminal lag. She sees where his hand is and steps back.

"Cool, it's not her fault," another man says wearily. He knocks back his grizzled hair. "Maybe they'll leave in some of the gut."

Delphi watches them go off to load the spools on the GTX transport for processing. Her hand roves over the breast the man had touched. Back under Carbondale, P. Burke has discovered something new about her Delphi-body.

About the difference between Delphi and her own grim carcass.

She's always known Delphi has almost no sense of taste or smell. They explained about that: Only so much bandwidth. You don't have to taste a suncar, do you? And the slight overall dimness of Delphi's sense of touch—she's familiar with that, too. Fabrics that would prickle P. Burke's own hide feel like a cool plastic film to Delphi.

But the blank spots. It took her a while to notice them. Delphi doesn't have much privacy; investments of her size don't. So she's slow about discovering there's certain definite places where her beastly P. Burke body *feels* things that Delphi's dainty flesh does not. H'mm! Channel space again, she thinks—and forgets it in the pure bliss of being Delphi.

You ask how a girl could forget a thing like that? Look. P. Burke is about as far as you can get from the concept *girl.* She's a female, yes—but for her, sex is a four-letter word spelled P-A-I-N. She isn't quite a virgin; you don't want the details. She'd been about twelve and the freak-lovers were bombed blind. When they came down they threw her out with a small hole in her anatomy and a mortal one elsewhere. She dragged off to buy her first and last shot and she can still hear the clerk's incredulous guffaws.

Do you see why Delphi grins, stretching her delicious little numb body in the sun she faintly feels? Beams, saying, "Please, I'm ready now."

Ready for what? For Barcelona like the sour man said, where his nature-thing is now making it strong in the amateur section of the Festival. A winner! Like he also said, a lot of strip-mines and dead fish have been scrubbed but who cares with Delphi's darling face so visible?

So it's time for Delphi's face and her other delectabilities to show on Barcelona's Playa Neuva. Which means switching her channel to the EurAf synchsat.

They ship her at night so the nanosecond transfer isn't even noticed by that insignificant part of Delphi that lives five hundred feet under Carbondale, so excited the nurse has to make sure she eats. The circuit switches while Delphi "sleeps," that is while P. Burke is out of the waldo cabinet.

The next time she plugs in to open Delphi's eyes it's no different—do you notice which relay boards your calls go through?

And now for the event that turns the sugarcube from Colorado into the PRINCESS.

Literally true, he's a prince, or rather an Infante of an old Spanish line that got shined up in the Neomonarchy. He's also eighty-one, with a passion for birds—the kind you see in zoos. Now it suddenly turns out that he isn't poor at all. Quite the reverse; his old sister laughs in their tax law-yer's face and starts restoring the family hacienda while the Infante totters out to court Delphi. And little Delphi begins to live the life of the gods.

What do gods do? Well, everything beautiful. But (re-member Mr. Cantle?) the main point is Things. Ever see a god empty-handed? You can't be a god without at least a magic girdle or an eight-legged horse. But in the old days some stone tablets or winged sandals or a chariot drawn by virgins would do a god for life. No more! Gods make it on novelty now. By Delphi's time the hunt for new god-gear is turning the earth and seas inside-out and sending frantic fingers to the stars. And what gods have, mortals desire.

So Delphi starts on a Euromarket shopping spree squired by her old Infante, thereby doing her bit to stave off social collapse.

Social what? Didn't you get it, when Mr. Cantle talked about a world where advertising is banned and fifteen bil-lion consumers are glued to their holocam shows? One ca-pricious self-powered god can wreck you.

Take the nose-filter massacre. Years, the industry worked years to achieve an almost invisible enzymatic filter. So a couple of pop-gods show up wearing nose-filters like *big purple bats*. By the end of the week the world market is screaming for purple bats. Then it switched to bird-heads and skulls. By the time the industry retooled the crazies had dropped bird-heads and gone to injection globes. Blood!

Multiply that by every consumer industry and you can see why it's economic to have a few controllable gods. Especially with the beautiful hunk of space R&D the Peace Department laid out for, and which the taxpayers are only too glad to have taken off their hands by an outfit like GTX which everybody knows is almost a public trust.

And so you—or rather, GTX—find a creature like P. Burke and give her Delphi. And Delphi helps keep things *orderly*, she does what you tell her to. Why? . . . That's right, Mr. Cantle never finished his speech.

But here come the tests of Delphi's button-nose twinkling in the torrent of news and entertainment. And she's noticed. The feedback shows a flock of viewers turning up the amps when this country baby gets tangled in her new colloidal body-jewels. She registers at a couple of major scenes, too, and when the Infante gives her a suncar, little Delphi trying out suncars is a tiger. There's a solid response in high-credit country. Mr. Cantle is humming his happy tune as he cancels a Benelux subnet option to guest her on a nude cook-show called Wok Venus.

And now for the superposh old-world wedding! The hacienda has Moorish baths and six-foot silver candelabras and real black horses and the Spanish Vatican blesses them. The final event is a grand gaucho ball with the old prince and his little Infante on a bowered balcony. She's a spectacular doll of silver lace, wildly launching toy doves at her new friends whirling by below.

The Infante beams, twitches his old nose to the scent of her sweet excitement. His doctor has been very helpful. Surely now, after he has been so patient with the suncars and all the nonsense—

The child looks up at him, saying something incomprehensible about "breath." He makes out that she's complaining about the three singers she had begged for.

"They've changed!" she marvels. "Haven't they changed? They're so dreary. I'm so happy now!"

And Delphi falls fainting against a gothic vargueno.

Her American duenna rushes up, calls help. Delphi's eyes are open, but Delphi isn't there. The duenna pokes among Delphi's hair, slaps her. The old prince grimaces. He has no idea what she is beyond an excellent solution to his tax problems, but he had been a falconer in his youth. There comes to his mind the small pinioned birds which were flung up to stimulate the hawks. He pockets the veined claw to which he had promised certain indulgences and departs to design his new aviary.

And Delphi also departs with her retinue to the Infante's newly discovered yacht. The trouble isn't serious. It's only that five thousand miles away and five hundred feet down P. Burke has been doing it too well.

They've always known she has terrific aptitude. Joe says he never saw a Remote take over so fast. No disorientations, no rejections. The psychomed talks about self-alienation. She's going into Delphi like a salmon to the sea.

She isn't eating or sleeping, they can't keep her out of the body-cabinet to get her blood moving, there are necroses under her grisly sit-down. Crisis!

So Delphi gets a long "sleep" on the yacht and P. Burke gets it pounded through her perforated head that she's endangering Delphi. (Nurse Fleming thinks of that, thus alienating the psychomed.)

They rig a pool down there (Nurse Fleming again) and chase P. Burke back and forth. And she loves it. So naturally when they let her plug in again Delphi loves it too. Every noon beside the yacht's hydrofoils darling Delphi clips along in the blue sea they've warned her not to drink. And every night around the shoulder of the world an ill-shaped thing in a dark barrow beats its way across a sterile pool.

So presently the yacht stands up on its foils and carries Delphi to the program Mr. Cantle has waiting. It's long-range; she's scheduled for at least two decades' product life. Phase One calls for her to connect with a flock of young ultra-riches who are romping loose between Brioni and Dja-karta where a competitor named PEV could pick them off.

A routine luxgear op see; no politics, no policy angles, and the main budget items are the title and the yacht, which was idle anyway. The storyline is that Delphi goes to accept some rare birds for her prince—who cares? The *point* is that the Haiti area is no longer radioactive and look!—the gods are there. And so are several new Carib West Happy Isles which can afford GTX rates, in fact two of them are GTX subsids.

But you don't want to get the idea that all these news-worthy people are wired-up robbies, for pity's sake. You don't need many if they're placed right. Delphi asks Joe about that when he comes down to Baranquilla to check her over. (P. Burke's own mouth hasn't said much for a while.)

"Are there many like me?"

"Nobody's like you, buttons. Look, are you still getting that Van Allen warble?"

"I mean, like Davy. Is he a Remote?"

(Davy is the lad who is helping her collect the birds. A sincere redhead who needs a little more exposure.)

"Davy? He's one of Matt's boys. Some psychojob. They haven't any channel."

"What about the real ones? Djuma van O, or Ali, or Jim Ten?"

"Djuma was born with a pile of GTX basic where her brain should be, she's nothing but a pain. Jimsy does what his astrologer tells him. Look, peanut, where do you get the idea you aren't real? You're the realest. Aren't you having joy?"

"Oh, Joe!" Flinging her little arms around him and his analyzer grids. "Oh, *me gusto mucho, muchissimo!*"

"Hey, hey." He pets her yellow head, folding the analyzer.

Four thousand miles north and five hundred feet down a forgotten hulk in a body-waldo glows.

And is she having joy. To waken out of the nightmare of being P. Burke and find herself a peri, a star-girl? On a yacht in paradise with no more to do than adorn herself and play with toys and attend revels and greet her friends—her, P. Burke, having friends!—and turn the right way for the holocams? Joy!

And it shows. One look at Delphi and the viewers know: DREAMS CAN COME TRUE.

Look at her riding pillion on Davy's sea-bike, carrying an apoplectic macaw in a silver hoop. *Oh, Morton, let's go there this winter!* Or learning the Japanese chinchona from that Kobe group, in a dress that looks like a blowtorch rising from one knee, and which should sell big in Texas. *Morton, is that real fire?* Happy, happy little girl!

And Davy. He's her pet and her baby and she loves to help him fix his red-gold hair. (P. Burke marveling, running Delphi's fingers through the curls.) Of course Davy is one of Matt's boys—not impotent exactly, but very *very* low drive. (Nobody knows exactly what Matt does with his bitty budget but the boys are useful and one or two have made names.) He's perfect for Delphi; in fact the psychomed lets her take him to bed like two kittens in a basket. Davy doesn't mind the fact that Delphi "sleeps" like the dead. That's when P. Burke is out of the body-waldo up at Carbondale, attending to her own depressing needs.

A funny thing about that. Most of her sleepy-time Delphi's just a gently ticking lush little vegetable waiting for P. Burke to get back on the controls. But now and again Delphi all by herself smiles a bit or stirs in her "sleep." Once she breathed a sound: "Yes."

Under Carbondale P. Burke knows nothing. She's asleep too, dreaming of Delphi, what else? But if the bushy Dr. Tesla had heard that single syllable his bush would have turned snow-white. Because Delphi is TURNED OFF.

He doesn't. Davy is too dim to notice and Delphi's staff boss, Hopkins, wasn't monitoring.

And they've all got something else to think about now, because the cold-fire dress sells half a million copies, and not only in Texas. The GTX computers already know it. When they correlate a minor demand for macaws in Alaska the problem comes to human attention: Delphi is something special.

It's a problem, see, because Delphi is targeted on a limited consumer bracket. Now it turns out she has mass-pop potential—those macaws in *Fairbanks*, man!—it's like trying to shoot mice with an ABM. A whole new ball game. Dr. Tesla and the fatherly Mr. Cantle start going around in headquarters circles and buddy-lunching together when they can get away from a seventh-level weasel boy who scares them both.

In the end it's decided to ship Delphi down to the GTX holocam enclave in Chili to try a spot on one of the mainstream shows. (Never mind why an Infante takes up acting.) The holocam complex occupies a couple of mountains where an observatory once used the clear air. Holocam total-environment shells are very expensive and electronically super-stable. Inside them actors can move freely without going off-register and the whole scene or any selected part will show up in the viewer's home in complete

3-di, so real you can look up their noses and much denser than you get from mobile rigs. You can blow a tit ten feet tall when there's no molecular skiffle around.

The enclave looks—well, take everything you know about Hollywood-Burbank and throw it away. What Delphi sees coming down is a neat giant mushroom-farm, domes of all sizes up to monsters for the big games and stuff. It's orderly. The idea that art thrives on creative flamboyance has long been torpedoed by proof that what art needs is computers. Because this showbiz has something TV and Hollywood never had—*automated inbuilt viewer feedback.* Samples, ratings, critics, polls? Forget it. With that carrier field you can get realtime response-sensor from every receiver in the world, served up at your console. That started as a thingie to give the public more influence on content.

Yes.

Try it, man. You're at the console. Slice to the sex-age-educ-econ-ethno-cetera audience of your choice and start. You can't miss. Where the feedback warms up, give 'em more of that. Warm—warmer—*hot!* You've hit it—the secret itch under those hides, the dream in those hearts. You don't need to know its name. With your hand controlling all the input and your eye reading all the response you can make them a god ... and somebody'll do the same for you.

But Delphi just sees rainbows, when she gets through the degaussing ports and the field relay and takes her first look at the insides of those shells. The next thing she sees is a team of shapers and technicians descending on her, and millisecond timers everywhere. The tropical leisure is finished. She's in gigabuck mainstream now, at the funnel maw of the unceasing hose that's pumping the sight and sound and flesh and blood and sobs and laughs and dreams of *reality* into the world's happy head. Little Delphi is going plonk into a zillion homes in prime time and nothing is left to chance. Work!

And again Delphi proves apt. Of course it's really P. Burke down under Carbondale who's doing it, but who remembers that carcass? Certainly not P. Burke, she hasn't spoken through her own mouth for months. Delphi doesn't even recall dreaming of her when she wakes up.

As for the show itself, don't bother. It's gone on so long no living soul could unscramble the plotline. Delphi's trial spot has something to do with a widow and her dead husband's brother's amnesia.

The bother comes after Delphi's spots begin to flash out along the world-hose and the feedback appears. You've guessed it, of course. Sensational! As you'd say, they IDENTIFY.

The report actually says something like InskinEmp with a string of percentages meaning that Delphi not only has it for anybody with a y-chromosome, but also for women and every thing in between. It's the sweet supernatural jackpot, the million-to-one.

Remember your Harlow? A sexpot, sure. But why did bitter hausfraus in Gary and Memphis know that the vanilla-ice-cream goddess with the white hair and crazy eyebrows was *their baby girl?* And write loving letters to Jean warning her that their husbands weren't good enough for her? Why? The GTX analysts don't know either, but they know what to do with it when it happens.

(Back in his bird sanctuary the old Infante spots it without benefit of computers and gazes thoughtfully at his bride in widow's weeds. It might, he feels, be well to accelerate the completion of his studies.)

The excitement reaches down to the burrow under Carbondale where P. Burke gets two medical exams in a week and a chronically inflamed electrode is replaced. Nurse

Fleming also gets an assistant who doesn't do much nursing but is very interested in access doors and identity tabs.

And in Chile little Delphi is promoted to a new home up among the stars' residential spreads and a private jitney to carry her to work. For Hopkins there's a new computer terminal and a full-time schedule man. What is the schedule crowded with?

Things.

And here begins the trouble. You probably saw that coming too.

"What does she think she is, a goddam *consumer rep*?" Mr. Cantle's fatherly face in Carbondale contorts.

"The girl's upset," Miss Fleming says stubbornly. "She *believes* that, what you told her about helping people and good new products."

"They are good products," Mr. Cantle snaps automatically, but his anger is under control. He hasn't got where he is by irrelevant reactions.

"She says the plastic gave her a rash and the glo-pills made her dizzy."

"Good god, she shouldn't swallow them," Doctor Tesla puts in agitatedly.

"You told her she'd use them," persists Miss Fleming. Mr. Cantle is busy figuring how to ease this problem to the weasel-faced young man. What, was it a goose that lays golden eggs?

Whatever he says to level Seven, down in Chile the offending products vanish. And a symbol goes into Delphi's tank matrix, one that means roughly *Balance unit resistance against PR index*. This means that, Delphi's complaints will be endured as long as her Pop Response stays above a certain level. (What happens when it sinks need not concern us.) And to compensate, the price of her exposure-time rises again. She's a regular on the show now and response is still climbing.

See her under the sizzling lasers, in a holocam shell set up as a walkway accident. (The show is guesting an acupuncture school expert.)

"I don't think this new body-lift is safe," Delphi's saying. "It's made a funny blue spot on me—look, Mr. Vere."

She wiggles to show where the mini-grav pak that imparts a delicious sense of weightlessness is attached.

"So don't leave it *on*, Dee. With your meat—watch that deck-spot, it's starting to synch."

"But if I don't wear it, it isn't honest. They should insulate it more or something, don't you see?"

The show's beloved old father, who is the casualty, gives a senile snigger.

"I'll tell them," Mr. Vere mutters. "Look now, as you step back bend like this so it just shows, see? And hold two beats."

Obediently Delphi turns, and through the dazzle her eyes connect with a pair of strange dark ones. She squints. A quite young man is lounging alone by the port, apparently waiting to use the chamber.

Delphi's used by now to young men looking at her with many peculiar expressions, but she isn't used to what she gets here. A jolt of something somber and knowing. *Secrets.*

"Eyes! Eyes, Dee!"

She moves through the routine, stealing peeks at the stranger. He stares back. He knows something.

When they let her go she comes shyly to him.

"Living wild, kitten." Cool voice, hot underneath.

"What do you mean?"

"Dumping on the product. You trying to get dead?"

"But it isn't right," she tells him. "They don't know, but I do, I've been wearing it."

His cool is jolted.

"You're out of your head."

"Oh, they'll see I'm right when they check it," she explains. "They're just so busy. When I tell them—"

He is staring down at little flower-face. His mouth opens, closes. "What are you doing in this sewer anyway? Who are you?"

Bewilderedly she says, "I'm Delphi."

"Holy Zen."

"What's wrong? Who are you, please?"

Her people are moving her out now, nodding at him.

"Sorry we ran over, Mister Uhunh," the script girl says.

He mutters something, but it's lost as her convoy bustles her toward the flower-decked jitney.

(Hear the click of an invisible ignition-train being armed?)

"Who was he?" Delphi asks her hair man.

The hair man is bending up and down from his knees as he works.

"Paul. Isham. Three," he says and puts a comb in his mouth.

"Who's that? I can't see."

He mumbles around the comb, meaning "Are you jiving?" Because she has to be, in the middle of the GTX enclave.

Next day there's a darkly smoldering face under a turban-towel when Delphi and the show's paraplegic go to use the carbonated pool.

She looks.

He looks.

And the next day, too.

(Hear that automatic sequencer cutting in? The system couples, the fuels begin to travel.)

Poor old Isham senior. You have to feel sorry for a man

who values order: when he begets young, genetic information is still transmitted in the old ape way. One minute it's a happy midget with a rubber duck—look around and here's this huge healthy stranger, opaquely emotional, running with God knows who. Questions are heard where there's nothing to question, and eruptions claiming to be moral outrage. When this is called to Papa's attention—it may take time, in that boardroom—Papa does what he can, but without immortality-juice the problem is worrisome.

And young Paul Isham is a bear. He's bright and articulate and tender-souled and incessantly active and he and his friends are choking with appallment at the world their fathers made. And it hasn't taken Paul long to discover that *his* father's house has many mansions and even the GTX computers can't relate everything to everything else. He noses out a decaying project which adds up to something like Sponsoring Marginal Creativity (the freelance team that "discovered" Delphi was one such grantee). And from there it turns out that an agile lad named Isham can get his hands on a viable packet of GTX holocam facilities.

So here he is with his little band, way down the mushroom-farm mountain, busily spooling a show which has no relation to Delphi's. It's built on bizarre techniques and unsettling distortions pregnant with social protest. An *underground* expression to you.

All this isn't unknown to his father, of course, but so far it has done nothing more than deepen Isham senior's apprehensive frown.

Until Paul connects with Delphi.

And by the time Papa learns this, those invisible hypergolics have exploded, the energy-shells are rushing out. For Paul, you see, is the genuine article. He's serious. He dreams. He even reads—for example, *Green Mansions*—and he wept fiercely when those fiends burned Rima alive.

When he hears that some new GTX pussy is making it big he sneers and forgets it. He's busy. He never connects the name with this little girl making her idiotic, doomed protest in the holocam chamber. This strangely simple little girl.

And she comes and looks up at him and he sees Rima, lost Rima the enchanted bird girl, and his unwired human heart goes twang.

And Rima turns out to be Delphi.

Do you need a map? The angry puzzlement. The rejection of the dissonance Rima-hustling-for-GTX-My-Father. Garbage, cannot be. The loitering around the pool to confirm the swindle . . . dark eyes hitting on blue wonder, jerky words exchanged in a peculiar stillness . . . the dreadful re-organization of the image into Rima-Delphi *in My Father's tentacles—*

You don't need a map.

Nor for Delphi either, the girl who loved her gods. She's seen their divine flesh close now, heard their unamplified voices call her name. She's played their god-games, worn their garlands. She's even become a goddess herself, though she doesn't believe it. She's not disenchanted, don't think that. She's still full of love. It's just that some crazy kind of *hope* isn't—

Really you can skip all this, when the loving little girl on the yellow-brick road meets a Man. A real human male burning with angry compassion and grandly concerned with human justice, who reaches for her with real male arms and—boom! She loves him back with all her heart.

A happy trip, see?

Except.

Except that it's really P. Burke four thousand miles away who loves Paul. P. Burke the monster, down in a dungeon smelling of electrode-paste. A caricature of a woman burning, melting, obsessed with true love. Trying over twenty-double-thousand miles of hard vacuum to reach her beloved through girl-flesh numbed by an invisible film. Feeling his arms around the body he thinks is hers, fighting through shadows to give herself to him. Trying to taste and smell him through beautiful dead nostrils, to love him back with a body that goes dead in the heart of the fire.

Perhaps you get P. Burke's state of mind?

She has phases. The trying, first. And the shame. The SHAME. *I am not what thou lovest.* And the fiercer trying. And the realization that there is no, no way, none. Never. *Never.* . . . A bit delayed, isn't it, her understanding that the bargain she made was forever? P. Burke should have noticed those stories about mortals who end up as grasshoppers.

You see the outcome—the funneling of all this agony into one dumb protoplasmic drive to fuse with Delphi. To leave, to close out the beast she is chained to. *To become Delphi.*

Of course it's impossible.

However her torments have an effect on Paul. Delphi-as-Rima is a potent enough love object, and liberating Delphi's mind requires hours of deeply satisfying instruction in the rottenness of it all. Add in Delphi's body worshipping his flesh, burning in the fire of P. Burke's savage heart—do you wonder Paul is involved?

That's not all.

By now they're spending every spare moment together and some that aren't so spare.

"Mister Isham, would you mind staying out of this sports sequence? The script calls for Davy here."

(Davy's still around, the exposure did him good.)

"What's the difference?" Paul yawns. "It's just an ad. I'm not blocking that thing."

Shocked silence at his two-letter word. The script girl swallows bravely.

"I'm sorry, sir, our directive is to do the *social sequence* exactly as scripted. We're having to respool the segments we did last week, Mister Hopkins is very angry with me."

"Who the hell is Hopkins? Where is he?"

"Oh, please, Paul. *Please.*"

Paul unwraps himself, saunters back. The holocam crew nervously check their angles. The GTX boardroom has a foible about having things *pointed* at them and theirs. Cold shivers, when the image of an Isham nearly went onto the world beam beside that Dialadinner.

Worse yet. Paul has no respect for the sacred schedules which are now a full-time job for ferret boy up at headquarters. Paul keeps forgetting to bring her back on time and poor Hopkins can't cope.

So pretty soon the boardroom data-ball has an urgent personal action-tab for Mr. Isham senior. They do it the gentle way, at first.

"I can't today, Paul."

"Why not?"

"They say I have to, it's *very* important."

He strokes the faint gold down on her narrow back. Under Carbondale, Pa., a blind mole-woman shivers.

"Important. Their importance. Making more gold. Can't you see? To them you're just a thing to get scratch with. A *huckster*. Are you going to let them screw you, Dee? Are you?"

"Oh, Paul—"

He doesn't know it but he's seeing a weirdie; Remotes aren't hooked up to make much tears.

"Just say no, Dee. No. Integrity. You have to."

"But they say it's my job—"

"Don't you believe I can take care of you, Dee? Baby,

baby, you're letting them rip us. You have to choose. Tell them, no."

"Paul . . . I w-will . . ."

And she does. Brave little Delphi (insane P. Burke). Saying "No, please, I promised, Paul."

They try some more, still gently.

"Paul, Mr. Hopkins told me the reason they don't want us to be together so much. It's because of who you are, your father."

She thinks his father is like Mr. Cantle, maybe.

"Oh great. Hopkins. I'll fix him. Listen, I can't think about Hopkins now. Ken came back today, he found out something."

They are lying on the high Andes meadow watching his friends dive their singing kites.

"Would you believe, on the coast the police have *electrodes in their heads*?"

She stiffens in his arms.

"Yeah, weird. I thought they only used PPs on criminals and the army. Don't you see, Dee—something has to be going on. Some movement. Maybe somebody's organizing. How can we find out?" He pounds the ground behind her. "We should make *contact!* If we could only find anything."

"The, the news . . . ?" she asks distractedly.

"The news." He laughs. "There's nothing in the news except what they want people to know. Half the country could burn up and nobody would know it if they didn't want. Dee, can't you take what I'm explaining to you? They've got the whole world programmed! Total control of communication. They've got everybody's minds wired in to think what they show them and want what they give them and they give them what they're programmed to want—you can't break in or out of it, you can't *get hold* of it anywhere. I don't think they even have a plan except to keep things going round and round—and God knows what's happening to the people or the earth or the other planets, maybe. One great big vortex of lies and garbage pouring round and round getting bigger and bigger and nothing can ever change. If people don't wake up soon we're through!"

He pounds her stomach softly.

"*You* have to break out, Dee."

"I'll try, Paul, I will—"

"You're mine. They can't have you."

And he goes to see Hopkins, who is indeed cowed.

But that night up under Carbondale the fatherly Mr. Cantle goes to see P. Burke.

P. Burke? On a cot in a utility robe like a dead camel in a tent, she cannot at first comprehend that he is telling *her* to break it off with Paul. P. Burke has never seen Paul. *Delphi* sees Paul. The fact is, P. Burke can no longer clearly recall that she exists apart from Delphi.

Mr. Cantle can scarely believe it either but he tries.

He points out the futility, the potential embarrassment for Paul. That gets a dim stare from the bulk on the bed. Then he goes into her duty to GTX, her job, isn't she grateful for the opportunity, etcetera. He's very persuasive.

The cobwebby mouth of P. Burke opens and croaks.

"No."

Nothing more seems to be forthcoming.

Mr. Cantle isn't dense, he knows an immovable obstacle when he bumps one. He also knows an irresistible force: GTX. The simple solution is to lock the waldo-cabinet until Paul gets tired of waiting for Delphi to wake up. But the cost, the schedules! And there's something odd here . . . he eyes the corporate asset hulking on the bed and his hunch-sense prickles.

You see, Remotes don't love. They don't have real sex, the circuits designed that out from the start. So it's been assumed that it's *Paul* who is diverting himself or something with the pretty little body in Chile. P. Burke can only be doing what comes natural to any ambitious gutter-meat. It hasn't occurred to anyone that they're dealing with the real hairy thing whose shadow is blasting out of every holoshow on earth.

Love?

Mr. Cantle frowns. The idea is grotesque. But his instinct for the fuzzy line is strong; he will recommend flexibility.

And so, in Chile:

"Darling, I don't have to work tonight! And Friday too— isn't that right, Mr. Hopkins?"

"Oh, great. When does she come up for parole?"

"Mr. Isham, please be reasonable. Our schedule—surely your own production people must be needing you?"

This happens to be true. Paul goes away. Hopkins stares after him wondering distastefully why an Isham wants to ball a waldo. (How sound are those boardroom belly-fears— garble creeps, creeps in!) It never occurs to Hopkins that an Isham might not know what Delphi is.

Especially with Davy crying because Paul has kicked him out of Delphi's bed.

Delphi's bed is under a real window.

"Stars," Paul says sleepily. He rolls over, pulling Delphi on top. "Are you aware that this is one of the last places on earth where people can see the stars? Tibet, too, maybe ..."

"Paul ..."

"Go to sleep. I want to see you sleep."

"Paul, I ... I sleep so *hard*, I mean, it's a joke how hard I am to wake up. Do you mind?"

"Yes."

But finally, fearfully, she must let go. So that four thousand miles north a crazy spent creature can crawl out to gulp concentrates and fall on her cot. But not for long. It's pink dawn when Delphi's eyes open to find Paul's arms around her, his voice saying rude, tender things. He's been kept awake. The nerveless little statue that was her Delphi-body nuzzled him in the night.

Insane hope rises, is fed a couple of nights later when he tells her she called his name in her sleep.

And that day Paul's arms keep her from work and Hopkins' wails go up to headquarters where the sharp-faced lad is working his sharp tailbone offpacking Delphi's program. Mr. Cantle defuses that one. But next week it happens again, to a major client. And ferret-face has connections on the technical side.

Now you can see that when you have a field of complexly heterodyned energy modulations tuned to a demand-point like Delphi there are many problems of standwaves and lashback and skiffle of all sorts which are normally balanced out with ease by the technology of the future. By the same token they can be delicately unbalanced too, in ways that feed back into the waldo operator with striking results.

"Darling—what the hell! What's wrong? DELPHI!"

Helpless shrieks, writhings. Then the Rima-bird is lying wet and limp in his arms, her eyes enormous.

"I . . . I wasn't supposed to . . ." she gasps faintly. "They told me not to . . ."

"Oh my god . . . *Delphi*."

And his hard fingers are digging in her thick yellow hair. Electronically knowledgeable fingers. They freeze.

"You're a *doll!* You're one of those. PP implants. They control you. I should have known. Oh God, I should have known."

"No, Paul," she's sobbing. "No, no, no—"

"Damn them. Damn them, what they've done—you're not *you*—"

He's shaking her, crouching over her in the bed and jerking her back and forth, glaring at the pitiful beauty.

"No!" She pleads (it's not true, that dark bad dream back there). "I'm Delphi!"

"My father. Filth, pigs—damn them, damn them, damn them."

"No, no," she babbles. "They were good to me—" P. Burke underground mouthing, "They were good to me—AAH-AAAAH!"

Another agony skewers her. Up north the sharp young man wants to make sure this so-tiny interference works. Paul can scarcely hang onto her, he's crying too. "I'll kill them."

His Delphi, a wired-up slave! Spikes in her brain, electronic shackles in his bird's heart. Remember when those savages burned Rima alive?

"I'll *kill* the man that's doing this to you."

He's still saying it afterward but she doesn't hear. She's sure he hates her now, all she wants is to die. When she finally understands that the fierceness is tenderness she thinks it's a miracle. *He knows—and he still loves!*

How can she guess that he's got it a little bit wrong?

You can't blame Paul—give him credit that he's even heard about pleasure-pain implants and snoops, which by their nature aren't mentioned much by those who know them most intimately. That's what he thinks is being used on Delphi, something to *control* her. And to listen—he burns at the unknown ears in their bed.

Of waldo-bodies and objects like P. Burke he has heard nothing.

So it never crosses his mind as he looks down at his violated bird, sick with fury and love, that he isn't holding *all* of her. Do you need to be told the mad resolve jelling in him now?

To free Delphi.

How? Well, he is after all Paul Isham III. And he even has an idea where the GTX neurolab is. In Carbondale.

But first things have to be done for Delphi, and for his own stomach. So he gives her back to Hopkins and departs in a restrained and discreet way. And the Chile staff is grateful and do not understand that his teeth don't normally show so much.

And a week passes in which Delphi is a very good, docile little ghost. They let her have the load of wildflowers Paul sends and the bland loving notes. (He's playing it coony.) And up in headquarters weasel boy feels that *his* destiny has clicked a notch onward floats the word up that he's handy with little problems.

And no one knows what P. Burke thinks is any way whatever, except that Miss Fleming catches her flushing her food down the can and next night she faints in the pool. They haul her out and stick her with IVs. Miss Fleming frets, she's seen expressions like that before. But she wasn't around when crazies who called themselves Followers of the Fish looked through flames to life everlasting. P. Burke is seeing Heaven on the far side of death too. Heaven is spelled P-a-u-l, but the idea's the same. *I will die and be born again in Delphi.*

Garbage, electronically speaking. No way.

Another week and Paul's madness has become a plan. (Remember, he does have friends.) He smolders, watching his love paraded by her masters. He turns out a scorching sequence for his own show. And finally, politely, he requests from Hopkins a morsel of his bird's free time, which duly arrives.

"—I thought you didn't want me anymore," she's repeating as they wing over mountain flanks in Paul's suncar. "Now you know—"

"Look at me!"

His hand covers her mouth and he's showing her a lettered card.

DON'T TALK THEY CAN HEAR EVERYTHING WE SAY. I'M TAKING YOU AWAY NOW.

She kisses his hand. He nods urgency, flipping the card.

DON'T BE AFRAID. I CAN STOP THE PAIN IF THEY TRY TO HURT YOU.

With his free hand he shakes out a silvery scrambler-mesh on a power pack. She is dumfounded.

THIS WILL CUT THE SIGNALS AND PROTECT YOU DARLING.

She's staring at him, her head going vaguely from side to side, No.

"Yes!" He grins triumphantly. "Yes!"

For a moment she ... wonders. That powered mesh will cut off the field, all right. It will also cut off Delphi. But he is *Paul*. Paul is kissing her, she can only seek him hungrily as he sweeps the suncar through a pass.

Ahead is an old jet ramp with a shiny bullet waiting to go. (Paul also has credits and a Name.) The little GTX patrol courier is built for nothing but speed. Paul and Delphi wedge in behind the pilot's extra fuel tank and there's no more talking when the torches start to scream.

They're screaming high over Quito before Hopkins starts to worry. He wastes another hour tracking the beeper on Paul's suncar. The suncar is sailing a pattern out to sea. By the time they're sure it's empty and Hopkins gets on the hot flue to headquarters the fugitives are a sourceless howl above Carib West.

Up at headquarters weasel boy gets the squeal. His first impulse is to repeat his previous play but then his brain snaps to. This one is too hot. Because, see, although in the long run they can make P. Burke do anything at all except

112

maybe *live*, instant emergencies can be tricky. And—Paul Isham III.

"Can't you order her back?"

They're all in the GTX tower monitor station, Mr. Cantle and ferret-face and Joe and a very neat man who is Mr. Isham senior's personal eyes and ears.

"No sir," Joe says doggedly. "We can read channels, particularly speech, but we can't interpolate organized pattern. It takes the waldo op to send one-to-one—"

"What are they saying?"

"Nothing at the moment, sir." The console jockey's eyes are closed. "I believe they are, ah, embracing."

"They're not answering," a traffic monitor says. "Still heading zero zero three zero—due north, sir."

"You're certain Kennedy is alerted not to fire on them?" the neat man asks anxiously.

"Yes sir."

"Can't you just turn her off?" The sharp-faced lad is angry. "Pull that beast out of the controls!"

"If you cut the transmission cold you'll kill the Remote," Joe explains for the third time. "Withdrawal has to be phased right, you have to fade over to the Remote's own autonomics. Heart, breathing, cerebellum would go blooey. If you pull Burke out you'll probably finish her too. It's a fantastic cybersystem, you don't want to do that."

"The investment." Mr. Cantle shudders.

Weasel boy puts his hand on the console jock's shoulder; it's the contact who arranged the No-no effect for him.

"We can at least give them a warning signal, sir." He licks his lips, gives the neat man his sweet ferret smile. "We know that does no damage."

Joe frowns, Mr. Cantle sighs. The neat man is murmuring into his wrist. He looks up. "I am authorized," he says reverently, "I am authorized to, ah, direct a signal. If this is the only course. But minimal, minimal."

Sharp-face squeezes his man's shoulder.

In the silver bullet shrieking over Charleston Paul feels Delphi arch in his arms. He reaches for the mesh, hot for action. She thrashes, pushing at his hands, her eyes roll. She's afraid of that mesh despite the agony. (And she's right.) Frantically Paul fights her in the cramped space, gets it over her head. As he turns the power up she burrows free under his arm and the spasm fades.

"They're calling you again, Mister Isham!" the pilot yells.

"Don't answer. Darling, keep this over your head damn it how can I—"

An AX90 barrels over their nose, there's a flash.

"Mister Isham! Those are Air Force jets!"

"Forget it," Paul shouts back. "They won't fire. Darling, don't be afraid."

Another AX90 rocks them.

"Would you mind pointing your pistol at my head where they can see it, sir?" the pilot howls.

Paul does so. The AX90s take up escort formation around them. The pilot goes back to figuring how he can collect from GTX, too, and after Goldsboro AB the escort peels away.

"Holding the same course," Traffic is reporting to the group around the monitor. "Apparently they've taken on enough fuel to bring them to towerport here."

"In that case it's just a question of waiting for them to dock." Mr. Cantle's fatherly manner revives a bit.

"Why can't they cut off that damn freak's life-support?" the sharp young man fumes. "It's ridiculous."

"They're working on it," Cantle assures him.

What they're doing, down under Carbondale, is arguing.

Miss Fleming's watchdog has summoned the bushy man to the waldo room.

"Miss Fleming, you will obey orders."

"You'll kill her if you try that, sir. I can't believe you meant it, that's why I didn't. We've already fed her enough sedative to affect heart action; if you cut any more oxygen she'll die in there."

The bushy man grimaces. "Get Doctor Quine here fast."

They wait, staring at the cabinet in which a drugged, ugly madwoman fights for consciousness, fights to hold Delphi's eyes open.

High over Richmond the silver pod starts a turn. Delphi is sagged into Paul's arm, her eyes swim up to him.

"Starting down now, baby. It'll be over soon, all you have to do is stay alive, Dee."

"...Stay alive..."

The traffic monitor has caught them. "Sir! They've turned off for Carbondale—Control has contact—"

"Let's go."

But the headquarters posse is too late to intercept the courier wailing into Carbondale. And Paul's friends have come through again. The fugitives are out through the freight dock and into the neurolab admin port before the guard gets organized. At the elevator Paul's face plus his handgun get them in.

"I want Doctor—what's his name, Dee? Dee!"

"...Tesla..." She's reeling on her feet.

"Doctor Tesla. Take me down to Tesla, fast."

Intercoms are squalling around them as they whoosh down, Paul's pistol in the guard's back. When the door slides open the bushy man is there.

"I'm Tesla."

"I'm Paul Isham. *Isham*. You're going to take your flaming implants out of this girl—now. Move!"

"What?"

"You heard me. Where's your operating room? Go!"

"But—"

"Move! Do I have to burn somebody?"

Paul waves the weapon at Dr. Quine, who has just appeared.

"No, no," says Tesla hurriedly. "But I can't, you know. It's impossible, there'll be nothing left."

"You screaming well can, right now. You mess up and I'll kill you," says Paul murderously. "Where is it, there? And wipe the creep that's on her circuits now."

He's backing them down the hall, Delphi heavy on his arm.

"Is this the place, baby? Where they did it to you?"

"Yes," she whispers, blinking at a door. "Yes . . ."

Because it is, see. Behind that door is the very suite where she was born.

Paul herds them through it into a gleaming hall. An inner door opens and a nurse and a gray man rush out. And freeze.

Paul sees there's something special about that inner door. He crowds them past it and pushes it open and looks in.

Inside is a big mean-looking cabinet with its front door panels ajar.

And inside that cabinet is a poisoned carcass to whom something wonderful, unspeakable, is happening. Inside is P. Burke the real living woman who knows that HE is there, coming closer—Paul whom she had fought to reach through forty thousand miles of ice—PAUL is here!—is yanking at the waldo doors—

The doors tear open and a monster rises up.

"Paul darling!" croaks the voice of love and the arms of love reach for him.

116

And he responds.

Wouldn't you, if a gaunt she-golem flab-naked and spouting wires and blood came at you—clawing you with metal-studded paws—

"Get away!" He knocks wires.

It doesn't much matter which wires, P. Burke has so to speak her nervous system hanging out. Imagine somebody jerking a handful of your medulla—

She crashes onto the floor at his feet, flopping and roaring *PAUL-PAUL-PAUL* in rictus.

It's doubtful he recognizes his name or sees her life coming out of her eyes at him. And at the last it doesn't go to him. The eyes find Delphi, fainting by the doorway, and die.

Now of course Delphi is dead, too.

There's total silence as Paul steps away from the thing by his foot.

"You killed her," Tesla says. "That was her."

"Your control." Paul is furious, the thought of that monster fastened into little Delphi's brain nauseates him. He sees her crumpling and holds out his arms. Not knowing she is dead.

And Delphi comes to him.

One foot before the other, not moving very well—but moving. Her darling face turns up. Paul is distracted by the terrible quiet, and when he looks down he sees only her tender little neck.

"Now you get the implants out," he warns them. Nobody moves.

"But, but she's dead," Miss Fleming whispers wildly.

Paul feels Delphi's life under his hand, they're talking about their monster. He aims his pistol at the gray man.

"You. If we aren't in your surgery when I count three I'm burning off this man's leg."

"Mr. Isham," Tesla says desperately, "you have just killed the person who animated the body you call Delphi. Delphi herself is dead. If you release your arm you'll see what I say is true."

The tone gets through. Slowly Paul opens his arm, looks down.

"Delphi?"

She totters, sways, stays upright. Her face comes slowly up.

"Paul . . ." Tiny voice.

"Your crotty tricks," Paul snarls at them. "Move!"

"Look at her eyes," Dr. Quine croaks.

They look. One of Delphi's pupils fills the iris, her lips writhe weirdly.

"Shock." Paul grabs her to him. "Fix her!" He yells at them, aiming at Tesla.

"For God's sake . . . bring it in the lab." Tesla quavers.

"Good-bye-bye," says Delphi clearly. They lurch down the hall, Paul carrying her, and meet a wave of people.

Headquarters has arrived.

Joe takes one look and dives for the waldo room, running into Paul's gun.

"Oh no, you don't."

Everybody is yelling. The little thing in his arm stirs, says plaintively, "I'm Delphi."

And all through the ensuing jabber and ranting she hangs on, keeps it up, the ghost of P. Burke or whatever whispering crazily "Paul . . . Paul . . . Please, I'm Delphi . . . Paul?"

"I'm here, darling, I'm here." He's holding her in the nursing bed. Tesla talks, talks, talks unheard.

"Paul . . . don't sleep . . ." the ghost-voice whispers. Paul is in agony, he will not accept, WILL NOT believe. Tesla runs down.

And then near midnight Delphi says roughly, "Ag-ag-ag—" and slips onto the floor, making a rough noise like a seal.

Paul screams. There's more of the *ag-ag* business and more gruesome convulsive disintegrations, until by two in the morning Delphi is nothing but a warm little bundle of vegetative functions hitched to some expensive hardware—the same that sustained her before her life began. Joe finally persuades Paul to let him at the waldo-cabinet. Paul stays by her long enough to see her face change in a dreadfully alien and coldly convincing way, and then he stumbles out bleakly through the group in Tesla's office.

Behind him Joe is working wet-faced, sweating to re-integrate the fantastic complex of circulation, respiration, endocrines, midbrain homeostasis, the patterned flux that was a human being—it's like saving an orchestra abandoned in midair. Joe is also crying a little; he alone had truly loved P. Burke. P. Burke, now a dead pile on a table, was the greatest cybersystem he has ever known, and he never forgets her.

The end, really.

You're curious? Sure, Delphi lives again. Next year she's back on the yacht getting sympathy for her tragic break-down. But there's a different chick in Chile, because while Delphi's new operator is competent, you don't get two P. Burkes in a row—for which GTX is duly grateful.

The real belly-bomb of course is Paul. He was *young*, see. Fighting abstract wrong. Now life has clawed into him and he goes through gut rage and grief and grows in human wisdom and resolve. So much so that you won't be surprised, some time later, to find him—where?

In the GTX boardroom, dummy. Using the advantage of his birth to radicalize the system. You'd call it "boring from within."

That's how he put it, and his friends couldn't agree more. It gives them a warm, confident feeling to know that Paul is up there. Sometimes one of them that is still around runs into him and gets a big hello.

And the sharp-faced lad?

Oh, he matures too. He learns fast, believe it. For instance, he's the first to learn that an obscure GTX research unit is actually getting something with their loopy temporal anomalizer project. True, he doesn't have a physics background, and he's bugged quite a few people. But he doesn't really learn about that until the day he stands where somebody points him during a test run—

—and wakes up lying on a newspaper headlined NIXON UNVEILS PHASE TWO.

Lucky he's a fast learner.

Believe it, zombie. When I say *growth* I mean growth. Capital appreciation. You can stop sweating. There's a great future there.

THE 57TH FRANZ KAFKA

BY RUDY RUCKER

20 JANUARY 1981.

Pain again, deep in the left side of my face. At some point in the night. I gave up pretending to sleep and sat by the window, staring down at the blind land-street and the deaf river.

The impossibility of connected thought. Several times I thought I heard the new body moving in the long basin.

It began snowing during the night. I opened both windows and hunched myself forward with my mouth open, drawing in deep, aching breaths. My hope: a perfect snowflake, if sucked down wholly and rapidly, might reach the black center of my lungs and freeze them solid. Imagine breathing water, breathing ice. Later, hearing the bells toll, I wept.

After Mema brought me my breakfast, she went out to clean away the melting snow. I stood well back from the window lest she see my cheers and gloating grimaces.

After clearing the sidewalk, she had not yet had enough

of wielding her scrub-broom, and stepped, repeatedly and at great risk, into the heavy land-street traffic, trying to clear off *our half*. She has, in the years since I dissolved the marriage, become an automaton. I realize this with finality when I see her stare uncomprehendingly after the splashing motor-wagons, which again and again cover *our half* of the street, and splatter her apron and her thick legs with the grey, crystalline frosting.

The suppressed laughter hurts my chest. I begin to cough and have to sit down on my bed. Here I sit, words crawling off my pen-point.

There are only four more pages left in this, the last volume of my fifty-seventh series of diaries. I must write less.

23 JANUARY 1981.

Three days of fever. Straightening my wet bedclothes, Mema found my special pictures, the Fast-Night groupings, and took them away. *What if Felice were to see them?*

I have more pictures hidden in the attic, pictures I press to my ribs while I pour all my food out into the long basin. The new body is not so far along as I had hoped. There are still only the clotted fibers. It is strange that I could have thought otherwise.

25 JANUARY 1981.

Last night the worst yet. Dream: again Reb Pessin showing me the Book of Qlippoth, the secrets of immortality. A high buzzing, as of a tremendous propeller, drowns out his voice. The surprising weight of the little book. He makes a false gesture, and I spread out in space instead of time. A whole city where everyone wears my face, streets of women, the offices. A street-car conductor leaning over me, shaking with laughter, "If I were you . . ."

Awake before dawn. For the first time real fear that the new body will not be ready. But going into the attic with a candle, I see that all is well. Even the skin is finished.

26 JANUARY 1981.

Real sleep at last. Waking up, an unnatural feeling of lightness. So many memories are gone already, gone over.

I drank two cups of black tea with breakfast. Mema had to go back down to the kitchen for the second. When she brought it up, I had forgotten the first breakfast already, and asked her where it was. This is all as it should be. Soon I can begin again.

Yesterday, in a mood of wild exaltation, I mailed my remaining special pictures to Felice, first scribbling her real name on some of the women's faces.

Now, cheerful and whistling from my sound sleep and my two cups of tea, I take pen in hand and compose another letter to her father:

Honored Herr B!

I am not surprised that you have failed to answer my letters of 24.XII.80, 26.XII.80, and 15.I.81. You need not apologize! It is only right and natural that a man in your position must take thought, *in the interests of his daughter*, before moving to bind a marriage contract. The questions of my finances, age and health are undoubtedly your unspoken concerns.

As regards the question of age: I am forty-one, and *will remain so*. Although your daughter is now but twenty, she will in the course of time become sixty. Until that age, I vow to have and hold her as sole love-object. Frau Mema, my housekeeper and ex-wife, can attest to this.

My financial security is assured by certain interlocking fixed-interest annuities. I do not need to work, and I despise to do so. My *brutto* yearly income is in excess of fifteen thousand thalers . . . not a figure to conjure with, but surely adequate for your little mouse's needs.

The state of my health is a predictable matter. At present it is bad, and it will grow a bit worse. But next month, and in the summer, I will once again be fresh and strong. There can be no doubt of this.

Would a marriage date of February 30 be acceptable to you?

With high respect,
Franz K. LVII.

29 JANUARY 1981.

All evening, Mema watched television in the parlor, directly under my bedroom. The police were here yesterday, sent by Felice's father.

They did not dare come up to me, and spoke only to Mema. I stood naked at the head of the stairs, baring my teeth and trembling with a fierce joy each time I glimpsed their green, peaked caps. It struck me that the caps are living beings which *wear policemen.*

The excitement made me very weak, and all day I left the bed only to empty my cavities into the long basin. It is time to complete the task, to open my veins. Mema knows that today is the day, and under my feet she rocks and watches green, peaked caps move across the television screen.

30 JANUARY 1981.

LVIII is still waiting in the long basin behind the thin attic wall.

Last night I took candle and long knife and leaned over the basin, staring down through the thick, gathered fluids. The candle-wax dripped and sprung into little saucers, white disks that drifted down to rest on Franz LVIII's closed eyelids. His mouth is set in a smile, as always.

I am not frightened of death, not after fifty-six times. But when my new body walks, the green, peaked caps will take it away. Herr B. must pay for this.

I have resolved to make him murder me. The exquisite uncertainty of *how he will do it*. I feel like a virgin bride.

Mema has gone to the butcher to buy two kilograms of blood-sausage. Tonight I will chew the sausage up for LVIII. My true blood must belong to Herr B.

31 JANUARY 1981.

The blood-sausage was everything I had ever dreamed it to be. Thick and dark, with the texture of excrement, the congealed pigs' blood is stuffed into a greasy casing made of the animals' own small intestines.

Leaning over the long basin, chewing and spitting up, I felt a disgust purer and more complete than anything I have experienced since the time of the camps.

The sausage-casing is stamped with repeated pictures of a pig wearing a crown and making obeisances. I have stretched the casing enough to wrap it around my waist, like the little tailor who killed seven with one blow.

The chewing of the sausage took a long time, and I fell asleep in a sort of ecstasy, with my forehead resting on the rim of the long basin. I awakened to a touch of LVIII's hand, tugging petulantly at my hair. I started back, uncertain where I was, and heard the church tower toll three.

Filled with an implacable strength, I descended the stairs. Mema lay sleeping on her cot in the kitchen. I unplugged the phone and brought it upstairs. Then I crawled under my bed to muffle the sound, and dialed Felice's number over and over.

The shining love-words dripped off my lips that still glistened with blood-sausage. My tongue felt slender, magically flexible, as if it could pierce the phone wires and the shell of her ear. After my second call, her father answered, and I gibbered like a golem, ever-new inspirations striking me with each call. I continued calling for two hours. They answered less and less often, and finally not at all. Now I have left my phone off the hook to keep theirs ringing.

Franz K. LVIII is sloshing about in the long basin, impatient for the final spark. The dawn strikes through my window and gilds this page, the last of this volume. Now, before Mema awakes, I must go to pound on Felice's door, a long knife in my hand.

BURNING CHROME

WILLIAM GIBSON

I t was hot, the night we burned Chrome. Out in the malls
and plazas, moths were batting themselves to death
against the neon, but in Bobby's loft the only light came
from a monitor screen and the green and red LEDs on the
face of the matrix simulator. I knew every chip in Bobby's
simulator by heart; it looked like your workaday Ono-
Sendai VII, the "Cyberspace Seven," but I'd rebuilt it so
many times that you'd have had a hard time finding a
square millimeter of factory circuitry in all that silicon.

We waited side by side in front of the simulator console,
watching the time display in the screen's lower left corner.

"Go for it," I said, when it was time, but Bobby was
already there, leaning forward to drive the Russian program
into its slot with the heel of his hand. He did it with the
tight grace of a kid slamming change into an arcade game,
sure of winning and ready to pull down a string of free
games.

A silver tide of phosphenes boiled across my field of
vision as the matrix began to unfold in my head, a 3-D
chessboard, infinite and perfectly transparent. The Russian
program seemed to lurch as we entered the grid. If anyone

else had been jacked into that part of the matrix, he might have seen a surf of flickering shadow roll out of the little yellow pyramid that represented our computer. The program was a mimetic weapon, designed to absorb local color and present itself as a crash-priority override in whatever context it encountered.

"Congratulations," I heard Bobby say. "We just became an Eastern Seaboard Fission Authority inspection probe. . . ." That meant we were clearing fiberoptic lines with the cybernetic equivalent of a fire siren, but in the simulation matrix we seemed to rush straight for Chrome's data base. I couldn't see it yet, but I already knew those walls were waiting. Walls of shadow, walls of ice.

Chrome: her pretty childface smooth as steel, with eyes that would have been at home on the bottom of some deep Atlantic trench, cold gray eyes that lived under terrible pressure. They said she cooked her own cancers for people who crossed her, rococo custom variations that took years to kill you. They said a lot of things about Chrome, none of them at all reassuring.

So I blotted her out with a picture of Rikki. Rikki kneeling in a shaft of dusty sunlight that slanted into the loft through a grid of steel and glass: her faded camouflage fatigues, her translucent rose sandals, the good line of her bare back as she rummaged through a nylon gear bag. She looks up, and a half-blond curl falls to tickle her nose. Smiling, buttoning an old shirt of Bobby's, frayed khaki cotton drawn across her breasts.

She smiles.

"Son of a bitch," said Bobby, "we just told Chrome we're an IRS audit and three Supreme Court subpoenas. . . . Hang on to your ass, Jack. . . ."

So long, Rikki. Maybe now I see you never.

And dark, so dark, in the halls of Chrome's ice.

* * *

Bobby was a cowboy, and ice was the nature of his game, *ice* from ICE, Intrusion Countermeasures Electronics. The matrix is an abstract representation of the relationships between data systems. Legitimate programmers jack into their employers' sector of the matrix and find themselves surrounded by bright geometries representing the corporate data.

Towers and fields of it ranged in the colorless nonspace of the simulation matrix, the electronic consensus-hallucination that facilitates the handling and exchange of massive quantities of data. Legitimate programmers never see the walls of ice they work behind, the walls of shadow that screen their operations from others, from industrial-espionage artists and hustlers like Bobby Quine.

Bobby was a cowboy. Bobby was a cracksman, a burglar, casing mankind's extended electronic nervous system, rustling data and credit in the crowded matrix, monochrome nonspace where the only stars are dense concentrations of information, and high above it all burn corporate galaxies and the cold spiral arms of military systems.

Bobby was another one of those young-old faces you see drinking in the Gentleman Loser, the chic bar for computer cowboys, rustlers, cybernetic second-story men. We were partners.

Bobby Quine and Automatic Jack. Bobby's the thin, pale dude with the dark glasses, and Jack's the mean-looking guy with the myoelectric arm. Bobby's software and Jack's hard; Bobby punches console and Jack runs down all the little things that can give you an edge. Or, anyway, that's what the scene watchers in the Gentleman Loser would've told you, before Bobby decided to burn Chrome. But they also might've told you that Bobby was losing his edge, slowing down. He was twenty-eight, Bobby, and that's old for a console cowboy.

Both of us were good at what we did, but somehow that one big score just wouldn't come down for us. I knew where to go for the right gear, and Bobby had all his licks down pat. He'd sit back with a white terry sweatband across his forehead and whip moves on those keyboards faster than you could follow, punching his way through some of the fanciest ice in the business, but that was when something happened that managed to get him totally wired, and that didn't happen often. Not highly motivated, Bobby, and I was the kind of guy who's happy to have the rent covered and a clean shirt to wear.

But Bobby had this thing for girls, like they were his private tarot or something, the way he'd get himself moving. We never talked about it, but when it started to look like he was losing his touch that summer, he started to spend more time in the Gentleman Loser. He'd sit at a table by the open doors and watch the crowd slide by, nights when the bugs were at the neon and the air smelled of perfume and fast food. You could see his sunglasses scanning those faces as they passed, and he must have decided that Rikki's was the one he was waiting for, the wild card and the luck changer. The new one.

I went to New York to check out the market, to see what was available in hot software.

The Finn's place has a defective hologram in the window, METRO HOLOGRAFIX, over a display of dead flies wearing fur coats of gray dust. The scrap's waist-high, inside, drifts of it rising to meet walls that are barely visible behind nameless junk, behind sagging pressboard shelves stacked with old skin magazines and yellow-spined years of *National Geographic*.

"You need a gun," said the Finn. He looks like a re-combo DNA project aimed at tailoring people for high-speed burrowing. "You're in luck. I got the new Smith and Wesson, the four-oh-eight Tactical. Got this xenon projector slung under the barrel, see, batteries in the grip, throw you a twelve-inch high-noon circle in the pitch dark at fifty yards. The light source is so narrow, it's almost impossible to spot. It's just like voodoo in a nightfight."

I let my arm clunk down on the table and started the fingers drumming; the servos in the hand began whining like overworked mosquitoes. I knew that the Finn really hated the sound.

"You looking to pawn that?" He prodded the Duralumin wrist joint with the chewed shaft of a felt-tip pen. "Maybe get yourself something a little quieter?"

I kept it up. "I don't need any guns, Finn."

"Okay," he said, "okay," and I quit drumming. "I only got this one item, and I don't even know what it is." He looked unhappy. "I got it off these bridge-and-tunnel kids from Jersey last week."

"So when'd you ever buy anything you didn't know what it was, Finn?"

"Wise ass." And he passed me a transparent mailer with something in it that looked like an audio cassette through the bubble padding. "They had a passport," he said. "They had credit cards and a watch. And that."

"They had the contents of somebody's pockets, you mean."

He nodded. "The passport was Belgian. It was also bo-gus, looked to me, so I put it in the furnace. Put the cards in with it. The watch was okay, a Porsche, nice watch."

It was obviously some kind of plug-in military program. Out of the mailer, it looked like the magazine of a small assault rifle, coated with nonreflective black plastic. The edges and corners showed bright metal; it had been knocking around for a while.

"I'll give you a bargain on it, Jack. For old times' sake."

I had to smile at that. Getting a bargain from the Finn was like God repealing the law of gravity when you have to carry a heavy suitcase down ten blocks of airport corridor.

"Looks Russian to me," I said. "Probably the emergency sewage controls for some Leningrad suburb. Just what I need."

"You know," said the Finn, "I got a pair of shoes older than you are. Sometimes I think you got about as much class as those yahoos from Jersey. What do you want me to tell you, it's the keys to the Kremlin? You figure out what the goddamn thing is. Me, I just sell the stuff."

I bought it.

Bodiless, we swerve into Chrome's castle of ice. And we're fast, fast. It feels like we're surfing the crest of the invading program, hanging ten above the seething glitch systems as they mutate. We're sentient patches of oil swept along down corridors of shadow.

Somewhere we have bodies, very far away, in a crowded loft roofed with steel and glass. Somewhere we have microseconds, maybe time left to pull out.

We've crashed her gates disguised as an audit and three subpoenas, but her defenses are specifically geared to cope with that kind of official intrusion. Her most sophisticated ice is structured to fend off warrants, writs, subpoenas. When we breached the first gate, the bulk of her data vanished behind core-command ice, these walls we see as leagues of corridor, mazes of shadow. Five separate landlines spurted May Day signals to law firms, but the virus had already taken over the parameter ice. The glitch systems gobble the distress calls as our mimetic subprograms scan anything that hasn't been blanked by core command.

The Russian program lifts a Tokyo number from the unscreened data, choosing it for frequency of calls, average length of calls, the speed with which Chrome returned those calls.

"Okay," says Bobby, "we're an incoming scrambler call from a pal of hers in Japan. That should help."

Ride 'em, cowboy.

Bobby read his future in women; his girls were omens, changes in the weather, and he'd sit all night in the Gentleman Loser, waiting for the season to lay a new face down in front of him like a card.

I was working late in the loft one night, shaving down a chip, my arm off and the little waldo jacked straight into the stump.

Bobby came in with a girl I hadn't seen before, and usually I feel a little funny if a stranger sees me working that way, with those leads clipped to the hard carbon studs that stick out of my stump. She came right over and looked at the magnified image on the screen, then saw the waldo moving under its vacuum-sealed dust cover. She didn't say anything, just watched. Right away I had a good feeling about her; it's like that sometimes.

"Automatic Jack, Rikki. My associate."

He laughed, put his arm around her waist, something in his tone letting me know that I'd be spending the night in a dingy room in a hotel.

"Hi," she said. Tall, nineteen or maybe twenty, and she definitely had the goods. With just those few freckles across the bridge of her nose, and eyes somewhere between dark amber and French coffee. Tight black jeans rolled to midcalf and a narrow plastic belt that matched the rose-colored sandals.

But now when I see her sometimes when I'm trying to sleep, I see her somewhere out on the edge of all this sprawl of cities and smoke, and it's like she's a hologram stuck behind my eyes, in a bright dress she must've worn once, when I knew her, something that doesn't quite reach her knees. Bare legs long and straight. Brown hair, streaked with blond, hoods her face, blown in a wind from somewhere, and I see her wave goodbye.

Bobby was making a show of rooting through a stack of audio cassettes. "I'm on my way, cowboy," I said, unclipping the waldo. She watched attentively as I put my arm back on.

"Can you fix things?" she asked.

"Anything, anything you want, Automatic Jack'll fix it." I snapped my Duralumin fingers for her.

She took a little simstim deck from her belt and showed me the broken hinge on the cassette cover.

"Tomorrow," I said, "no problem."

And my oh my, I said to myself, sleep pulling me down the six flights to the street, *what'll Bobby's luck be like with a fortune cookie like that? If his system worked, we'd be striking it rich any night now.* In the street I grinned and yawned and waved for a cab.

Chrome's castle is dissolving, sheets of ice shadow flickering and fading, eaten by the glitch systems that spin out from the Russian program, tumbling away from our central logic thrust and infecting the fabric of the ice itself. The glitch systems are cybernetic virus analogs, self-replicating and voracious. They mutate constantly, in unison, subverting and absorbing Chrome's defenses.

Have we already paralyzed her, or is a bell ringing somewhere, a red light blinking? Does she know?

Rikki Wildside, Bobby called her, and for those first few weeks it must have seemed to her that she had it all, the whole teeming show spread out for her, sharp and bright under the neon. She was new to the scene, and she had all the miles of malls and plazas to prowl, all the shops and clubs, and Bobby to explain the wild side, the tricky wiring on the dark underside of things, all the players and their names and their games. He made her feel at home.

"What happened to your arm?" she asked me one night in the Gentleman Loser, the three of us drinking at a small table in a corner.

"Hang-gliding," I said, "accident."

"Hang-gliding over a wheatfield," said Bobby, "place called Kiev. Our Jack's just hanging there in the dark, under a Nightwing parafoil, with fifty kilos of radar jammer between his legs, and some Russian asshole accidentally burns his arm off with a laser."

I don't remember how I changed the subject, but I did.

I was still telling myself that it wasn't Rikki who was getting to me, but what Bobby was doing with her. I'd known him for a long time, since the end of the war, and I knew he used women as counters in a game, Bobby Quine versus fortune, versus time and the night of cities. And Rikki had turned up just when he needed something to get him going, something to aim for. So he'd set her up as a symbol for everything he wanted and couldn't have, everything he'd had and couldn't keep.

I didn't like having to listen to him tell me how much he loved her, and knowing he believed it only made it worse. He was a past master at the hard fall and the rapid recovery, and I'd seen it happen a dozen times before. He might as well have had NEXT printed across his sunglasses in green Day-Glo capitals, ready to flash out at the first interesting face that flowed past the tables in the Gentleman Loser.

I knew what he did to them. He turned them into emblems, sigils on the map of his hustlers life, navigation beacons he could follow through a sea of bars and neon. What else did he have to steer by? He didn't love money, in and of itself, not enough to follow its lights. He wouldn't work for power over other people; he hated the responsibility it brings. He had some basic pride in his skill, but that was never enough to keep him pushing.

So he made do with women.

When Rikki showed up, he needed one in the worst way. He was fading fast, and smart money was already whispering that the edge was off his game. He needed that one big score, and soon, because he didn't know any other kind of life, and all his clocks were set for hustler's time, calibrated in risk and adrenaline and that supernal dawn calm that comes when every move's proved right and a sweet lump of someone else's credit clicks into your own account.

It was time for him to make his bundle and get out; so Rikki got set up higher and farther away than any of the others ever had, even though—and I felt like screaming it at him—she was right there, alive, totally real, human, hungry, resilient, bored, beautiful, excited, all the things she was. . . .

Then he went out one afternoon, about a week before I made the trip to New York to see the Finn. Went out and left us there in the loft, waiting for a thunderstorm. Half the skylight was shadowed by a dome they'd never finished, and the other half showed sky, black and blue with clouds. I was standing by the bench, looking up at the sky, stupid with the hot afternoon, the humidity, and she touched me, touched my shoulder, the half-inch border of taut pink scar that the arm doesn't cover. Anybody else ever touched me there, they went on to the shoulder, the neck. . . .

But she didn't do that. Her nails were lacquered black, not pointed, but tapered oblongs, the lacquer only a shade darker than the carbon-fiber laminate that sheathes my arm. And her hand went down the arm, black nails tracing a weld in the laminate, down to the black anodized elbow joint, out to the wrist, her hand soft-knuckled as a child's, fingers spreading to lock over mine, her palm against the perforated Duralumin.

Her other palm came up to brush across the feedback pads, and it rained all afternoon, raindrops drumming on the steel and soot-stained glass above Bobby's bed.

Ice walls flick away like supersonic butterflies made of shade. Beyond them, the matrix's illusion of infinite space. It's like watching a tape of a prefab building going up; only the tape's reversed and run at high speed, and these walls are torn wings.

Trying to remind myself that this place and the gulfs beyond are only representations, that we aren't "in" Chrome's computer, but interfaced with it, while the matrix simulator in Bobby's loft generates this illusion . . . The core data begin to emerge, exposed, vulnerable. . . . This is the far side of ice, the view of the matrix I've never seen before, the view that fifteen million legitimate console operators see daily and take for granted.

The core data tower around us like vertical freight trains, color-coded for access. Bright primaries, impossibly bright in that transparent void, linked by countless horizontals in nursery blues and pinks.

But ice still shadows something at the center of it all: the heart of all Chrome's expensive darkness, the very heart . . .

* * *

It was late afternoon when I got back from my shopping expedition to New York. Not much sun through the skylight, but an ice pattern glowed on Bobby's monitor screen, a 2-D graphic representation of someone's computer defenses, lines of neon woven like an Art Deco prayer rug. I turned the console off, and the screen went completely dark.

Rikki's things were spread across my workbench, nylon bags spilling clothes and makeup, a pair of bright red cowboy boots, audio cassettes, glossy Japanese magazines about simstim stars. I stacked it all under the bench and then took my arm off, forgetting that the program I'd bought from the Finn was in the right-hand pocket of my jacket, so that I had to fumble it out left-handed and then get it into the padded jaws of the jeweler's vise.

The waldo looks like an old audio turntable, the kind that played disc records, with the vise set up under a transparent dust cover. The arm itself is just over a centimeter long, swinging out on what would've been the tone arm on one of those turntables. But I don't look at that when I've clipped the leads to my stump; I look at the scope, because that's my arm there in black and white, magnification 40×.

I ran a tool check and picked up the laser. It felt a little heavy; so I scaled my weight-sensor input down to a quarter-kilo per gram and got to work. At 40 × the side of the program looked like a trailer truck.

It took eight hours to crack: three hours with the waldo and the laser and four dozen taps, two hours on the phone to a contact in Colorado, and three hours to run down a lexicon disc that could translate eight-year-old technical Russian.

Then Cyrillic alphanumerics started reeling down the monitor, twisting themselves into English halfway down. There were a lot of gaps, where the lexicon ran up against specialized military acronyms in the readout I'd bought from my man in Colorado, but it did give me some idea of what I'd bought from the Finn.

I felt like a punk who'd gone out to buy a switchblade and come home with a small neutron bomb.

Screwed again, I thought. *What good's a neutron bomb in a streetfight?* The thing under the dust cover was right out of my league. I didn't even know where to unload it, where to look for a buyer. Someone had, but he was dead, someone with a Porsche watch and a fake Belgian passport, but I'd never tried to move in those circles. The Finn's muggers from the 'burbs had knocked over someone who had some highly arcane connections.

The program in the jeweler's vise was a Russian military icebreaker, a killer-virus program.

It was dawn when Bobby came in alone. I'd fallen asleep with a bag of takeout sandwiches in my lap.

"You want to eat?" I asked him, not really awake, holding out my sandwiches. I'd been dreaming of the program, of its waves of hungry glitch systems and mimetic subprograms; in the dream it was an animal of some kind, shapeless and flowing.

He brushed the bag aside on his way to the console, punched a function key. The screen lit with the intricate pattern I'd seen there that afternoon. I rubbed sleep from my eyes with my left hand, one thing I can't do with my right. I'd fallen asleep trying to decide whether to tell him about the program. Maybe I should try to sell it alone, keep the money, go somewhere new, ask Rikki to go with me.

"Whose is it?" I asked.

He stood there in a black cotton jump suit, an old leather jacket thrown over his shoulders like a cape. He hadn't shaved for a few days, and his face looked thinner than usual.

"It's Chrome's," he said.

My arm convulsed, started clicking, fear translated to the myoelectrics through the carbon studs. I spilled the sandwiches; limp sprouts, and bright yellow dairy-produce slices on the unswept wooden floor.

"You're stone crazy," I said.

"No," he said, "you think she rumbled it? No way. We'd be dead already. I locked on to her through a triple-blind rental system in Mombasa and an Algerian comsat. She knew somebody was having a look-see, but she couldn't trace it."

If Chrome had traced the pass Bobby had made at her ice, we were good as dead. But he was probably right, or she'd have had me blown away on my way back from New York. "Why her, Bobby? Just give me one reason...."

Chrome: I'd seen her maybe half a dozen times in the Gentleman Loser. Maybe she was slumming, or checking out the human condition, a condition she didn't exactly aspire to. A sweet little heart-shaped face framing the nastiest pair of eyes you ever saw. She'd looked fourteen for as long as anyone could remember, hyped out of anything like a normal metabolism on some massive program of serums and hormones. She was as ugly a customer as the street ever produced, but she didn't belong to the street anymore. She was one of the Boys, Chrome, a member in good standing of the local Mob subsidiary. Word was, she'd gotten started as a dealer, back when synthetic pituitary hormones were still proscribed. But she hadn't had to move hormones for a long time. Now she owned the House of Blue Lights.

"You're flat-out crazy, Quine. You give me one sane reason for having that stuff on your screen. You ought to dump it, and I mean *now*...."

"Talk in the Loser," he said, shrugging out of the leather jacket. "Black Myron and Crow Jane. Jane, she's up on all the sex lines, claims she knows where the money goes. So she's arguing with Myron that Chrome's the controlling interest in the Blue Lights, not just some figurehead for the Boys."

" 'The Boys,' Bobby," I said. "That's the operative word there. You still capable of seeing that? We don't mess with the Boys, remember? That's why we're still walking around."

"That's why were still poor, partner." He settled back into the swivel chair in front of the console, unzipped his jump suit, and scratched his skinny white chest. "But maybe not for much longer."

"I think maybe this partnership just got itself permanently dissolved."

Then he grinned at me. That grin was truly crazy, feral and focused, and I knew that right then he really didn't give a shit about dying.

"Look," I said, "I've got some money left, you know? Why don't you take it and get the tube to Miami, catch a hopper to Montego Bay. You need a rest, man. You've got to get your act together."

"My act, Jack," he said, punching something on the keyboard, "never has been this together before." The neon prayer rug on the screen shivered and woke as an animation program cut in, ice lines weaving with hypnotic frequency, a living mandala. Bobby kept punching, and the movement slowed; the pattern resolved itself, grew slightly less complex, became an alternation between two distant configurations. A first-class piece of work, and I hadn't thought he was still that good. "Now," he said, "there, see it? Wait. There. There again. And there. Easy to miss. That's it. Cuts in every hour and twenty minutes with a squirt transmission to their comsat. We could live for a year on what she pays them weekly in negative interest."

"Whose comsat?"

"Zürich. Her bankers. That's her bankbook, Jack. That's where the money goes. Crow Jane was right."

I stood there. My arm forgot to click.

"So how'd you do in New York, partner? You get anything that'll help me cut ice? We're going to need whatever we can get."

I kept my eyes on his, forced myself not to look in the direction of the waldo, the jeweler's vise. The Russian program was there, under the dust cover.

Wild cards, luck changers.

"Where's Rikki?" I asked him, crossing to the console, pretending to study the alternating patterns on the screen.

"Friends of hers," he shrugged, "kids, they're all into simstim." He smiled absently. "I'm going to do it for her, man."

"I'm going out to think about this, Bobby. You want me to come back, you keep your hands off the board."

"I'm doing it for her," he said as the door closed behind me. "You know I am."

And down now, down, the program a roller coaster through this fraying maze of shadow walls, gray cathedral spaces between the bright towers. Headlong speed.

Black ice. Don't think about it. Black ice.

Too many stories in the Gentleman Loser; black ice is a part of the mythology. Ice that kills. Illegal, but then aren't we all? Some kind of neural-feedback weapon, and you connect with it only once. Like some hideous Word that eats the mind from the inside out. Like an epileptic spasm that goes on and on until there's nothing left at all...

And we're diving for the floor of Chrome's shadow castle.

Trying to brace myself for the sudden stopping of

breath, a sickness and final slackening of the nerves. Fear
of that cold Word waiting, down there in the dark.

I went out and looked for Rikki, found her in a café with a
boy with Sendai eyes, half-healed suture lines radiating
from his bruised sockets. She had a glossy brochure spread
open on the table, Tally Isham smiling up from a dozen
photographs, the Girl with the Zeiss Ikon Eyes.

Her little simstim deck was one of the things I'd stacked
under my bench the night before, the one I'd fixed for her
the day after I'd first seen her. She spent hours jacked into
that unit, the contact band across her forehead like a gray
plastic tiara. Tally Isham was her favorite, and with the contact band on, she was gone, off somewhere in the recorded
sensorium of simstim's biggest star. Simulated stimuli: the
world—all the interesting parts, anyway—as perceived by
Tally Isham. Tally raced a black Fokker ground-effect plane
across Arizona mesa tops. Tally dived the Truk Island pre-
serves. Tally partied with the superrich on private Greek
islands, heartbreaking purity of those tiny white seaports at
dawn.

Actually she looked a lot like Tally, same coloring and
cheekbones. I thought Rikki's mouth was stronger. More
sass. She didn't want to *be* Tally Isham, but she coveted the
job. That was her ambition, to be in simstim. Bobby just
laughed it off. She talked to me about it, though. "How'd I
look with a pair of these?" she'd ask, holding a full-page
headshot, Tally Isham's blue Zeiss Ikons lined up with her
own amber-brown. She'd had her corneas done twice, but
she still wasn't 20-20; so she wanted Ikons. Brand of the
stars. Very expensive.

"You still window-shopping for eyes?" I asked as I sat
down.

"Tiger just got some," she said. She looked tired, I thought.

Tiger was so pleased with his Sendais that he couldn't help smiling, but I doubted whether he'd have smiled otherwise. He had the kind of uniform good looks you get after your seventh trip to the surgical boutique; he'd probably spend the rest of his life looking vaguely like each new season's media front-runner; not too obvious a copy, but nothing too original, either.

"Sendai, right?" I smiled back.

He nodded. I watched as he tried to take me in with his idea of a professional simstim glance. He was pretending that he was recording. I thought he spent too long on my arm. "They'll be great on peripherals when the muscles heal," he said, and I saw how carefully he reached for his double espresso. Sendai eyes are notorious for depth-perception defects and warranty hassles, among other things.

"Tiger's leaving for Hollywood tomorrow."

"Then maybe Chiba City, right?" I smiled at him. He didn't smile back. "Got an offer, Tiger? Know an agent?"

"Just checking it out," he said quietly. Then he got up and left. He said a quick goodbye to Rikki, but not to me.

"That kid's optic nerves may start to deteriorate inside six months. You know that, Rikki? Those Sendais are illegal in England, Denmark, lots of places. You can't replace nerves."

"Hey, Jack, no lectures." She stole one of my croissants and nibbled at the tip of one of its horns.

"I thought I was your adviser, kid."

"Yeah. Well, Tiger's not too swift, but everybody knows about Sendais. They're all he can afford. So he's taking a chance. If he gets work, he can replace them."

"With these?" I tapped the Zeiss Ikon brochure. "Lot of

money, Rikki. You know better than to take a gamble like that."

She nodded. "I want Ikons."

"If you're going up to Bobby's, tell him to sit tight until he hears from me."

"Sure. It's business?"

"Business," I said. But it was craziness.

I drank my coffee, and she ate both my croissants. Then I walked her down to Bobby's. I made fifteen calls, each one from a different pay phone.

Business. Bad craziness.

All in all, it took us six weeks to set the burn up, six weeks of Bobby telling me how much he loved her. I worked even harder, trying to get away from that.

Most of it was phone calls. My fifteen initial and very oblique inquiries each seemed to breed fifteen more. I was looking for a certain service Bobby and I both imagined as a requisite part of the world's clandestine economy, but which probably never had more than five customers at a time. It would be one that never advertised.

We were looking for the world's heaviest fence, for a non-aligned money laundry capable of dry-cleaning a meg-abuck on-line cash transfer and then forgetting about it.

All those calls were a waste, finally, because it was the Finn who put me on to what we needed. I'd gone up to New York to buy a new blackbox rig, because we were going broke paying for all those calls.

I put the problem to him as hypothetically as possible.

"Macao," he said.

"Macao?"

"The Long Hum family. Stockbrokers."

He even had the number. You want a fence, ask another fence.

The Long Hum people were so oblique that they made

my idea of a subtle approach look like a tactical nuke-out. Bobby had to make two shuttle runs to Hong Kong to get the deal straight. We were running out of capital, and fast. I still don't know why I decided to go along with it in the first place; I was scared of Chrome, and I'd never been all that hot to get rich.

I tried telling myself that it was a good idea to burn the House of Blue Lights because the place was a creep joint, but I just couldn't buy it. I didn't like the Blue Lights, because I'd spent a supremely depressing evening there once, but that was no excuse for going after Chrome. Actually I halfway assumed we were going to die in the attempt. Even with that killer program, the odds weren't exactly in our favor.

Bobby was lost in writing the set of commands we were going to plug into the dead center of Chrome's computer. That was going to be my job, because Bobby was going to have his hands full trying to keep the Russian program from going straight for the kill. It was too complex for us to rewrite, and so he was going to try to hold it back for the two seconds I needed.

I made a deal with a streetfighter named Miles. He was going to follow Rikki the night of the burn, keep her in sight, and phone me at a certain time. If I wasn't there, or didn't answer in just a certain way, I'd told him to grab her and put her on the first tube out. I gave him an envelope to give her, money and a note.

Bobby really hadn't thought about that, much, how things would go for her if we blew it. He just kept telling me he loved her, where they were going to go together, how they'd spend the money.

"Buy her a pair of Ikons first, man. That's what she wants. She's serious about that simstim scene."

"Hey," he said, looking up from the keyboard, "she

won't need to work. We're going to make it, Jack. She's my luck. She won't ever have to work again."

"Your luck," I said. I wasn't happy. I couldn't remember when I had been happy. "You seen your luck around lately?"

He hadn't, but neither had I. We'd both been too busy.

I missed her. Missing her reminded me of my one night in the House of Blue Lights, because I'd gone there out of missing someone else. I'd gotten drunk to begin with, then I'd started hitting Vasopressin inhalers. If your main squeeze has just decided to walk out on you, booze and Vasopressin are the ultimate in masochistic pharmacology; the juice makes you maudlin and the Vasopressin makes you remember, I mean really remember. Clinically they use the stuff to counter senile amnesia, but the street finds its own uses for things. So I'd bought myself an ultraintense replay of a bad affair; trouble is, you get the bad with the good. Go gunning for transports of animal ecstasy and you get what you said, too, and what she said to that, how she walked away and never looked back.

I don't remember deciding to go to the Blue Lights, or how I got there, hushed corridors and this really tacky decorative waterfall trickling somewhere, or maybe just a hologram of one. I had a lot of money that night; somebody had given Bobby a big roll for opening a three-second window in someone else's ice.

I don't think the crew on the door liked my looks, but I guess my money was okay.

I had more to drink there when I'd done what I went there for. Then I made some crack to the barman about closet necrophiliacs, and that didn't go down too well. Then this very large character insisted on calling me War Hero, which I didn't like. I think I showed him some tricks with the arm, before the lights went out, and I woke up two days later in a basic sleeping module somewhere else. A cheap place, not even room to hang yourself. And I sat there on that narrow foam slab and cried.

Some things are worse than being alone. But the thing they sell in the House of Blue Lights is so popular that it's almost legal.

At the heart of darkness, the still center, the glitch systems shred the dark with whirlwinds of light, translucent razors spinning away from us; we hang in the center of a silent slow-motion explosion, ice fragments falling away forever, and Bobby's voice comes in across light-years of electronic void illusion—

"Burn the bitch down. I can't hold the thing back—"

The Russian program, rising through towers of data, blotting out the playroom colors. And I plug Bobby's home-made command package into the center of Chrome's cold heart. The squirt transmission cuts in, a pulse of condensed information that shoots straight up, past the thickening tower of darkness, the Russian program, while Bobby struggles to control that crucial second. An unformed arm of shadow twitches from the towering dark, too late.

We've done it.

The matrix folds itself around me like an origami trick.

And the loft smells of sweat and burning circuitry.

I thought I heard Chrome scream, a raw metal sound, but I couldn't have.

Bobby was laughing, tears in his eyes. The elapsed-time figure in the corner of the monitor read 07:24:05. The burn had taken a little under eight minutes.

And I saw that the Russian program had melted in its slot.

We'd given the bulk of Chrome's Zürich account to a dozen world charities. There was too much there to move, and we knew we had to break her, burn her straight down, or she might come after us. We took less than ten percent for ourselves and shot it through the Long Hum setup in Macao. They took sixty percent of that for themselves and kicked what was left back to us through the most convoluted sector of the Hong Kong exchange. It took an hour before our money started to reach the two accounts we'd opened in Zürich.

I watched zeros pile up behind a meaningless figure on the monitor. I was rich.

Then the phone rang. It was Miles. I almost blew the code phrase.

"Hey, Jack, man, I dunno—what's it all about, with this girl of yours? Kinda funny thing here . . ."

"What? Tell me."

"I been on her, like you said, tight but out of sight. She goes to the Loser, hangs out, then she gets a tube. Goes to the House of Blue Lights—"

"She what?"

"Side door. *Employees* only. No way I could get past their security."

"Is she there now?"

"No, man, I just lost her. It's insane down here, like the Blue Lights just shut down, looks like for good, seven kinds of alarms going off, everybody running, the heat out in riot gear. . . . Now there's all this stuff going on, insurance guys, real-estate types, vans with municipal plates. . . ."

"Miles, where'd she go?"

"Lost her, Jack."

"Look, Miles, you keep the money in the envelope, right?"

"You serious? Hey, I'm real sorry. I—"

I hung up.

"Wait'll we tell her," Bobby was saying, rubbing a towel across his bare chest.

"You tell her yourself, cowboy. I'm going for a walk."

So I went out into the night and the neon and let the crowd pull me along, walking blind, willing myself to be just a segment of that mass organism, just one more drifting chip of consciousness under the geodesics. I didn't think, just put one foot in front of another, but after a while I did think, and it all made sense. She'd needed the money.

I thought about Chrome, too. That we'd killed her, murdered her, as surely as if we'd slit her throat. The night that carried me along through the malls and plazas would be hunting her now, and she had nowhere to go. How many enemies would she have in this crowd alone? How many would move, now they weren't held back by fear of her money? We'd taken her for everything she had. She was back on the street again. I doubted she'd live till dawn.

Finally I remembered the café, the one where I'd met Tiger.

Her sunglasses told the whole story, huge black shades with a telltale smudge of fleshtone paintstick in the corner of one lens. "Hi. Rikki," I said, and I was ready when she took them off.

Blue. Tally Isharn blue. The clear trademark blue they're famous for, ZEISS IKON ringing each iris in tiny capitals, the letters suspended there like flecks of gold.

"They're beautiful," I said. Paintstick covered the bruising. No scars with work that good. "You made some money."

"Yeah, I did." Then she shivered. "But I won't make any more, not that way."

"I think that place is out of business."

"Oh." Nothing moved in her face then. The new blue eyes were still and very deep.

"It doesn't matter. Bobby's waiting for you. We just pulled down a big score."

"No. I've got to go. I guess he won't understand, but I've got to go."

I nodded, watching the arm swing up to take her hand; it didn't seem to be part of me at all, but she held on to it like it was.

"I've got a one-way ticket to Hollywood. Tiger knows some people I can stay with. Maybe I'll even get to Chiba City."

She was right about Bobby. I went back with her. He didn't understand. But she'd already served her purpose, for Bobby, and I wanted to tell her not to hurt for him, because I could see that she did. He wouldn't even come out into the hallway after she had packed her bags. I put the bags down and kissed her and messed up the paintstick, and something came up inside me the way the killer program had risen above Chrome's data. A sudden stopping of the breath, in a place where no word is. But she had a plane to catch.

Bobby was slumped in the swivel chair in front of his monitor, looking at his string of zeros. He had his shades on, and I knew he'd be in the Gentleman Loser by nightfall, checking out the weather, anxious for a sign, someone to tell him what his new life would be like. I couldn't see it being very different. More comfortable, but he'd always be waiting for that next card to fall.

I tried not to imagine her in the House of Blue Lights, working three-hour shifts in an approximation of REM sleep, while her body and a bundle of conditioned reflexes took care of business. The customers never got to complain that she was faking it, because those were real orgasms. But she felt them, if she felt them at all, as faint silver flares somewhere out on the edge of sleep. Yeah, it's so popular, it's almost legal. The customers are torn between needing someone and wanting to be alone at the same time, which has probably always been the name of that particular game, even before we had the neuroelectronics to enable them to have it both ways.

I picked up the phone and punched the number for her airline. I gave them her real name, her flight number. "She's changing that," I said, "to Chiba City. That's right. Japan." I thumbed my credit card into the slot and punched my ID code. "First class." Distant hum as they scanned my credit records. "Make that a return ticket."

But I guess she cashed the return fare, or else she didn't need it, because she hasn't come back. And sometimes late at night I'll pass a window with posters of simstim stars, all those beautiful, identical eyes staring back at me out of faces that are nearly as identical, and sometimes the eyes are hers, but none of the faces are, none of them ever are, and I see her far out on the edge of all this sprawl of night and cities, and then she waves goodbye.

BLOOD MUSIC

BY GREG BEAR

There is a principle in nature I don't think anyone has pointed out before. Each hour, a myriad of trillions of little live things—bacteria, microbes, "animalcules"—are born and die, not counting for much except in the bulk of their existence and the accumulation of their tiny effects. They do not perceive deeply. They don't suffer much. A hundred billion, dying, would not begin to have the same importance as a single human death.

Within the ranks of magnitude of all creatures, small as microbes or great as humans, there is an equality of "elan," just as the branches of a tall tree, gathered together, equal the bulk of the limbs below, and all the limbs equal the bulk of the trunk.

That, at least, is the principle. I believe Vergil Ulam was the first to violate it.

It had been two years since I'd last seen Vergil. My memory of him hardly matched the tan, smiling, well-dressed gentleman standing before me. We had made a lunch appointment over the phone the day before, and now faced each other in the wide double doors of the employee's cafeteria at the Mount Freedom Medical Center.

"Vergil?" I asked. "My God, Vergil!"

"Good to see you, Edward." He shook my hand firmly. He had lost ten or twelve kilos and what remained seemed tighter, better proportioned. At the university, Vergil had been the pudgy, shock-haired, snaggle-toothed whiz kid who hot-wired doorknobs, gave us punch that turned our piss blue, and never got a date except with Eileen Termagent, who shared many of his physical characteristics.

"You look fantastic," I said, "Spend a summer in Cabo San Lucas?"

We stood in line at the counter and chose our food. "The tan," he said, picking out a carton of chocolate milk, "is from spending three months under a sun lamp. My teeth were straightened just after I last saw you. I'll explain the rest, but we need a place to talk where no one will listen close."

I steered him to the smoker's corner, where three die-hard puffers were scattered among six tables.

"Listen, I mean it," I said as we unloaded our trays. "You've changed. You're looking good."

"I've changed more than you know." His tone was motion-picture ominous, and he delivered the line with a theatrical lift of his brows. "How's Gail?"

Gail was doing well, I told him, teaching nursery school. We'd married the year before. His gaze shifted down to his food—pineapple slice and cottage cheese, piece of banana cream pie—and he said, his voice almost cracking, "Notice something else?"

I squinted in concentration. "Uh."

"Look closer."

"I'm not sure. Well, yes, you're not wearing glasses. Contacts?"

"No. I don't need them anymore."

"And you're a snappy dresser. Who's dressing you now? I hope she's as sexy as she is tasteful."

"Candice isn't—wasn't—responsible for the improvements in my clothes," he said. "I just got a better job, more money to throw around. My taste in clothes is better than my taste in food, as it happens." He grinned the old Vergil self-deprecating grin, but ended it with a peculiar leer. "At any rate, she's left me, I've been fired from my job, I'm living on savings."

"Hold it," I said. "That's a bit crowded. Why not do a linear breakdown? You got a job. Where?"

"Genetron Corp.," he said. "Sixteen months ago."

"I haven't heard of them."

"You will. They're putting out common stock in the next month. It'll shoot off the board. They've broken through with MABs. Medical—"

"I know what MABs are," I interrupted. "At least in theory. Medically Applicable Biochips."

"They have some that work."

"What?" It was my turn to lift my brows.

"Microscopic logic circuits. You inject them into the human body, they set up shop where they're told and troubleshoot. With Dr. Michael Bernard's approval."

That was quite impressive. Bernard's reputation was spotless. Not only was he associated with the genetic engineering biggies, but he had made news at least once a year in his practice as a neurosurgeon before retiring. Covers on *Time, Mega, Rolling Stone.*

"That's supposed to be secret—stock, breakthrough, Bernard, everything." He looked around and lowered his voice. "But you do whatever the hell you want. I'm through with the bastards."

I whistled. "Make me rich, huh?"

"If that's what you want. Or you can spend some time with me before rushing off to your broker."

"Of course." He hadn't touched the cottage cheese or pie. He had, however, eaten the pineapple slice and drunk the chocolate milk. "So tell me more."

"Well, in med school I was training for lab work. Bio-chemical research. I've always had a bent for computers, too. So I put myself through my last two years—"

"By selling software packages to Westinghouse," I said.

"It's good my friends remember. That's how I got in-volved with Genetron, just when they were starting out. They had big money backers, all the lab facilities I thought anyone would ever need. They hired me, and I advanced rapidly.

"Four months and I was doing my own work. I made some breakthroughs," he tossed his hand nonchalantly, "then I went off on tangents they thought were premature. I persisted and they took away my lab, handed it over to a certifiable flatworm. I managed to save part of the experi-ment before they fired me. But I haven't exactly been cau-tious . . . or judicious. So now it's going on outside the lab."

I'd always regarded Vergil as ambitious, a trifle cracked, and not terribly sensitive. His relations with authority fig-ures had never been smooth. Science, for him, was like the woman you couldn't possibly have, who suddenly opens her arms to you, long before you're ready for mature love— leaving you afraid you'll forever blow the chance, lose the prize, screw up royally. Apparently, he had. "Outside the lab? I don't get you."

"Edward, I want you to examine me. Give me a thor-ough physical. Maybe a cancer diagnostic. Then I'll explain more."

"You want a five-thousand-dollar exam?"

"Whatever you can do. Ultrasound, NMR, thermogram, everything."

"I don't know if I can get access to all that equipment. NMR full-scan has only been here a month or two. Hell, you couldn't pick a more expensive way—"

"Then ultrasound. That's all you'll need."

"Vergil, I'm an obstetrician, not a glamour-boy lab-tech. OB-GYN, butt of all jokes. If you're turning into a woman, maybe I can help you."

He leaned forward, almost putting his elbow into the pie, but swinging wide at the last instant by scant milli-meters. The old Vergil would have hit it square. "Examine me closely and you'll . . ." He narrowed his eyes and shook his head. "Just examine me."

"So I make an appointment for ultrasound. Who's going to pay?"

"I'm on Blue Shield." He smiled and held up a medical credit card. "I messed with the personnel files at Genetron. Anything up to a hundred thousand dollars medical, they'll never check, never suspect."

He wanted secrecy, so I made arrangements. I filled out his forms myself. As long as everything was billed properly, most of the examination could take place without official notice. I didn't charge for my services. After all, Vergil had turned my piss blue. We were friends.

He came in late at night. I wasn't normally on duty then, but I stayed late, waiting for him on the third floor of what the nurses called the Frankenstein wing. I sat on an orange plastic chair. He arrived, looking olive-colored under the fluorescent lights.

He stripped, and I arranged him on the table. I noticed, first off, that his ankles looked swollen. But they weren't puffy. I felt them several times. They seemed healthy, but looked odd. "Hm," I said.

I ran the paddles over him, picking up areas difficult for the big unit to hit, and programmed the data into the imaging system. Then I swung the table around and inserted it into the enameled orifice of the ultrasound diagnostic unit, the hum-hole, so called by the nurses.

I integrated the data from the hum-hole with that from the paddle sweeps and rolled Vergil out, then set up a video frame. The image took a second to integrate, then flowed into a pattern showing Vergil's skeleton.

Three seconds of that—my jaw gaping—and it switched to his thoracic organs, then his musculature, and finally, vascular system and skin.

"How long since the accident?" I asked, trying to take the quiver out of my voice.

"I haven't been in an accident," he said. "It was deliberate."

"Jesus, they beat you, to keep secrets?"

"You don't understand me, Edward. Look at the images again. I'm not damaged."

"Look, there's thickening here," I indicated the ankles, "and your ribs—that crazy zigzag pattern of interlocks. Broken sometime, obviously. And—"

"Look at my spine," he said. I rotated the image in the video frame.

Buckminster Fuller, I thought. It was fantastic. A cage of triangular projections, all interlocking in ways I couldn't begin to follow, much less understand. I reached around and tried to feel his spine with my fingers. He lifted his arms and looked off at the ceiling.

"I can't find it," I said. "It's all smooth back there." I let go of him and looked at his chest, then prodded his ribs. They were sheathed in something rough and flexible. The harder I pressed, the tougher it became. Then I noticed another change.

"Hey," I said. "You don't have any nipples." There were tiny pigment patches, but no nipple formations at all.

"See?" Vergil asked, shrugging on the white robe. "I'm being rebuilt from the inside out."

In my reconstruction of those hours, I fancy myself saying, "So tell me about it." Perhaps mercifully, I don't remember what I actually said.

He explained with his characteristic circumlocutions. Listening was like trying to get to the meat of a newspaper article through a forest of sidebars and graphic embellishments.

I simplify and condense.

Genetron had assigned him to manufacturing prototype biochips, tiny circuits made out of protein molecules. Some were hooked up to silicon chips little more than a micrometer in size, then sent through rat arteries to chemically keyed locations, to make connections with the rat tissue and attempt to monitor and even control lab-induced pathologies.

"*That* was something," he said. "We recovered the most complex microchip by sacrificing the rat, then debriefed it—hooked the silicon portion up to an imaging system. The computer gave us bar graphs, then a diagram of the chemical characteristics of about eleven centimeters of blood vessel . . . then put it all together to make a picture. We zoomed down eleven centimeters of rat artery. You never saw so many scientists jumping up and down, hugging each other, drinking buckets of bug juice." Bug juice was lab ethanol mixed with Dr Pepper.

Eventually, the silicon elements were eliminated completely in favor of nucleoproteins. He seemed reluctant to explain in detail, but I gathered they found ways to make huge molecules—as large as DNA, and even more complex—into electrochemical computers, using ribosome-like structures as "encoders" and "readers," and RNA as "tape." Vergil was able to mimic reproductive separation and reassembly in his nucleoproteins, incorporating program changes at key points by switching nucleotide pairs. "Genetron wanted me to switch over to supergene engineering, since that was the coming thing everywhere else. Make all kinds of critters, some out of our imagination. But I had different ideas." He twiddled his finger around his ear and made theremin sounds. "Mad scientist time, right?" He laughed, then sobered. "I injected my best nucleoproteins into bacteria to make duplication and compounding easier. Then I started to leave them inside, so the circuits could interact with the cells. They were heuristically programmed; they taught themselves more than I programmed them. The cells fed chemically coded information to the computers, the computers processed it and made decisions, the cells became smart. I mean, smart as planaria, for starters. Imagine an *E. coli* as smart as a planarian worm!"

I nodded. "I'm imagining."

"Then I really went off on my own. We had the equipment, the techniques; and I knew the molecular language. I could make really dense, really complicated biochips by compounding the nucleoproteins, making them into little brains. I did some research into how far I could go, theoretically. Sticking with bacteria, I could make them a biochip with the computing capacity of a sparrow's brain. Imagine how jazzed I was! Then I saw a way to increase the complexity a thousandfold, by using something we regarded as a nuisance—quantum chitchat between the fixed elements of the circuits. Down that small, even the slightest change could bomb a biochip. But I developed a program that actually predicted and took advantage of electron tunneling. Emphasized the heuristic aspects of the computer, used the chitchat as a method of increasing complexity."

"You're losing me," I said.

"I took advantage of randomness. The circuits could repair themselves, compare memories, and correct faulty elements. The whole schmeer. I gave them basic instructions: Go forth and multiply. Improve. By God, you should have seen some of the cultures a week later! It was amazing. They were evolving all on their own, like little cities. I destroyed them all. I think one of the petri dishes would have grown legs and walked out of the incubator if I'd kept feeding it."

"You're kidding." I looked at him. "You're not kidding."

"Man, they *knew* what it was like to improve! They knew where they had to go, but they were just so limited, being in bacteria bodies, with so few resources."

"How smart were they?"

"I couldn't be sure. They were associating in clusters of a hundred to two hundred cells, each cluster behaving like an autonomous unit. Each cluster might have been as smart as a rhesus monkey. They exchanged information through their pili, passed on bits of memory, and compared notes. Their organization was obviously different from a group of monkeys. Their world was so much simpler, for one thing. With their abilities, they were masters of the petri dishes. I put phages in with them; the phages didn't have a chance. They used every option available to change and grow."

"How is that possible?"

"What?" He seemed surprised I wasn't accepting everything at face value.

"Cramming so much into so little. A rhesus monkey is not your simple little calculator, Vergil."

"I haven't made myself clear," he said, obviously irritated. "I was using nucleoprotein computers. They're like

DNA, but all the information can interact. Do you know how many nucleotide pairs there are in the DNA of a single bacteria?"

It had been a long time since my last biochemistry lesson. I shook my head.

"About two million. Add in the modified ribosome structures—fifteen thousand of them, each with a molecular weight of about three million—and consider the combinations and permutations. The RNA is arranged like a continuous loop paper tape, surrounded by ribosomes ticking off instructions and manufacturing protein chains . . ." His eyes were bright and slightly moist. "Besides, I'm not saying every cell was a distinct entity. They cooperated."

"How many bacteria in the dishes you destroyed?"

"Billions. I don't know." He smirked. "You got it, Edward. Whole planetsful of *E. coli*."

"But they didn't fire you then?"

"No. They didn't know what was going on, for one thing. I kept compounding the molecules, increasing their size and complexity. When bacteria were too limited, I took blood from myself, separated out white cells, and injected them with the new biochips. I watched them, put them through mazes and little chemical problems. They were whizzes. Time is a lot faster at that level—so little distance for the messages to cross, and the environment is much simpler. Then I forgot to store a file under my secret code in the lab computers. Some managers found it and guessed what I was up to. Everybody panicked. They thought we'd have every social watchdog in the country on our backs because of what I'd done. They started to destroy my work and wipe my programs. Ordered me to sterilize my white cells. Christ." He pulled the white robe off and started to get dressed. "I only had a day or two. I separated out the most complex cells—"

"How complex?"

"They were clustering in hundred-cell groups, like the bacteria. Each group as smart as a ten-year-old kid, maybe." He studied my face for a moment. "Still doubting? Want me to run through how many nucleotide pairs there are in a mammalian cell? I tailored my computers to take advantage of the white cells' capacity. Ten billion nucleotide pairs, Edward. Ten E-f––ing ten. And they don't have a huge body to worry about, taking up most of their thinking time."

"Okay," I said. "I'm convinced. What did you do?"

"I mixed the cells back into a cylinder of whole blood and injected myself with it." He buttoned the top of his shirt and smiled thinly at me. "I'd programmed them with every drive I could, talked as high a level as I could using just enzymes and such. After that, they were on their own."

"You programmed them to go forth and multiply, improve?" I repeated.

"I think they developed some characteristics picked up by the biochips in their *E. coli* phases. The white cells could talk to one another with extruded memories. They almost certainly found ways to ingest other types of cells and alter them without killing them."

"You're crazy."

"You can see the screen! Edward, I haven't been sick since. I used to get colds all the time. I've never felt better."

"They're inside you, finding things, changing them."

"And by now, each cluster is as smart as you or I."

"You're absolutely nuts."

He shrugged. "They fired me. They thought I was going to get revenge for what they did to my work. They ordered me out of the labs, and I haven't had a real chance to see what's been going on inside me until now. Three months."

"So . . ." My mind was racing. "You lost weight because they improved your fat metabolism. Your bones are stronger, your spine has been completely rebuilt—"

"No more backaches even if I sleep on my old mattress."

"Your heart looks different."

"I didn't know about the heart," he said, examining the frame image from a few inches. "About the fat—I was thinking about that. They could increase my brown cells, fix up the metabolism. I haven't been as hungry lately. I haven't changed my eating habits that much—I still want the same old junk—but somehow I get around to eating only what I need. I don't think they know what my brain is yet. Sure, they've got all the glandular stuff—but they don't have the *big* picture, if you see what I mean. They don't know *I'm* in there. But boy, they sure did figure out what my reproductive organs are."

I glanced at the image and shifted my eyes away.

"Oh, they look pretty normal," he said, hefting his scrotum obscenely. He snickered. "But how else do you think I'd land a real looker like Candice? She was just after a one-night stand with a techie. I looked okay then, no tan but trim, with good clothes. She'd never screwed a techie before. Joke time, right? But my little geniuses kept us up half the night. I think they made improvements each time. I felt like I had a goddamned fever."

His smile vanished. "But then one night my skin started to crawl. It really scared me. I thought things were getting out of hand. I wondered what they'd do when they crossed the blood-brain barrier and found out about *me*—about the brain's real function. So I began a campaign to keep them under control. I figured, the reason they wanted to get into the skin was the simplicity of running circuits across a surface. Much easier than trying to maintain chains of communication in and around muscles, organs, vessels. The skin was much more direct. So I bought a quartz lamp." He caught my puzzled expression. "In the lab, we'd break down the protein in biochip cells by exposing them to ultraviolet light. I alternated sun lamp with quartz treatments. Keeps them out of my skin, so far as I can tell, and gives me a nice tan."

"Give you skin cancer, too," I commented.

"They'll probably take care of that. Like police."

"Okay, I've examined you, you've told me a story I still find hard to believe . . . what do you want me to do?"

"I'm not as nonchalant as I act, Edward. I'm worried. I'd like to find some way to control them before they find out about my brain. I mean, think of it, they're in the trillions by now, each one smart. They're cooperating to some extent. I'm probably the smartest thing on the planet, and they haven't even begun to get their act together yet. I don't really want them to take over." He laughed very unpleasantly. "Steal my soul, you know? So think of some treatment to block them. Maybe we can starve the little buggers. Just think on it." He buttoned his shirt. "Give me a call." He handed me a slip of paper with his address and phone number. Then he went to the keyboard and erased the image on the frame, dumping the memory of the examination. "Just you," he said. "Nobody else for now. And please . . . hurry."

It was three o'clock in the morning when Vergil walked out of the examination room. He'd allowed me to take blood samples, then shaken my hand—his palm damp, nervous—and cautioned me against ingesting anything from the specimens.

Before I went home, I put the blood through a series of tests. The results were ready the next day.

I picked them up during my lunch break in the afternoon, then destroyed all the samples. I did it like a robot. It took me five days and nearly sleepless nights to accept what I'd seen. His blood was normal enough, though the machines diagnosed the patient as having an infection. High levels of leukocytes—white blood cells—and histamines. On the fifth day, I believed.

Gail was home before I, but it was my turn to fix dinner. She slipped one of the school's disks into the home system and showed me video art her nursery kids had been creating. I watched quietly, ate with her in silence.

I had two dreams, part of my final acceptance. The first that evening—which had me up thrashing in my sheets—I witnessed the destruction of the planet Krypton, Superman's home world. Billions of superhuman geniuses went screaming off in walls of fire. I related the destruction to my sterilizing the samples of Vergil's blood.

The second dream was worse: I dreamed that New York City was raping a woman. By the end of the dream, she was giving birth to little embryo cities, all wrapped up in translucent sacs, soaked with blood from the difficult labor.

I called him on the morning of the sixth day. He answered on the fourth ring. "I have some results," I said. "Nothing conclusive. But I want to talk with you. In person."

"Sure," he said. "I'm staying inside for the time being." His voice was strained; he sounded tired.

Vergil's apartment was in a fancy high-rise near the lake shore. I took the elevator up, listening to little advertising jingles and watching dancing holograms display products, empty apartments for rent, the building's hostess discussing social activities for the week.

Vergil opened the door and motioned me in. He wore a checked robe with long sleeves and carpet slippers. He clutched an unlit pipe in one hand, his fingers twisting it back and forth as he walked away from me and sat down, saying nothing.

"You have an infection," I said.

"Oh?"

"That's all the blood analyses tell me. I don't have access to the electron microscopes."

"I don't think it's really an infection," he said. "After all, they're my own cells. Probably something else . . . sign of their presence, of the change. We can't expect to understand everything that's happening."

I removed my coat. "Listen," I said, "you have me worried now." The expression on his face stopped me: a kind of frantic beatitude. He squinted at the ceiling and pursed his lips.

"Are you stoned?" I asked.

He shook his head, then nodded once, very slowly. "Listening," he said.

"To what?"

"I don't know. Not sounds . . . exactly. Like music. The heart, all the blood vessels, friction of blood along the arteries, veins. Activity. Music in the blood." He looked at me plaintively. "Why aren't you at work?"

"My day off. Gail's working."

"Can you stay?"

I shrugged. "I suppose." I sounded suspicious. I was glancing around the apartment, looking for ashtrays, packs of papers.

"I'm not stoned, Edward," he said. "I may be wrong, but I think something big is happening. I think they're finding out who I am."

I sat down across from Vergil, staring at him intently. He didn't seem to notice. Some inner process was involving him. When I asked for a cup of coffee, he motioned to the kitchen. I boiled a pot of water and took a jar of instant from the cabinet. With cup in hand, I returned to my seat. He was twisting his head back and forth, eyes open. "You always knew what you wanted to be, didn't you?" he asked me.

"More or less."

"A gynecologist. Smart moves. Never false moves. I was different. I had goals, but no direction. Like a map without roads, just places to be. I didn't give a shit for anything, anyone but myself. Even science. Just a means. I'm surprised I got so far. I even hated my folks."

He gripped his chair arms.

"Something wrong?" I asked.

"They're talking to me," he said. He shut his eyes.

For an hour he seemed to be asleep. I checked his pulse, which was strong and steady, felt his forehead—slightly cool—and made myself more coffee. I was looking through a magazine, at a loss what to do, when he opened his eyes again. "Hard to figure exactly what time is like for them," he said. "It's taken them maybe three, four days to figure out language, key human concepts. Now they're on to it. On to me. Right now."

"How's that?"

He claimed there were thousands of researchers hooked up to his neurons. He couldn't give details. "They're damned efficient, you know," he said. "They haven't screwed me up yet."

"We should get you into the hospital now."

"What in hell could they do? Did you figure out any way to control them? I mean, they're my own cells."

"I've been thinking. We could starve them. Find out what metabolic differences—"

"I'm not sure I want to be rid of them," Vergil said. "They're not doing any harm."

"How do you know?"

He shook his head and held up one finger. "Wait. They're trying to figure out what space is. That's tough for them. They break distances down into concentrations of chemicals. For them, space is like intensity of taste."

"Vergil—"

"Listen! Think, Edward!" His tone was excited but even. "Oh-serve! Something big is happening inside me. They talk to one another across the fluid, through membranes. They tailor something—viruses?—to carry data stored in nucleic acid chains. I think they're saying 'RNA.' That makes sense. That's one way I programmed them. But plasmid-like structures, too. Maybe that's what your machines think is a sign of infection—all their chattering in my blood, packets of data. Tastes of other individuals. Peers. Superiors. Subordinates."

"Vergil, I'm listening, but I still think you should be in a hospital."

"This is my show, Edward," he said. "I'm their universe. They're amazed by the new scale." He was quiet again for a time. I squatted by his chair and pulled up the sleeve to his robe. His arm was crisscrossed with white lines. I was about to go to the phone and call for an ambulance when he stood and stretched. "Do you realize," he said, "how many body cells we kill each time we move?"

"I'm going to call for an ambulance," I said.

"No, you aren't." His tone stopped me. "I told you, I'm not sick; this is my show. Do you know what they'd do to me in a hospital? They'd be like cavemen trying to fix a computer the same way they fix a stone ax. It would be a farce."

"Then what the hell am I doing here?" I asked, getting angry. "I can't do anything. I'm one of those cavemen."

"You're a friend," Vergil said, fixing his eyes on me. I had the impression I was being watched by more than just Vergil. "I want you here to keep me company." He laughed. "But I'm not exactly alone."

He walked around the apartment for two hours, fingering things, looking out windows, making himself lunch slowly and methodically. "You know, they can actually feel their own thoughts," he said about noon. "I mean, the cytoplasm seems to have a will of its own, a kind of subconscious life counter to the rationality they've only recently acquired. They hear the chemical 'noise' or whatever of the molecules fitting and unfitting inside."

At two o'clock, I called Gail to tell her I would be late. I was almost sick with tension but I tried to keep my voice level. "Remember Vergil Ulam? I'm talking with him right now."

"Everything okay?" she asked.

Was it? Decidedly not. "Fine," I said.

"Culture!" Vergil said, peering around the kitchen wall at me. I said good-bye and hung up the phone. "They're always swimming in that bath of information. Contributing to it. It's a kind of gestalt-thing, whatever. The hierarchy is absolute. They send tailored phages after cells that don't interact properly. Viruses specified to individuals or groups. No escape. One gets pierced by the virus, the cell blebs outward, it explodes and dissolves. But it's not just a dictatorship, I think they effectively have more freedom than in a democracy. I mean, they vary so differently from individual to individual. Does that make sense? They vary in different ways than we do."

"Hold it," I said, gripping his shoulders. "Vergil, you're pushing me close to the edge. I can't take this much longer. I don't understand, I'm not sure I believe—"

"Not even now?"

"Okay, let's say you're giving me the, the right interpretation. Giving it to me straight. The whole thing's true. Have you bothered to figure out all the consequences yet? What all this means, where it might lead?"

He walked into the kitchen and drew a glass of water from the tap, then returned and stood next to me. His expression had changed from childish absorption to sober concern. "I've never been very good at that."

"Aren't you afraid?"

"I was. Now I'm not sure." He fingered the tie of his robe. "Look, I don't want you to think I went around you, over your head or something. But I met with Michael Bernard yesterday. He put me through his private clinic, took specimens. Told me to quit the lamp treatments. He called this morning, just before you did. He says it all checks out. And he asked me not to tell anybody." He paused and his expression became dreamy again. "Cities of cells," he continued. "Edward, they push pili-like tubes through the tissues, spread information—"

"Stop it!" I shouted. "Checks out? What checks out?"

"As Bernard puts it, I have 'severely enlarged macrophages' throughout my system. And he concurs on the anatomical changes. So it's not just our common delusion."

"What does he plan to do?"

"I don't know. I think he'll probably convince Genetron to reopen the lab."

"Is that what you want?"

"It's not just having the lab again. I want to show you. Since I stopped the lamp treatments. I'm still changing." He undid his robe and let it slide to the floor. All over his body, his skin was criss-crossed with white lines. Along his back, the lines were starting to form ridges.

"My God," I said.

"I'm not going to be much good anywhere else but the lab soon. I won't be able to go out in public. Hospitals wouldn't know what to do, as I said."

"You're ... you can talk to them, tell them to slow down," I said, aware how ridiculous that sounded.

"Yes, indeed I can, but they don't necessarily listen."

"I thought you were their god or something."

"The ones hooked up to my neurons aren't the big wheels. They're researchers, or at least serve the same function. They know I'm here, what I am, but that doesn't mean they've convinced the upper levels of the hierarchy."

"They're disputing?"

"Something like that. It's not all that bad, anyway. If the lab is reopened, I have a home, a place to work." He glanced out the window, as if looking for someone. "I don't have anything left but them. They aren't afraid, Edward. I've never felt so close to anything before." The beatific smile again. "I'm responsible for them. Mother to them all."

"You have no way of knowing what they're going to do."

He shook his head.

"No, I mean it. You say they're like a civilization—"

"Like a thousand civilizations."

"Yes, and civilizations have been known to screw up. Warfare, the environment—"

I was grasping at straws, trying to restrain a growing panic. I wasn't competent to handle the enormity of what was happening. Neither was Vergil. He was the last person I would have called insightful and wise about large issues.

"But I'm the only one at risk."

"You don't know that. Jesus, Vergil, look what they're *doing* to you!"

"To me, all to me!" he said. "Nobody else."

I shook my head and held up my hands in a gesture of defeat. "Okay, so Bernard gets them to reopen the lab, you move in, become a guinea pig. What then?"

"They treat me right. I'm more than just good old Vergil Ulam now. I'm a goddamned galaxy, a super-mother."

"Super-host, you mean." He conceded the point with a shrug.

I couldn't take any more. I made my exit with a few

flimsy excuses, then sat in the lobby of the apartment building, trying to calm down. Somebody had to talk some sense
into him. Who would he listen to? He had gone to Bernard . . .

And it sounded as if Bernard was not only convinced,
but very interested. People of Bernard's stature didn't coax
the Vergil Ulams of the world along, not unless they felt it
was to their advantage.

I had a hunch, and I decided to play it. I went to a pay
phone, slipped in my credit card, and called Genetron.

"I'd like you to page Dr. Michael Bernard," I told the
receptionist.

"Who's calling, please?"

"This is his answering service. We have an emergency
call and his beeper doesn't seem to be working."

A few anxious minutes later, Bernard came on the line.
"Who the hell is this?" he asked quietly. "I don't have an
answering service."

"My name is Edward Milligan. I'm a friend of Vergil
Ulam's. I think we have some problems to discuss."

We made an appointment to talk the next morning.

I went home and tried to think of excuses to keep me
off the next day's hospital shift. I couldn't concentrate on
medicine, couldn't give my patients anywhere near the attention they deserved.

Guilty, anxious, angry, afraid.

That was how Gail found me. I slipped on a mask of calm
and we fixed dinner together. After eating, we watched the
city lights come on in late twilight through the bayside window, holding on to each other. Odd winter starlings pecked
at the yellow lawn in the last few minutes of light, then flew
away with a rising wind which made the windows rattle.

"Something's wrong," Gail said softly. "Are you going

to tell me, or just act like everything's normal?"

"It's just me," I said. "Nervous. Work at the hospital."

"Oh, lord," she said, sitting up. "You're going to divorce me for that Baker woman." Mrs. Baker weighed three hundred and sixty pounds and hadn't known she was pregnant until her fifth month.

"No," I said, listless.

"Rapturous relief," Gail said, touching my forehead lightly. "You know this kind of introspection drives me crazy."

"Well, it's nothing I can talk about yet, so . . ." I patted her hand.

"That's disgustingly patronizing," she said, getting up. "I'm going to make some tea. Want some?" Now she was miffed, and I was tense with not telling.

Why not just reveal all? I asked myself. An old friend of mine was turning himself into a galaxy.

I cleared away the table instead. That night, unable to sleep, I looked down on Gail in bed from my sitting position, pillow against the wall, and tried to determine what I knew was real, and what wasn't.

I'm a doctor, I told myself. A technical, scientific profession. I'm supposed to be immune to things like future shock.

Vergil Ulam was turning into a galaxy.

How would it feel to be topped off with a trillion Chinese? I grinned in the dark, and almost cried at the same time. What Vergil had inside him was unimaginably stranger than Chinese. Stranger than anything I—or Vergil—could easily understand. Perhaps ever understand.

But I knew what was real. The bedroom, the city lights faint through gauze curtains. Gail sleeping. Very important. Gail, in bed, sleeping.

The dream came again. This time the city came in

through the window and attacked Gail. It was a great, spiky lighted-up prowler and it growled in a language I couldn't understand, made up of auto horns, crowded noises, construction bedlam. I tried to fight it off, but it got to her—and turned into a drift of stars, sprinkling all over the bed, all over everything. I jerked awake and stayed up until dawn, dressed with Gail, kissed her, savored the reality of her human, unviolated lips.

And went to meet with Bernard. He had been loaned a suite in a big downtown hospital; I rode the elevator to the sixth floor, and saw what fame and fortune could mean.

The suite was tastefully furnished, fine serigraphs on wood-paneled walls, chrome and glass furniture, cream-colored carpet, Chinese brass, and wormwood-grain cabinets and tables.

He offered me a cup of coffee, and I accepted. He took a seat in the breakfast nook, and I sat across from him, cradling my cup in moist palms. He was dapper, wearing a gray suit; had graying hair and a sharp profile. He was in his mid-sixties and he looked quite a bit like Leonard Bernstein.

"About our mutual acquaintance," he said. "Mr. Ulam. Brilliant. And, I won't hesitate to say, courageous."

"He's my friend. I'm worried about him."

Bernard held up one finger. "Courageous—and a bloody damned fool. What's happening to him should never have been allowed. He may have done it under duress, but that's no excuse. Still, what's done is done. He's talked to you, I take it."

I nodded. "He wants to return to Genetron."

"Of course. That's where all his equipment is. Where his home probably will be while we sort this out."

"Sort it out—how? What use is it?" I wasn't thinking too clearly. I had a slight headache.

"I can think of a large number of uses for small, super-dense computer elements with a biological base. Can't you? Genetron has already made breakthroughs, but this is something else again."

"What do you envision?"

Bernard smiled. "I'm not really at liberty to say. It'll be revolutionary. We'll have to get him in lab conditions. Animal experiments have to be conducted. We'll have to start from scratch, of course. Vergil's . . . um . . . colonies can't be transferred. They're based on his white blood cells. So we have to develop colonies that won't trigger immune reactions to other animals."

"Like an infection?" I asked.

"I suppose there are comparisons. But Vergil is not infected."

"My tests indicate he is."

"That's probably the bits of data floating around in his blood, don't you think?"

"I don't know."

"Listen, I'd like you to come down to the lab after Vergil is settled in. Your expertise might be useful to us."

Us. He was working with Genetron hand in glove. Could he be objective? "How will you benefit from all this?"

"Edward, I have always been at the forefront of my profession. I see no reason why I shouldn't be helping here. With my knowledge of brain and nerve functions, and the research I've been conducting in neurophysiology—"

"You could help Genetron hold off an investigation by the government," I said.

"That's being very blunt. Too blunt, and unfair."

"Perhaps. Anyway, yes. I'd like to visit the lab when Vergil's settled in. If I'm still welcome, bluntness and all." He looked at me sharply. I wouldn't be playing on *his* team; for a moment, his thoughts were almost nakedly apparent.

"Of course," Bernard said, rising with me. He reached out to shake my hand. His palm was damp. He was as nervous as I was, even if he didn't look it.

I returned to my apartment and stayed there until noon, reading, trying to sort things out. Reach a decision. What was real, what I needed to protect.

There is only so much change anyone can stand. Innovation, yes, but slow application. Don't force. Everyone has the right to stay the same until they decide otherwise.

The greatest thing in science since . . .

And Bernard would force it. Genetron would force it. I couldn't handle the thought. "Neo-Luddite," I said to myself. A filthy accusation.

When I pressed Vergil's number on the building security panel, Vergil answered almost immediately. "Yeah," he said. He sounded exhilarated now. "Come on up. I'll be in the bathroom. Door's unlocked."

I entered his apartment and walked through the hallway to the bathroom. Vergil was in the tub, up to his neck in pinkish water. He smiled vaguely at me and splashed his hands. "Looks like I slit my wrists, doesn't it?" he said softly. "Don't worry. Everything's fine now. Genetron's going to take me back. Bernard just called." He pointed to the bathroom phone and intercom.

I sat down on the toilet and noticed the sun lamp fixture standing unplugged next to the linen cabinets. The bulbs sat in a row on the edge of the sink counter. "You're sure that's what you want," I said, my shoulders slumping.

"Yeah, I think so," he said. "They can take better care of me. I'm getting cleaned up, go over there this evening. Bernard's picking me up in his limo. Style. From here on in, everything's style."

The pinkish color in the water didn't look like soap. "Is

that bubble bath?" I asked. Some of it came to me in a rush then and I felt a little weaker: what had occurred to me was just one more obvious and necessary insanity.

"No," Vergil said. I knew that already.

"No," he repeated, "it's coming from my skin. They're not telling me everything, but I think they're sending out scouts. Astronauts." He looked at me with an expression that didn't quite equal concern; more like curiosity as to how I'd take it.

The confirmation made my stomach muscles tighten as if waiting for a punch. I had never even considered the possibility until now, perhaps because I had been concentrating on other aspects. "Is this the first time?" I asked.

"Yeah," he said. He laughed. "I've half a mind to let the little buggers down the drain. Let them find out what the world's really about."

"They'd go everywhere," I said.

"Sure enough."

"How . . . how are you feeling?"

"I'm feeling pretty good now. Must be billions of them." More splashing with his hands. "What do you think? Should I let the buggers out?"

Quickly, hardly thinking, I knelt down beside the tub. My fingers went for the cord on the sun lamp and I plugged it in. He had hot-wired doorknobs, turned my piss blue, played a thousand dumb practical jokes and never grown up, never grown mature enough to understand that he was just brilliant enough to really affect the world; he would never learn caution.

He reached for the drain knob. "You know, Edward, I—"

He never finished. I picked up the fixture and dropped it into the tub, jumping back at the flash of steam and sparks. Vergil screamed and thrashed and jerked and then everything was still, except for the low, steady sizzle and the smoke wafting from his hair.

I lifted the toilet and vomited. Then I clenched my nose and went into the living room. My legs went out from under me and I sat abruptly on the couch.

After an hour, I searched through Vergil's kitchen and found bleach, ammonia, and a bottle of Jack Daniel's. I returned to the bathroom, keeping the center of my gaze away from Vergil. I poured first the booze, then the bleach, then the ammonia into the water. Chlorine started bubbling up and I left, closing the door behind me.

The phone was ringing when I got home. I didn't answer. It could have been the hospital. It could have been Bernard. Or the police. I could envision having to explain everything to the police. Genetron would stonewall; Bernard would be unavailable.

I was exhausted, all my muscles knotted with tension and whatever name one can give to the feelings one has after—

Committing genocide?

That certainly didn't seem real. I could not believe I had just murdered a hundred trillion intelligent beings. Snuffed a galaxy. It was laughable. But I didn't laugh.

It was not at all hard to believe I had just killed one human being, a friend. The smoke, the melted lamp rods, the drooping electrical outlet and smoking cord.

Vergil.

I had dunked the lamp into the tub with Vergil.

I felt sick. Dreams, cities raping Gail (and what about his girlfriend, Candice?). Letting the water filled with them out. Galaxies sprinkling over us all. What horror. Then again, what potential beauty—a new kind of life, symbiosis and transformation.

Had I been thorough enough to kill them all? I had a

moment of panic. Tomorrow, I thought, I will sterilize his apartment. Somehow. I didn't even think of Bernard.

When Gail came in the door, I was asleep on the couch. I came to, groggy, and she looked down at me.

"You feeling okay?" she asked, perching on the edge of the couch. I nodded.

"What are you planning for dinner?" My mouth wasn't working properly. The words were mushy. She felt my forehead.

"Edward, you have a fever," she said. "A very high fever."

I stumbled into the bathroom and looked in the mirror. Gail was close behind me. "What is it?" she asked.

There were lines under my collar, around my neck. White lines, like freeways. They had already been in me a long time, days.

"Damp palms," I said. So obvious.

I think we nearly died. I struggled at first, but within minutes I was too weak to move. Gail was just as sick within an hour.

I lay on the carpet in the living room, drenched in sweat. Gail lay on the couch, her face the color of talcum, eyes closed, like a corpse in an embalming parlor. For a time I thought she was dead. Sick as I was, I raged—hated, felt tremendous guilt at my weakness, my slowness to understand all the possibilities. Then I no longer cared. I was too weak to blink, so I closed my eyes and waited.

There was a rhythm in my arms, my legs. With each pulse of blood, a kind of sound welled up within me. A sound like an orchestra thousands strong, but not playing in unison; playing whole seasons of symphonies at once. Music in the blood. The sound or whatever became harsher, but more coordinated, wavetrains finally cancelling into silence, then separating into harmonic beats.

The beats seemed to melt into me, into the sound of my own heart.

First, they subdued our immune responses. The war—and it was a war, on a scale never before known on Earth, with trillions of combatants—lasted perhaps two days.

By the time I regained enough strength to get to the kitchen faucet, I could feel them working on my brain, trying to crack the code and find the god within the protoplasm. I drank until I was sick, then drank more moderately and took a glass to Gail. She sipped at it. Her lips were cracked, her eyes bloodshot and ringed with yellowish crumbs. There was some color in her skin. Minutes later, we were eating feebly in the kitchen.

"What in hell was *that?*" was the first thing she asked. I didn't have the strength to explain, so I shook my head. I peeled an orange and shared it with her. "We should call a doctor," she said. But I knew we wouldn't. I was already receiving messages; it was becoming apparent that any sensation of freedom we had was illusory.

The messages were simple at first. Memories of commands, rather than the commands themselves, manifested themselves in my thoughts. We were not to leave the apartment—a concept which seemed quite abstract to those in control, even if undesirable—and we were not to have contact with others. We would be allowed to eat certain foods, and drink tap water, for the time being.

With the subsidence of the fevers, the transformations were quick and drastic. Almost simultaneously, Gail and I were immobilized. She was sitting at the table, I was kneeling on the floor. I was able barely to see her in the corner of my eye.

Her arm was developing pronounced ridges.

They had learned inside Vergil; their tactics within the two of us were very different. I itched all over for about two hours—two hours in hell—before they made the breakthrough and found me. The effort of ages on their time scale paid off and they communicated smoothly and directly with this great, clumsy intelligence which had once controlled their universe.

They were not cruel. When the concept of discomfort and its undesirability was made clear, they worked to alleviate it. They worked too effectively. For another hour, I was in a sea of bliss, out of all contact with them.

With dawn the next day, we were allowed freedom to move again; specifically, to go to the bathroom. There were certain waste products they could not deal with. I voided those—my urine was purple—and Gail followed suit. We looked at each other vacantly in the bathroom. Then she managed a slight smile. "Are they talking to you?" she asked. I nodded. "Then I'm not crazy."

For the next twelve hours, control seemed to loosen on some levels. During that time, I managed to pencil the majority of this manuscript. I suspect there was another kind of war going on in me. Gail was capable of our previous limited motion, but no more.

When full control resumed, we were instructed to hold each other. We did not hesitate.

"Eddie . . ." she whispered. My name was the last sound I ever heard from outside.

Standing, we grew together. In hours, our legs expanded and spread out. Then extensions grew to the windows to take in sunlight, and to the kitchen to take water from the sink. Filaments soon reached to all corners of the room, stripping paint and plaster from the walls, fabric and stuffing from the furniture.

By the next dawn, the transformation was complete.

I no longer have any clear view of what we look like. I suspect we resemble cells—large, flat and filamented cells, draped purposefully across most of the apartment. The great shall mimic the small.

I have been asked to carry on recording, but soon that will not be possible. Our intelligence fluctuates daily as we are absorbed into the minds within. Each day, our individuality declines. We are, indeed, great clumsy dinosaurs. Our memories have been taken over by billions of them, and our personalities have been spread through the transformed blood.

Soon there will be no need for centralization.

I am informed that already the plumbing has been invaded. People throughout the building are undergoing transformation.

Within the old time frame of weeks, we will reach the lakes, rivers, and seas in force.

I can barely begin to guess the results. Every square inch of the planet will teem with thought. Years from now, perhaps much sooner, they will subdue their own individuality—what there is of it.

New creatures will come, then. The immensity of their capacity for thought will be inconceivable.

All my hatred and fear is gone now.

I leave them—us—with only one question.

How many times has this happened, elsewhere? Travelers never came through space to visit the Earth. They had no need.

They had found universes in grains of sand.

TILL HUMAN
VOICES WAKE US

BY LEWIS SHINER

They were at forty feet, in darkness. Inside the narrow circle of his dive light, Campbell could see coral polyps feeding, their ragged edges transformed into predatory flowers.

If anything could have saved us, he thought, this week should have been it.

Beth's lantern wobbled as she flailed herself away from the white-petaled spines of a sea urchin. She wore nothing but a white T-shirt over her bikini, despite Campbell's warnings, and he could see gooseflesh on her thighs. Which is as much of her body, he thought, as I've seen in...how long? Five weeks? Six? He couldn't remember the last time they'd made love.

As he moved his light away he thought he saw a shape in the darkness. He thought: shark, and felt a quick constriction of fear in his throat. He swung the light back again and saw her.

She was frozen by the glare, like any wild animal. Her long, straight hair floated up from her shoulders and blended into the darkness; the ends of her bare breasts were eliptical and purple in the night water.

Her legs merged into a green, scaly tail.

Campbell listened to his breath rasp into the regulator. He could see the width of her cheekbones, the paleness of her eyes, the frightened tremor of the gills around her neck.

Then reflex took over and he brought up his Nikonos and fired. The flare of the strobe shocked her to life. She shuddered, flicked her crescent tail toward him, and disappeared.

A sudden, inexplicable longing overwhelmed him. He dropped the camera and swam after her, legs pumping, pulling with both arms. As he reached the edge of a hundred foot drop-off, he swept the light in an arc that picked up a final glimpse of her, heading down and to the west. Then she was gone.

He found Beth on the surface, shivering and enraged. "What the hell was the idea of leaving me alone like that? I was scared to death. You heard what that guy said about sharks. . . ."

"I saw something," Campbell said.

"Fan-fucking-tastic." She rode low in the water, and Campbell watched her catch a wave in her open mouth. She spat it out and said, "Were you taking a look, or just running away?"

"Blow up your vest," Campbell said, feeling numb, desolate, "before you drown yourself." He turned his back to her and swam for the boat.

Showered, sitting outside his cabin in the moonlight, Campbell began to doubt himself.

Beth was already cocooned in a flannel nightgown near her edge of the bed. She would lie there, Campbell knew, sometimes not even bothering to close her eyes, until he was asleep.

His recurring, obsessive daydreams were what had brought him here to the island. How could he be sure he hadn't hallucinated that creature out on the reef?

He'd told Beth that they'd been lucky to be picked for the vacation, that he'd applied for it months before. In fact, his fantasies had so utterly destroyed his concentration at work that the company had ordered him to come to the island or submit to a complete course of psych testing.

He'd been more frightened than he was willing to admit. The fantasies had progressed from the mild violence of smashing his CRT screen to a bizarre, sinister image of himself floating outside his shattered office windows, not falling the forty stories to the street, just drifting there in the whitish smog.

High above him Campbell could see the company bar, glittering like a chrome-and-steel monster just hatched from its larval stage.

He shook his head. Obviously he needed some sleep. Just one good night's rest, he told himself, and things would start getting back to normal.

In the morning Campbell went out on the dive boat while Beth slept in. He was distracted, clumsy, and bothered by shadows in his peripheral vision.

The dive master wandered over while they were changing tanks and asked him, "You nervous about something?"

"No," Campbell said. "I'm fine."

"There's no sharks on this part of the reef, you know."

"It's not that," Campbell said. "There's no problem. Really."

He read the look in the dive master's eyes: another case of shell shock. The company must turn them out by the dozens, Campbell thought. The stressed-out executives and the boardroom victims, all with the same glazed expressions.

That afternoon they dove a small wreck at the east end of the island. Beth paired off with another woman, so Campbell stayed with his partner from the morning, a balding pilot from the Cincinnati office.

The wreck was no more than a husk, an empty shell, and Campbell floated to one side as the others crawled over the rotting wood. His sense of purpose had disappeared, left him wanting only the weightlessness and lack of color of the deep water.

After dinner he followed Beth out onto the patio. He'd lost track of how long he'd been watching the clouds over the dark water, when she said, "I don't like this place."

Campbell shifted his eyes back to her. She was sleek and pristine in the white linen jacket, the sleeves pushed up to her elbows, her still-damp hair twisted into a chignon and spiked with an orchid. She had been sulking into her brandy since they'd finished dinner, and once again she'd astonished him with her ability to exist in a completely separate mental universe from his own. "Why not?"

"It's fake. Unreal. This whole island." She swirled the brandy but didn't drink any of it. "What business does an American company have owning an entire island? What happened to the people that used to live here?"

"In the first place," Campbell said, "it's a multinational company, not just American. And the people are still living here, only now they've got jobs instead of starving to death." As usual, Beth had him on the defensive, but he wasn't as thrilled with the Americanization of the island as he wanted to be. He'd imagined natives with guitars and congas, not portable stereos that blasted electronic reggae and neo-funk. The hut where he and Beth slept was some kind of geodesic dome, air-conditioned and comfortable, but he missed the sound of the ocean.

"I just don't like it," Beth said. "I don't like top secret projects that they have to keep locked up behind electric fences. I don't like the company flying people out here for vacations the way they'd throw a bone to a dog."

Or a straw to a drowning man, Campbell thought. He was as curious as anybody about the installation at the west end of the island, but of course that wasn't the point. He and Beth were walking through the steps of a dance that Campbell now saw would inevitably end in divorce. Their friends had all been divorced at least once, and an eighteen-year marriage probably seemed as anachronistic to them as a 1957 Chevy.

"Why don't you just admit it?" Campbell said. "The only thing you really don't like about the island is the fact that you're stuck here with me."

She stood up, and Campbell felt, with numbing jealousy, the stares of men all around them focus on her. "I'll see you later," she said, and heads turned to follow the clatter of her sandals.

Campbell ordered another *Salva Vida*, watching her walk downhill. The stairs were lit with Japanese lanterns and surrounded by wild purple and orange flowers. By the time she reached the sandbar and the line of cabins, she was no more than a shadow, and Campbell had finished most of the beer.

Now that she was gone, he felt drained and a little dizzy. He looked at his hands, still puckered from the long hours in the water, at the cuts and bruises of three days of physical activity. Soft hands, the hands of a company man, a desk man. Hands that would push a pencil or type on a CRT for another twenty years, then retire to the remote control of a big-screen TV.

The thick, caramel-tasting beer was starting to catch up to him. He shook his head and got up to find the bathroom.

His reflection shimmered and melted in the warped mirror over the bathroom sink. He realized he was stalling, staying away from the chill, sterile air of the cabin as long as he could.

And then there were the dreams. They'd gotten worse since he'd come to the island, more vivid and disturbing every night. He couldn't remember details, only slow, erotic sensations along his skin, a sense of floating in thick, crystalline water, of rolling in friction-less sheets. He'd awaken from them gasping for air like a drowning fish, his penis swollen and throbbing.

He brought another beer back to his table, not really wanting it, just needing it to hold in his hands. His attention kept wandering to a table on a lower level, where a rather plain young woman sat talking with two men in glasses and dress shirts. He couldn't understand what was so familiar about her until she tilted her head in a puzzled gesture and he recognized her. The broad cheekbones, the pale eyes.

He could hear the sound of his own heart. Was it just some kind of prank, then? A woman in a costume? But what about the gill lines he'd seen on her neck? How, in God's name, had she moved so quickly?

She stood up, made apologetic gestures to her friends. Campbell's table was near the stairs, and he saw she would have to pass him on her way out. Before he could stop to think about it, he stood up, blocking her exit, and said, "Excuse me?"

"Yes?" She was not that physically attractive, he thought, but he was drawn to her anyway, in spite of the heaviness of her waist, her solid, shortish legs. Her face was older, tireder than the one he'd seen out on the reef. But similar, too close for coincidence. "I wanted to . . . could I buy you a drink?" Maybe, he thought, I'm just losing my mind.

She smiled, and her eyes crinkled warmly. "I'm sorry. It's really very late, and I have to be at work in the morning."

"Please," Campbell said. "Just for a minute or two." He could see her suspicion, and behind that a faint glow of flattered ego. She wasn't used to being approached by men, he realized, "I just want to talk with you."

"You're not a reporter, are you?"

"No, nothing like that." He searched for something reassuring. "I'm with the company. The Houston office."

The magic words, Campbell thought. She sat down in Beth's chair and said, "I don't know if I should have any more. I'm about half-looped as it is."

Campbell nodded, said, "You work here, then."

"That's right."

"Secretary?"

"Biologist," she said, a little sharply. "I'm Dr. Kimberly." When he didn't react to the name, she softened it by adding, "Joan Kimberly."

"I'm sorry," Campbell said. "I always thought biologists were supposed to be homely." The flirtation came easily. She had the same beauty as the creature on the reef, a sort of fierce shyness and alien sensuality, but in the woman they were more deeply buried.

My God, Campbell thought, I'm actually doing this, actually trying to seduce this woman. He glanced at the swelling of her breasts, knowing what they would look like without the blue oxford shirt she wore, and the knowledge became a warmth in his groin.

"Maybe I'd better have that drink," she said. Campbell signaled the waiter.

"I can't imagine what it would be like to live here," he said. "To see this every day."

"You get used to it," she said. "I mean, it's still unbearably beautiful sometimes, but you still have your work, and your life goes on. You know?"

"Yes," Campbell said. "I know exactly what you mean."

She let Campbell walk her home. Her loneliness and vulnerability were like a heavy perfume, so strong that it repelled him at the same time that it pulled him irresistibly toward her.

She stopped at the doorway of her cabin, another geodesic, but this one set high on the hill, buried in a grove of palms and bougainvillaea. The sexual tension was so strong that Campbell could feel his shirtfront trembling.

"Thank you," she said, her voice rough. "You're very easy to talk to."

He could have turned away then, but he couldn't seem to unravel himself. He put his arms around her, and her mouth bumped against his, awkwardly. Then her lips began to move and her tongue flicked out eagerly. She fumbled the door open without moving away from him, and they nearly fell into the house.

He pushed himself up on extended arms and watched her moving beneath him. The moonlight through the trees was green and watery, falling in slow waves across the bed. Her breasts swayed heavily as she arched and twisted her back, the breath bubbling in her throat. Her eyes were clenched tight, and her legs wrapped around his and held them, like a long, forked tail.

* * *

Before dawn he slid out from under her limp right arm and got into his clothes. She was still asleep as he let himself out.

He'd meant to go back to his cabin, but instead he found himself climbing to the top of the island's rocky spine to wait for the sun to come up.

He hadn't even showered. Kimberly's perfume and musk clung to his hands and crotch like sexual stigmata. It was Campbell's first infidelity in eighteen years of marriage, a final, irreversible act.

He knew most of the jargon. Midlife crisis and all of that. He'd probably seen Kimberly there at the bar some other night and not consciously remembered her, projected her face onto a fantasy with obvious Freudian water/rebirth connotations.

In the dim, fractionated light of the sunrise, the lagoon was gray, the line of the barrier reef a darker smudge broken by whitecaps that curved like scales on the skin of the ocean. Dry palm fronds rustled in the breeze, and the island birds began to chirp and stutter themselves awake. A shadow broke from one of the huts on the beach below and climbed toward the road, weighted down with a large suitcase and a flight bag. Above her, in the asphalt lot at the top of the stairs, a taxi coasted silently to a stop and doused its lights.

If he had run, he could have reached her, and maybe he could even have stopped her, but the hazy impulse never became strong enough to reach his legs. Instead, he sat until the sun was hot on his neck and his eyes were dazzled into blindness by the white sand and water.

On the north side of the island, facing the mainland, the village of Espejo sprawled in the mud for the use of the resort and the company. A dirt track ran down the middle of it, oily water standing in the ruts. The cinder block houses on concrete piers and the Fords rusting in the yards reminded Campbell of an American suburb in the fifties; warped by nightmare.

The locals who worked in the company's kitchens and swept the company's floors lived here, and their kids scuffled in alleys that smelled of rotting fish or lay in the shade and threw rocks at three-legged dogs. An old woman sold Saint Francis flour sack shirts from ropes tied between pilings of her house. Under an awning of corrugated green plastic, bananas lay in heaps and flies swarmed over haunches of beef and next door was a *farmacia* with a faded yellow Kodak sign that promised "One Day Service."

Campbell blinked and found his way to the back, where a ten- or eleven-year-old boy was reading *La Novela Policiaca*. The boy set the comic on the counter and said, "Yes, sir?"

"How soon can you develop these?" Campbell asked, shoving the film cartridge toward him.

"*¿Mande?*"

Campbell gripped the edge of the counter. "Ready today?" he asked slowly.

"Tomorrow. This time."

Campbell took a twenty out of his wallet and held it face down on the scarred wood. "This afternoon?"

"*Momentito.*" The boy tapped, something out on a computer terminal at his right hand. The dry clatter of the keys filled Campbell with distaste. "Tonight, O.K.?" the boy said. "*A las seis.*" He touched the dial of his watch and said, "Six."

"All right," Campbell said. For another five dollars he bought a pint of Canadian Club, and then he went back onto the street. He felt like a sheet of weakly colored glass, as if the sun shone clear through him. He was a fool, of course, to be taking this kind of chance with the film, but he needed that picture.

He had to know.

He anchored the boat as close as possible to where it had been the night before. He had two fresh tanks and about half the bottle of whiskey left.

Diving drunk and alone was against every rule anyone had ever tried to teach him, but the idea of a simple, clean death by drowning seemed ludicrous to Campbell, not even worth consideration.

His diving jeans and sweatshirt, still damp and salty from the night before, were suffocating him. He got into his tank as quickly as he could and rolled over the side.

The cool water revived him, washed him clean. He purged the air from his vest and dropped straight to the bottom. Dulled by whiskey and lack of sleep, he floundered for a moment in the sand before he could get his buoyancy neutralized.

At the edge of the drop-off he hesitated, then swam to his right, following the edge of the cliff. From his physical condition, he was burning air faster than he wanted to; going deeper would only make it worse.

The bright red of a Coke can winked at him from a coral head. He crushed it and stuck it in his belt, suddenly furious with the company and its casual rape of the island, with himself for letting them manipulating him, with Beth for leaving him, with the entire world and human race. He kicked hard, driving himself through swarms of jack and blue tang, hardly noticing the twisted, brilliantly colored landscape that moved beneath him.

Some of the drunkenness burned off in the first burst of energy, and he gradually slowed, wondering what he possibly could hope to accomplish. It was useless, he thought.

He was chasing a phantom. But he didn't turn back.

He was still swimming when he hit the net.

It was nearly invisible, a web of monfilament in one-foot squares, strong enough to hold a shark or a school of porpoises. He tested it with the serrated edge of his diver's knife, with no luck.

He was close to the west end of the island, where the company kept their research facility. The net followed the line of the reef as far down as he could see, and extended out into the open water.

She was real, he thought. They built this to keep her in. But how did she get past it?

When he'd last seen her she'd been heading down. Campbell checked his seaview gauge, saw that he had less than five hundred pounds of air left. Enough to take him down to a hundred feet or so and right back up. The sensible thing to do was to return to the boat and bring a fresh tank back with him.

He went down anyway.

He could see the fine wires glinting as he swam past them. They seemed bonded to the coral itself, by some process he could not even imagine. He kept his eyes moving between the depth gauge and the edge of the net. Much deeper than a hundred feet and he would have to worry about decompression as well as an empty tank.

At 110 feet he tripped his reserve lever. Three hundred pounds and counting. All the reds had disappeared from the coral, leaving only blues and purples. The water was noticeably darker, colder, and each breath seemed to roar into his lungs like a geiser. Ten more feet, he told himself, and at 125 he saw the rip in the net.

He snagged his backpack on the monofilament and had to back off and try again, fighting panic. He could already feel the constriction in his lungs again, as if he were trying to breathe with a sheet of plastic over his mouth. He'd seen tanks that had been sucked so dry that the sides caved in. They found them on divers trapped in rock-slides and tangled in fishing line.

His tank slipped free and he was through, following his bubbles upward. The tiny knot of air in his lungs expanded as the pressure around him let up, but not enough to kill his need to breathe. He pulled the last of the air out of the tank and forced himself to keep exhaling, forcing the nitrogen out of his tissues.

At fifty feet he slowed and angled toward a wall of coral, turned the corner, and swam into a sheltered lagoon.

For a few endless seconds he forgot that he had no air.

The entire floor of the lagoon was laid out in squares of greenery—kelp, mosses, and something that looked like giant cabbage. A school of red snappers circled past him, herded by a metal box with a blinking light on the end of one long antenna. Submarines with spindly mechanical arms worked the ocean floor, thinning the vegetation and darkening the water with chemicals. Two or three dolphins were swimming side by side with human divers, and they seemed to be talking to each other.

His lungs straining, Campbell turned his back on them and kicked for the surface, trying to stay as close to the rocks as he could. He wanted to stop for a minute at ten feet, to give at least a nod to decompression, but it wasn't possible. His air was gone.

He broke the surface less than hundred feet from a concrete dock. Behind him was a row of marker buoys that traced the line of the net all the way out to sea and around the far side of the lagoon.

The dock lay deserted and steaming in the sun. Without a fresh tank, Campbell had no chance of getting out the way he's come in; if he tried to swim out on the surface, he'd be as conspicuous as a drowning man. He had to find another tank or another way out.

Hiding his gear under a sheet of plastic, he crossed the hot concrete slab to the building behind it, a wide, low warehouse full of wooden crates. A rack of diving gear was built into the left-hand wall, and Campbell was just starting for it when he heard a voice behind him.

"Hey you! Hold it!"

Campbell ducked behind a wall of crates, saw a tiled hallway opening into the back of the building, and ran for it. He didn't get more than three or four steps before a uniformed guard stepped out and pointed a .38 at his chest.

You can leave him with me."

"Are you sure, Dr. Kimberly?"

"I'll be all right," she said. "I'll call you if there's any trouble."

Campbell collapsed in a plastic chair across from her desk. The office was strictly functional, waterproof, and mildew-resistant. A long window behind Kimberly's head showed the lagoon and the row of marker buoys.

"How much did you see?" she asked.

"I don't know. I saw what looked like farms. Some machinery."

She slid a photograph across the desk to him. It showed a creature with a woman's breasts and the tail of a fish. The face was close enough to Kimberly's to be her sister.

Or her clone's.

Campbell suddenly realized the amount of trouble he was in.

"The boy at the *farmacia* works for us," Kimberly said.

Campbell nodded. Of course he did. Where else would he get a computer? "You can have the picture," Campbell said, blinking the sweat out of his eyes. "And the negative."

"Let's be realistic," she said, tapping the keys of her CRT and studying the screen. "Even if we let you keep your job, I don't see how we could hold your marriage together. And then you have two kids to put through college. . . ." She shook her head. "Your brain is full of hot information. There are too many people who would pay to have it, and there're just too many ways you can be manipulated. You're not much of a risk, *Mister* Campbell." She radiated hurt and betrayal, and he wanted to slink away from her in shame.

She got up and looked out the window. "We're building the future here," she said. "A future we couldn't even imagine fifteen years ago. And that's just too valuable to let one person screw up. Plentiful food, cheap energy, access to a computer net for the price of TV set, a whole new form of government—"

"I've seen your future," Campbell said. "Your boats have killed the reef for over a mile around the hotel. Your Coke cans are lying all over the coral beds. Your marriages don't last and your kids are on drugs and your TV is garbage. I'll pass."

"Did you see that boy in the drugstore? He's learning calculus on that computer, and his parents can't even read and write. We're testing a vaccine on human subjects that will probably cure leukemia. We've got laser surgery and transplant techniques that are revolutionary. Literally."

"Is that where *she* came from?" Campbell asked, pointing to the photograph.

Kimberly's voice dropped. "It's synergistic, don't you see? To do the transplants we had to be able to clone cells from the donor. To clone cells we had to have laser manipulation of the genes. . . ."

"They cloned your cells? Just for practice?"

She nodded slowly. "Something happened. She grew, but she stopped developing, kept her embryonic form from the waist down. There was nothing we could do except . . . make the best of it."

Campbell took a longer look at the picture. No, not the romantic myth he had first imagined. The tail was waxy-looking in the harsh light of the strobe, the fins more clearly undeveloped legs. He stared at the photo in queasy fascination. "You could have let her die."

"No. She was mine. I don't have much, and I wouldn't give her up." Kimberly's fists clenched at her sides. "She's not happy, she knows who I am. In her own way I suppose she cares for me." She paused, looking at the floor. "I'm a lonely woman, Campbell. But of course you know that."

Campbell's throat was dry. "What about me?" he rasped, and managed to swallow. "Am I going to die?"

"No," she said. "Not you, either. . . ."

Campbell swam for the fence. His memories were cloudy and he had trouble focusing his thoughts, but he could visualize the gap in the net and the open ocean beyond. He kicked easily down to 120 feet, the water cool and comforting on his naked skin. Then he was through drifting gently away from the noise and stink of the island, toward some primal vision of peace and timelessness.

His gills rippled smoothly as he swam.

FREEZONE

JOHN SHIRLEY

Freezone floated in the Atlantic Ocean, a city afloat in the wash of international cultural confluence.

Freezone was anchored about a hundred miles north of Sidi Ifni, a drowsy city on the coast of Morocco, in a warm, gentle current, and in a sector of the sea only rarely troubled by large storms. What storms arose here spent their fury on the maze of concrete wave baffles Freezone Admin had spent years building up around the artificial island.

Originally, Freezone had been just another offshore drilling project. The massive oil deposit a quarter mile below the artificial island was still less than a quarter tapped out. The drilling platform was owned jointly by the Moroccan government and a Texas-based petroleum and electronic products company, Texcorp. The company that bought Disneyland and Disneyworld and Disneyworld II—all three of which had closed in the wake of the CSD: the Computer Storage Depression. Also called the Dissolve Depression.

A group of Arab terrorists—at least, the US State Department claimed that's who did it—had arranged a well-placed electromagnetic pulse from a small hydrogen bomb hidden aboard a routine orbital shuttle. The shuttle was vaporized in the blast, as well as two satellites, one of them manned; but when the CSD hit, no one took time to mourn the dead.

The orbital bomb had almost triggered Armageddon: three Cruise missiles had to be aborted, and fortunately two more were shot down by the Soviets before the terrorist cell took credit for the upper-atmosphere blast. Most of the bomb's blast had been directed upward; what came downward, though, was the side effect of the blast: the EMP. An electromagnetic pulse that—just as had been predicted in the 1970s—traveled through thousands of miles of wires and circuitry on the continent below the H-blast. The Defense Department was shielded; the banking system, for the most part, was not. The pulse wiped out 93 percent of the newly formed American Banking Credit Adjustment Bureau. ABCAB had handled 76 percent of the nation's buying and credit transferal. Most of what was bought, was bought through ABCAB or ABCAB-related companies . . . until the EMP wiped out ABCAB's memory storage, the pulse overburdening the circuits, melting them, and literally frying the data storage chips. And thereby kicking the crutches out from under the American economy. Hundreds of thousands of bank accounts were "suspended" until records could be restored—causing a run on the remaining banks. The insurance companies and the federal guarantee programs were overwhelmed. They just couldn't cover the loss.

The States had already been in trouble. The nation had lost its economic initiative in the 1980s and 1990s: its undereducated and badly trained workers, its corrupt, greedy unions, and its lower manufacturing standards made US industry unable to compete with the Asian and South American manufacturing booms. The EMP credit dissolve kicked the nation over the rim of recession into the pit of depression. And made the rest of the world laugh. The Arab terrorist cell responsible—hard-core Islamic Fundamentalists—had been composed of seven men. Seven men who crippled a nation.

But America still had its enormous military spread, its electronics and medical innovators. And the war economy kept it humming. Like a man with cancer taking amphetamines for a last burst of strength. While the endless malls and housing projects, built cheaply and in need of constant upkeep, got shabbier, uglier, and trashier by the day. And more dangerous.

The States just weren't safe for the rich any more. The resorts, the amusement parks, the exclusive affluent neighborhoods all crumbled under the attrition of perennial strikes and persistent terrorist attacks. The swelling mass of the poor—growing since the 1980s—resented the recreations of the rich. And the middle-class buffer was shrinking to insignificance.

There were still enclaves in the States where you could get lost in the media churn, hypnotized by the flashcards of desire into a TV-trance version of the American Dream as ten thousand companies vied for your attention, begged you to buy and keep buying. Places that were walled city-states of middle-class illusions.

But the affluent could feel the crumbling of their kingdom. They didn't feel safe in the States. They needed someplace outside, somewhere controlled. Europe was out now; Central and South America too risky. The Pacific theater was another war zone.

So that's where Freezone came in.

A Texas entrepreneur—who hadn't had his money in AB-CAB—saw the possibilities in the community that had grown up around the enormous complex of offshore drilling platforms. A paste-jewel necklace of brothels and arcades and cabarets had crystallized on derelict ships permanently anchored around the platforms. Two hundred hookers and three hundred casino dealers worked the international melange of men who worked the oil rigs. The entrepreneur made a deal with the Moroccan government. He bought the rusting hulks and the shanty nightclubs. And he fired everyone.

The Texan owned a plastics company; the company had developed a light, super-tough plastic that the entrepreneur used in the rafts on which the new floating city was built. The community was now seventeen square miles of urban raft, protected with one of the meanest security forces in the world. Freezone dealt in pleasant distractions for the rich in the exclusive section and—in the second-string places around the edge—for technickis from the drill rigs. The second-string places also sheltered a few semi-illicit hangers-on and a few hundred performers.

Like Rickenharp.

Rick Rickenharp stood against the south wall of the Semiconductor, letting the club's glare and blare wash over him and mentally writing a song. The song went something like, "Glaring blare, lightning stare/Nostalgia for the electric chair."

Then he thought, Fucking drivel.

And he was doing his best to look cool but vulnerable, hoping one of the females flashing through the crowd would remember having seen him in the band the night before, would try to chat him up, play groupie. But they were mostly into wire dancers.

And *no fucking way* Rickenharp was going to wire into minimono.

Rickenharp was a rock classicist. He wore a black leather motorcycle jacket that was some fifty-five years old, said to have been worn by John Cale when he was still in the Velvet Underground. The seams were beginning to pop; three studs were missing from the chrome trimming. The elbows and collar edges were worn through the black dye to the brown animal the leather had come from. But the leather was second skin to Rickenharp. He wore nothing under it. His bony, hairless chest showed translucent blue-white beneath the broken zippers. He wore blue jeans that were only ten years old but looked older than the coat; he wore genuine Harley Davidson boots. Earrings clustered up and down his long, slightly too prominent ears, and his rusty brown hair looked like a cannon-shell explosion.

And he wore dark glasses.

And he did all this because it was gratingly unfashionable.

His band hassled him about it. They wanted their lead-git and frontman minimono.

"If we're gonna go minimono, we oughta just sell the fucking guitars and go wires," Rickenharp had told them.

And the drummer had been stupid and tactless enough to say, "Well, fuck, man, maybe we *should* go to wires."

Rickenharp had said, "Maybe we should get a fucking drum machine too, you fucking Neanderthal!" and kicked the drum seat over, sending Murch into the cymbals with a fine crashing, so that Rickenharp added, "You should get that good a sound outta those cymbals on stage. Now we know how to do it."

Murch had started to throw his sticks at him, but then he'd remembered how you had to have them lathed up special because they didn't make them any more, so he'd said, "Suck my ass, bigshot!" and got up and walked out, not for the first time. But that was the first time it meant anything, and only some heavy ambassadorial action on the part of Ponce had kept Murch from leaving the band.

The call from their agent had set the whole thing off. That's what it really was. Agency was streamlining its repertoire. Rickenharp was out. The last two LP's hadn't sold, and in fact the engineers claimed that live drums didn't record well on the miniaturized soundcaps that passed for records now. Rickenharp's holovid and the videos weren't getting airplay.

Anyway, Vid-Co was probably going out of business. Another business sucked into the black hole of the depression. "So it ain't our fault the stuff's not selling," Rickenharp said. "We got fans but we can't get the distribution to reach 'em."

José had said, "Bullshit, we're out of the Grid and you know it. All that was carrying us was the nostalgia wave anyway. You can't get more'n two hits out of a revival, man."

Julio the bassist had said something in technicki jargon that Rickenharp hadn't bothered to translate because it was so stupid—he'd suggested they hire a wiredancer for a frontman—and when Rickenharp had ignored him he'd gotten pissed and it was *his* turn to walk out. Fucking touchy technickis anyway.

And now the band was in abeyance. Their train was stopped between stations. They had a gig opening for a wire act and Rickenharp didn't want to do it, but they had a contract and there were a lot of rock nostalgia freaks on Freezone, so maybe that was their audience anyway and he owed it to them. Blow the goddamn wires off the stage.

He looked around the Semiconductor and wished the Retro-Club was still open. There'd been a strong retro presence at the RC, even some rockabillies, and some of the rockabillies actually knew what rockabilly sounded like. The Semiconductor was a minimono scene.

The minimono crowd wore their hair long, fanned out

between the shoulders and narrowing to a point at the crown of the head, and straight, absolutely straight, stiff, so from the back each head had a black or gray or red or white tepee-shape. Those, in monochrome, were the only acceptable colors. Flat tones and no streaks. Their clothes were stylistic extensions of their hairstyles. Minimono was a reaction to flare. And to the chaos of the war, and the war economy, and the amorphous shifting of the Grid. The flare style was going, dying.

Rickenharp had always been contemptuous of the trendy flares, but he preferred them to minimono. Flare had energy, anyway.

Flare had grown up out of the teased-up, anticontrol styles popular in the last part of the twentieth century. A flare was expected to wear his hair *up*, as far over the top of his head as possible and in some way that *expressed*, that emphasized the wearer's individuality, originality. The more colors the better. You weren't "an individual" unless you had an expressive flare. Screw shapes, hooks, aureolas, layered multicolored snarls. Fortunes were made in flare hair-shaping shops and lost when it began to go out of fashion. But it had lasted longer than most fashions; it had endless variation and the appeal of its energy to sustain it. A lot of people copped out of the necessity of inventing individual expression by adopting a politically standard flare. Shape your hair like the insignia for your favorite downtrodden third-world country (back when they were downtrodden, before the new marketing axis). Flares were so much trouble most people took to having flare wigs prepared to wear when they went out. And their drugs were styled to fit the fashion. Excitative neurotransmitters of all kinds—antidepressants, drugs that made you seem to glow. The wealthier flares had nimbus belts, creating artificial auroras. The hipper flares considered this to be tastelessly narcissistic, which was a joke to nonflares, since all flares were floridly vain.

Rickenharp had never colored or shaped his hair, except to encourage its punk spikiness.

But Rickenharp wasn't a punk. He identified with pre-punk, late 1950s, mid-1960s, early 1970s. Rickenharp was an anachronism. He was simply a hard-core rocker, as out of place in the Semiconductor as bebop would have been in the 1980s dance clubs.

Rickenharp looked around at the flat-black, flat-gray, monochrome tunics and jumpsuits, the black wristfones, the cookie-cutter sameness; at the uniform tans and ubiquitous FirStep Colony-shaped earrings (only one, always in the left ear). The high-tech-fetishist minimonos were said to aspire toward a place in the orbiting space Colony the way Rastas had dreamed of a return to Ethiopia. Rickenharp thought it was funny that the Soviets had blockaded the Colony. Funny to see the normally dronelike, antiflamboyant min-imonos quietly simmering on ampheticool, standing in tense groups, hissing about the Soviets, in why-doesn't-somebody-do-something outrage.

The stultifying regularity of their canned music banged from the walls and pulsed from the floor. Lean against the wall and you felt a drill-bit vibration of it in your spine.

There were a few hardy, defiant flares here, and flares were Rickenharp's best hope for getting laid. They tended to respect old rock.

The music ceased; a voice boomed "Joel NewHope!" and spots lit the stage. The first wire act had come on. Ricken-harp glanced at his watch. It was ten. He was due to open for the headline act at eleven thirty. Rickenharp pictured the club emptying as he hit the stage. He wasn't long for this club. But maybe enough variant crowd would show. Fringe scenes can add up.

NewHope hit the stage. A wire act. He was anorexic and

surgically sexless: radical minimono. A fact advertised by his nudity: he wore only gray and black spray-on sheathing. How did the guy piss? Rickenharp wondered. Maybe it was out of that faint crease at his crotch. A dancing mannequin. His sexuality was clipped to the back of his head: a single chrome electrode that activated the pleasure center of the brain during the weekly legally controlled catharsis. But he was so skinny—hey, who knows, maybe he went to a black-market cerebrostim to interface with the pulser. Though minimonos were supposed to be into stringent law-and-order.

The wires jacked into NewHope's arms and legs and torso fed to impulse-translation pickups on the stage floor, making him look like a puppet with its strings inverted. But he was the puppeteer. The long, funereal wails pealing from hidden speakers were triggered by the muscular contractions of his arms and legs and torso. He wasn't bad for a mini-mono, Rickenharp thought condescendingly. You could make out the melody, the tune shaped by his dancing, and it had a shade more complexity than the M'n'Ms usually had.... The M'n'M crowd moved into their geometrical dance configurations, somewhere between disco dancing and square dance, Busby Berkeley kaleidoscopings worked out according to formulas you were simply expected to know if you had the nerve to participate. Try to dance free-style in their interlocking choreography, and sheer social rejection, on the wings of body language, would hit you like an arctic wind.

Sometimes Rickenharp did an acid dance in the midst of the minimono configuration, just for the hell of it, just to revel in their rejection. But the band had made him stop that. Don't alienate the audience at our only gig, man. Probably our *last* fucking gig....

The wiredancer rippled out bagpipelike riffs over the taped rhythm section. The walls came alive.

A good rock club—in 1965 or 1975 or 1985 or 1995 or 2020—should be narrow, dark, close, claustrophobic. The walls should either be starkly monochrome—all black and mirrored, say—or deliberately garish. Camp, layered with whatever was the contemporary avant-garde or gaudy graffiti.

The Semiconductor showed both sides. It started out butch, its walls glassy black; during the concert it went in gaudy drag as the sound-sensitive walls reacted to the music with color streaking, wavelengthing in oscilloscope patterns, shades of blue-white for high end, red and purple for bass and percussion. Reacting vividly, hypnotically, to each note. The minimonos disliked reactive walls. They called it kitschy and "vid."

The dancer spazzed the stage, and Rickenharp grudgingly watched, trying to be fair. Thinking, It's another kind of rock 'n' roll, is all. Like a Christian watching a Buddhist ceremony—telling himself, "Oh well, it's all manifestations of the One God in the end." ... Rickenharp thinking,: But real rock is better. *Real rock is coming back*, he'd tell almost anyone who'd listen. Almost no one would.

A chaoticist came in, and he watched her, feeling less alone. Chaoticists were much closer to real rockers. She was a skinhead, with the sides of her head painted. Skirt made of at least two hundred rags of synthetic material sewn to her leather belt—a sort of grass skirt of bright rags. Bare breasts, nipples pierced with thin screws. The minimonos looked at her in disgust; they were prudish, and calling attention to one's breasts was decidedly gauche with the M'n'Ms. She smiled sunnily back at them. Her handsome Semitic features were slashed randomly with paint. Her makeup looked like a spin painting. Her teeth were filed.

Rickenharp swallowed hard, looking at her. Damn, she was *his type.*

Only . . . only she wore a blue mesc sniffer. The sniffer's inverted question mark ran from its hook at her right ear to just under her right nostril. Now and then she tilted her head to it and sniffed a little blue powder.

Rickenharp had to look away. Silently cursing.

He'd written a song called "Trying to Stay Clean."

Blue mesc. Or syncoke. Or heroin. Or amphetamorphine. Or XT2. But mostly he went for blue mesc. And blue mesc was addictive. And it was sooooo *good.*

Blue mesc, also called boss blue. It was all the best effects of mescaline and cocaine together, framed in the gelatinous sweetness of Quaaludes. But, unlike coke, not much crash. Only . . . only stop taking it after a period of steady use and the world drained of meaning for you. There was no actual withdrawal sickness. There was only a deeply resonant depression, a sense of worthlessness that seemed to settle like dust and maggot dung into each individual cell of the user's body. Not the same as a coke crash, but . . .

But some people called blue mesc "the suicide ticket."

It could make you feel like a coal miner when the mine shaft caved in; like you were buried in yourself.

Rickenharp had pulled therapy, paid for by his parents—he'd squandered the money from his only major hit on boss blue and dope. He'd just barely made it clean. And lately, at least before the band squabbles, he'd begun feeling like life was worth living again.

Watching the girl with the sniffer walk past, watching her use, Rickenharp felt stricken, lost, as if he'd seen something to remind him of a lost lover. An ex-user's syndrome. Pain from the guilt of having jilted your drug.

And he could imagine the sweet burn of the stuff in his nostrils, the backward-sweet pharmaceutical taste of it in the back of your palate; or, if you banged it, the explosion of pure fluorescent confidence, confidence you could feel somatically, the way you'd feel a woman's lips on your cock. The autoerotic feedback loop of blue mesc. Imagining it, he had a shadow of the sensation, a tantalizing ghost of the rush. In memory he could taste it, smell it, feel it. . . . Seeing her *use* brought back a hundred iridescent memories. An almost irrepressible longing. (While some small voice in the back of his head tried to get his attention, tried to warn him, *Hey, remember the shit makes you want to kill yourself when you run out; remember it makes you stupidly overconfident and boorish; remember it eats your internal organs* . . . a small, dwindling voice. . . .)

The girl was looking at him. A flicker of invitation in her eyes.

He wavered.

The small voice got louder.

Told him, *Rickenharp if you go to her, go with her, you'll end up using.*

He turned away with an anguished internal wrenching. Stumbled through the wash of sound and lights and monochrome people to the dressing room. To guitar and earphones and the safer, sonic world.

Rickenharp was listening to a collector's-item Velvet Underground tape from 1968. It was capped into his Earmite. The song was "White Light/White Heat." The guitarists were doing things that would make Baron Frankenstein say, "There are some things man was not meant to know." He screwed the Earmite a little deeper so that the vibrations would shiver the bone around his ear, chills that lapped through him in harmony with the guitar chords. He'd picked a visorclip to go with the music: a documentary on expressionist painters. Listening to the Velvets and looking at Edvard Munch. Man!

And then Julio dug a finger into his shoulder.

"Happiness is transient," Rickenharp muttered, as he flipped the visorclip back. The visor looked like the strap-and-mirror affairs doctors once wore, only the screen that snapped down over the eyes was rectangular, like a rearview mirror. Some visors came with a clip-on camera eye and fieldstim. The fieldstim you wore over your back, snugged to the skin, as if it were a sheer corset. The camera picked up an image of the street you were walking down and routed it to the fieldstim, which tickled your back in the pattern of whatever the camera saw. Some part of your mind assembled a rough image of the street out of that. Developed for blind people in the 1980s. Now used by viddy addicts who walked or drove the streets wearing visors, watching TV, reflexively navigating by using the fieldstim, their eyes blocked off by the screen but never quite bumping into anyone. But Rickenharp didn't use a fieldstim.

So he had to look at Julio with his own eyes. "What you want?"

" 'N ten," Julio slurred. Julio the technicki bassist. In ten. They went on in ten minutes.

José, Ponce, Julio, Murch: Rhythm guitar and backup vocals, Keyboards, Bass, Drums.

Rickenharp nodded and reached up to flip the visor back into place, but Ponce flicked the switch on the visor's headset. The visor image shrank like a landscape vanishing down a tunnel behind a train, and Rickenharp felt as if his stomach were shrinking inside him at the same rate. He knew what was coming down. "Okay," he said, turning to look at them. *"What?"*

They were in the dressing room. The walls were black with graffiti. All rock club dressing rooms will always be black with graffiti. Flayed with it, scourged with it. Like the flat declaration THE PARASITES RULE, the cheerful petulance of SYMBIOSIS 666 GOT FUCKING BORED HERE, the oblique existentialism of THE ALKLOID BROTHERS LOVE YOU ALL BUT THINK YOU WOULD BE BETTER OFF DEAD, and the enigmatic ones like SYNC 66 CLICKS NOW. It looked like the patterning of badly wrinkled wallpaper. It was in layers. It was a palimpsest. Hallucinatory stylization as if tracing the electron firings of the visual cortex.

The walls, in the few places they were visible under the graffiti, were a gray-painted pressboard. There was just enough room for Rickenharp's band, sitting around on broken-backed kitchen chairs and one desk chair with three legs. Crowded between the chairs were the instruments in their cases. The edges of the cases were frayed, the false leather peeling. Half the snaps broken.

Rickenharp looked at the band, looked clockwise from one face to the next, taking a poll from their expressions: José on his left, a bruised look to his eyes, the rings under his eyes compositionally harmonious with his double handful of earrings; his hair a triple mohawk, the center spine red, the outer two white and blue; a smoky crystal ring on his left index finger that matched—he knew it matched—his smoky crystal amber eyes. Rickenharp and José had been close. Each looked at the other a little accusingly. There was a lovers' sulkiness between them, though they'd never been lovers. José was hurt because Rickenharp didn't want to make the transition: Rickenharp was putting his own taste in music before the survival of the band. Rickenharp was hurt because José wanted to go minimono wire act, a betrayal of the spiritual ethos of the band; and because José was willing to sacrifice Rickenharp. Replace him with a wire dancer. They both knew it, though it had never been said. Most of what passed between them was semiotically transmitted with the studied indirection of the terminally cool. Now, José looked bad news. His head was tilted as if his neck were broken. His eyes lusterless.

Ponce had gone minimono, at least in his look, and they'd had a ferocious fight over that. Ponce was slender and fox-faced, and now he was battleship gray from head to toe, including hair and skin tint. In the smoky atmosphere of the club he sometimes vanished completely.

He wore silver contact lenses. He stared at a ten-slivered funhouse reflection in his mirrored fingernails. Flat-out glum.

Julio, yeah, he liked to give Rickenharp shit, and he wanted the change. Sure, he was loyal to Rickenharp, up to a point. But he was also a conformist. He'd argue for Rickenharp maybe, but he'd go with the consensus. Julio had lush curly black Puerto Rican hair piled prowlike over his head. He had a woman's profile and a woman's long-lashed eyes. He had a silver-stud earring, and he wore classic retrorock black leather like Rickenharp. He twisted the skull ring on his thumb, returning a scowl for its grin, staring at it as if deeply worried that one of its fake-ruby red glass eyes was about to come out.

Murch was a thick slug of a guy with a glass crew cut. He was a mediocre drummer, but he was a drummer, a species of musician almost extinct. "Murch's rare as a dodo," Rickenharp said once, "and that's not all he's got in common with a dodo." Murch wore horn-rimmed dark glasses, and there was a bottle of Southern Comfort on his knee. The Southern Comfort was part of his outfit. It went with his cowboy boots. So he thought.

Murch was looking at Rickenharp in open contempt. He didn't have the brains to dissemble.

"Fuck you, Murch," Rickenharp said.

"Whuh? I didn't say nothing."

"You don't have to. I can smell your thoughts. Enough to gag a faggot maggot." Rickenharp stood and looked at the others. "I know what's on your mind. Give me this: one last good gig. After that you can have it how you want."

Tension lifted its wings and flew away.

Another bird settled over the room. Rickenharp saw it in his mind's eye: a thunderbird. Half made of an Indian tepee painting of a thunderbird, and half of chrome T-bird parts. When it spread its wings the pinfeathers glistened like polished bumpers. There were two headlights on its chest, and when the band picked up their instruments to go out to the stage, the headlights switched on.

Rickenharp carried his Stratocaster in its black case. The case was bandaged with duct tape and peeling with faded stickers. But the Strat was spotless. It was transparent. Its lines curved hot like a sports car.

They walked down a white plastibrick corridor toward the stage. The corridor narrowed after the first turn, so they had to walk sideways, holding the instruments out in front of them. Space was precious on Freezone.

The stagehand saw Murch go out first, and he signaled the DJ, who cut the tape and announced the band through the PA. Old-fashioned, like Rickenharp requested: "Please welcome . . . *Rickenharp.*"

There was no answering roar from the crowd. There were a few catcalls and a smattering of applause.

Good, you bitch, fight me, Rickenharp thought, waiting for the band to take up their positions. He'd go on stage last. After they'd set up the spot for him. Always.

Rickenharp squinted from the wings to see past the glare of lights into the dark snakepit of the audience. Only about half minimono now. That was good; that gave him a chance to put this one over.

The band took its place. Pressed their automatic tuners, fiddled with dials.

Rickenharp was pleasantly surprised to see that the stage was lit with soft red floods, which was what he'd requested. Maybe the lighting director was one of his fans. Maybe the band wouldn't fuck this one up. Maybe everything would fall into place. Maybe the lock on the cage door would tumble into the right combination, the cage door would open, the T-Bird would fly.

He could hear some of the audience whispering about Murch. Most of them had never seen a live drummer before, except for salsa. Rickenharp caught a scrap of technicki jargon: *"Whuzziemack wizzut?"* What's he make with that? meaning, What are those things he's adjusting? The drums.

Rickenharp took the Strat out of its case and strapped it on. He adjusted the strap. He pressed the tuner. He didn't need to plug in; when he walked onto the stage, the amp's reception field would trigger, transmit the Strat's signal to the stack of Marshalls behind the drummer. A shame, in a way, about miniaturization of electronics: the amps were small, though just as loud as twentieth-century amps and speakers. But they looked less imposing. The audience was muttering about the Marshalls, too. Most of them hadn't seen old-fashioned amps. "What're those for?"

Murch looked at Rickenharp. Rickenharp nodded.

Murch thudded 4/4, alone for a moment. Then the bass took it up, laid down a sonic stratum that was kind of off-center strutting. And the keyboards laid down the sheets of infinity.

Now he could walk on stage. It was like there'd been an abyss between Rickenharp and the stage, and the bass and drum and keyboards working together made a bridge to cross the abyss. He walked over the bridge and into the warmth of the floods. He could feel the heat of the lights on his skin. It was like stepping from an air-conditioned room into the tropics. The music suffered deliciously in a tropical lushness. The pure white spotlight caught and held him, focusing on his guitar, as per his directions, and he thought, Good, the lighting guy really is with me.

He felt as if he could feel what the guitar felt. The guitar ached to be touched.

Without consciously knowing it, Rickenharp was moving to the music. Not too much. Not in the pushy, look-at-me way that some performers had. The way they had of trying to *force* enthusiasm from the audience, every move looking artificial.

No, Rickenharp was a natural. The music flowed through him physically, unimpeded by anxieties or ego knots. His ego was there; it was the fuel for his personal Olympian torch. But it was as immaculate as a pontiff's robes.

The band sensed it. Rickenharp was in rare form tonight. Because he was freed. The tensions were gone because he knew it was the end of the line: The band had received its death sentence. Now, Rickenharp was as unafraid as a true suicide. He had the courage of despair.

The band sensed it and let it happen. The chemistry was there, this time, when Ponce and José came into the verse section, José with a sinuous riffing picked low, almost on the chrome plate that clamped the strings, Ponce with a magnificently redundant theme washed through the brass mode of the synthesizer. The whole band felt the chemistry like a pleasing electric shock, the pleasurable shock of individual egos becoming a group ego. Something beyond sexual pleasure.

The audience was listening, but they were resisting. They didn't want to like it. Still, the place was crowded—

because of the club's rep, not because of Rickenharp—and all those packed-in bodies make a kind of sensitive atmospheric exoskeleton, and he knew that made them vulnerable. He knew what to touch.

Feeling the Good Thing begin to happen, Rickenharp looked confident but not quite arrogant. He was too arrogant to show arrogance.

The audience looked at Rickenharp as a man will look at a smug adversary just before a hand-to-hand fight and wonder, Why's he so smug, what does he know?

He knew about timing. And he knew there were feelings even the most aloof among them couldn't control, once those feelings were released; and he knew how to release them.

Rickenharp hit a chord. He let it shimmer through the room and he looked out at them. He made eye contact.

He liked seeing the defiant stares, because that was going to make his victory more complete.

Because he *knew*. He'd played five gigs with the band in the last two weeks, and for all five gigs the atmosphere had been strained, the chemistry had been there only in spates. Like a Jacob's ladder where the two poles aren't properly lined up for the sparks to jump.

And like a horniness it had built up in them, like sexual energy, dammed behind their private resentments; and now it was pouring through the dam, and the band shook with the release of it as Rickenharp thundered into his progression and began to sing. . . .

The audience stared at him with insistent hostility, but Rickenharp liked it when the girl played pretend-to-rape-me. *Force it into their ears, man.*

The band was fuel-injecting into the combustion chamber of the room; Rickenharp was sparking the combustion, causing the audience to react, to press the piston, and . . .

they were racing. Rickenharp was at the wheel. He was taking them somewhere, and each song was a landscape he swept them through. Strumming over the vocals, he sang,

> You want easy overnight action
> want it casually
> A neat little chain reaction
> and a little sympathy
> You say it's just consolation
> In the end it's a compensation
> for insecurity
>> That way there's no surprises
>> That way no one gets hurt
>> No moral question tries us
>> No blood on satin shirts
>> But for me, yeah for me
>> PAIN IS EVERYTHING!
>> Pain is all there is
>> Babe take some of mine
>> or lick some of his
>> PAIN IS EVERYTHING
>> Pain is all there is
>> Pain is EVERYTHING . . .

*From "An Interview with Rickenharp: The Boy Methuselah,"
in Guitar Player Magazine, May 2017.*

GPM: Rick, you keep talking about group dynamics, but I have a feeling you don't mean dynamics in the usual musical sense.

RICKENHARP: The right way to create a band is for the members to simply find one another, the way lovers do. In bars or whatever. The members of the band are like five chemicals that come together with a specific chemical reaction. If the chemistry is right, the audience becomes involved in this—this kind of—well, a social chemical reaction.

GPM: Could it be that all this is an illusion of your psychology? I mean, your need for a really organically whole group?

RICKENHARP: (after a long pause): To an extent. It's true I need something like that. I need to belong. I mean—okay, I'm a "nonconformist," but still, on some level I got a need to belong. Maybe rock bands are a surrogate family. The family unit is shot to hell, so ... the band is my family. I'd do anything to keep it together. I need these guys. I'd be like a kid whose mom and dad and brothers and sisters were killed if I lost this band.

And he sang,

"PAIN IS EVERYTHING
Pain is all there is
Babe take some of mine
Suck some of his
Yeah, said PAIN IS EVERYTHING—"

Singing it insolently, half shouting, half warbling at the end of each note, with that fuck-you-bitch tone, performing that magic act, shouting a melody. He could see doors opening in their faces, even the minimonos, even the neutrals, all the flares, the rebs, the chaoticists, the preps, the retros. Forgetting their subcultural classifications in the organic, orgasmic unification of the music. He was basted in sweat under the lights, he was squeezing sounds with his fingers, and it was as if he could feel the sounds taking shape in his hands the way a sculptor feels clay shaping under his fingers, and it was like there was no gap between his hearing the sound in his head and its coming out of the speakers. His brain, his body, his fingers had closed the gap, was one supercooled circuit breaker fused shut.

Some part of him was looking for the chaoticist trim he'd spotted earlier. He was faintly disappointed when he didn't see her. He told himself, You ought to be happy, you had a narrow escape, she would've got you back into boss blue.

But when he saw her press to the front and nod at him ever so slightly in that smug insider's way, he was simply glad, and he wondered what his subconscious was planning for him. . . . All those thoughts were flickers. Most of the time his conscious mind was completely focused on the sound and on the business of acting out the sound for the audience. He was playing out of sorrow, the sorrow of loss. His family was going to die, and he played tunes that touched the chord of loss, in everyone. . . .

And the band was supernaturally tight. The gestalt was there, uniting them, and he pressed its tongs home into the collective body of the audience and took them where he wanted to take them, and he thought: The band feels good, but it's not going to help when the gig's over.

It was like a divorced couple having a good time in bed but knowing that wouldn't make the marriage right again. In fact, the good time was a function of having given up.

But in the meantime there were fireworks.

By the last tune in the set, the electricity was so thick in the club that—as José had said once, with a rocker's melodrama—"if you could cut it, it would bleed." The dope and smashweed and tobacco smoke moiling the air seemed to conspire with the stage lights to create an atmosphere of magical apartness. With each song-keyed shift in the light, red to blue to white to sulfurous yellow, a corresponding emotional wavelength rippled through the room. The energy

built, and Rickenharp discharged it, his Strat the lightning
rod.

And then the set ended.

Rickenharp bashed out the last five notes alone, nailing
a climax onto the air. Then he walked offstage, hardly hearing the roar from the crowd. He found himself half running
down the grimy plastibrick corridor, and then he was in the
dressing room and didn't remember getting there. Everything felt more real than usual. His ears were ringing like
Quasimodo was getting off in his belfry.

He heard footsteps and turned, working up what he was
going to say to the band. But it was the girl chaoticist and
someone else, and then a third coming in after the someone
else.

The someone else was a skinny guy with brown hair
that was naturally messy, not messy as part of one of the
cultural subcurrents. His mouth hung a little ajar, and one
of his incisors was decayed black. His nose was windburned
and the backs of his bony hands were gnarled with veins.
The third was Japanese: small, brown-eyed, nondescript, his
expression mild, just a shade more friendly than neutral.
The skinny Caucasian guy wore an army jacket sans insignia, shiny jeans, and rotting tennis shoes. His hands were
nervous, like there was something he was used to holding
in them that wasn't there now. An instrument? Maybe.

The Japanese guy wore a Japanese Action Suit, sky-blue
and neat as a pin. His hands looked comfortable empty.
Only there was a lump on his hip—something he could reach
by putting his right arm across his body and through the
zipper down the front of the suit—and Rickenharp was
pretty sure it was a gun. There was one thing all three of
them had in common: they looked half starved.

Rickenharp shivered—his gloss of sweat cooling on
him—but forced himself to say, "Whusappnin'?" It was

wooden in his mouth. He was looking past them, waiting for the band.

"Band's in the wings," the chaoticist said. "The bass player said, 'Telm getzassoutere.'"

Rickenharp had to smile at her mock of Julio's techni-cki; Tell him, get his ass out here.

Them some of the druggy feeling washed away and he heard the shouts and he realized they wanted an encore.

"Jeez, an encore," he said without thinking. "Been so fucking long."

" 'Ey, mate," the skinny guy said, pronouncing *mate* like *mite*. Brit or Aussie. "Oi sawr you at Stone'enge five years ago when you 'ad your second 'it."

Rickenharp winced a little when the guy said *your second hit*, inadvertently underlining the fact that Rickenharp had had only two, and everyone knew he wasn't likely to have any more.

"I'm Carmen," the chaoticist said. "This is Willow and Yukio."

Yukio was standing sideways from the others, and something about the way he did it told Rickenharp he was watching down the corridor without seeming to.

Carmen saw Rickenharp looking at Yukio and said, "Cops are coming down."

"Why?" Rickenharp asked. "The club's licensed."

"Not for you or the club. For us."

He looked at her and said, "Hey, I don't need to get busted." He picked up his guitar and went into the hall. "I got to do my encore before they lose interest."

She followed along, into the hall and the echo of the encore stomps, and asked, "Can we hang out in the dressing room for a while?"

"Yeah, but it ain't sacrosanct. You come back here, the cops can too." They were in the wings now. Rickenharp signaled to Murch and the band started playing.

She said, "These aren't exactly cops. They probably don't know these kinds of places; they'd look for us in the crowd, not the dressing room."

"You're an optimist. I'll tell the bouncer to stand here, and if he sees anyone else start to come back, he'll tell 'em it's empty back here 'cause he just checked."

"Thanks." She went back to the dressing room. He spoke to the bouncer and went on stage. Feeling drained, the guitar heavy on him. But he picked up on the energy level in the room and it carried him through two encores. He left them wanting more, which is the way to do it, and, sticky with sweat, walked back to his dressing room.

They were still there: Carmen, Yukio, Willow.

"Is there a stage door?" Yukio asked. "Into alley?"

Rickenharp nodded. "Wait in the hall; I'll come out and show you in a minute."

Yukio nodded, and they went into the hall. The band came in, filed past Carmen and Yukio and the Brit without much noticing them, assuming they were backstage hangout flotsam, except Murch stared at Carmen's tits and swaggered a bit, twirling his drumsticks.

The band sat around laughing in the dressing room and slapping palms, lighting several kinds of smokes. They didn't offer Rickenharp any; they knew he didn't use it.

Rickenharp was packing his guitar away when José said, "You blew good."

"You mean he gave you good head?" Murch said, and Julio snickered.

"Yeah," Ponce said, "the guy gives good head, good collarbone, good kidneys—"

"Good kidneys? Rick sucks on your kidneys? I think I'm gonna puke."

And the usual puerile band banter, because they were

still high from a good set and putting off what they knew had to come, till Rickenharp said, "What you want to talk about, José?"

José looked at him, and the others shut up.

"I know there's something on your mind," Rickenharp said softly.

José said, "Well, it's like—there's an agent Ponce knows, and this guy could take us on. He's a technicki agent and we'd be taking on a technicki circuit, but we'd work our way back from there, that's a good base. But this guy says we have to get a wire act in."

"You guys been busy," Rickenharp said, shutting the guitar case.

José shrugged. "Hey, we ain't been doing it behind your back; we didn't hear from the guy till yesterday night. We didn't have a real chance to talk to you till now, so—uh, we have the same personnel but we change costumes, change the band's name, write new tunes—"

"We'd lose it," Rickenharp said. Feeling caved in. "We'd lose the thing we got. You won't have it, doing that shit, because it's all superimposed."

"Rock 'n' roll is not a fucking religion," José said.

"No, it's not a religion, it's a way to sound. Now, here's *my* 'posal: we write new songs in the same style as always. We did good tonight. It could be the beginning of a turn-around for us. We stay here, build on the base audience we established tonight."

It was like throwing coins into the Grand Canyon. You couldn't even hear them hit bottom.

The band just looked back at him.

"Okay," Rickenharp said. "Okay. We've been through this ten fucking times. Okay. That's all." He'd had an exit speech worked out for this moment, but it caught in his throat. He turned to Murch and said, "You think they're going to keep you on, they tell you that?" Bullshit! They'll be doing it without a drummer, man. You better learn to program, fast." Then he looked at José. "Fuck you, José." He said it quietly.

He turned to Julio, who was looking at the far wall as if to decipher some particularly cryptic piece of graffiti. "Julio, you can have my amp, I'll be traveling light."

He turned and, carrying his guitar, walked out, leaving silence behind him.

He nodded at Yukio and led them to the stage door.

At the door, Carmen said, "Any chance you could help us find a little cover?"

Rickenharp needed company, bad. He nodded and said, "Yeah—if you'll give me a hit of that mesc."

She said, "Sure." And they went into the alley.

Rickenharp put on his dark glasses, because of the way the Walk tugged at him.

The Walk wound through the interlinked Freezone outfloats for a half mile, looping up and back, through a hairpin canyon of arcades crusted with neon and gloflake. It was involuted, intensified by layering and a blaze of colored light.

Rickenharp and Carmen walked through the sticky-warm night almost in step. Yukio walked behind, Willow walked ahead. Rickenharp felt like part of a jungle patrol formation. And he had another feeling: that they were being followed, or watched. Maybe it was suggestion, from seeing Yukio and Willow glance over their shoulders now and then. . . .

Rickenharp felt a ripple of kinetic force under his feet, an arc of wallow moving in languid whiplash through the flexible street stuff, telling him that the breakers were up today, the baffles around the artificial island feeling the strain.

The arcade ran three levels above the narrow street; each level had its own sidewalk balcony; people stood at the railing to look down at the segmented snake of street traffic. The stack of arcades funneled a rich wash of scents to Rickenharp: the french-fried toastiness of the fast food; the sweet harshness of smokes—smashweed smoke, gynosmoke, tobacco smoke—the cloy of perfumes; the mixed odors of fish-ka-bob stands, urine, rancid beer, popcorn, sea air; and the faint ozone smell of the small electric cars jockeying on the street. His first time here, Rickenharp had thought the place smelled wrong for a red-light cluster. "It's wimpy," he'd said. Then he'd realized he was missing the bass bottom of carbon monoxides. There were no combustion cars on Freezone.

The sounds splashed over Rickenharp in a warm wave of cultural fecundity; pop tunes from thudders and beat boxes swelled in volume as they passed, the guys carrying the boxes insignificant in comparison to the noise they carried, the shanky tripping of protosalsa or the calculatedly redundant pulse of minimono.

Rickenharp and Carmen walked beneath a fiberglass arch—so covered with graffiti its original commemorative meaning was lost—and ambled down the milky walkway under the second-story arcade boardwalk. The multinational crowd thickened as they approached the heart of the Walk. The soft lights glowing upward from beneath the polystyrene walkway gave the crowd a 1940s-horror-movie look, and even through the dark glasses the place tugged at Rickenharp with a thousand subliminal come-hithers.

Rickenharp was still riding the blue mesc surf, but the wave was beginning to break; he could feel it crumbling under him. He looked at Carmen. She glanced back at him, and they understood one another. She looked around, then nodded toward the darkened doorway of a defunct movie theater, a trash-cluttered recess twenty feet off the street. They went into the doorway; Yukio and Willow stood with their backs to the door, blocking the view from the street, so that Rickenharp and Carmen could each do a double hit of blue mesc. There was a kind of little-kid pleasure in stepping into seclusion to do drugs, a rush of outlaw in-crowd romance to it. On the second sniff the graffiti on the padlocked, fiberglass doors seemed to writhe with significance. "I'm running low," Carmen said, checking her mesc bottle.

Rickenharp didn't want to think about that. His mind was racing now, and he felt himself click into the boss blue verbal mode. "You see that graffiti? 'You're gonna die young because the ITE took the second half of your life.' You know what that means? I didn't know what ITE was till yesterday, I used to see those things and wonder and then somebody said—"

"Immortality something or other," she said, licking blue mesc off her sniffer.

"Immortality Treatment Elite. Supposedly some people keeping an immortality treatment to themselves because the government doesn't want the public to live too long and overpopulate the place. Another bullshit conspiracy theory."

"You don't believe in conspiracies?"

"I don't know—some. Nothing that farfetched. But—I think people are being manipulated all the time. Even here: this place tugs at you, you know. Like—"

Willow said, "Roit, we'll 'ave our sociology class later, children, you gotter? Where's this plice with the lad can get us off the island, mite?"

"Come on," Rickenharp said, leading them back into the flow of the crowd. But seamlessly picking up his blue mesc rap. "I mean, this place is a Times Square, right? You ever

read the old novels about that place? That was the arche-
type. Or some places in Bangkok. I mean, these places are
carefully arranged. Maybe subconsciously. But arranged as
carefully as Japanese florals, only with the inverse esthetic.
Sure, every whining, self-righteous, tight-assed evangelist
who ever preached about the diabolical seductiveness of
places like this was right—in a way—was fully justified
'cause, yeah, the places titillate and they seduce and they
vampirize people. Yeah, they're Venus flytraps. Architectural Svengalis. Yes to all the clichés about the bad part of
town. All the reverend preachers: Reverend Iko, Reverend—
what's his name?—Smilin' Rick Crandall—"

She looked sharply at him. He wondered why, but the
mesc swept him on.

"—all the preachers are right, but the reason they're right
is why they're wrong, too. Everything here is trying to sell
you something. Lots of light and whirligig suction to seduce
you into throwing your energy into it—in the form of
money. People mostly come here to buy or be titillated up
to the verge of buying. The tension between wanting to buy
and the resistance to buying can give you a charge. That's
what I get into: I let it tickle my glands, but I hold back
from paying into it. You know? Just constant titillation but
no cumming because you waste your money or you get a
social disease or mugged or sold bad drugs or something. . . .
I mean, anything sold here is pointless bullshit. But it's
harder for me to resist tonight. . . ." Unspoken: *Because I'm
stoned.* "Makes you susceptible. Receptive to subliminals
worked into the design of signs, that gaudy kinetics, those
fucking on-off bulbs—makes you flash on the old computer-
thinking models, binomial thinking, on-off, on-off, *blink-
blink*—all those neon tubes, pulling you like the hypnotist's
spiral pendant in the old movies. . . . And the kinds of colors
they use, the energy of the signs, the rate of pulse, the rate

of on-offing in the bulbs, all of it's engineered according to principles of psychology the people who make them don't even know they're using, colors that hint about, you know, glandular discharges and tingly chemical flows to the plea-sure center . . . like obscenities you pay for in the painted mouth of a whore . . . like video games . . . I mean—"

"I know what you mean," she said, in desperation buy-ing a wax-paper cup of beer. "You must be thirsty after that monologue. Here." She shoved the foaming cup under his nose.

"Talking too much. Sorry." He drank off half the beer in three gulps, took a breath, finished it, and it was paradise for a moment in his throat. A wave of quietude soothed him—and then evaporated as the blue mesc burned through again. Yeah, he was wired.

"I don't mind listening to you talk," she said, "except you might say too much, and I'm not sure if we're being scanned."

He nodded sheepishly, and they walked on. He crushed the cup in his hand, began methodically to shred it as they went.

Rickenharp luxuriated in the colors of the place, colors that mixed and washed over the crowd, making the stream of hats and heads into a living swatch of iridescent ging-ham, shining the cars into multicolored lumps of mobile ice.

You take the word *lurid*, Rickenharp thought, and you put it raw in a vat filled with the juice of the word *appeal*. You leave it and let the acids of appeal leach the colors out of lurid, so that you get a kind of gasoline rainbow on the surface of the vat. You extract the petro rainbow with cheesecloth, strain it into a glass tube, and dilute heavily with oil of cartoon innocence and extract of pure subjectiv-ity. Now run a current through the glass tube and all the other tubes of the neon signs interlacing Freezone's Walk.

The Walk, stretching ahead of them, was itself almost a tube of colored lights, converging in a kaleidoscope; the concave fronts of the buildings to either side were flashing with a dozen varieties of signs. The sensual flow of neon data in primary colors was broken at cunningly irregular intervals by stark trademark signs á la Times Square: CANON and ATARI and NIKE and COCA-COLA and WARNER AMEX and SEIKO and SONY and NASA CHEMCO and BRAZILIAN EXPORTS INT and EXXON and NESSIO. In all of that, only one hint of the war: two unlit signs, FABRIZZIO and ALLINNE, an Italian and a French company, killed by the Soviet blockades. The signs were unlit, dead.

They passed a TV-shirt shop; tourists walked out with their chests flashing moving video imagery, microthin circuitry and chips woven into the shirtfront playing the sequence of your choice.

Sidewalk hawkers of every race sold beta candy spiked with beta endorphin; sold shellfish from Freezone's own beds, tempura'd and skewered; sold holocube pornography key rings; sold instapix of you and your wife, or is that your boyfriend? . . . Despite the nearness of Africa, black Africans were few here; Freezone Admin considered them a security risk. The tourists were mostly Japanese, Canadian, Brazilian—riding the crest of the Brazilian boom—South Koreans, Chinese, Arabs, Israelis, and a smattering of Americans. Damned few Americans any more, with the depression.

The atmosphere was hothouse. It was a multicolored steam bath. The air was sultry, the various smokes of the place warping the neon glow, filtering and smearing the colors of signs and TV shirts and Day-Glo jewelry. High up, between the not-quite-fitted jigsaw parts of signs and lights and pleasure houses' video signs displaying purulently sexual imagery, were blue-black slices of night sky. At street level the jumble was given shape and borders by the doors opening on either side: by the in-and-out currents of people using the doors to check out malls and stimsmoke parlors and memento shops and cubey theaters and, especially, tingler galleries.

Dealers drifted up like reef fish, nibbling and moving on, pausing to offer, "Dee Aitch, gotcher good Dee Aitch"— DH, Direct Hookup, illegal cerebral pleasure center stimulation. And drugs, cocaine and various smokable herbs, stims, and downs; about half the dealers were burn artists, selling baking soda or pseudostims. The dealers tended to hang on to Rickenharp and Carmen because they looked like users, and Carmen was wearing a sniffer. Blue mesc and sniffers were illegal, but so were lots of things the Freezone cops ignored. You could wear a sniffer and carry the stuff, but the understanding was, You don't use it openly, you step into someplace discreet.

And whores of both sexes cruised the street, flagrantly soliciting. Freezone Admin was supposed to regulate all prostitution, but black-market pros were tolerated as long as somebody paid off the beat security and they didn't get too numerous.

The crowd streaming past was a perpetually unfolding revelation of human variety. It unfolded again and a specialty pimp appeared, pushing a teenage boy and girl ahead of him; they had to hobble because they were straitjacket-packaged in black-rubber bondage gear. Their faces were ciphers in blank black-rubber full-face masks; aluminum racks held their mouths wide open, intended to be inviting, but to Rickenharp they looked like victims of a mad orthodontist.

Studded down the streets were Freezone security guards in bullet-proofed uniforms that made Rickenharp think of baseball umpires, faces caged in helmets, guns locked by

combination into their holsters; they were said to be trained
to open the four-digit combination in one second.

Mostly they stood around, gossipped on their helmet
radios. Now two of them hassled a sidewalk three-card-
monte artist—a withered little black guy who couldn't afford
the baksheesh—pushing him back and forth between them,
bantering one another through helmet amplifiers, their
voices booming over the discothud from the speakers on the
'sette shops:

"WHAT THE FUCK YOU DOING ON MY BEAT SCUM-
BAG. HEY BILL, YOU KNOW WHAT THIS GUY'S DOING ON
MY BEAT."

"FUCK NO I DUNNO WHAT'S HE DOING ON YOUR
BEAT."

"HE'S MAKING ME SICK WITH THIS RIP-OFF MONTE
BULLSHIT IS WHAT HE'S DOING."

One of them hit the guy too hard with the waldo-
enhanced arm of his riot suit, and the monte dealer spun to
the ground like a top running out of momentum, out cold.

"LOITERING ON THE ZONE'S WALKS, YOU SEE THAT
BILL."

"I SEE IT AND IT MAKES ME SICK JIM."

The bulls dragged the little guy by the ankle to a
lozenge-shaped kiosk in the street and pushed him into a
man capsule. They sealed the capsule, scribbled out a report,
pasted it onto the capsule's hard plastic hull. Then they
shoved the man capsule into the kiosk's chute. The capsule
was sucked by mail-tube principle to Freezone Lockup.

"Looks like they're using some kind of garbage disposal
to get rid of people here," Carmen said when they were past
the cops.

Rickenharp looked at her. "You weren't nervous walking
by the cops. So it's not them, huh?"

"Nope."

"You wanna tell me who it is we're supposed to be avoiding?"

"Uh-uh."

"How do you know these out-of-town cops you're worried about haven't gone to the locals and recruited some help?"

"Yukio says they won't, they don't want anybody to scan what they're doing here because Freezone Admin don't like 'em."

"Mmm. . . ."

Rickenharp guessed: the *who it is* was the Second Alliance. The Second Alliance International Security Corporation, the crypto-fascists moving in throughout the wreckage of Europe. The SA played the role of multinational police, taking over, imposing their idea of order, where NATO's demoralized legions collapsed. The grasp of the SA and their sympathizers reached farther and wider as the war ground hopelessly on. Never yet to Freezone—Freezone's independent boss would have liked to see the SA gassed. They couldn't operate here—except covertly.

The fucking SA bulls! Shit! . . . The blue mesc worked with Rickenharp's paranoia. Adrenaline spurted, making his heart bang. He began to feel claustrophobic in the crowd. Began to see patterns in the movement around him, patterns charged with meaning superimposed by his fear-galvanized mind. Patterns that taunted him with *The SA's close behind.* He felt a stomach-churning combination of horror and elation.

All night he'd worked hard at suppressing thoughts of the band. And of his failure to make the band work. *He'd lost the band.* And it was almost impossible to make anyone understand why that was, to him, like a man losing his wife and children. And there was the career. All those years of pushing for that band, struggling to program a place for it

in the media Grid. Shot to hell now, and his identity with
it. He knew somehow that it would be futile to try to put
together another band. The Grid just didn't want him, and
he didn't want the fucking Grid. And the elation was this:
The ugly pit of displacement inside him closed up, was just
gone, when he thought about the SA bulls. The bulls threatened his life, and the threat caught him up in something
that made it possible to forget about the band. *He'd found
a way out.*

But the horror was there too. If he got caught up with
the SA's enemies . . . if the SA bulls got hold of him. . . .

Fuck it. What else did he have?

He grinned at Carmen, and she looked blankly back at
him, wondering what the grin meant.

So now what? he asked himself. Get to the OmeGaity.
Find Frankie. Frankie was the doorway.

But it was taking so long to get there. Thinking, The
drug's fucking with your sense of duration. Heightened perception makes it seem to take longer.

The crowd seemed to get thicker, the air hotter, the music louder, the lights brighter. It was getting to Rickenharp.
He began to lose the ability to make the distinction between
things in his mind and things around him. He began to see
himself as an enzyme molecule floating in some macrocos-
mic bloodstream. The sort of things that always OD'd him
when he did an energizing drug in a sensory-overflow environment.

What am I?

Sizzling orange-neon arrows on the marquee overhead
seemed to crawl off the marquee, slither down the wall,
down into the sidewalk, snaking to twine around his ankles,
to try to tug him into a tingler emporium. The emporium's
display holos writhed with fleshy intertwinings; breasts and
buttocks projected out at him, and he responded against his

will, like all the clichés, getting hard in his pants: visual stimuli; monkey see, monkey respond. He thought, Bell rings and dog salivates.

He looked over his shoulder. Who was that guy with the sunglasses back there? Why was he wearing sunglasses at night? Maybe he's an SA—

Noooo, man: *I'm* wearing sunglasses at night. Means nothing.

He tried to shrug off the paranoia, but somehow it was twined into the undercurrent of sexual excitement. Every time he saw a whore or a pornographic video sign, the paranoia hooked into him as a kind of scorpion stinger on the tail of his adolescent surge of arousal. And he could feel his nerve ends begin to extrude from his skin.

Who am I? Am I the crowd?

(Realizing that after having been clean so long, his blue mesc tolerance was low.)

He saw Carmen look at something in the street, then whisper urgently to Yukio.

"What's the matter?" Rickenharp asked.

She whispered, "You see that silver thing? Kind of a silvery fluttering? There—over the cab. . . . Just look, I can't point."

He looked into the street. A cab was pulling up at the curb. Its electric motor whined as it nosed through a heap of refuse. Its windows were dialed to mercuric opacity. Above and a little behind it a chrome bird hovered, its wings a hummingbird blur. It was about thrush-sized, and it had a camera lens instead of a head. There was some kind of insignia on its aluminum chest. He couldn't make it out. "I see it. I can't tell what it is."

"I think it's run from in that cab. That's like them. Come on."

She ducked into a tingler gallery; Willow and Yukio and

Rickenharp followed her. They had to buy user tokens to get in. They bought the minimum, four apiece. A bald, jowly old dude at the counter counted the tokens without looking, his eyes locked on a wrist-TV screen. On his wrist a miniature newscaster was saying in a small tinny voice, "... attempted assassination today of the Second Alliance director, the Reverend Rick Crandall...." Something mumbled, distorted. "Crandall is in serious condition and heavily guarded at Freezone Medicenter. The surprise presence of Crandall at a meeting at the Freezone Fuji Hilton—"

They scooped up their tokens and went into the gallery. Rickenharp heard Willow mutter to Yukio, "The bastard's still alive."

Rickenharp put two and two together.

The tingler gallery was predominantly fleshtone, every available vertical surface taken up by emulsified nude humanity, usually photos as ghastly as Polaroids. As you passed from one photo or holo to the next, you saw the people in them were inverted or splayed or toyed with, turned in a thousand variations on coupling, as if a child had been playing with unclothed dolls and left them scattered. A sodden red light hummed in each booth; the light snagged you, a wavelength calculated to produce sexual curiosity. In each "privacy booth" was a screen and a tingler. The tingler looked like a twentieth-century vacuum cleaner hose with an oversized salt-shaker top on one end. You watched the pictures, listened to the sounds, and ran the tingler over your erogenous zones; the tingler stimulated the appropriate nerve ends with a subcutaneously penetrative electric field, very precisely attenuated. You could pick out the guys in the health-club showers who'd used a tingler too long. Use it more than the "recommended thirty-five-minute limit" and it made your skin look and feel sunburned.... Another five tokens in the machines triggered an oxygen mask that dropped from a ceiling trap to pump out a combination of amyl nitrate and pheromones.

"To phrase it in the classic manner," Yukio said abruptly, "is there another way out of here?"

Rickenharp nodded. "Yeah. This place's on the corner, so chances are it's got two entrances, one around the corner from the first. And maybe an alley exit. . . ."

Willow was staring at a teaser blurb under a still image of two men, a woman, and a goat. He took a step closer, squinting at the goat as if searching out a family resemblance, and the booth sensed his nearness: the images on the sample placard began to move, bending, licking, penetrating, reshaping themselves with a weirdly formalized awkwardness; the booth's light increased its red glow, puffed out a tease of pheromone and amyl nitrate, trying to seduce him.

"Well, where *is* the other door?" Carmen hissed.

"Huh?" Rickenharp looked at her. "Oh! I'm sorry, I'm so—uh—I'm not sure." He glanced over his shoulder, lowered his voice. "The spy-bird didn't follow us in."

Yukio murmured, "The electric fields on the tinglers confuse the bird's guidance systems. But we must keep a step ahead."

Rickenharp looked around—but the maze of black booths and fleshtones seemed to twist back on itself, to turn ponderously, as if going down some cubistic drain. . . .

"*I* will find the other door," Yukio said. Rickenharp followed him gratefully. He wanted *out*.

They hurried through the narrow hall between tingler booths. The customers moved pensively—or strolled with excessive nonchalance—from one booth to another, reading the blurbs, scanning the imagery, sorting through fetishistic indexings for their personal libido codes, not looking at one another except peripherally, carefully avoiding personal-space margins, as if afraid of the volatility of dormant sexual elasticity.

Chuffing, sighing music played from somewhere; the red lights were like the glow of blood in a hand held over a bright light. But the place was rigorously Calvinistic in its obstacle course of tacit regulations. And here and there, at the turns in the hot, narrow passageways between rows of booths, bored nonuniformed security guards rocked on their heels and told the browsers, No loitering, please, you can purchase tokens at the front desk.

Rickenharp flashed that the place wanted to drain his sexuality, as if the vacuum-cleaner hoses in the booths were going to vacuum his orgone energy, leave him chilled as a gelding.

Get the fuck out of here, he told himself.

Then he saw EXIT, and they rushed for it, through it.

They were in an alley. They looked up, around, half expecting to see the bird. No bird. Only the gray intersection of styroconcrete planes, stunningly monochrome after the hungry chromatics of the tingler gallery.

They walked out to the end of the alley, stood for a moment watching the crowd churn by both ways. It was like standing on the bank of a torrent. Then they stepped into it, Rickenharp fantasizing that he was getting wet with the liquefied flesh of the rush of humanity as he steered by sheer instinct to his original objective: the OmeGaity.

They pushed through the peeling black pressboard doors into the dark mustiness of the OmeGaity's entrance hall, and Rickenharp gave Carmen his coat to hide her bare breasts. "Men only, in here," he said, "but if you don't shove your femaleness into their line of sight, they might let us slide."

Carmen pulled the jacket on, zipped it up—very carefully—and Rickenharp gave her his dark glasses.

Rickenharp banged on the window of the screening kiosk beside the locked door that led into the cruising rooms. Beyond the glass, someone looked up from a TV screen. "Hey, Carter," Rickenharp said.

"Hey." Carter grinned at him. Carter was, by his own admission, "a trendy faggot." He was flexicoated battleship gray with white trim, a minimono style. But the real M'n'Ms would have spurned him for wearing a luminous earring—it blinked through a series of words in tiny green letters: Fuck...you...if...you...don't...like...it....Fuck... you...if—they'd have considered that unforgivably "griddy." And anyway Carter's wide, froggish face didn't fit the svelte minimono look. He looked at Carmen. "No girls, Harpie."

"Drag queen," Rickenharp said. He slipped a folded twenty-newbux note through the slot in the window. "Okay?"

"Okay, but she takes her chances in there," Carter said, shrugging. He tucked the twenty in his charcoal bikini briefs.

"Sure."

"You hear about Geary?"

"Nope."

"Snuffed himself with China White 'cause he got green-pissed."

"Oh, shit." Rickenharp's skin crawled. His paranoia flared up again, and to soothe it he said, "Well, I'm not gonna be licking anybody's anything. I'm looking for Frankie."

"That asshole. He's there, holding court or something. But you still got to pay admission, honey."

"Sure," Rickenharp said.

He took another twenty newbux out of his pocket, but Carmen put a hand on his arm and said, "We'll cover this one." She slapped a twenty down.

Carter took it, chuckling. "Man, that queen got some real nice larynx work." Knowing damn well she was a girl. "You still playing at the—"

"I lost the gig," Rickenharp cut in, trying to head off the pain. The boss blue had peaked and left him feeling like he was made out of cardboard inside, like any pressure might make him buckle. His muscles twitched now and then, fretful as restive children scuffing feet. He was crashing. He needed another hit. When you were up, things showed you their frontsides, their upsides; when you peaked, things showed you their hideous insides. When you were down, things showed you their backsides, their downsides. File it away for lyrics.

Carter pressed the buzzer that unlocked the door. It razzed them as they walked through.

Inside it was dim, hot, humid.

"I think your blue was cut with coke or meth or something," Rickenharp told Carmen as they walked past the dented lockers. " 'Cause I'm crashing harder than I should be."

"Yeah, probably.... What'd he mean, 'he got green-pissed'?"

"Positive test for AIDS-three, the AIDS that kills you in six weeks. You drop this testing pill in your urine and if the urine turns green you got AIDS. There's no cure for the new AIDS, so the guy...." He shrugged.

"What the 'ell is this place?" Willow asked.

In a low voice Rickenharp told him, "It's a kind of bathless gay baths, man. Cruising places for 'mos. But about half the people are straights who ran out of bux at the casinos, use it for a cheap place to sleep, you know?"

"Yeah? And 'ow come you know all about it, 'ey?"

Rickenharp smirked. "You calling me a homo?"

Someone in a darkened alcove to one side laughed at that.

Willow was arguing with Yukio in an undertone. "Oi don't like it, that's all, fucking faggots got a million fucking diseases. Some geezer 'oo looks like a side o' beef with a tan going to wank off on me leg."

"We just walk through, we don't touch," Yukio said. "Rickenharp knows what to do."

Rickenharp thought, Hope so. Maybe Frankie could get them safely off Freezone, maybe not.

The walls were black pressboard. It was a maze like a tingler gallery but in the negative. There was a more ordinary red light; there was the peculiar scent that lots of skin on skin generates—and the accretion of various smokes, aftershaves, cheap soap, and an ingrained stink of sweat. And underneath, KY jelly, and poppers, and semen gone rancid. The walls stopped at ten feet up and the shadows gathered the ceiling into themselves, far overhead. It was a converted warehouse space, with a strange vibe of stratification: claustrophobia layered under agoraphobia. They passed mossy-dark cruising warrens. Faces blurred by anonymity turned to monitor them as they passed, expressions cool as TV cameras.

Such places had not changed significantly in fifty years. Some were shabbier than others. The shabbier ones had stopped-up toilets and badly focused 16-mm pornography and a drunken whine from the speakers that passed for porn soundtracks. And the OmeGaity was one of the shabbier ones.

They passed through the game room with its stained pool tables and stammering video games, its prized-open vending machines. Peeling from the walls between the machines were posters of men as exquisitely fem as they were overbearingly macho—caricatures with oversized genitals and muscles that seemed a kind of sexual organ, faces like California surfers. Carmen bit her finger to keep from laughing at them, marveling at the idiosyncratic narcissism of the place.

They passed through a cruising room designed to look like a barn. Two men ministered to one another on a wooden bench inside a "horse stall." Wet fleshy noises. Willow and Yukio looked away. Carmen stared at the gay sex in fascination. Rickenharp walked past without reacting, led the way through other midnight nests of pawing men; past men sleeping on benches and couches, snorting with annoyance and sleepily slapping unwanted hands away. And found Frankie in the TV lounge.

The TV lounge was bright, well-lit, the walls cheerful yellow. There were motel-standard living-room lamps on end tables, a couch, a regular color TV showing a rock video channel, and a bank of TV monitors on the wall. It was like emerging from the underworld. Frankie was sitting on the couch, waiting for customers.

Frankie dealt on a portaterminal he'd plugged into a grid socket. The buyer gave him an account number or credit card; Frankie checked the account, transferred the funds into his own (registered as "consultancy fees"), and handed over the packets.

The walls of the lounge were inset with video monitors; one showed the orgy room, another a porn tape, another ran a Grid network satellite channel. On that one a newscaster was yammering about the intended assassination of Crandall, this time in technicki; Rickenharp hoped Frankie wouldn't notice it and make the connection. Frankie the Mirror was into taking profit from whatever came along, and the SA paid for information.

Frankie sat on the torn blue vinyl couch, hunched over the pocket-sized terminal on the coffee table. Frankie's customer was a disco 'mo with a blue sharkfin flare, steroid muscles, and a white karate robe; the guy was standing to one side, staring at the little black canvas bag of blue packets on the coffee table as Frankie completed the transaction.

Frankie was black. His bald scalp had been painted with reflective chrome; his head was a mirror, reflecting the TV screens in fish-eye miniature. He wore a pinstriped three-piece gray suit. A real one, but rumpled and stained like he'd slept in it, maybe fucked in it. He was smoking a Nat Sherman cigaretello, down to the gold filter. His synthcoke eyes were demonically red. He flashed a yellow grin at Rickenharp. He looked at Willow, Yukio, and Carmen, made a mocking scowl. "Fucking narcs—get more fancy with their setups every day. Now they got four agents in here, one of them looks like my man Rickenharp, other three look like two refugees and a computer designer. But that Jap hasn't got a camera. Gives him away."

"What's this 'ere about—" Willow began.

Rickenharp made a dismissive gesture that said, *He isn't serious, dumbshit.* "I got two purchases to make," he announced and looked at Frankie's buyer. The buyer took his packet and melted back into the warrens.

"First off," Rickenharp said, taking his card from his wallet, "I need some blue blow, three grams."

"You got it, homeboy." Frankie ran a lightpen over the card, then punched in a request for data on that account. The terminal asked for the private code number. Frankie handed the terminal to Rickenharp, who punched in his code, then erased it from visual. Then he punched to transfer funds to Frankie's account. Frankie took the terminal and double-checked the transfer. The terminal showed Rickenharp's adjusted balance and Frankie's gain.

"That's gonna eat up half your account, Harpie," Frankie said.

"I got some prospects."

"I heard you and José parted company."

"How'd you get that so fast?"

"Ponce was here buying."

"Yeah, well—now I've dumped the dead weight, my prospects are even better." But as he said it he felt dead weight in his gut.

" 'S your bux, man." Frankie reached into the canvas carry-on, took out three pre-weighed bags of blue powder. He looked faintly amused. Rickenharp didn't like the look. It seemed to say, *I knew you'd come back, you sorry little wimp.*

"Fuck off, Frankie," Rickenharp said, taking the packets.

"What's this sudden squall of discontent, my child?"

"None of your business, you smug bastard."

Frankie's smugness output tripled. He glanced speculatively at Carmen and Yukio and Willow. "There's something more, right?"

"Yeah. We got a problem. My friends here—they're getting off the raft. They need to slip out the back way so Tom and Huck don't see 'em."

"Hmm. What kind of net's out for them?"

"It's a private outfit. They'll be watching the copter port, everything legit—"

"We had another way off," Carmen said suddenly, "but it was blown—"

Yukio silenced her with a look. She shrugged.

"Ver-ry mysterious," Frankie said. "But there are safety limits to curiosity. Okay. Three grand gets you three berths on my next boat out. My boss's sending a team to pick up a shipment. I can probably get 'em on there. That's going *east*, though. You know? Not west or north or south. One direction and one only."

"That's what we need," Yukio said, smiling, nodding.

Like he was talking to a travel agent. "East. Someplace Mediterranean."

"Malta," Frankie said. "Island of Malta. Best I can do."

Yukio nodded. Willow shrugged. Carmen assented by her silence.

Rickenharp was sampling the goods. In the nose, to the brain, and right to work. Frankie watched him placidly. Frankie was a connoisseur of the changes drugs made in people. He watched the change of expression on Rickenharp's face. He watched Rickenharp's shift into egodrive.

"We're *gonna* need *four* berths, Frankie," Rickenharp said.

Frankie raised an eyebrow. "You better decide after that shit wears off."

"I decided before I took it," Rickenharp said, not sure if it was true.

Carmen was staring at him.

He took her by the arm and said, "Talk to you a minute?" He led her out of the lounge, into the dark hallway. The skin of her arm was electrically sweet under his fingers. He wanted more. But he dropped his hand from her and said, "Can you get the bux?"

She nodded. "I got a fake card, dips into—well, it'll get it for us. I mean, for me and Yukio and Willow. I'd have to get authorization to bring you. And I can't do that."

"I won't help you get out otherwise."

"You don't know—"

"Yeah, I do. I'm ready to go. I just go back and get my guitar."

"The guitar'll be a burden where we're going. We're going into occupied territory, to get where we want to be. You'd have to leave the guitar."

He almost wavered at that. "I'll check it into a locker. Pick it up someday." He couldn't play it anyway without every note sounding wrong because of the pain he played through now. "Thing is—if they watched us with that bird, they saw me with you. They'll assume I'm part of it. Look, I know what you're doing. The SA's looking for you. Right? So that means you're—"

"Okay, hold it, shit, keep your voice down. Look—I can see where maybe they marked you, so you got to get off the raft too. Okay, you go with us to Malta. But then you—"

"I got to stay with you. The SA's everywhere. They marked me."

She took a deep breath and let it out in a soft whistle through her teeth. She stared at the floor. "You can't do it." She looked at him. "You're not the type. You're a fucking *artist*."

He laughed. "You say that like it's the lowest insult you can come up with. Look—I can do it. I'm going to do it. The band is dead. I need to—" He shrugged helplessly. Then he reached up and took her sunglasses off, looked at her shadowed eyes. "And when I get you alone I'm going to batter your cervix into jelly."

She punched him hard in the shoulder. It hurt. But she was smiling. "You think that kind of talk turns me on? Well, it does. But it's not going to get you into my pants. And as for going with us—what do you think this is? You've seen too many movies."

"The SA's marked me. What else can I do?"

"That's not a good enough reason to . . . to become part of this thing. You've got to really believe in it, because *it's hard*. This is not a celebrity game show."

"Jesus. Give me a break. I know what I'm doing."

That was bullshit. He was trashed. He was blown. He thought, *My computer's experiencing a power surge. All circuits wiped out. Hell, then burn out the rest.*

He was living a fantasy. But he wasn't going to admit it. He repeated, "I know what I'm doing."

She snorted. She stared at him. "Okay," she said.

And after that everything was different.

DOGFIGHT

WILLIAM GIBSON AND
MICHAEL SWANWICK

He meant to keep on going, right down to Florida. Work passage on a gunrunner, maybe wind up conscripted into some ratass rebel army down in the war zone. Or maybe, with that ticket good as long as he didn't stop riding, he'd just never get off—Greyhound's Flying Dutchman. He grinned at his faint reflection in cold, greasy glass while the downtown lights of Norfolk slid past, the bus swaying on tired shocks as the driver slung it around a final corner. They shuddered to a halt in the terminal lot, concrete lit gray and harsh like a prison exercise yard. But Deke was watching himself starve, maybe in some snowstorm out of Oswego, with his cheek pressed up against that same bus window, and seeing his remains swept out at the next stop by a muttering old man in faded coveralls. One way or the other, he decided, it didn't mean shit to him. Except his legs seemed to have died already. And the driver called a twenty-minute stopover—Tidewater Station, Virginia. It was an old cinder-block building with two entrances to each rest room, holdover from the previous century.

Legs like wood, he made a halfhearted attempt at ghost-
ing the notions counter, but the black girl behind it was
alert, guarding the sparse contents of the old glass case as
though her ass depended on it. *Probably does*, Deke thought,
turning away. Opposite the washrooms, an open doorway
offered GAMES, the word flickering feebly in biofluorescent
plastic. He could see a crowd of the local kickers clustered
around a pool table. Aimless, his boredom following him
like a cloud, he stuck his head in. And saw a biplane, wings
no longer than his thumb, blossom bright orange flame.
Corkscrewing, trailing smoke, it vanished the instant it
struck the green-felt field of the table.

"Tha's right, Tiny," a kicker bellowed, "you *take* that
sumbitch!"

"Hey," Deke said. "What's going on?"

The nearest kicker was a bean pole with a black mesh
Peterbilt cap. "Tiny's defending the Max," he said, not taking his eyes from the table.

"Oh, yeah? What's that?" But even as he asked, he saw
it: a blue enamel medal shaped like a Maltese cross, the
slogan *Pour le Mérite* divided among its arms.

The Blue Max rested on the edge of the table, directly
before a vast and perfectly immobile bulk wedged into a
fragile-looking chrome-tube chair. The man's khaki work
shirt would have hung on Deke like the folds of a sail, but
it bulged across that bloated torso so tautly that the buttons
threatened to tear away at any instant. Deke thought of
southern troopers he'd seen on his way down; of that weird,
gut-heavy endotype balanced on gangly legs that looked
like they'd been borrowed from some other body. Tiny
might look like that if he stood, but on a larger scale—a
forty-inch jeans inseam that would need a woven-steel
waistband to support all those pounds of swollen gut. If Tiny
were ever to stand at all—for now Deke saw that that shiny

frame was actually a wheelchair. There was something disturbingly childlike about the man's face, an appalling suggestion of youth and even beauty in features almost buried in fold and jowl. Embarrassed, Deke looked away. The other man, the one standing across the table from Tiny, had bushy sideburns and a thin mouth. He seemed to be trying to push something with his eyes, wrinkles of concentration spreading from the corners. . . .

"You dumbshit or what?" The man with the Peterbilt cap turned, catching Deke's Indo proleboy denims, the brass chains at his wrists, for the first time. "Why don't you get your ass lost, fucker. Nobody wants your kind in here." He turned back to the dogfight.

Bets were being made, being covered. The kickers were producing the hard stuff, the old stuff, liberty-headed dollars and Roosevelt dimes from the stamp-and-coin stores, while more cautious bettors slapped down antique paper dollars laminated in clear plastic. Through the haze came a trio of red planes, flying in formation. Fokker D VIIs. The room fell silent. The Fokkers banked majestically under the solar orb of a two-hundred-watt bulb.

The blue Spad dove out of nowhere. Two more plunged from the shadowy ceiling, following closely. The kickers swore, and one chuckled. The formation broke wildly. One Fokker dove almost to the felt, without losing the Spad on its tail. Furiously, it zigged and zagged across the green flatlands but to no avail. At last it pulled up, the enemy hard after it, too steeply—and stalled, too low to pull out in time.

A stack of silver dimes was scooped up.

The Fokkers were outnumbered now. One had two Spads on its tail. A needle-spray of tracers tore past its cockpit. The Fokker slip-turned right, banked into an Immelmann, and was behind one of its pursuers. It fired, and the biplane fell, tumbling.

"Way to go, Tiny!" The kickers closed in around the table.

Deke was frozen with wonder. It felt like being born all over again.

Frank's Truck Stop was two miles out of town on the Commercial Vehicles Only route. Deke had tagged it, out of idle habit, from the bus on the way in. Now he walked back between the traffic and the concrete crash guards. Articulated trucks went slamming past, big eight-segmented jobs, the wash of air each time threatening to blast him over. CVO stops were easy makes. When he sauntered into Frank's, there was nobody to doubt that he'd come in off a big rig, and he was able to browse the gift shop as slowly as he liked. The wire rack with the projective wetware wafers was located between a stack of Korean cowboy shirts and a display for Fuzz Buster mudguards. A pair of Oriental dragons twisted in the air over the rack, either fighting or fucking, he couldn't tell which. The game he wanted was there: a wafer labeled SPADS & FOKKERS. It took him three seconds to boost it and less time to slide the magnet—which the cops in D.C. hadn't even bothered to confiscate—across the universal security strip.

On the way out, he lifted two programming units and a little Batang facilitator-remote that looked like an antique hearing aid.

He chose a highstack at random and fed the rental agent the line he'd used since his welfare rights were yanked. Nobody ever checked up; the state just counted occupied rooms and paid.

The cubicle smelled faintly of urine, and someone had

scrawled Hard Anarchy Liberation Front slogans across the walls. Deke kicked trash out of a corner, sat down, back to the wall, and ripped open the wafer pack.

There was a folded instruction sheet with diagrams of loops, rolls, and Immelmanns, a tube of saline paste, and a computer list of operational specs. And the wafer itself, white plastic with a blue biplane and logo on one side, red on the other. He turned it over and over in his hand: SPADS & FOKKERS, FOKKERS & SPADS. Red or blue. He fitted the Batang behind his ear after coating the inductor surface with paste, jacked its fiberoptic ribbon into the programmer, and plugged the programmer into the wall current. Then he slid the wafer into the programmer. It was a cheap set, Indonesian, and the base of his skull buzzed uncomfortably as the program ran. But when it was done, a sky-blue Spad darted restlessly through the air a few inches from his face. It almost glowed, it was so real. It had the strange inner life that fanatically detailed museum-grade models often have but it took all of his concentration to keep it in existence. If his attention wavered at all, it lost focus, fuzzing into a pathetic blur.

He practiced until the battery in the earset died, then slumped against the wall and fell asleep. He dreamed of flying, in a universe that consisted entirely of white clouds and blue sky, with no up and down, and never a green field to crash into.

He woke to a rancid smell of frying krillcakes and winced with hunger. No cash, either. Well, there were plenty of student types in the stack. Bound to be one who'd like to score a programming unit. He hit the hall with the boosted spare. Not far down was a door with a poster on it: THERE'S A HELL OF A GOOD UNIVERSE NEXT DOOR. Under that was a starscape with a cluster of multicolored pills, torn from an ad for some pharmaceutical company, pasted over an inspirational shot of the "space colony" that had been under construction since before he was born. LET'S GO, the poster said, beneath the collaged hypnotics.

He knocked. The door opened, security slides stopping it at a two-inch slice of girlface. "Yeah?"

"You're going to think this is stolen." He passed the programmer from hand to hand. "I mean because it's new, virtual cherry, and the bar code's still on it. But listen, I'm not gonna argue the point. No. I'm gonna let you have it for only like half what you'd pay anywhere else."

"Hey, wow, *really*, no kidding?" The visible fraction of mouth twisted into a strange smile. She extended her hand, palm up, a loose fist. Level with his chin. "Lookahere!"

There was a hole in her hand, a black tunnel that ran right up her arm. Two small red lights. Rat's eyes. They scurried toward him—growing, gleaming. Something gray streaked forward and leaped for his face.

He screamed, throwing hands up to ward it off. Legs twisting, he fell, the programmer shattering under him.

Silicate shards skittered as he thrashed, clutching his head. Where it hurt, it hurt—it hurt very badly indeed.

'Oh, my God!" Slides unsnapped, and the girl was hovering over him. "Here, listen, come on." She dangled a blue hand towel. "Grab on to this and I'll pull you up."

He looked at her through a wash of tears. Student. That fed look, the oversize sweatshirt, teeth so straight and white they could be used as a credit reference. A thin gold chain around one ankle (fuzzed, he saw, with baby-fine hair). Choppy Japanese haircut. Money. "That sucker was gonna be my dinner," he said ruefully. He took hold of the towel and let her pull him up.

She smiled but skittishly backed away from him. "Let

me make it up to you," she said. "You want some food? It was only a projection, okay?"

He followed her in, wary as an animal entering a trap.

"Holy shit," Deke said, "this is *real cheese.* . . ." He was sitting on a gutsprung sofa, wedged between a four-foot teddy bear and a loose stack of floppies. The room was ankle-deep in books and clothes and papers. But the food she magicked up—Gouda cheese and tinned beef and honest-to-God greenhouse wheat wafers—was straight out of the Arabian Nights.

"Hey," she said. "We know how to treat a prole boy right, huh?" Her name was Nance Bettendorf. She was seventeen. Both her parents had jobs—greedy buggers—and she was an engineering major at William and Mary. She got top marks except in English. "I guess you must really have a thing about rats. You got some kind of phobia about rats?"

He glanced sidelong at her bed. You couldn't see it, really; it was just a swell in the ground cover. "It's not like that. It just reminded me of something else, is all."

"Like what?" She squatted in front of him, the big shirt riding high up one smooth thigh.

"Well . . . did you ever see the—" his voice involuntarily rose and rushed past the words—"*Washington Monument?* Like at night? It's got these two little . . . red lights on top, aviation markers or something, and I, and I. . . ." He started to shake.

"You're afraid of the Washington Monument?" Nance whooped and rolled over with laughter, long tanned legs kicking. She was wearing crimson bikini panties.

"I would die rather than look at it again," he said levelly.

She stopped laughing then, sat up, studied his face. White, even teeth worried at her lower lip, like she was dragging up something she didn't want to think about. At last she ventured, "Brainlock?"

"Yeah," he said bitterly. "They told me I'd never go back to D.C. And then the fuckers laughed."

"What did they get you for?"

"I'm a thief." He wasn't about to tell her that the actual charge was career shoplifting.

"Lotta old computer hacks spent their lives programming machines. And you know what? The human brain is not a goddamn bit like a machine, no way. They just don't program the same." Deke knew this shrill, desperate rap, this long, circular jive that the lonely string out to the rare listener; knew it from a hundred cold and empty nights spent in the company of strangers. Nance was lost in it, and Deke, nodding and yawning, wondered if he'd even be able to stay awake when they finally hit that bed of hers.

"I built that projection I hit you with myself," she said, hugging her knees up beneath her chin. "It's for muggers, you know? I just happened to have it on me; and I threw it at you 'cause I thought it was so funny, you trying to sell me that shit little Indojavanese programmer." She hunched forward and held out her hand again. "Look here." Deke cringed. "No, no, it's okay, I swear it, this is different." She opened her hand.

A single blue flame danced there, perfect and ever-changing. "Look at that," she marveled. "Just look. I programmed that. It's not some diddly little seven-image job either. It's a continuous two-hour loop, seven thousand, two hundred seconds, never the same twice, each instant as individual as a fucking snowflake!"

The flame's core was glacial crystal, shards and facets flashing up, twisting and gone, leaving behind near-subliminal images so bright and sharp that they cut the eye.

Deke winced. People mostly. Pretty little naked people, fucking. "How the hell did you do that?"

She rose, bare feet slipping on slick magazines, and melodramatically swept folds of loose printout from a raw plywood shelf. He saw a neat row of small consoles, austere and expensive-looking. Custom work. "This is the real stuff I got here. Image facilitator. Here's my fast-wipe module. This is a brainmap one-to-one function analyzer." She sang off the names like a litany. "Quantum flicker stabilizer. Program splicer. An image assembler . . ."

"You need all that to make one little flame?"

"You betcha. This is all state of the art, professional projective wetware gear. It's years ahead of anything you've seen."

"Hey," he said, "you know anything about SPADS & FOK-KERS?"

She laughed. And then, because he sensed the time was right, he reached out to take her hand.

"Don't you touch me, motherfuck, don't you *ever touch me!*" Nance screamed, and her head slammed against the wall as she recoiled, white and shaking with terror.

"Okay!" He threw up his hands. "Okay! I'm nowhere near you. Okay?"

She cowered from him. Her eyes were round and unblinking; tears built up at the corners, rolled down ashen cheeks. Finally, she shook her head. "Hey, Deke. Sorry. I should've told you."

"Told me what?" But he had a creepy feeling . . . already knew. The way she clutched her head. The weakly spasmodic way her hands opened and closed. "You got a brainlock, too."

"Yeah." She closed her eyes. "It's a chastity lock. My asshole parents paid for it. So I can't stand to have anybody touch me or even stand too close." Eyes opened in blind hate. "I didn't even *do* anything. Not a fucking thing. But they've both got jobs and they've so horny for me to have a career that they can't piss straight. They're afraid I'd neglect my studies if I got, you know, involved in sex and stuff. The day the brainlock comes off I am going to fuck the vilest, greasiest, hairiest . . ."

She was clutching her head again. Deke jumped up and rummaged through the medicine cabinet. He found a jar of B-complex vitamins, pocketed a few against need, and brought two to Nance, with a glass of water. "Here." He was careful to keep his distance. "This'll take the edge off."

"Yeah, yeah," she said. Then, almost to herself, "You must really think I'm a jerk."

The games room in the Greyhound station was almost empty. A lone, long-jawed fourteen-year-old was bent over a console, maneuvering rainbow fleets of submarines in the murky grid of the North Atlantic.

Deke sauntered in, wearing his new kicker drag, and leaned against a cinder-block wall made smooth by countless coats of green enamel. He'd washed the dye from his proleboy butch, boosted jeans and T-shirt from the Goodwill, and found a pair of stompers in the sauna locker of a highstack with cutrate security.

"Seen Tiny around, friend?"

The subs darted like neon guppies. "Depends on who's asking."

Deke touched the remote behind his left ear. The Spad snap-rolled over the console, swift and delicate as a dragonfly. It was beautiful; so perfect, so *true* it made the room seem an illusion. He buzzed the grid, millimeters from the glass, taking advantage of the programmed ground effect.

The kid didn't even bother to look up. "Jackman's," he said. "Down Richmond Road, over by the surplus."

Deke let the Spad fade in midclimb.

Jackman's took up most of the third floor of an old brick building. Deke found Best Buy War Surplus first, then a broken neon sign over an unlit lobby. The sidewalk out front was littered with another kind of surplus—damaged vets, some of them dating back to Indochina. Old men who'd left their eyes under Asian suns squatted beside twitching boys who'd inhaled mycotoxins in Chile. Deke was glad to have the battered elevator doors sigh shut behind him.

A dusty Dr. Pepper clock at the far side of the long, spectral room told him it was a quarter to eight. Jackman's had been embalmed twenty years before he was born, sealed away behind a yellowish film of nicotine, of polish and hair oil. Directly beneath the clock, the flat eyes of somebody's grandpappy's prize buck regarded Deke from a framed, blown-up snapshot gone the slick sepia of cockroach wings. There was the click and whisper of pool, the squeak of a work boot twisting on linoleum as a player leaned in for a shot. Somewhere high above the green-shaded lamps hung a string of crepe-paper Christmas bells faded to dead rose. Deke looked from one cluttered wall to the next. No facilitator.

"Bring one in, should we need it," someone said. He turned, meeting the mild eyes of a bald man with steel-rimmed glasses. "My name's Cline. Bobby Earl. You don't look like you shoot pool, mister." But there was nothing threatening in Bobby Earl's voice or stance. He pinched the steel frames from his nose and polished the thick lenses with a fold of tissue. He reminded Deke of a shop instructor who'd patiently tried to teach him retrograde biochip installation. "I'm a gambler," he said, smiling. His teeth were white plastic. "I know I don't much look it."

"I'm looking for Tiny," Deke said.

"Well," replacing the glasses, "you're not going to find

him. He's gone up to Bethesda to let the V.A. clean his plumbing for him. He wouldn't fly against you any how."

"Why not?"

"Well, because you're not on the circuit or I'd know your face. You any good?" When Deke nodded, Bobby Earl called down the length of Jackman's, "Yo, Clarence! You bring out that facilitator. We got us a flyboy."

Twenty minutes later, having lost his remote and what cash he had left, Deke was striding past the broken soldiers of Best Buy.

"Now you let me tell you, boy," Bobby Earl had said in a fatherly tone as, hand on shoulder, he led Deke back to the elevator. "You're not going to win against a combat vet—you listening to me? I'm not even especially good, just an old grunt who was on hype fifteen, maybe twenty times. Ol' Tiny, he was a *pilot.* Spent his entire enlistment hyped to the gills. He's got membrane attenuation real bad . . . you ain't never going to beat him."

It was a cool night. But Deke burned with anger and humiliation.

"Jesus, that's crude," Nance said as the Spad strafed mounds of pink underwear., Deke, hunched up on the couch, yanked her flashy little Braun remote from behind his ear.

"Now don't you get on my case too, Miss rich-bitch gonna-have-a-job—"

"Hey, lighten up! It's nothing to do with you—it's just *tech.* That's a really primitive wafer you got there. I mean, on the street maybe it's fine. But compared to the work I do at school, it's—hey. You ought to let me rewrite it for you."

"Say what?"

"Lemme beef it up. These suckers are all written in hexadecimal, see, 'cause the industry programmers are all washed-out computer hacks. That's how they think. But let me take it to the reader-analyzer at the department, run a few changes on it, translate it into a modern wetlanguage. Edit out all the redundant intermediaries. That'll goose up your reaction time, cut the feedback loop in half. So you'll fly faster and better. Turn you into a real pro, Ace!" She took a hit off her bong, then doubled over laughing and choking.

"Is that legit?" Deke asked dubiously.

"Hey, why do you think people buy gold-wire remotes? For the prestige? Shit. Conductivity's better, cuts a few nanoseconds off the reaction time. And reaction time is the name of the game, kiddo."

"No," Deke said. "If it were that easy, people'd already have it. Tiny Montgomery would have it,. He'd have the best."

"Don't you ever *listen*?" Nance set down the bong; brown water slopped onto the floor. "The stuff I'm working with is three years ahead of anything you'll find on the street."

"No shit," Deke said after a long pause. "I mean, you can do that?"

It was like graduating from a Model T to a ninety-three Lotus. The Spad handled like a dream, responsive to Deke's slightest thought. For weeks he played the arcades, with not a nibble. He flew against the local teens and by ones and threes shot down their planes. He took chances, played flash. And the planes tumbled. . . .

Until one day Deke was tucking his seed money away, and a lanky black straightened up from the wall. He eyed the laminateds in Deke's hand and grinned. A ruby tooth gleamed. "You know," the man said, "I *heard* there was a casper who could fly-going up against the kiddies."

* * *

"Jesus," Deke said, spreading Danish butter on a kelp stick. "I wiped the *floor* with those spades. They were good, too."

"That's nice, honey," Nance mumbled. She was working on her finals project, sweating data into a machine.

"You know, I think what's happening is I got real talent for this kind of shit. You know? I mean, the program gives me an edge, but I got the stuff to take advantage of it. I'm really getting a rep out there, you know?" Impulsively, he snapped on the radio. Scratchy Dixieland brass blared.

"Hey," Nance said. "Do you *mind*?"

"No, I'm just—" He fiddled with the knobs, came up with some slow, romantic bullshit. "There. Come on, stand up. Let's dance."

"Hey, you know I can't—"

"Sure you can, sugarcakes." He threw her the huge teddy bear and snatched up a patchwork cotton dress from the floor. He held it by the waist and sleeve, tucking the collar under his chin. It smelled of patchouli, more faintly of sweat. "See, I stand over here, you stand over there. We dance. Get it?"

Blinking softly, Nance stood and clutched the bear tightly. They danced then, slowly, staring into each other's eyes. After a while, she began to cry. But still, she was smiling.

Deke was daydreaming, imaging he was Tiny Montgomery wired into his jumpjet. Imagined the machine responding to his slightest neural twitch, reflexes cranked *way* up, hype flowing steadily into his veins.

Nance's floor became jungle, her bed a plateau in the Andean foothills, and Deke flew his Spad at forced speed, as if it were a full-wired interactive combat machine. Computerized hypos fed a slow trickle of high-performance enhancement mélange into his bloodstream. Sensors were wired directly into his skull—pulling a supersonic snapturn in the green-blue bowl of sky over Bolivian rain forest. Tiny would have *felt* the airflow over control surfaces.

Below, grunts hacked through the jungle with hype-pumps strapped above elbows to give them that little extra death-dance fury in combat, a shot of liquid hell in a blue plastic vial. Maybe they got ten minutes' worth in a week. But coming in at treetop level, reflexes cranked to the max, flying so low the ground troops never spotted you until you were on them, phosgene agents released, away and gone before they could draw a bead . . . it took a constant trickle of hype just to maintain. And the direct neuron interface with the jumpjet was a two-way street. The onboard computers monitored biochemistry and decided when to open the sluice gates and give the human component a killer jolt of combat edge.

Dosages like that ate you up. Ate you good and slow and constant, etching the brain surfaces, eroding away the brain-cell membranes. If you weren't yanked from the air promptly enough, you ended up with brain-cell attenuation—with reflexes too fast for your body to handle and your fight-or-flight reflexes fucked real good. . . .

"I aced it, proleboy!"

"Hah?" Deke looked up, startled, as Nance slammed in, tossing books and bag onto the nearest heap.

"My finals project—I got exempted from exams. The prof said he'd never seen anything like it. Uh, hey, dim the lights, wouldja? The colors are weird on my eyes."

He obliged. "So show me. Show me this wunnerful thing."

"Yeah, okay." She snatched up his remote, kicked clear standing space atop the bed, and struck a pose. A spark flared into flame in her hand. It spread in a quicksilver line up her arm, around her neck, and it was a snake, with triangular head and flickering tongue. Molten colors, oranges and reds. It slithered between her breasts. "I call it a firesnake," she said proudly.

Deke leaned close, and she jerked back.

"Sorry. It's like your flame, huh? I mean, I can see these tiny little fuckers in it."

"Sort of." The firesnake flowed down her stomach. "Next month I'm going to splice two hundred separate flame programs together with meld justification in between to get the visuals. Then I'll tap the mind's body image to make it self-orienting. So it can crawl all over your body without your having to mind it. You could wear it dancing."

"Maybe I'm dumb. But if you haven't done the work yet, how come I can see it?"

Nance giggled. "That's the best part—half the work isn't done yet. Didn't have the time to assemble the pieces into a unified program. Turn on that radio, huh? I want to dance." She kicked off her shoes. Deke tuned in something gutsy. Then, at Nance's urging, turned it down, almost to a whisper.

"I scored two hits of hype, see." She was bouncing on the bed, weaving her hands like a Balinese dancer. "Ever try the stuff? In-credible. Gives you like absolute concentration. Look here." She stood *en pointe*. "Never done that before."

"Hype," Deke said. "Last person I heard of got caught with that shit got three years in the infantry. How'd you score it?"

"Cut a deal with a vet who was in grad school. She bombed out last month. Stuff gives me perfect visualization. I can hold the projection with my eyes shut. It was a snap assembling the program in my head."

"On just two hits, huh?"

"One hit. I'm saving the other. Teach was so impressed he's sponsoring me for a job interview. A recruiter from I. G.

Feuchtwaren hits campus in two weeks. That cap is gonna sell him the program *and* me. I'm gonna cut out of school two years early, straight into industry, do not pass jail, do not pay two hundred dollars."

The snake curled into a flaming tiara. It gave Deke a funny-creepy feeling to think of Nance walking out of his life.

"I'm a witch," Nance sang, "a wetware witch." She shucked her shirt over her head and sent it flying. Her fine, high breasts moved freely, gracefully, as she danced. "I'm gonna make it"—now she was singing a current pop hit— "to the . . . top!" Her nipples were small and pink and aroused. The firesnake licked at them and whipped away.

"Hey. Nance," Deke said uncomfortably. "Calm down a little, huh?"

"I'm celebrating!" She hooked a thumb into her shiny gold panties. Fire swirled around hand and crotch. "I'm the virgin goddess, baby, and I have the pow-er!" Singing again.

Deke looked away. "Gotta go now," he mumbled. Gotta go home and jerk off. He wondered where she'd hidden that second hit. Could be anywhere.

There was a protocol to the circuit, a tacit order of deference and precedence as elaborate as that of a Mandarin court. It didn't matter that Deke was hot, that his rep was spreading like wildfire. Even a name flyboy couldn't just challenge whom he wished. He had to climb the ranks. But if you flew every night. If you were always available to anybody's challenge. And if you were good . . . well, it was possible to climb fast.

Deke was one plane up. It was tournament fighting, three planes against three. Not many spectators, a dozen maybe, but it was a good fight, and they were noisy. Duke was immersed in the manic calm of combat when he realized suddenly that they had fallen silent. Saw the kickers stir and exchange glances. Eyes flicked past him. He heard the elevator doors close. Coolly, he disposed of the second of his opponent's planes, then risked a quick glance over his shoulder.

Tiny Montgomery had just entered Jackman's. The wheelchair whispered across browning linoleum, guided by tiny twitches of one imperfectly paralyzed hand. His expression was stern, blank, calm.

In that instant, Deke lost two planes. One to deresolution—gone to blur and canceled out by the facilitator—and the other because his opponent was a real fighter. Guy did a barrel roll, killing speed and slipping to the side, and strafed Deke's biplane as it shot past. It went down in flames. Their last two planes shared altitude and speed, and as they turned, trying for position, they naturally fell into a circling pattern.

The kickers made room as Tiny wheeled up against the table. Bobby Earl Cline trailed after him, lanky and casual. Deke and his opponent traded glances and pulled their machines back from the pool table so they could hear the man out. Tiny smiled. His features were small, clustered in the center of his pale, doughy face. One finger twitched slightly on the chrome handrest. "I heard about you." He looked straight at Deke. His voice was soft and shockingly sweet, a baby-girl little voice. "I heard you're good."

Deke nodded slowly. The smile left Tiny's face. His soft, fleshy lips relaxed into a natural pout, as if he were waiting for a kiss. His small, bright eyes studied Deke without malice. "Let's see what you can do, then."

Deke lost himself in the cool game of war. And when the enemy went down in smoke and flame, to explode and vanish against the table, Tiny wordlessly turned his chair, wheeled it into the elevator, and was gone.

As Deke was gathering up his winnings, Bobby Earl eased up to him and said, "The man wants to play you."

"Yeah?" Deke was nowhere near high enough on the circuit to challenge Tiny. "What's the scam?"

"Man who was coming up from Atlanta tomorrow canceled. Ol' Tiny, he was spoiling to go up against somebody new. So it looks like you get your shot at the Max."

"Tomorrow? Wednesday? Doesn't give me much prep time."

Bobby Earl smiled gently. "I don't think that makes no nevermind."

"How's that, Mr. Cline?"

"Boy, you just ain't got the *moves*, you follow me? Ain't got no surprises. You fly just like some kinda beginner, only faster and slicker. You follow what I'm trying to say?"

"I'm not sure I do. You want to put a little action on that?"

"Tell you truthful," Cline said, "I been hoping on that." He drew a small black notebook from his pocket and licked a pencil stub. "Give you five to one. They's nobody gonna give no fairer odds than that."

He looked at Deke almost sadly. "But Tiny, he's just naturally better'n you, and that's all she wrote, boy. He lives for that goddamned game, ain't *got* nothing else. Can't get out of that goddamned chair. You think you can best a man who's fighting for his life, you are just lying to yourself."

Norman Rockwell's portrait of the colonel regarded Deke dispassionately from the Kentucky Fried across Richmond Road from the coffee bar. Deke held his cup with hands that were cold and trembling. His skull hummed with fatigue. Cline was right, he told the colonel. I can go up against

Tiny, but I can't win. The colonel stared back, gaze calm and level and not particularly kindly, taking in the coffee bar and Best Buy and all his drag-ass kingdom of Richmond Road. Waiting for Deke to admit to the terrible thing he had to do.

"The bitch is planning to leave me *anyway*," Deke said aloud. Which made the black countergirl look at him funny, then quickly away.

"Daddy called!" Nance danced into the apartment, slamming the door behind her. "And you know what? He says if I can get this job and hold it for six months, he'll have the brain-lock reversed. Can you *believe* it? Deke?" She hesitated. "You okay?"

Deke stood. Now that the moment was on him, he felt unreal, like he was in a movie or something. "How come you never came home last night?" Nance asked.

The skin on his face was unnaturally taut, a parchment mask. "Where'd you stash the hype, Nance? I need it."

"Deke," she said, trying a tentative smile that instantly vanished. "Deke, that's mine. My hit. I need it. For my in-terview."

He smiled scornfully. "You got money. You can always score another cap."

"Not by Friday! Listen, Deke, this is really important. My whole life is riding on this interview. I need that cap. It's all I got!"

"Baby, you got the fucking world! Take a look around you—six ounces of blond Lebanese hash! Little anchovy fish in tins. Unlimited medical coverage, if you need it." She was backing away from him, stumbling against the static waves of unwashed bedding and wrinkled glossy magazines that crested at the foot of her bed. "Me, I never had a glimmer of any of this. Never had the kind of edge it takes to get along. Well, this one time I am gonna. There is a match in two hours that I am going to fucking well win. Do you hear me?" He was working himself into a rage, and that was good. He needed it for what he had to do.

Nance flung up an arm, palm open, but he was ready for that and slapped her hand aside, never even catching a glimpse of the dark tunnel, let alone those little red eyes. Then they were both falling, and he was on top of her, her breath hot and rapid in his face. "Deke! Deke! I *need* that shit, Deke, my *interview*, it's the only...I gotta... gotta..." She twisted her face away... crying into the wall. "Please, God, please don't..."

"Where did you stash it?"

Pinned against the bed under his body, Nance began to spasm, her entire body convulsing in pain and fear.

"Where is it?"

Her face was bloodless, gray corpse flesh, and horror burned in her eyes. Her lips squirmed. It was too late to stop now; he'd crossed over the line. Deke felt revolted and nauseated, all the more so because on some unexpected and unwelcome level, he was *enjoying* this.

"Where is it, Nance?" And slowly, very gently, he began to stroke her face.

Deke summoned Jackman's elevator with a finger that moved as fast and straight as a hornet and landed daintily as a butterfly on the call button. He was full of bouncy energy, and it was all under control. On the way up, he whipped off his shades and chuckled at his reflection in the finger-smudged chrome. The blacks of his eyes were like pinpricks, all but invisible, and still the world was neon bright.

Tiny was waiting. The cripple's mouth turned up at the corners into a sweet smile as he took in Deke's irises, the exaggerated calm of his motions, the unsuccessful attempt to mine an undrugged clumsiness. "Well," he said in that girlish voice, "looks like I have a treat in store for me."

The Max was draped over one tube of the wheelchair. Deke took up position and bowed, not quite mockingly. "Let's fly." As challenger, he flew defense. He materialized his planes at a conservative altitude, high enough to dive, low enough to have warning when Tiny attacked. He waited.

The crowd tipped him. A fatboy with brilliantined hair looked startled, a hollow-eyed cracker started to smile. Murmurs rose. Eyes shifted slow-motion in heads frozen by hyped-up reaction time. Took maybe three nanoseconds to pinpoint the source of attack. Deke whipped his head up, and—

Sonofabitch, he was *blind!* The Fokkers were diving straight from the two-hundred-watt bulb, and Tiny had suckered him into staring right at it. His vision whited out. Deke squeezed lids tight over welling tears and frantically held visualization. He split his flight, curving two biplanes right, one left. Immediately twisting each a half-turn, then back again. He had to dodge randomly—he couldn't tell where the hostile warbirds were.

Tiny chuckled. Deke could hear him through the sounds of the crowd, the cheering and cursing and slapping down of coins that seemed to syncopate independent of the ebb and flow of the duel.

When his vision returned an instant later, a Spad was in flames and falling. Fokkers tailed his surviving planes, one on one and two on the other. Three seconds into the game and he was down one.

Dodging to keep Tiny from pinning tracers on him, he looped the single-pursued plane about and drove the other toward the blind spot between Tiny and the light bulb.

Tiny's expression went very calm. The faintest shadow

of disappointment—of contempt, even—was swallowed up by tranquility. He tracked the planes blandly, waiting for Deke to make his turn.

Then, just short of the blind spot, Deke shoved his Spad into a drive, the Fokkers overshooting and banking wildly to either side, twisting around to regain position.

The Spad swooped down on the third Fokker, pulled into position by Deke's other plane. Fire strafed wings and crimson fuselage. For an instant nothing happened, and Deke thought he had a fluke miss. Then the little red mother veered left and went down, trailing black, oily smoke.

Tiny frowned, small lines of displeasure marring the perfection of his mouth. Deke smiled. One even, and Tiny held position.

Both Spads were tailed closely. Deke swung them wide, and then pulled them together from opposite sides of the table. He drove them straight for each other, neutralizing Tiny's advantage . . . neither could fire without endangering his own planes. Deke cranked his machines up to top speed, slamming them at each other's nose.

An instant before they crashed, Deke sent the planes over and under one another, opening fire on the Fokkers and twisting away. Tiny was ready. Fire filled the air. Then one blue and one red plane soared free, heading in opposite directions. Behind them, two biplanes tangled in midair. Wings touched, slewed about, and the planes crumpled. They fell together, almost straight down, to the green felt below.

Ten seconds in and four planes down. A black vet pursed his lips and blew softly. Someone else shook his head in disbelief.

Tiny was sitting straight and a little forward in his wheelchair, eyes intense and unblinking, soft hands plucking feebly at the grips. None of that amused and detached bullshit now; his attention was riveted on the game. The kickers, the table, Jackman's itself, might not exist at all for him. Bobby Earl Cline laid a hand on his shoulder; Tiny didn't notice. The planes were at opposite ends of the room, laboriously gaining altitude. Deke jammed his against the ceiling, dim through the smoky haze. He spared Tiny a quick glance, and their eyes locked. Cold against cold. "Let's see your best," Deke muttered through clenched teeth.

They drove their planes together.

The hype was peaking now, and Deke could see Tiny's tracers crawling through the air between the planes. He had to put his Spad into the line of fire to get off a fair burst, then twist and bank so the Fokker's bullets would slip by his undercarriage. Tiny was every bit as hot, dodging Deke's fire and passing so close to the Spad their landing gears almost tangled as they passed.

Deke was looping his Spad in a punishingly tight turn when the hallucinations hit. The felt writhed and twisted— became the green hell of Bolivian rain forest that Tiny had flown combat over. The walls receded to gray infinity, and he felt the metal confinement of a cybernetic jumpjet close in around him.

But Deke had done his homework. He was expecting the hallucinations and knew he could deal with them. The military would never pass on a drug that couldn't be fought through. Spad and Fokker looped into another pass. He could read the tensions in Tiny Montgomery's face, the echoes of combat in deep jungle sky. They drove their planes together, feeling the torqued tensions that fed straight from instrumentation to hindbrain, the adrenaline pumps kicking in behind the armpits, the cold, fast freedom of airflow over jetskin mingling with the smells of hot metal and fear sweat. Tracers tore past his face, and he pulled back, seeing the Spad zoom by the Fokker again, both untouched. The kickers were just going ape, waving hats and stomping feet, acting like God's own fools. Deke locked glances with Tiny again.

Malice rose up in him, and though his every nerve was taut as the carbon-crystal whiskers that kept the jumpjets from falling apart in superman turns over the Andes, he counterfeited a casual smile and winked, jerking his head slightly to one side, as if to say "Looka here."

Tiny glanced to the side.

It was only for a fraction of a second, but that was enough. Deke pulled as fast and tight an Immelmann—right on the edge of theoretical tolerance—as had ever been seen on the circuit, and he was hanging on Tiny's tail.

Let's see you get out of this one, sucker.

Tiny rammed his plane straight down at the green, and Deke followed after. He held his fire. He had Tiny where he wanted him.

Running. Just like he'd been on his every combat mission. High on exhilaration and hype, maybe, but running scared. They were down to the felt now, flying treetop-level. Break, Deke thought, and jacked up the speed. Peripherally, he could see Bobby Earl Cline, and there was a funny look on the man's face. A pleading kind of look. Tiny's composure was shot; his face was twisted and tormented.

Now Tiny panicked and dove his plane in among the crowd. The biplanes looped and twisted between the kickers. Some jerked back involuntarily, and others laughingly swatted at them with their hands. But there was a hot glint of terror in Tiny's eyes that spoke of an eternity of fear and confinement, two edges sawing away at each other endlessly. . . .

The fear was death in the air, the confinement a locking away in metal, first of the aircraft, then of the chair. Deke could read it all in his face: Combat was the only out Tiny had had, and he'd taken it every chance he got. Until some anonymous *nationalista* with an antique SAM tore him out of that blue-green Bolivian sky and slammed him straight down to Richmond Road and Jackman's and the smiling killer boy he faced this one last time across the faded cloth.

Deke rocked up on his toes, face burning with that million-dollar smile that was the trademark of the drug that had already fried Tiny before anyone ever bothered to blow him out of the sky in a hot tangle of metal and mangled flesh. It all came together then. He saw that flying was all that held Tiny together. That daily brush of fingertips against death, and then rising up from the metal coffin, alive again. He'd been holding back collapse by sheer force of will. Break that willpower, and mortality would come pouring out and drown him. Tiny would lean over and throw up in his own lap.

And Deke drove it home . . .

There was a moment of stunned silence as Tiny's last plane vanished in a flash of light. "I did it," Deke whispered. Then, louder, "Son of a bitch, I did it!"

Across the table from him, Tiny twisted in his chair, arms jerking spastically; his head lolled over on one shoulder. Behind him, Bobby Earl Cline stared straight at Deke, his eyes hot coals.

The gambler snatched up the Max and wrapped its ribbon around a stack of laminateds. Without warning, he flung the bundle at Deke's face. Effortlessly, casually, Deke plucked it from the air.

For an instant, then, it looked like the gambler would come at him, right across the pool table. He was stopped by a tug on his sleeve. "Bobby Earl," Tiny whispered, his voice choking with humiliation, "you gotta get me . . . out of here. . . ."

Stiffly, angrily, Cline wheeled his friend around, and then away, into shadow.

Deke threw back his head and laughed. By God, he felt good! He stuffed the Max into a shirt pocket, where it hung cold and heavy. The money he crammed into his jeans. Man, he had to jump with it, his triumph leaping up through him like a wild thing, fine and strong as the flanks of a buck in the deep woods he'd seen from a Greyhound once, and for this one moment it seemed that everything was worth it somehow, all the pain and misery he'd gone through to finally win.

But Jackman's was silent. Nobody cheered. Nobody crowded around to congratulate him. He sobered, and silent, hostile faces swam into focus. Not one of these kickers was on his side. They radiated contempt, even hatred. For an interminably drawn-out moment the air trembled with potential violence ... and then someone turned to the side, hawked up phlegm, and spat on the floor. The crowd broke up, muttering, one by one drifting into the darkness.

Deke didn't move. A muscle in one leg began to twitch, harbinger of the coming hype crash. The top of his head felt numb, and there was an awful taste in his mouth. For a second he had to hang on to the table with both hands to keep from falling down forever, into the living shadow beneath him, as he hung impaled by the prize buck's dead eyes in the photo under the Dr. Pepper clock.

A little adrenaline would pull him out of this. He needed to celebrate. To get drunk or stoned and talk it up, going over the victory time and again, contradicting himself, making up details, laughing and bragging. A starry old night like this called for big talk.

But standing there with all of Jackman's silent and vast and empty around him, he realized suddenly that he had nobody left to tell it to.

Nobody at all.

GREEN DAYS IN BRUNEI

BY BRUCE STERLING

Two men were fishing from the corroded edge of an offshore oil rig. After years of decrepitude, the rig's concrete pillars were thick with barnacles and waving fronds of seaweed. The air smelled of rust and brine.

"Sorry to disturb your plans," the minister said. "But we can't just chat up the Yankees every time you hit a little contretemps." The minister reeled in and revealed a bare hook. He cursed mildly in his native Malay. "Hand me another bait, there's a good fellow."

Turner Choi reached into the wooden bait bucket and gave the minister a large dead prawn. "But I need that phone link," Turner said. "Just for a few hours. Just long enough to access the net in America and download some better documentation."

"What ghastly jargon," said the minister, who was formally known as the Yang Teramat Pehin Orang Kaya Amar Diraja Dato Seri Paduka Abdul Kahar. He was minister of industrial policy for the Sultanate of Brunei Darussalam, a tiny nation on the northern shore of the island of Borneo.

The titles of Brunei's aristocracy were in inverse proportion to the country's size.

"It'd save us a lot of time, Tuan Minister," Turner said. "Those robots are programmed in an obsolete language, forty years old. Strictly Neanderthal."

The minister deftly baited his hook and flicked it out in a long spinning cast. "You knew before you came here how the sultanate feels about the world information order. You shall just have to puzzle out this conundrum on your own,"

"But you're making weeks, months maybe, out of a three-hour job!" Turner said.

"My dear fellow, this is Borneo," the minister said benignly. "Stop looking at your watch and pay some attention to catching us dinner."

Turner sighed and reeled in his line. Behind them, the rig's squatter population of Dayak fisherfolk clustered on the old helicopter pad, mending nets and chewing betel-nut.

It was another slow Friday in Brunei Darussalam. Across the shallow bay, Brunei Town rose in tropical sunlight, its soaring high-rises festooned with makeshift solar roofs, windmills, and bulging greenhouse balconies. The golden-domed mosque on the waterfront was surrounded by the towering legacy of the twentieth-century oil boom: boxlike office blocks, now bizarrely transmuted into urban farms.

Brunei Town, the sultanate's capital, had a hundred thousand citizens: Malays, Chinese, Ibans, Dayaks, and a sprinkling of Europeans. But it was a city under a hush. No cars. No airport. No television. From a distance it reminded Turner of an old Western fairy tale: Sleeping Beauty, the jury-rigged high-rises with their cascading greenery like a hundred castles shrouded in thorns. The Bruneians seemed like sleeping-walkers, marooned from the world, wrapped in the enchantment of their ideology.

Turner baited his hook again, restive at being away from

the production line. The minister seemed more interested in converting him than in letting him work. To the Bruneians, the robots were just another useless memento of their long-dead romance with the West. The old robot assembly line hadn't been used in twenty years, since the turn of the century.

And yet the royal government had decided to retrofit the robot line for a new project. For technical help, they had applied to Kyocera, aJapanese multinational corporation. Kyocera had sent Turner Choi, one of their new recruits, a twenty-six-year-old Chinese Canadian CAD-CAM engineer from Vancouver.

It wasn't much of a job—a kind of industrial archeology whose main tools were chicken-wire and a ball-peen hammer—but it was Turner's first and he meant to succeed. The Bruneians were relaxed to the point of coma, but Turner Choi had his future ahead of him with Kyocera. In the long run, it was Kyocera who would judge his work here. And Turner was running out of time.

The minister, whooping in triumph, hauled hard on his line. A fat, spotted fish broke the surface, flopping on the hook. Turner decided to break the rules and to hell with it.

The local neighborhood organization, the *kampong*, was showing a free movie in the little park fourteen stories below Turner's window. Bright images crawled against the bleak white Bauhaus wall of a neighboring high-rise.

Turner peered down through the blinds. He had been watching the flick all night as he finished his illegal tinkering.

The Bruneians, like Malays everywhere, adored ghost stories. The film's protagonist, or chief horror (Turner wasn't sure which) was an acrobatic monkey-demon with razor-sharp forearms. It had burst into a depraved speakeasy and was slaughtering drunkards with a tremendous windmilling flurry of punches, kicks, and screeches. Vast meaty sounds of combat, like colliding freight trains packed with beef, drifted faintly upward.

Turner sat before his bootleg keyboard, and sighed. He'd known it would come to this ever since the Bruneians had confiscated his phone at the customs. For five months he'd politely tried to work his way around it. Now he had only three months left. He was out of time and out of patience.

The robots were okay, under caked layers of yellowing grease. They'd been roped down under tarps for years. But the software manuals were a tattered ruin.

Just thinking about it gave Turner a cold sinking feeling. It was a special, private terror that had dogged him since childhood. It was the fear he felt when he had to confront his grandfather.

He thought of his grandfather's icy and pitiless eyes, fixed on him with that "Hong Kong Bad Cop" look. In the 1970s, Turner's grandfather had been one of the infamous "millionaire sergeants" of the Hong Kong police, skimming the cream of the Burmese heroin trade. He'd emigrated in the Triad bribery scandals of 1973.

After forty-seven years of silk suits and first class flights between his mansions in Taipei and Vancouver, Grandfather Choi still had that cold eye and that grim shakedown look. It was an evil memory for Turner, of being weighed and found wanting.

The documentation was hopeless, crumbling and mildewed, alive with silverfish. The innocent Bruneians hadn't realized that the information it held was the linchpin of the whole enterprise. The sultanate had bought the factory long ago, with the last gush of Brunei's oil money, as a stylish, doomed gesture in Western industrial chic. Somehow, robots had never really caught on in Borneo.

But Turner had to seize this chance. He had to prove that he could make it on his own, without Grandfather Choi and the stifling weight of his money.

For days, Turner had snooped around down on the waterfront, with its cubbyholed rows of Chinese junkshops. It was Turner's favorite part of Brunei Town, a white-elephant's graveyard of dead tech. The wooden and bamboo shops were lined with dead, blackened televisions like decaying teeth.

There, he'd set about assembling a bootleg modern phone. He'd rescued a water-stained keyboard and screen from one of the shops. His modem and recorder came from work. On the waterfront he'd found a Panamanian freighter whose captain would illegally time-share on his satellite navigation dish.

Brunei Town was full of phone booths that no one ever seemed to use, grimy old glass-and-plastic units labeled in Malay, English, and Mandarin. A typical payphone stood on the street outside Turner's high-rise. It was an old twentieth-century job with a coin-feed and a rotary dial, and no video screen.

In the dead of night he'd crept down there to install a radio link to his apartment on the fourteenth floor. Someone might trace his illegal call back to the phone booth, but no farther. With the radio link, his own apartment would stay safe.

But when he'd punch-jacked the payphone's console off, he'd found that it already had a bootleg link hooked up. It was in fine working order, too. He'd seen then that he wasn't alone, and that Brunei, despite all its rhetoric about the Neo-Colonial World Information Order, was not entirely free of the global communications net. Brunei was wired too, just like the West, but the net had gone underground.

All those abandoned payphones had taken on a new and

mildly sinister significance for him since that discovery, but he wasn't going to kick. All his plans were riding on his chance to get through.

Now he was ready. He re-checked the satellite guide in the back ofhis ASME Handbook. Arabsat 7 was up, in its leisurely low-orbit ramble over the tropics. Turner dialed from his apartment down through the payphone outside, then patched in through the Panamanian dish. Through Arabsat he hooked up to an American geosynchronous sat and down into the American ground net. From there he direct-dialed his brother's house.

Georgie Choi was at breakfast in Vancouver, dressed in a French-cuffed pinstripe shirt and varsity sweater. Behind him, Turner's sleek sister-in-law, Marjorie, presided over a table crowded with crisp linen napkins and silver cutlery. Turner's two young nieces decorously spread jam on triangles of toast.

"Is it you, Turner?" Georgie said. "I'm not getting any video."

"I couldn't get a camera," Turner said. "I'm in Brunei— phone quarantine, remember? I had to bootleg it just to get sound."

A monsoon breeze blew up outside Turner's window. The windpower generators bolted to the high-rise walls whirred into life, and threw broad bars of raw static across the screen. Georgie's smooth brow wrinkled gracefully. "This reception is terrible! You're not even in stereo." He smiled uncertainly. "No matter, we'll make do. We haven't heard from you in ages. Things all right?"

"They will be," Turner said. "How's Grandfather?"

"He's flown in from Taipei for dialysis and his blood change," Georgie said. "He hates hospitals, but I had good news for him." He hesitated. "We have a new great-grandchild on the way."

Marjorie glanced up and bestowed one of her glittering wifely smiles on the camera. "That's fine," Turner said reflexively. Children were a touchy subject with Turner. He had not yet married, despite his family's endless prodding and nagging.

He thought guiltily that he should have spent more time with Georgie's children. Georgie was already in some upscale never-neverland, all leather-bound law and municipal politics, but it wasn't his kids' fault. Kids were innocent. "Hi kids," he said in Mandarin. "I'll bring you something you'll like."

The younger girl looked up, her elegant child's mouth crusted with strawberry jam. "I want a shrunken head," she said in English.

"You see?" Georgie said with false joviality. "This is what comes of running off to Borneo."

"I need some modem software," Turner said, avoiding the issue. Grandfather hadn't approved of Borneo. "Could you get it off the old Hayes in my room?"

"If you don't have a modem protocol, how can I send you a program?" Georgie said.

"Print it out and hold it up to the screen," Turner explained patiently. "I'll record it and type it in later by hand."

"That's clever," Georgie said. "You engineers."

He left to set it up. Turner talked guardedly to Marjorie. He had never been able to figure the woman out. Turner would have liked to know how Marjorie really felt about cold-eyed Bad Cop Grandfather and his eight million dollars in Triad heroin money.

But Marjorie was so coolly elegant, so brilliantly designed, that Turner had never been able to bring himself to probe her real feelings. It would have been like popping open some factory-sealed peripheral that was still under warranty, just so you could sneak a look at the circuit boards.

Even he and Georgie never talked frankly any more. Not since Grandfather's health had turned shaky. The prospect of finally inheriting that money had left a white hush over his family like fifteen feet of Canadian snow.

The horrible old man relished the competition for his favor. He insisted on it. Grandfather had a second household in Taipei; Turner's uncle and cousins. If Grandfather chose them over his Canadian brood, Georgie's perfect life would go to pieces.

A childhood memory brushed Turner: Georgie's toys, brightly painted little Hong Kong wind-ups held together with folded tin flaps. As a child, Turner had spent many happy, covert hours dexterously prying Georgie's toys apart.

Marjorie chatted about Turner's mother, a neurotic widow who ran an antique store in Atlanta. Behind her, a Chinese maid began clearing the table, glancing up at the camera with the spooked eyes of an immigrant fresh off the boat.

Turner was used to phone cameras, and though he didn't have one he kept a fixed smile through habit. But he could feel himself souring, his face knotting up in that inherited Bad Cop glare. Turner had his Grandfather's face, with hollow cheeks, and sunken eyes under heavy, impressive brows.

But Canada, Turner's birthplace, had left its mark on him. Years of steak and Wonder Bread had given him a six-foot frame and the build of a linebacker.

Georgie came back with the printout. Turner said goodbye and cut the link.

He pulled up the blinds for the climax of the movie downstairs. The monkey-demon massacred a small army of Moslem extremists in the corroded remnants of a Shell refinery. Moslem fanatics had been stock villains in Brunei since the failure of their coup of '98.

The last of the reel flickered loose. Turner unpinned a banana-leaf wrapping and dug his chopsticks into a midnight snack of rice fried with green pineapple. He leaned on the open window, propping one booted foot on the massive windowbox with its dense ranks of onions and pepper plants.

The call to Vancouver had sent a shiver of culture shock through him. He saw his apartment with new eyes. It was decorated with housewarming gifts from other members of his *kampong*. A flat leather shadow-puppet, all perforations and curlicues. A gold-framed photo of the sultan shaking hands with the king of England. A hand-painted glass ant farm full of inch-long Borneo ants, torpid on molasses. And a young banyan bonsai tree from the *kampong* headman.

The headman, an elderly Malay, was a political wardheeler for Brunei's ruling party, the Greens, or "Partai Ekolojasi." In the West, the Greens had long ago been co-opted into larger parties. But Brunei's Partai Ekolojasi had twenty years of deep roots.

The banyan tree came with five pages of meticulous instructions on care and feeding, but despite Turner's best efforts the midget tree was yellowing and shedding leaves. The tree was not just a gift; it was a test, and Turner knew it. The *kampong* smiled, but they had their ways of testing, and they watched.

Turner glanced reflexively at his deadbolt on the door. The locks were not exactly forbidden, but they were frowned on. The Greens had converted Brunei's old office buildings into huge multilayered village long-houses. Western notions of privacy were unpopular.

But Turner needed the lock for his work. He had to be

discreet. Brunei might seem loose and informal, but it was still a one-party state under autocratic rule.

Twenty years earlier, when the oil crash had hit, the monarchy had seemed doomed. The Muslim insurgents had tried to murder them outright. Even the Greens had had bigger dreams then. Turner had seen their peeling, forgotten wall posters, their global logo of the Whole Earth half-buried under layered years of want-ads and soccer schedules.

The Royal Family had won through, a symbol of tradition and stability. They'd weathered the storm of the Muslim insurgence, and stifled the Greens' first wild ambitions. After five months in Brunei, Turner, like the Royals, had grasped Brunei's hidden dynamics. It was *adat*, Malay custom, that ruled. And the first law of *adat* was that you didn't embarrass your neighbors.

Turner unpinned his favorite movie poster, a big promotional foursheet for a Brunei historical epic. In garish four-color printing, a boatload of heroic Malay pirates gallantly advanced on a sinister Portuguese galleon. Turner had carved a hideout in the sheetrock wall behind the poster. He stowed his phone gear.

Somebody tried the door, hit the deadbolt, and knocked softly. Turner hastily smoothed the poster and pinned it up.

He opened the door. It was his Australian neighbor, McGinty, a retired newscaster from Melbourne. McGinty loved Brunei for its utter lack of televisions. It was one of the last places on the planet in which one could truly get away from it all.

McGinty glanced up and down the hall, stepped inside, and reached into his loose cotton blouse. He produced a cold quart can of Foster's Lager. "Have a beer, chum?"

"Fantastic!" Turner said. "Where'd you get it?"

McGinty smiled evasively. "The bloody fridge is on the

blink, and I thought you'd fancy one while they're still cold."

"Right," Turner said, popping the top. "I'll have a look at your fridge as soon as I destroy this evidence." The *kampong* ran on a web of barter and mutual obligation. Turner's skills were part of it. It was tiresome, but a Foster's Lager was good pay. It was a big improvement over the liquid brain damage from the illegal stills down on Floor 4.

They went to McGinty's place. McGinty lived next door with his aged parents; four of them, for his father and mother had divorced and both remarried. The ancient Australians thrived in Brunei's somnolent atmosphere, pottering about the *kampong* gardens in pith helmets, gurkha shorts, and khaki bush vests. McGinty, like many of his generation, had never had children. Now in retirement he seemed content to shepherd these older folk, plying them with megavitamins and morning Tai Chi exercises.

Turner stripped the refrigerator. "It's your compressor," he said. "I'll track you down one on the waterfront. I can jury-rig something. You know me. Always tinkering."

McGinty looked uncomfortable, since he was now in Turner's debt. Suddenly he brightened. "There's a party at the privy councilor's tomorrow night. Jimmy Brooke. You know him?"

"Heard of him," Turner said. He'd heard rumors about Brooke: hints of corruption, some long-buried scandal. "He was a big man when the Partai got started, right? Minister of something."

"Communications."

Turner laughed. "That's not much of a job around here."

"Well, he still knows a lot of movie people." McGinty lowered his voice. "And he has a private bar. He's chummy with the Royal Family. They make allowances for him."

"Yeah?" Turner didn't relish mingling with McGinty's

social circle of wealthy retirees, but it might be smart, politically. A word with the old com minister might solve a
lot of his problems. "Okay," he said. "Sounds like fun."

The privy councilor, Yang Amat Mulia Pengiran Indera Ne-
gara Pengiran Jimmy Brooke, was one of Brunei's odder
relics. He was a British tax exile, a naturalized Bruneian,
who had shown up in the late '90s after the oil crash. His
wealth had helped cushion the blow and had won him a
place in the government.

Larger and better-organized governments might have
thought twice about co-opting this deaf, white-haired eccentric, a washed-up pop idol with a parasitic retinue of
balding bohemians. But the aging rock star, with his decaying glamor, fit in easily with the comic-opera glitter of Brunei's tiny aristocracy. He owned the old Bank of Singapore
office block, a *kampong* of remarkable looseness where pec-
cadillos flourished under Brooke's noblesse oblige.

Monsoon rain pelted the city. Brooke's henchmen,
paunchy bodyguards in bulging denim, had shut the glass
doors of the penthouse and turned on the air conditioning.
The party had close to a hundred people, mostly retired
Westerners from Europe and Australia. They had the stifling
clubbiness of exiles who have all known each other too
long. A handful of refugee Americans, still powdered and
rouged with their habitual video makeup, munched imported beer nuts by the long mahogany bar.

The Bruneian actress Dewi Serrudin was holding court
on a rattan couch, surrounded by admirers. Cinema was a
lost art in the West, finally murdered and buried by video;
but Brunei's odd policies had given it a last toe-hold. Turner,
who had a mild, long-distance crush on the actress, edged
up between two hopeful *émigrés:* a portly Madrasi producer

in dhoti and jubbah, and a Hong Kong chop-socky director in a black frogged cotton jacket.

Miss Serrudin, in a gold lamé blouse and a skirt of antique ultrasuede, was playing the role to the hilt, chattering brightly and chain-burning imported Rothmans in a jade holder. She had the ritual concentration of a Balinese dancer evoking postures handed down through the centuries. And she was older than he'd thought she was.

Turner finished his whiskey sour and handed it to one of Brooke's balding gofers. He felt depressed and lonely. He wandered away from the crowd, and turned down a hall at random. The walls were hung with gold albums and old, yellowing pub-shots of Brooke and his band, all rhinestones and platform heels, their flying hair lavishly backlit with klieg lights.

Turner passed a library, and a billiards room where two wrinkled, turbaned Sikhs were racking up a game of snooker. Further down the hall, he glanced through an archway, into a sunken conversation pit lavishly carpeted with ancient, indestructible synthetic plush.

A bony young Malay woman in black jeans and a satin jacket sat alone in the room, reading a month-old issue of NEW MUSICAL EXPRESS. It was headlined "Leningrad Pop Cuts Loose!" Her sandaled feet were propped on a coffee table next to a beaten silver platter with a pitcher and an ice-bucket on it. Her bright red, shoulder-length hair showed two long inches of black roots.

She looked up at him in blank surprise. Turner hesitated at the archway, then stepped into the room. "Hi," he said.

"Hello. What's your *kampong?*"

"Citibank Building," Turner said. He was used to the question by now. "I'm with the industrial ministry, consulting engineer. I'm a Canadian. Turner Choi."

She folded the newspaper and smiled. "Ah, you're the bloke who's working on the robots."

"Word gets around," Turner said, pleased.

She watched him narrowly. "Seria Bolkiah Mu'izzaddin Waddaulah."

"Sorry, I don't speak Malay."

"That's my name," she said.

Turner laughed. "Oh Lord. Look, I'm just a no-neck Canuck with hay in my hair. Make allowances, okay?"

"You're a Western technician," she said. "How exotic. How is your work progressing?"

"It's a strange assignment," Turner said. He sat on the couch at a polite distance, marveling at her bizarre accent. "You've spent some time in Britain?"

"I went to school there." She studied his face. "You look rather like a Chinese Keith Richards."

"Sorry, don't know him."

"The guitarist of the Rolling Stones."

"I don't keep up with the new bands;" Turner said. "A little Russian pop, maybe." He felt a peculiar tension in the situation. Turner glanced quickly at the woman's hands. No wedding ring, so that wasn't it.

"Would you like a drink?" the woman said. "It's grape juice."

"Sure," Turner said. "Thanks." She poured gracefully: innocent grape juice over ice. She was a Moslem, Turner thought, despite her dyed hair. Maybe that was why she was oddly standoffish.

He would have to bend the rules again. She was not conventionally pretty, but she had the kind of neurotic intensity that Turner had always found fatally attractive. And his love life had suffered in Brunei; the *kampongs* with their prying eyes and village gossip had cramped his style.

He wondered how he could arrange to see her. It wasn't

a question of just asking her out to dinner—it all depended on her *kampong*. Some were stricter than others. He might end up with half-a-dozen veiled Muslim chaperones—or maybe a gang of muscular cousins and brothers with a bad attitude about Western lechers.

"When do you plan to start production, Mr. Choi?"

Turner said, "We've built a few fishing skiffs already, just minor stuff. We have bigger plans once the robots are up."

"A real factory," she said. "Like the old days."

Turner smiled, seeing his chance. "Maybe you'd like a tour of the plant?"

"It sounds romantic," she said. "Those robots are free labor. They were supposed to take the place of our free oil when it ran out. Brunei used to be rich, you know. Oil paid for everything. The Shellfare state, they used to call us." She smiled wistfully.

"How about Monday?" Turner said.

She looked at him, surprised, and suddenly blushed. "I'm afraid not."

Turner caught her eye. It's not me, he thought. It was something in the way—*adat* or something. "It's all right," he said gently. "I'd like to see you, is that so bad? Bring your whole *kampong* if you want."

"My *kampong* is the Palace," she said.

"Uh-oh." Suddenly he had that cold feeling again.

"You didn't know," she said triumphantly. "You thought I was just some rock groupie."

"Who are you, then?"

"I'm the Duli Yang Maha Mulia Diranee . . . Well, I'm the princess. Princess Seria." She smiled.

"Good lord." He had been sitting and flirting with the royal princess of Brunei. It was bizarre. He half expected a troupe of bronzed eunuchs to burst in, armed with scimitars. "You're the sultan's daughter?"

"You mustn't think too much of it," she said. "Our country is only two thousand square miles. It's so small that it's a family business, that's all. The mayor of your Vancouver rules more people than my family does."

Turner sipped his grape juice to cover his confusion. Brunei was a Commonwealth country, after all, with a British-educated aristocracy. The sultan had polo ponies and cricket pitches. But still, a princess . . .

"I never said I was from Vancouver," he told her. "You knew who I was all along."

"Brunei doesn't have many tall Chinese in lumberjack shirts." She smiled wickedly. "And those boots."

Turner glanced down. His legs were armored in knee-high engineering boots, a mass of shiny leather and buckles: His mother had bought them for him, convinced that they would save his life from snakebite in savage Borneo. "I promised I'd wear them," he said. "Family obligation."

She looked sour. "You, too? That sounds all too familiar, Mr. Choi." Now that the spell of anonymity was broken, she seemed flustered. Their quick rapport was grinding to a halt. She lifted the music paper with a rustle of pages. He saw that her nails were gnawed down to the quick.

For some perverse reason this put Turner's libido jarringly back into gear. She had that edgy flyaway look that spelled trouble with a capital "T." Ironically, she was just his type.

"I know the mayor's daughter in Vancouver," he said deliberately. "I like the local version a lot better."

She met his eyes. "It's really too bad about family obligations. . . ."

The privy councilor appeared suddenly in the archway. The wizened rock star wore a cream-colored seersucker suit with ruby cufflinks. He was a cadaverous old buzzard with rheumy eyes and a wattled neck. A frizzed mass of snow-white hair puffed from his head like cotton from an aspirin bottle.

"Highness," he said loudly. "We need a fourth at bridge."

Princess Seria stood up with an air of martyrdom. "I'll be right with you," she shouted.

"And who's the young man?" said Brooke, revealing his dentures in an uneasy smile.

Turner stepped nearer. "Turner Choi, Tuan Privy Councilor," he said loudly. "A privilege to meet you, sir."

"What's your *kampong*, Mr. Chong?"

"Mr. Choi is working on the robot shipyard!" the princess said.

"The what? The shipyard? Oh, splendid." Brooke seemed relieved.

"I'd like a word with you, sir," Turner said. "About communications."

"About what?" Brooke cupped one hand to his ear.

"The phone net, sir! A line out!"

The princess looked startled. But Brooke, still not understanding, nodded blankly. "Ah yes. Very interesting . . . My entourage and I will bop by some day when you have the line up! I love the sound of good machines at work!"

"Sure," Turner said, recognizing defeat. "That would be, uh, groovy."

"Brunei is counting on you, Mr. Chong," Brooke said, his wrinkled eyes gleaming with bogus sincerity. "Good to see you here. Enjoy yourself." He shook Turner's hand, pressing something into his palm. He winked at Turner and escorted the Princess out into the hall.

Turner looked at his hand. The old man had given him

a marijuana cigarette. Turner shook himself, laughed, and threw it away.

Another slow Monday in Brunei Town. Turner's work crew meandered in around midmorning. They were Bruneian Chinese, toting wicker baskets stuffed with garden-fresh produce, and little lacquered lunchboxes with *satay* shishkabobs and hot shrimp paste. They started the morning's food barter, chatting languidly in Malay-accented Mandarin.

Turner had very little power over them. They were hired by the Industrial Ministry, and paid little or nothing. Their labor was part of the invisible household economy of the *kampongs*. They worked for *kampong* perks, like chickens or movie tickets.

The shipyard was a cavernous barn with overhead pulley tracks and an oil-stained concrete floor. The front section, with its bare launching rails sloping down to deep water, had once been a Dayak *kampong*. The Dayaks had spraybombed the concrete-block walls with giant neon-bright murals of banshees dead in childbirth, and leaping cricket-spirits with evil dayglo eyes.

The back part was two-story, with the robots' machine shop at ground level and a glass-fronted office upstairs that looked down over the yard.

Inside, the office was decorated in crass '80s High-Tech Moderne, with round-cornered computer desks between sleek modular partitions, all tubular chrome and grainy beige plastic. The plastic had aged hideously in forty years, absorbing a gray miasma of fingerprints and soot.

Turner worked alone in the neck-high maze of curved partitions, where a conspiracy of imported clerks and programmers had once efficiently sopped up the last of Brunei's oil money. He was typing up the bootlegged modem software on the IBM, determined to call America and get the production line out of the Stone Age.

The yard reeked of hot epoxy as the crew got to work. The robots were one-armed hydraulic jobs, essentially glorified tea-trolleys with single, swivel-jointed manipulators. Turner had managed to get them up to a certain crude level of donkey-work: slicing wood, stirring glue, hauling heavy bundles of lumber.

But, so far, the crew handled all the craft-work. They laminated the long strips of shaved lumber into sturdy panels of epoxied plywood. They bent the wet panels into hull and deck shapes, steam-sealing them over curved molds. They lapped and veneered the seams, and painted good-luck eye-symbols on the bows.

So far, the plant had produced nothing larger than a twenty-foot skiff. But on the drawing boards was a series of freighter-sized floating *kampongs*, massive sail-powered trimarans for the deep ocean, with glassed-in greenhouse decks.

The ships would be cheap and slow, like most things in Brunei, but pleasant enough, Turner supposed. Lots of slow golden afternoons on the tropical seas, with plenty of fresh fruit. The whole effort seemed rather pointless, but at least it would break Brunei's isolation from the world, and give them a crude merchant fleet.

The foreman, a spry old Chinese named Leng, shouted for Turner from the yard. Turner saved his program, got up, and looked down through the office glass. The minister of industrial policy had arrived, tying up an ancient fiberglass speedboat retrofitted with ribbed lateen sails.

Turner hurried down, groaning to himself, expecting to be invited off for another avuncular lecture. But the minister's zen-like languor had been broken. He came almost directly to the point, pausing only to genially accept some coconut milk from the foreman.

"It's His Highness the Sultan," the minister said. "Someone's put a bee in his bonnet about these robots. Now he wants to tour the plant."

"When?" Turner said.

"Two weeks," said the minister. "Or maybe three."

Turner thought it over, and smiled. He sensed the princess's hand in this and felt deeply flattered.

"I say," the minister said. "You seem awfully pleased for a fellow who was predicting disaster just last Friday."

"I found another section of the manual," Turner lied glibly. "I hope to have real improvements in short order."

"Splendid," said the minister. "You remember the prototype we were discussing?"

"The quarter-scale model?" Turner said. "Tuan Minister, even in miniature, that's still a fifty-foot trimaran."

"Righto. How about it? Do you think you could scatter the blueprints about, have the robots whir by looking busy, plenty of sawdust and glue?"

Politics, Turner thought. He gave the minister his Bad Cop look. "You mean some kind of Potemkin village. Don't you want the ship built?"

"I fail to see what pumpkins have to do with it," said the minister, wounded. "This is a state occasion. We shall have the newsreel cameras in. Of course build the ship. I simply want it impressive, that's all."

Impressive, Turner thought. Sure. If Seria was watching, why not?

Luckily the Panamanian freighter was still in port, not leaving till Wednesday. Armed with his new software, Turner tried another bootleg raid at ten P.M. He caught a Brazilian comsat and tied into Detroit.

Reception was bad, and Doris had already moved twice. But he found her finally in a seedy condominium in the Renaissance Center historical district.

"Where's your video, man?"

"It's out," Turner lied, not wanting to burden his old girlfriend with two years of past history. He and Doris had lived together in Toronto for two semesters, while he studied CAD-CAM. Doris was an automotive designer, a rust-belt refugee from Detroit's collapse.

For Turner, school was a blissful chance to live in the same pair of jeans for days on end, but times were tough in the Rust Belt and Doris had lived close to the bone. He'd ended up footing the bills, which hadn't bothered him (Bad Cop money), but it had preyed on Doris's mind. Months passed, and she spent more each week. He picked up her bills without a word, and she quietly went over the edge. She ended up puking drunk on her new satin sheets, unable to go downstairs for the mail without a line of coke.

But then word had come of his father's death. His father's antique. Maserati had slammed head-on into an automated semi-trailer rig. Turner and his brother had attended the cremation in a drizzling Vancouver rain. They put the ashes on the family altar and knelt before little gray ribbons of incense smoke. Nobody said much. They didn't talk about Dad's drinking. Grandfather wouldn't have liked it.

When he'd gone back to Toronto, he found that Doris had packed up and left.

"I'm with Kyocera now," he told her. "The consulting engineers,"

"You got a job, Turner?" she said, brushing back a frizzed tangle of blonde hair. "It figures. Poor people are standing in line for a chance to do dishes." She frowned.

"What kind of hours you keeping, man? It's seven A.M. You caught me without my vid makeup."

She turned the camera away and walked out of sight. Turner studied her apartment: concrete blocks and packing crates, vinyl beanbag chairs, peeling walls festooned with printout. She was still on the Net, all right. Real Net-heads resented every penny not spent on information.

"I need some help, Doris. I need you to find me someone who can system-crack an old IBM robotics language called AML."

"Yeah?" she called out. "Ten percent agent's fee?"

"Sure. And this is on the hush, okay? Not Kyocera's business, just mine."

He heard her shouting from the condo's cramped bathroom. "I haven't heard from you in two years! You're not mad that I split, huh?"

"No."

"It wasn't that you were Chinese, okay? I mean, you're about as Chinese as maple syrup, right? It's just, the high life was making my sinuses bleed."

Turner scowled. "Look, it's okay. It was a temporary thing."

"I was crazy then. But I've been hooked up to a good shrink program, it's done wonders for me, really." She came back to the screen; she'd put on rouge and powder. She smiled and touched her cheek. "Good stuff, huh? The kind the President uses."

"You look fine."

"My shrink makes me jog every day. So, how you doin', man? Seeing anybody?"

"Not really." He smiled. "Except a princess of Borneo."

She laughed. "I thought you'd settle down by now, man. With some uptown family girl, right? Like your brother and what's-her-face."

"Didn't work out that way."

"You like crazy women, Turner, that's your problem. Remember the time your mom dropped by? She's a fruit-cake, that's why."

"Aw, Jesus Christ, Doris," Turner said. "If I need a shrink, I can download one."

"Okay," she said, hurt. She touched a remote control. A television in the corner of the room flashed into life with a crackle of video music. Doris didn't bother to watch it. She'd turned it on by reflex, settling into the piped flow of cable like a hot bath. "Look, I'll see what I can scare you up on the Net. AML language, right? I think I know a—"

BREAK.

The screen went blank. Alphanumerics flared up: EN-TERING (C) HAT MODE

The line zipped up the screen. Then words spelled out in 80-column, glowing bright green. WHAT ARE YOU DO-ING ON THIS LINE??

SORRY, Turner typed.

ENTER YOUR PASSWORD:

Turner thought fast. He had blundered into the Brunei underground net. He'd known it was possible, since he was using the pre-rigged payphone downstairs. MAPLE SYRUP, he typed at random.

CHECKING. . . . THAT IS NOT A VALID PASSWORD.

SIGNING OFF, Turner typed.

WAIT, said the screen. WE DON'T TAKE LURKERS LIGHTLY HERE. WE HAVE BEEN WATCHING YOU. THIS IS THE SECOND TIME YOU HAVE ACCESSED A SATELLITE. WHAT ARE YOU DOING IN OUR NET??

Turner rested one finger on the off switch.

More words spilled out. WE KNOW WHO YOU ARE, "MAPLE SYRUP." YOU ARE TURNER CHONG.

"Turner *Choi*," Turner said aloud. Then he remembered

the man who had made that mistake. He felt a sudden surge of glee. He typed: OKAY, YOU'VE GOT ME—TUAN COUNCILOR JIMMY BROOKE!

There was a long blank space. Then: CLEVER, Brooke typed. SERIA TOLD YOU. SERIA, ARE YOU ON THIS LINE??

I WANT HER NUMBER!! Turner typed at once.

THEN LEAVE A (M)ESSAGE FOR "GAMELAN ROCKER," Brooke typed. I AM "NET HEADHUNTER."

THANKS, Turner typed.

I'LL LOG YOU ON, MAPLE SYRUP. SINCE YOU'RE ALREADY IN, YOU'D BETTER BE IN ON OUR TERMS. BUT JUST REMEMBER: THIS IS OUR ELECTRIC KAMPONG, SO YOU LIVE BY OUR RULES. OUR "ADAT," OKAY?

I'LL REMEMBER, SIR.

AND NO MORE BOOTLEG SATELLITE LINKS, YOU'RE SCREWING UP OUR GROUND LINES.

OKAY, Turner typed.

YOU CAN RENT TIME ON OUR OWN DISHES. NEXT TIME CALL 85-1515 DIRECTLY. OUR GAMES SECTION COULD USE SOME UPLOADS, BY THE WAY.

The words flashed off, replaced by the neatly ranked commands of a computer bulletin board. Turner accessed the message section, but then sat sweating and indecisive. In his mind, his quick message to Seria was rapidly ramifying into a particularly touchy and tentative love letter.

This was good, but it wasn't how he'd planned it. He was getting in over his head. He'd have to think it through.

He logged off the board. Doris's face appeared at once. "Where the hell have you been, man?"

"Sorry," Turner said.

"I've found you some old geezer out in Yorktown Heights," she said. "He says he used to work with Big Blue back in prehistory."

"It's always some old geezer," Turner said in resignation.

Doris shrugged. "Whaddya expect, man? Birth control got everybody else."

Down in the yard, the sultan of Brunei chatted with his minister as technicians in sarongs and rubber sandals struggled with their huge, ancient cameras. The sultan wore his full regalia, a high-collared red military jacket with gold-braided shoulderboards, heavy with medals and pins. He was an elderly Malay with a neatly clipped white mustache and sad, wise eyes.

His son, the crown prince, had a silk ascot and an air force pilot's jacket. Turner had heard that the prince was nuts about helicopters. Seria's formal wear looked like a jazzed-up Girl Guide's outfit, with a prim creased skirt and a medal-clustered shoulder-sash.

Turner was alone in the programming room, double-checking one of the canned routines he's downloaded from America. They'd done wonders for the plant already; the robots had completed one hull of the trimaran. The human crew was handling the delicate work: the glassed-in greenhouse. Braced sections of glass now hung from ceiling pulleys, gleaming photogenically in geodesic wooden frames.

Turner studied his screen.

IF QMONITOR(FMONS(2)) EQ O THEN RETURN('TOO SMALL')

TOGO = GRIPPER-OPENING + MIN-OFS-QPOSITION-(GRIPPER)

DMOVE(XYZ#(GRIPPER),   (−TOGO/2*HANDFRAME)(2,2))#(TOGO), FMONS(2));

This was more like it! Despite its low-powered crudity, AML was becoming obsessive with him, its rhythms sticking like poetry. He picked up his coffee-cup, thinking: REACH-GRASP-TOGO = (MOUTH) + SIP; RETURN.

The sluggishness of Brunei had vanished overnight once

he'd hooked to the Net. The screen had eaten up his life. A month had passed since his first bootleg run. All day he worked on AML; at night he went home to trade electronic mail with Seria.

Their romance had grown through the Net; not through modern video, but through the ancient bulletin board's anonymous green text. Day by day it became more intense, for it was all kept in a private section of memory, and nothing could be taken back. There were over a hundred messages on their secret disks, starting coolly and teasingly, and working slowly up through real passion to a kind of mutual panic.

They hadn't planned it to happen like this. It was part of the dynamic of the Net. For Seria, it had been a rare chance to escape her role and talk to an interesting stranger. Turner was only looking for the kind of casual feminine solace that had never been hard to find. The Net had tricked them.

Because they couldn't see each other. Turner realized now that no woman had ever known and understood him as Seria did, for the simple reason that he had never had to talk to one so much. If things had gone as they were meant to in the West, he thought, they would have chased their attraction into bed and killed it there. Their two worlds would have collided bruisingly, and they would have smiled over the orange juice next morning and mumbled tactful goodbyes.

But that wasn't how it had happened. Over the weeks, it had all come pouring out between them: his family, her family, their resentment, his loneliness, her petty constraints, all those irritants that ulcerate a single person, but are soothed by two. Bizarrely, they had more in common than he could have ever expected. Real things, things that mattered.

The painfully simple local Net filtered human relations down to a single channel of printed words, leaving only a high-flown Platonic essence. Their relationship had grown into a classic, bloodless, spiritual romance in its most intense and dangerous sense. Human beings weren't meant to live such roles. It was the stuff of high drama because it could very easily drive you crazy.

He had waited on tenterhooks for her visit to the shipyard. It had taken a month instead of two weeks, but he'd expected as much. That was the way of Brunei.

"Hello, Maple Syrup."

Turner started violently and stood up. "Seria!"

She threw herself into his arms with a hard thump. He staggered back, hugging her. "No kissing," she said hastily. "Ugh, it's nasty."

He glanced down at the shipyard and hauled her quickly out of sight of the window. "How'd you get up here?"

"I sneaked up the stairs. They're not looking. I had to see you. The real you, not just words on a screen."

"This is crazy." He lifted her off the ground, squeezing her hard. "God, you feel wonderful."

"So do you. Ouch, my medals, be careful."

He set her back down. "We've got to do better than this. Look, where can I see you?"

She gripped his hands feverishly. "Finish the boat, Turner. Brooke wants it, his new toy. Maybe we can arrange something." She pulled his shirt tail out and ran her hands over his midriff. Turner felt a rush of arousal so intense that his ears rang. He reached down and ran his hand up the back of her thigh. "Don't wrinkle my skirt!" she said, trembling. "I have to go on camera!"

Turner said, "This place is nowhere. It isn't right for you, you need fast cars and daiquiris and television and jet trips to the goddamn Bahamas."

"So romantic," she whispered hotly. "Like rock stars, Turner. Huge stacks of amps and mobs at the airport. Turner, if you could see what I'm wearing under this, you'd go crazy."

She turned her face away. "Stop trying to kiss me! You Westerners are weird. Mouths are for eating."

"You've got to get used to Western things, precious."

"You can't take me away, Turner. My people wouldn't let you."

"We'll think of something. Maybe Brooke can help."

"Even Brooke can't leave," she said. "All his money's here. If he tried, they would freeze his funds. He'd be penniless."

"Then I'll stay here," he said recklessly. "Sooner or later we'll have our chance."

"And give up all your money, Turner?"

He shrugged. "You know I don't want it."

She smiled sadly. "You tell me that now, but wait till you see your real world again."

"No, listen—"

Lights flashed on in the yard.

"I have to go, they'll miss me. Let go, let go." She pulled free of him with vast, tearing reluctance. Then she turned and ran.

In the days that followed, Turner worked obsessively, linking subroutines like data tinkertoys, learning as he went along, adding each day's progress to the master program. Once it was all done, and he had weeded out the redundance, it would be self-sustaining. The robots would take over, transforming information into boats. He would be through. And his slow days in Brunei would be history.

After his job, he'd vaguely planned to go to Tokyo, for a sentimental visit to Kyocera corporate headquarters. He'd been recruited through the Net; he'd never actually seen anyone from Kyocera in the flesh.

That was standard practice. Kyocera's true existence was as data, not as real estate. A modern multinational company was not its buildings or its stock. Its real essence was its ability to pop up on a screen, and to funnel that special information known as money through the global limbo of electronic banking.

He'd never given this a second thought. It was old hat. But filtering both work and love-life through the screen had left him feeling Netburned. He took to long morning walks through Brunei Town after marathon sessions at the screen, stretching cramped muscles and placing his feet with a dazed AML deliberation: TOGO = DMOVE(KNEE) + QPOSITION(FOOT).

He felt ghostlike in the abandoned streets; Brunei had no nightlife to speak of, and a similar lack of muggers and predators. Everybody was in everyone else's lap, doing each other's laundry, up at dawn to the shrieks of *kampong* roosters. People gossiped about you if you were a mugger. Pretty soon you'd have nightsoil duty and have to eat bruised mangos.

When the rain caught him, as it often did in the early morning, he would take shelter in the corner bus stations. The bus stops were built of tall glass tubes, aquaculture cylinders, murky green soups full of algae and fat, sluggish carp.

He would think about staying then, sheltered in Brunei forever, like a carp behind warm glass. Like one of those little bonsai trees in its cramped and cosy little pot, with people always watching over you, trimming you to fit. That was Brunei for you: the whole East, really: wonderful community, but people always underfoot and in your face. . . .

But was the West any better? Old people locked away

in bursting retirement homes . . . Soaring unemployment, with no one knowing when some robot or expert system would make him obsolete . . . People talking over televisions when they didn't know the face of the man next door. . . .

Could he really give up the West, he wondered, abandon his family, ruin his career? It was the craziest sort of romantic gesture, he thought, because even if he was brave or stupid enough to break all the rules, she wouldn't. Seria would never escape her *adat*. Being royalty was worse than Triad.

A maze of plans spun through his head like an error-trapping loop, always coming up empty. He would sit dazedly and watch the fish circle in murky water, feeling like a derelict, and wondering if he was losing his mind.

Privy Councilor Brooke bought the boat. He showed up suddenly at the shipyard one afternoon, with his claque of followers. They'd brought a truckload of saplings in tubs of dirt. They began at once to load them aboard the greenhouse, clumping up and down the stepladders to the varnished deck.

Brooke oversaw the loading for a while, checking a deck plan from the pocket of his white silk jacket. Then he jerked his thumb at the glassed-in front of the data center. "Let's go upstairs for a little talk, Turner."

Mercifully, Brooke had brought his hearing aid. They sat in two of the creaking, musty swivel-chairs. "It's a good ship," Brooke said.

"Thanks."

"I knew it would be. It was my idea, you know."

Turner poured coffee. "It figures," he said.

Brooke cackled. "You think it's a crazy notion, don't you? Using robots to build tubs out of cheap glue and scrubwood. But your head's on backwards, boy. You engineers are all mystics. Always goosing God with some new Tower of Babel. Masters of nature, masters of space and time. Aim at the stars, and hit London."

Turner scowled. "Look, Tuan Councilor, I did my job. Nothing in the contract says I have to share your politics."

"No," Brooke said. "But the sultanate could use a man like you. You're a *bricoleur*, Chong. You can make do. You can retrofit. That's what *bricolage* is—it's using the clutter and rubble to make something worth having. Brunei's too poor now to start over with fresh clean plans. We've got nothing but the junk the West conned us into buying, every last bloody Coke can and two-car garage. And now we have to live in the rubble, and make it a community. It's a tough job, *bricolage*. It takes a special kind of man, a special eye, to make the ruins bloom."

"Not me," Turner said. He was in one of his tough-minded moods. Something about Brooke made him leery. Brooke had a peculiar covert sleaziness about him. It probably came from a lifetime of evading drug laws.

And Turner had been expecting this final push; people in his *kampong* had been dropping hints for weeks. They didn't want him to leave; they were always dropping by with pathetic little gifts. "This place is one big hothouse," he said. "Your little *kampongs* are like orchids, they can only grow under glass. Brunei's already riddled with the Net. Someday it'll break open your glass bubble, and let the rest of the world in. Then a hard rain's gonna fall."

Brooke stared. "You like Bob Dylan?"

"Who?" Turner said, puzzled.

Brooke, confused, sipped his coffee, and grimaced. "You've been drinking this stuff? Jesus, no wonder you never sleep."

Turner glowered at him. Nobody in Brunei could mind

their own business. Eyes were everywhere, with tongues to match. "You already know my real trouble."

"Sure." Brooke smiled with a yellowed gleam of dentures. "I have this notion that I'll sail upriver, lad. A little shakedown cruise for a couple of days. I could use a technical adviser; if you can mind your manners around royalty."

Turner's heart leapt. He smiled shakily. "Then I'm your man, Councilor."

They bashed a bottle of nonalcoholic grape juice across the center bow and christened the ship the *Mambo Sun*. Turner's work crew launched her down the rails and stepped the masts. She was crewed by a family of Dayaks from one of the offshore rigs, an old woman with four sons. They were the dark, beautiful descendants of headhunting pirates, dressed in hand-dyed sarongs and ancient plastic baseball caps. Their language was utterly incomprehensible.

The *Mambo Sun* rode high in the water, settling down into her new element with weird drumlike creaks from the hollow hulls. They put out to sea in a stiff offshore breeze.

Brooke stood with spry insouciance under the towering jib sail, snorting at the sea air. "She'll do twelve knots," he said with satisfaction. "Lord, Turner, it's great to be out of the penthouse and away from that crowd of flacks."

"Why do you put up with them?"

"It comes with the money, lad. You should know that."

Turner said nothing. Brooke grinned at him knowingly. "Money's power, my boy. Power doesn't go away. If you don't use it yourself, someone else will use you to get it."

"I hear they've trapped you here with that money," Turner said. "They'll freeze your funds if you try to leave."

"I let them trap me," Brooke said. "That's how I won their trust." He took Turner's arm. "But you let me know if you have money troubles here. Don't let the local Islamic Bank fast-talk you into anything. Come see me first."

Turner shrugged him off. "What good has it done you? You're surrounded with yes-men."

"I've had my crew for forty years." Brooke sighed nostalgically. "Besides, you should have seen them in '98, when the streets were full of Moslem fanatics screaming for blood. Molotovs burning everywhere, pitched battles with the blessed Chinese, the sultan held hostage. . . . My crew didn't turn a hair. Held the mob off like a crowd of teenyboppers when they tried to rush my building. They had grit, those lads."

An ancient American helicopter buzzed overhead, its orange seafloats almost brushing the mast. Brooke yelled to the crew in their odd language; they furled the sails and set anchor, half a mile offshore. The chopper wheeled expertly and settled down in a shimmering circle of wind-flattened water. One of the Dayaks threw them a weighted line.

They hauled in. "Permission to come aboard, sir!" said the crown prince. He and Seria wore crisp nautical whites. They clambered from the float up a rope ladder and onto the deck. The third passenger, a pilot, took the controls. The crew hauled anchor and set sail again; the chopper lifted off.

The prince shook Turner's hand. "You know my sister, I believe."

"We met at the filming," Turner said.

"Ah yes. Good footage, that."

Brooke, with miraculous tact, lured the prince into the greenhouse. Seria immediately flung herself into Turner's arms. "You haven't written in two days," she hissed.

"I know," Turner said. He looked around quickly to make sure the Dayaks were occupied. "I keep thinking about Vancouver. How I'll feel when I'm back there."

"How you left your Sleeping Beauty behind in the castle of thorns? You're such a romantic, Turner."

"Don't talk like that. It hurts."

She smiled. "I can't help being cheerful. We have two days together, and Omar gets seasick."

The river flowed beneath their hulls like thin gray grease. Jungle leaned in from the banks; thick, clotted green mats of foliage over skinny, light-starved trunks, rank with creepers. It was snake country, leech country, a primeval reek stewing in deadly humidity, with air so thick that the raucous shrieks of birds seemed to cut it like ripsaws. Bugs whirled in dense mating swarms over rafts of slime. Suspicious, sodden logs loomed in the gray mud. Some logs had scales and eyes.

The valley was as crooked as an artery, snaking between tall hills smothered in poisonous green. Sluggish wads of mist wreathed their tops. Where the trees failed, sheer cliffs were shrouded in thick ripples of ivy. The sky was gray, the sun a muddy glow behind tons of haze.

The wind died, and Brooke fired up the ship's tiny alcohol engine. Turner stood on the central bow as they sputtered upstream. He felt glazed and dreamy. Culture shock had seized him; none of it seemed real. It felt like television. Reflexively, he kept thinking of Vancouver, sailboat trips out to clean pine islands.

Seria and the prince joined him on the bow. "Lovely, isn't it?" said the prince. "We've made it a game preserve. Someday there will be tigers again."

"Good thinking, Your Highness," Turner said.

"The city feeds itself, you know. A lot of the old paddies and terraces have gone back to jungle." The prince smiled with deep satisfaction.

With evening, they tied up at a dock by the ruins of a

riverine city. Decades earlier, a flood had devastated the town, leaving shattered walls, where vines snaked up trellises of rusting reinforcement rods. A former tourist hotel was now a ranger station.

They all went ashore to review the troops: Royal Malay Rangers in jungle camo, and a visiting crew of Swedish ecologists from the World Wildlife Fund. The two aristocrats were gung-ho for a bracing hike through the jungle. They chatted amiably with the Swedes as they soaked themselves with gnat and leech repellent. Brooke pleaded his age, and Turner managed to excuse himself.

Behind the city rose a soaring radio aerial and the rain-blotched white domes of satellite dishes.

"Jamming equipment," said Brooke with a wink. "The sultanate set it up years ago. Islamic, Malaysian, Japanese—you'd be surprised how violently people insist on being listened to."

"Freedom of speech," Turner said.

"How free is it when only rich nations can afford to talk? The Net's expensive, Turner. To you it's a way of life, but for us it's just a giant megaphone for Coca-Cola. We built this to block the shouting of the outside world. It seemed best to set the equipment here in the ruins, out of harm's way. This is a good place to hide secrets." Brooke sighed. "You know how the corruption spreads. Anyone who touches it is tempted. We use these dishes as the nerve center of our own little Net. You can get a line out here—a real one, with video. Come along, Turner. I'll stand Maple Syrup a free call to civilization, if you like."

They walked through leaf-littered streets, where pigs and lean, lizard-eyed chickens scattered from underfoot. Turner saw a tattooed face, framed in headphones, at a shattered second-story window. "The local Murut tribe," Brooke said, glancing up. "They're a bit shy."

The central control room was a small white concrete blockhouse surrounded by sturdy solar-panel racks. Brooke opened a tarnished padlock with a pocket key, and shot the bolt. Inside, the windowless blockhouse was faintly lit by the tiny green and yellow power-lights of antique disk drives and personal computers. Brooke flicked on a desk lamp and sat on a chair cushioned with moldy foam rubber. "All automated, you see? The government hasn't had to pay an official visit in years. It keeps everyone out of trouble."

"Except for your insiders," Turner said.

"We *are* trouble," said Brooke. "Besides, this was my idea in the first place." He opened a musty wicker chest and pulled a video camera from a padded wrapping of cotton batik. He popped it open, sprayed its insides with silicone lubricant, and propped it on a tripod. "All the comforts of home." He left the blockhouse.

Turner hesitated. He'd finally realized what had bothered him about Brooke. Brooke was *hip*. He had that classic hip attitude of being in on things denied to the uncool. It was amazing how sleazy and suspicious it looked on someone who was *really old*.

Turner dialed his brother's house. The screen remained dark. "Who is it?" Georgie said.

"Turner."

"Oh." A long moment passed; the screen flashed on to show Georgie in a maroon silk houserobe, his hair still flattened from the pillow. "That's a relief. We've been having some trouble with phone flashers."

"How are things?"

"He's dying, Turner."

Turner stared. "Good God."

"I'm glad you called." Georgie smoothed his hair shakily. "How soon can you get here?"

"I've got a job here, Georgie."

Georgie frowned. "Look, I don't blame you for running. You wanted to live your own life; okay, that's fine. But this is *family business*, not some two-bit job in the middle of nowhere."

"Goddammit," Turner said, pleading, "I *like* it here, Georgie."

"I know how much you hate the old bastard. But he's just a dying old man now. Look, we hold his hands for a couple of weeks, and it's all ours, understand? The Riviera, man."

"It won't work, Georgie," Turner said, clutching at straws. "He's going to screw us."

"That's why I need you here. We've got to double-team him, understand?" Georgie glared from the screen. "Think of my kids, Turner. We're your family, you owe us."

Turner felt growing despair. "Georgie, there's a woman here..."

"Christ, Turner."

"She's not like the others. Really."

"Great. So you're going to marry this girl, right? Raise kids."

"Well..."

"Then what are you wasting my time for?"

"Okay," Turner said, his shoulders slumping. "I gotta make arrangements. I'll call you back."

The Dayaks had gone ashore. The prince blithely invited the Swedish ecologists on board. They spent the evening chastely sipping orange juice and discussing Krakatoa and the swamp rhinoceros.

After the party broke up, Turner waited a painful hour and crept into the deserted greenhouse.

Seria was waiting in the sweaty green heat, sitting cross-legged in watery moonlight crosshatched by geodesics, brushing her hair. Turner joined her on the mat. She wore an erotic red synthetic nightie (some groupie's heirloom from the legion of Brooke's women), crisp with age. She was drenched in perfume.

Turner touched her fingers to the small lump on his forearm, where a contraceptive implant showed beneath his skin. He kicked his jeans off.

They began in caution and silence, and ended, two hours later, in the primeval intimacy of each other's musk and sweat. Turner lay on his back, with her head pillowed on his bare arm, feeling a sizzling effervescence of deep, cellular pleasure.

It had been mystical. He felt as if some primal feminine energy had poured off her body and washed through him, to the bone. Everything seemed different now. He had discovered a new world, the kind of world a man could spend a lifetime in. It was worth ten years of a man's life just to lie here and smell her skin.

The thought of having her out of arm's reach, even for a moment, filled him with a primal anxiety close to pain. There must be a million ways to make love, he thought languidly. As many as there are to talk or think. With passion. With devotion. Playfully, tenderly, frantically, soothingly. Because you want to, because you need to.

He felt an instinctive urge to retereat to some snug den—anywhere with a bed and a roof—and spend the next solid week exploring the first twenty or thirty ways in that million.

But then the insistent pressure of reality sent a trickle of reason into him. He drifted out of reverie with a stabbing conviction of the perversity of life. Here was all he wanted—all he asked was to pull her over him like a blanket and shut out life's pointless complications. And it wasn't going to happen.

He listened to her peaceful breathing and sank into black depression. This was the kind of situation that called for wild romantic gestures, the kind that neither of them were going to make. They weren't allowed to make them. They weren't in his program, they weren't in her *adat*, they weren't in the plans.

Once he'd returned to Vancouver, none of this would seem real. Jungle moonlight and erotic sweat didn't mix with cool piny fogs over the mountains and the family mansion in Churchill Street. Culture shock would rip his memories away, snapping the million invisible threads that bind lovers.

As he drifted toward sleep, he had a sudden lucid flash of precognition: himself, sitting in the back seat of his brother's Mercedes, letting the machine drive him randomly around the city. Looking past his reflection in the window at the clotted snow in Queen Elizabeth Park, and thinking: *I'll never see her again.*

It seemed only an instant later that she was shaking him awake. "Shh!"

"What?" he mumbled.

"You were talking in your sleep." She nuzzled his ear, whispering. "What does 'Set-position Q-move' mean?"

"Jesus," he whispered back. "I was dreaming in AML." He felt the last fading trail of nightmare then, some unspeakable horror of cold iron and helpless repetition. "My family," he said. "They were all robots."

She giggled.

"I was trying to repair my grandfather."

"Go back to sleep, darling."

"No." He was wide awake now. "We'd better get back."

"I hate that cabin. I'll come to your tent on deck."

"No, they'll find out. You'll get hurt, Seria." He stepped back into his jeans.

"I don't care. This is the only time we'll have." She struggled fretfully into the red tissue of her nightie.

"I want to be with you," he said. "If you could be mine, I'd say to hell with my job and my family."

She smiled bitterly. "You'll think better of it, later. You can't throw away your life for the sake of some affair. You'll find some other woman in Vancouver. I wish I could kill her."

Every word rang true, but he still felt hurt. She shouldn't have doubted his willingness to totally destroy his life. "You'll marry too, someday. For reasons of state."

"I'll never marry," she said aloofly. "Someday I'll run away from all this. My grand romantic gesture."

She would never do it, he thought with a kind of aching pity. She'll grow old under glass in this place. "One grand gesture was enough," he said. "At least we had this much."

She watched him gloomily. "Don't be sorry you're leaving, darling. It would be wrong of me to let you stay. You don't know all the truth about this place. Or about my family."

"All families have secrets. Yours can't be any worse than mine."

"My family is different." She looked away. "Malay royalty are sacred, Turner. Sacred and unclean. We are aristocrats, shields for the innocent. . . . Dirt and ugliness strikes the shield, not our people. We take corruption on ourselves. Any crimes the State commits are our crimes, understand? They belong to our family."

Turner blinked. "Well, what? Tell me, then. Don't let it come between us."

"You're better off not knowing. We came here for a reason, Turner. It's a plan of Brooke's."

"That old fraud?" Turner said, smiling. "You're too romantic about Westerners, Seria. He looks like hot stuff to you, but he's just a burnt-out crackpot."

She shook her head. "You don't understand. It's different in your West." She hugged her slim legs and rested her chin on her knee. "Someday I will get out."

"No," Turner said, "it's *here* that it's different. In the West families disintegrate, money pries into everything. People don't belong to each other there, they belong to money and their institutions ... Here at least people really care and watch over each other ..."

She gritted her teeth. "Watching. Yes, always. You're right, I have to go."

He crept back through the mosquito netting of his tent on deck, and sat in the darkness for hours, savoring his misery. Tomorrow the prince's helicopter would arrive to take the prince and his sister back to the city. Soon Turner would return as well, and finish the last details, and leave. He played out a fantasy: cruising back from Vanc with a fat cashier's check. Tea with the sultan. *Er, look, Your Highness, my granddad made it big in the heroin trade, so here's two mill. Just pack the girl up in excelsior, she'll love it as an engineer's wife, believe me. . . .*

He heard the faint shuffle of footsteps against the deck. He peered through the tentflap, saw the shine of a flashlight. It was Brooke. He was carrying a valise.

The old man looked around surreptitiously and crept down over the side, to the dock. Weakened by hours of brooding, Turner was instantly inflamed by Brooke's deviousness. Turner sat still for a moment, while curiosity and misplaced fury rapidly devoured his common sense. Common sense said Brunei's secrets were none of his business, but common sense was making his life hell. Anything was better than staying awake all night wondering. He struggled quickly into shirt and jeans and boots.

He crept over the side, spotted Brooke's white suit in a patch of moonlight, and followed him. Brooke skirted the edge of the ruins, and took a trail into the jungle; full of ominous vines and the promise of snakes. Beneath a spongy litter of leaves and moss, the trail was asphalt. It had been a highway, once.

Turner shadowed Brooke closely; realizing gratefully that the deaf old man couldn't hear the crunching of his boots. The trail led uphill, into the interior. Brooke cursed goodnaturedly as a group of grunting hogs burst across the trail. Half a mile later he rested for ten long minutes in the rusting hulk of a Land Rover, while vicious gnats feasted on Turner's exposed neck and hands.

They rounded a hill and came across an encampment. Faint moonlight glittered off twelve-foot barbed wire and four dark watchtowers. The undergrowth had been burned back for yards around. There were barracks inside.

Brooke walked nonchalantly to the gate. The place looked dead. Turner crept nearer, sheltered by darkness.

The gate opened. Turner crawled forward between two bushes, craning his neck.

A watchtower spotlight clacked on and framed him in dazzling light from forty yards away. Someone shouted at him through a bullhorn, in Malay. Turner lurched to his feet, blinded, and put his hands high. "Don't shoot!" he yelled, his voice cracking. "Hold your fire!"

The light flickered out. Turner stood blinking in darkness, then watched four little red fireflies crawling across his chest. He realized what they were and reached higher, his spine icy. Those little red fireflies were laser sights for automatic rifles.

The guards were on him before his eyesight cleared. Dim forms in jungle camo. He saw the wicked angular magazines of their rifles, leveled at his chest. Their heads were bulky: they wore night-sight goggles.

They handcuffed him and hustled him forward toward the camp. "You guys speak English?" Turner said. No answer. "I'm a Canadian, okay?"

Brooke waited, startled, beyond the gate. "Oh," he said. "It's you. What sort of dumbshit idea was this, Turner?"

"A really bad one," Turner said sincerely.

Brooke spoke to the guards in Malay. They lowered their guns; one freed his hands. They stalked off unerringly back into the darkness.

"What *is* this place?" Turner said.

Brooke turned his flashlight on Turner's face. "What does it look like, jerk? It's a political prison." His voice was so cold from behind the glare that Turner saw, in his mind's eye, the sudden flash of a telegram. DEAR MADAM CHOI, REGRET TO INFORM YOU THAT YOUR SON STEPPED ON A VIPER IN THE JUNGLES OF BORNEO AND YOUR BOOTS DIDN'T SAVE HIM. . . .

Brooke spoke quietly. "Did you think Brunei was all sweetness and light? It's a nation, damn it, not your toy train set. All right, stick by me and keep your mouth shut."

Brooke waved his flashlight. A guard emerged from the darkness and led them around the corner of the wooden barracks, which was set above the damp ground on concrete blocks. They walked up a short flight of steps. The guard flicked an exterior switch and the cell inside flashed into harsh light. The guard peered through close-set bars in the heavy ironbound door, then unlocked it with a creak of hinges.

Brooke murmured thanks and carefully shook the guard's hand. The guard smiled below the ugly goggles and slipped his hand inside his camo jacket.

"Come on," Brooke said. They stepped into the cell. The door clanked shut behind them.

A dark-skinned old man was blinking wearily in the sudden light. He sat up in his iron cot and brushed aside yellowed mosquito netting, reaching for a pair of wire-rimmed spectacles on the floor. He wore gray-striped prison canvas: drawstring trousers and a rough, buttoned blouse. He slipped the spectacles carefully over his ears and looked up. "Ah," he said. "Jimmy."

It was a bare cell: wooden floor, a chamberpot, a battered aluminum pitcher and basin. Two wire shelves above the bed held books in English and a curclicued alphabet Turner didn't recognize.

"This is Dr. Vikram Moratuwa," Brooke said. "The founder of the Partai Ekolojasi. This is Turner Choi, a prying young idiot."

"Ah," said Moratuwa. "Are we to be cellmates, young man?"

"He's not under arrest," Brooke said. "Yet." He opened his valise. "I brought you the books."

"Excellent," said Moratuwa, yawning. He had lost most of his teeth. "Ah, Mumford, Florman, and Lévi-Strauss. Thank you, Jimmy."

"I think it's okay," Brooke said, noticing Turner's stricken look. "The sultan winks at these little charity visits, if I'm discreet. I think I can talk you out of trouble, even though you put your foot in it."

"Jimmy is my oldest friend in Brunei," said Moratuwa. "There is no harm in two old men talking."

"Don't you believe it," Brooke said. "This man is a dangerous radical. He wanted to dissolve the monarchy. And him a privy councilor, too."

"Jimmy, we did not come here to be aristocrats. That is not Right Action."

Turner recognized the term. "You're a Buddhist?"

"Yes. I was with Sarvodaya Shramadana, the Buddhist technological movement. Jimmy and I met in Sri Lanka, where the Sarvodaya was born."

"Sri Lanka's a nice place to do videos," Brooke said. "I was still in the rock biz then, doing production work. Finance. But it was getting stale. Then I dropped in on a Sarvodaya rally, heard him speak. It was damned exciting!" Brooke grinned at the memory. "He was in trouble there, too. Even thirty years ago, his preaching was a little too pure for anyone's comfort."

"We were not put on this earth to make things comfortable for ourselves," Moratuwa chided. He glanced at Turner. "Brunei flourishes now, young man. We have the techniques, the expertise, the experience. It is time to fling open the doors and let Right Action spread to the whole earth! Brunei was our greenhouse, but the fields are the greater world outside."

Brooke smiled. "Choi is building the boats."

"Our Ocean Arks?" said Moratuwa. "Ah, splendid."

"I sailed here today on the first model."

"What joyful news. You have done us a great service, Mr. Choi."

"I don't understand," Turner said. "They're just sailboats."

Brooke smiled. "To you, maybe. But imagine you're a Malaysian dock worker living on fish meal and single-cell protein. What're you gonna think of a ship that costs nothing to build, nothing to run, and gives away free food?"

"Oh," said Turner slowly.

"Your sailboats will carry our Green message around the globe," Moratuwa said. "We teachers have a saying: 'I hear and I forget; I see and I remember; I do and I understand.' Mere preaching is only words. When people see our floating *kampongs* tied up at docks around the world, then they can touch and smell and live our life aboard those ships, then they will truly understand our Way."

"You really think that'll work?" Turner said.

"That is how we started here," Moratuwa said. "We had textbooks on the urban farm, textbooks developed in your own West, simple technologies anyone can use. Jimmy's building was first Green *kampong*, our demonstration model. We found many to help us. Unemployment was severe, as it still is throughout the world. But idle hands can put in skylights, haul nightsoil, build simple windmills. It is not elegant, but it is food and community and pride."

"It was a close thing between our Partai and the Moslem extremists," Brooke said. "They wanted to burn every trace of the West—we wanted to retrofit. We won. People could see and touch the future we offered. Food tastes better than preaching."

"Yes, those poor Moslem fellows," said Moratuwa. "Still here after so many years. You must talk to the sultan about an amnesty, Jimmy."

"They shot his brother in front of his family," Brooke said. "Seria saw it happen. She was only a child."

Turner felt a spasm of pain for her. She had never told him.

But Moratuwa shook his head. "The royals went too far in protecting their power. They tried to bottle up our Way, to control it with their royal *adat*. But they cannot lock out the world forever, and lock up those who want fresh air. They only imprison themselves. Ask your Seria." He smiled. "Buddha was a prince also, but he left his palace when the world called out."

Brooke laughed sourly. "Old troublemakers are stubborn." He looked at Turner. "This man's still loyal to our old dream, all that wild-eyed stuff that's buried under twenty years. He could be out of here with a word, if he promised to be cool and follow the *adat*. It's a crime to keep him in here. But the royal family aren't saints, they're politicians. They can't afford the luxury of innocence."

Turner thought it through, sadly. He realized now that he had found the ghost behind those huge old Green Party wallposters, those peeling Whole Earth sermons buried under sports ads and Malay movie stars. This was the man who had saved Seria's family—and this was where they had put him. "The sultan's not very grateful," Turner said.

"That's not the problem. You see, my friend here doesn't really give a damn about Brunei. He wants to break the greenhouse doors off, and never mind the trouble to the locals. He's not satisfied to save one little postage-stamp country. He's got the world on his conscience."

Moratuwa smiled indulgently. "And my friend Jimmy has the world in his computer terminal. He is a wicked Westerner. He has kept the simple natives pure, while he is drenched in whiskey and the Net."

Brooke winced. "Yeah. Neither one of us really belongs here. We're both goddamn outside agitators, is all. We came here together. His words, my money—we thought we could change things everywhere. Brunei was going to be our laboratory. Brunei was just small enough, and desperate enough, to listen to a couple of crackpots." He tugged at his hearing aid and glared at Turner's smile. "You're no prize either, Choi. Y'know, I was wrong about you. I'm glad you're leaving."

"Why?" Turner said, hurt.

"You're too straight, and you're too much trouble. I checked you out through the Net a long time ago—I know all about your granddad the smack merchant and all that Triad shit. I thought you'd be cool. Instead you had to be the knight in shining armor—bloody robot, that's what you are."

Turner clenched his fists. "Sorry I didn't follow your program, you old bastard."

"She's like a daughter to me," Brooke said. "A quick bump-and-grind, okay, we all need it, but you had to come on like Prince Charming. Well, you're getting on that chopper tomorrow, and it's back to Babylon for you, kid."

"Yeah?" Turner said defiantly. "Or else, huh? You'd put me in this place?"

Brooke shook his head. "I won't have to. Think it over, Mr. Choi. You know damn well where you belong."

It was a grim trip back. Seria caught his mood at once. When she saw his bad cop scowl, her morning-after smile died like a moth in a killing bottle. She knew it was over. They didn't say much. The roar of the copter blades would have drowned it anyway.

The shipyard was crammed with the framework of a massive Ocean Ark. It had been simple to scale the process up with the programs he'd downloaded. The work crew was overjoyed, but Turner's long-expected triumph had turned to ashes for him. He printed out a letter of resignation and took it to the minister of industry.

The minister's *kampong* was still expanding. They had webbed off a whole city block under great tent-like sheets of translucent plastic, which hung from the walls of tall buildings like giant dew-soaked spiderwebs. Women and children were casually ripping up the streets with picks and hoes, revealing long-smothered topsoil. The sewers had been grubbed up and diverted into long troughs choked with watercress.

The minister lived in a long flimsy tent of cotton batik. He was catching an afternoon snooze in a woven hammock anchored to a high-rise wall and strung to an old lamp post.

Turner woke him up.

"I see," the minister yawned, slipping on his sandals. "Illness in the family, is it? You have my sympathies. When may we expect you back?"

Turner shook his head. "The job's done. Those 'bots will be pasting up ships from now till doomsday."

"But you still have two months to run. You should oversee the line until we're sure we have the beetles out."

"Bugs," Turner said. "There aren't any." He knew it was true. Building ships that simple was monkey-work. Humans could have done it.

"There's plenty of other work here for a man of your talents."

"Hire someone else."

The minister frowned. "I shall have to complain to Kyocera."

"I'm quitting them, too."

"Quitting your multinational? At this early stage in your career? Is that wise?"

Turner closed his eyes and summoned his last dregs of patience. "Why should I care? Tuan Minister, I've never ever *seen* them."

Turner cut a last deal with the bootleg boys down on Floor 4 and sneaked into his room with an old gas can full of rice beer. The little screen on the end of the nozzle was handy for filtering out the thickest dregs. He poured himself a long one and looked around the room. He had to start packing.

He began stripping the walls and tossing souvenirs onto his bed, pausing to knock back long shuddery glugs of warm rice beer. Packing was painfully easy. He hadn't brought much. The room looked pathetic. He had another beer.

His bonsai tree was dying. There was no doubt of it now.

The cramping of its tiny pot was murderous. "You poor little bastard," Turner told it, his voice thick with self-pity. On impulse, he broke its pot with his boot. He carried the tree gently across the room, and buried its gnarled roots in the rich black dirt of the windowbox. "There," he said, wiping his hands on his jeans. "Now *grow*, dammit!"

It was Friday night again. They were showing another free movie down in the park. Turner ignored it and called Vancouver.

"No video again?" Georgie said.

"No."

"I'm glad you called, anyway. It's bad, Turner. The Taipei cousins are here. They're hovering around the old man like a pack of buzzards."

"They're in good company, then."

"Jesus, Turner! Don't say that kind of crap! Look, Honorable Grandfather's been asking about you every day. How soon can you get here?"

Turner looked in his notebook. "I've booked passage on a freighter to Labuan Island. That's Malaysian territory. I can get a plane there, a puddle-jumper to Manila. Then a Japan Air jet to Midway and another to Vanc. That puts me in at, uh, eight P.M. your time Monday."

"Three *days?*

"There are no *planes* here, Georgie."

"All right, if that's the best you can do. It's too bad about this video. Look, I want you to call him at the hospital, okay? Tell him you're coming."

"Now?" said Turner, horrified.

Georgie exploded. "I'm sick of doing your explaining, man! Face up to your goddamn obligations, for once! The least you can do is call him and play good boy grandson! I'm gonna call-forward you from here."

"Okay, you're right," Turner said. "Sorry, Georgie, I know it's been a strain."

Georgie looked down and hit a key. White static blurred, a phone rang, and Turner was catapulted to his Grandfather's bedside.

The old man was necrotic. His cheekbones stuck out like wedges, and his lips were swollen and blue. Stacks of monitors blinked beside his bed. Turner spoke in halting Mandarin. "Hello, Grandfather. It's your grandson, Turner. How are you?"

The old man fixed his horrible eyes on the screen. "Where is your picture, boy?"

"This is Borneo, Grandfather. They don't have modern telephones."

"What kind of place is that? Have they no respect?"

"It's politics, Grandfather."

Grandfather Choi scowled. A chill of terror went through Turner. Good God, he thought, I'm going to look like that when I'm old. His grandfather said, "I don't recall giving my permission for this."

"It was just eight months, Grandfather."

"You prefer these barbarians to your own family, is that it?"

Turner said nothing. The silence stretched painfully. "They're not barbarians," he blurted at last.

"What's that, boy?"

Turned switched to English. "They're British Commonwealth, like Hong Kong was. Half of them are Chinese."

Grandfather sneered and followed him to English. "Why they need you, then?"

"They need me," Turner said tightly, "because I'm a trained engineer."

His Grandfather peered at the blank screen. He looked feeble suddenly, confused. He spoke Chinese. "Is this some sort of trick? My son's boy doesn't talk like that. What is that howling I hear?"

The movie was reaching a climax downstairs. Visceral crunches and screaming. It all came boiling up inside Turner then. "What's it sound like, old man? A Triad gang war?"

His grandfather turned pale. "That's it, boy. Is all over for you."

"Great," Turner said, his heart racing. "Maybe we can be honest, just this once."

"My money bought you diapers, boy."

"Fang-pa," Turner said. "Dog's-fart. You made our lives hell with that money. You turned my dad into a drunk and my brother into an ass-kisser. That's blood money from junkies and I wouldn't take it if you begged me!"

"You talk big, boy, but you don't show the face," the old man said. He raised one shrunken fist, his bandaged forearm trailing tubes. "If you were here I give you a good beating."

Turner laughed giddily. He felt like a hero. "You old fraud! Go on, give the money to Uncle's kids. They're gonna piss on your altar every day, you stupid old bastard."

"They're good children, not like you."

"They hate your guts, old man. Wise up."

"Yes, they hate me," the old man admitted gloomily. The truth seemed to fill him with grim satisfaction. He nestled his head back into his pillow like a turtle into its shell. "They all want more money, more, more, more. You want it, too, boy, don't lie to me."

"Don't need it," Turner said airily. "They don't use money here."

"Barbarians," his grandfather said. "But you need it when you come home."

"I'm staying here," Turner said. "I *like* it here. I'm free here, understand? Free of the money and free of the family and free of you!"

"Wicked boy," his grandfather said. "I was like you once. I did bad things to be free." he sat up in bed, glowering. "But at least I helped my family."

"I could never be like you," Turner said.

"You wait till they come after you with their hands out," his grandfather said, stretching out one wrinkled palm. "The end of the world couldn't hide you from them."

"What do you mean?"

His grandfather chuckled with an awful satisfaction. "I leave you all the money, Mr. Big Freedom. You see what you do then when you're in my shoes."

"I don't want it!" Turner shouted. "I'll give it all to charity!"

"No you won't," his grandfather said. "You'll think of your duty to your family, like I had to. From now on *you* take care of them, Mr. Runaway, Mr. High and Mighty."

"I won't!" Turner said. "You can't!"

"I'll die happy now," his grandfather said, closing his eyes. He lay back on the pillow and grinned feebly. "It worth it just to see the look on their faces."

"You can't make me!" Turner yelled. "I'll never go back, understand? I'm staying—"

The line went dead.

Turner shut down his phone and stowed it away.

He had to talk to Brooke. Brooke would know what to do. Somehow. Turner would play off one old man against the other.

Turner still felt shocked by the turn of events, but beneath his confusion he felt a soaring confidence. At last he had faced down his grandfather. After that, Brooke would be easy. Brooke would find some loophole in the Bruneian government that would protect him from the old man's legacy. Turner would stay safe in Brunei. It was the best place in the world to frustrate the banks of the Global Net.

But Brooke was still on the river, on his boat.

Turner decided to meet Brooke the moment he docked in town. He couldn't wait to tell Brooke about his decision to stay in Brunei for good. He was feverish with excitement. He had wrenched his life out of the program now; everything was different. He saw everything from a fresh new angle, with a *bricoleur's* eyes. His whole life was waiting for a retrofit.

He took the creaking elevator to the ground floor. In the park outside, the movie crowd was breaking up. Turner hitched a ride in the pedicab of some teenagers from a waterfront *kampong*. He took the first shift pedaling, and got off a block away from the dock Brooke used.

The cracked concrete quays were sheltered under a long, rambling roof of tin and geodesic bamboo. Half-a-dozen fishing smacks floated at the docks, beside an elderly harbor dredge. Brooke's first boat, a decrepit pleasure cruiser, was in permanent drydock with its diesel engine in pieces.

The headman of the dock *kampong* was a plump, motherly Malay grandmother. She and her friends were having a Friday night quilting bee, repairing canvas sails under the yellow light of an alcohol lamp.

Brooke was not expected back until morning. Turner was determined to wait him out. He had not asked permission to sleep out from his *kampong*, but after a long series of garbled translations he established that the locals would vouch for him later. He wandered away from the chatter of Malay gossip and found a dark corner.

He fell back on a floury pile of rice bags, watching from the darkness, unable to sleep. Whenever his eyes closed, his brain ran a loud interior monologue, rehearsals for his talk with Brooke.

The women worked on, wrapped in the lamp's mild glow. Innocently, they enjoyed themselves, secure in their usefulness. Yet Turner knew machines could have done the sewing faster and easier. Already, through reflex, as he watched, some corner of his mind pulled the task to computerized pieces, thinking: simplify, analyze, reduce.

But to what end? What was it really for, all that tech he'd learned? He'd become an engineer for reasons of his own. Because it offered a way out for him, because the gift for it had always been there in his brain and hands and eyes.... Because of the rewards it offered him. Freedom, independence, money, the rewards of the West.

But what control did he have? Rewards could be snatched away without warning. He'd seen others go to the wall when their specialties ran dry. Education and training were no defense. Not today, when a specialist's knowledge could be programmed into a computerized expert system.

Was he really any safer than these Bruneians? A thirty-minute phone call could render these women obsolete—but a society that could do their work with robots would have no use for their sails. Within their little greenhouse, their miniature world of gentle technologies, they had more control than he did.

People in the West talked about the "technical elite"—and Turner knew it was a damned lie. Technology roared on, running full-throttle on the world's last dregs of oil, but no one was at the wheel, not really. Massive institutions, both governments and corporations, fumbled for control, but couldn't understand. They had no hands-on feel for tech and what it meant, for the solid feeling in a good design.

The "technical elite" were errand boys. They didn't decide how to study, what to work on, where they could be most useful, or to what end. Money decided that. Technicians were owned by the abstract ones and zeros in bankers' microchips, paid out by silk-suit hustlers who'd never touched a wrench. Knowledge wasn't power, not really, not for engineers. There were too many abstractions in the way.

But the gift was real—Brooke had told him so, and now Turner realized it was true. That was the reason for engineering. Not for money, because there was more money in shuffling paper. Not for power, that was in management. For the gift itself.

He leaned back in darkness, smelling tar and rice dust. For the first time, he truly felt he understood what he was doing. Now that he had defied his family and his past, he saw his work in a new light. It was something bigger than just his private escape hatch. It was a worthy pursuit on its own merits: a thing of dignity.

It all began to fall into place for him then, bringing with it a warm sense of absolute rightness. He yawned, nestling his head into the burlap.

He would live here and help them. Brunei was a new world, a world built on a human scale, where people mattered. No, it didn't have the flash of a hot CAD-CAM establishment with its tons of goods and reams of printout; it didn't have that technical sweetness and heroic scale.

But it was still good work. A man wasn't a Luddite because he worked for people instead of abstractions. The green technologies demanded *more* intelligence, more reason, more of the engineer's true gift. Because they went against the blind momentum of a dead century, with all its rusting monuments of arrogance and waste.…

Turner squirmed drowsily into the scrunchy comfort of the rice bags, in the fading grip of his epiphany. Within him, some unspoken knot of division and tension eased, bringing a new and deep relief. As always, just before sleep, his thoughts turned to Seria. Somehow, he would deal with that too. He wasn't sure just how yet, but it could wait. It was different now that he was staying. Everything was working out. He was on a roll.

Just as he drifted off, he half-heard a thrashing scuffle as a *kampong* cat seized and tore a rat behind the bags.

A stevedore shook him awake next morning. They needed the rice. Turner sat up, his mouth gummy with hangover. His T-shirt and jeans were caked with dust.

Brooke had arrived. They were loading provisions aboard his ship: bags of rice, dried fruit, compost fertilizer. Turner, smiling, hoisted a bag over his shoulder and swaggered up the ramp on board.

Brooke oversaw the loading from a canvas deck chair. He was unshaven, nervously picking at a gaudy acoustic guitar. He started violently when Turner dropped the bag at his feet.

"Thank God you're here!" he said. "Get out of sight!" He grabbed Turner's arm and hustled him across the deck into the greenhouse.

Turner stumbled along reluctantly. "What the hell? How'd you know I was coming here?"

Brooke shut the greenhouse door. He pointed through a dew-streaked pane at the dock. "See that little man with the black songkak hat?"

"Yeah?"

"He's from the Ministry of Islamic Banking. He just came from your *kampong*, looking for you. Big news from the gnomes of Zurich. You're hot property now, kid."

Turner folded his arms defiantly. "I've made my decision, Tuan Councilor. I threw it over. Everything. My family, the West . . . I don't want that money. I'm turning it down! I'm staying."

Brooke ignored him, wiping a patch of glass with his sleeve. "If they get their hooks into your cash flow, you'll never get out of here." Brooke glanced at him, alarmed. "You didn't sign anything, did you?"

Turner scowled. "You haven't heard a word I've said, have you?"

Brooke tugged at his hearing aid. "What? These damn batteries ... Look, I got spares in my cabin. We'll check it out, have a talk." He waved Turner back, opened the greenhouse door slightly, and shouted a series of orders to the crew in their Dayak dialect. "Come on," he told Turner.

They left by a second door, and sneaked across a patch of open deck, then down a flight of plywood steps into the center hull.

Brooke lifted the paisley bedspread of his cabin bunk and hauled out an ancient steamer chest. He pulled a jingling set of keys from his pocket and opened it. Beneath a litter of ruffled shirts, a shaving kit, and cans of hair spray, the trunk was packed to the gills with electronic contraband: coax cables, multiplexers, buffers and converters, shiny plug-in cards still in their heat-sealed baggies, multiplugged surge suppressors wrapped in tentacles of black extension cord. "Christ," Turner said. He heard a gentle thump as the ship came loose, followed by a rattle of rigging as the crew hoisted sail.

After a long search, Brooke found batteries in a cloisonné box. He popped them into place.

Turner said, "Admit it. You're surprised to see me, aren't you? Still think you were wrong about me?"

Brooke looked puzzled. "Surprised? Didn't you get Seria's message on the Net?"

"What? No. I slept on the docks last night."

"You missed the message?" Brooke said. He mulled it over. "Why are you here, then?"

"You said you could help me if I ever had money trouble," Turner said. "Well, now's the time. You gotta figure some way to get me out of this bank legacy. I know it doesn't look like it, but I've broken with my family for good. I'm gonna stay here, try to work things out with Seria."

Brooke frowned. "I don't understand. You want to stay with Seria?"

"Yes, here in Brunei, with her!" Turner sat on the bunk and waved his arms passionately. "Look, I know I told you that Brunei was just a glass bubble, sealed off from the world, and all that. But I've changed now! I've thought it through, I understand things. Brunei's important! It's small, but it's the ideas that matter, not the scale. I can get along, I'll fit in—you said so yourself."

"What about Seria?"

"Okay, that's part of it," Turner admitted. "I know she'll never leave this place. I can defy my family and it's no big deal, but she's Royalty. She wouldn't leave here, any more than you'd leave all your money behind. So you're both trapped here. All right. I can accept that." Turner looked up, his face glowing with determination. "I know things won't be easy for Seria and me, but it's up to me to make the sacrifice. Someone has to make the grand gesture. Well, it might as well be me."

Brooke was silent for a moment, then thumped him on the shoulder. "This is a new Turner I'm seeing. So you faced down the old smack merchant, huh? You're quite the hero!"

Turner felt sheepish. "Come on, Brooke."

"And turning down all that nice money, too."

Turner brushed his hands together, dismissing the idea. "I'm sick of being manipulated by old geezers."

Brooke rubbed his unshaven jaw and grinned. "Kid, you've got a lot to learn." He walked to the door. "But that's okay, no harm done. Everything still works out. Let's go up on deck and make sure the coast is clear."

Turner followed Brooke to his deck chair by the bamboo railing. The ship sailed rapidly down a channel between mud flats. Already they'd left the waterfront, paralleling a shoreline densely fringed with mangroves. Brooke sat down and opened a binocular case. He scanned the city behind them.

Turner felt a lightheaded sense of euphoria as the triple bows cut the water. He smiled as they passed the first off-shore rig. It looked like a good place to get some fishing done.

"About this bank," Turner said. "We have to face them some time—what good is this doing us?"

Brooke smiled without looking up from his binoculars. "Kid, I've been planning this day a long time. I'm running it on a wing and a prayer. But hey, I'm not proud, I can adapt. You've been a lot of trouble to me, stomping in where angels fear to tread, in those damn boots of yours. But I've finally found a way to fit you in. Turner, I'm going to re-trofit your life."

"Think so?" Turner said. He stepped closer, looming over Brooke. "What are you looking for, anyway?"

Brooke sighed. "Choppers. Patrol boats."

Turner had a sudden terrifying flash of insight. "You're leaving Brunei. Defecting!" He stared at Brooke. "You bastard! You kept me on board!" He grabbed the rail, then began tearing at his heavy boots, ready to jump and swim for it.

"Don't be stupid!" Brooke said. "You'll get her in a lot of trouble!" He lowered the binoculars. "Oh Christ, here comes Omar."

Turner followed his gaze and spotted a helicopter, rising gnatlike over the distant high-rises. "Where is Seria?"

"Try the bow."

"You mean she's here? She's leaving too?" He ran forward across the thudding deck.

Seria wore bell-bottomed sailor's jeans and a stained nylon windbreaker. With the help of two of the Dayak crew, she was installing a meshwork satellite dish in an anchored iron plate in the deck. She had cut away her long dyed hair; she looked up at him, and for a moment he saw a stranger. Then her face shifted, fell into a familiar focus. "I thought I'd never see you again, Turner. That's why I had to do it."

Turner smiled at her fondly, too overjoyed at first for her words to sink in. "Do what, angel?"

"Tap your phone, of course. I did it because I was jealous, at first. I had to be sure. You know. But then when I knew you were leaving, well, I had to hear your voice one last time. So I heard your talk with your Grandfather. Are you mad at me?"

"You tapped my phone? You heard all that?" Turner said.

"Yes, darling. You were wonderful. I never thought you'd do it."

"Well," Turner said, "I never thought you'd pull a stunt like this, either."

"Some had to make a grand gesture," she said. "It was up to me, wasn't it? But I explained all that in my message."

"So you're defecting? Leaving your family?" Turner knelt beside her, dazed. As he struggled to fit it all together, his eyes focussed on a cross-threaded nut at the base of the dish. He absently picked up a socket wrench. "Let me give you a hand with that," he said through reflex.

Seria sucked on a barked knuckle. "You didn't get my last message, did you? You came here on your own!"

"Well, yeah," Turner said. "I decided to stay. You know. With you."

"And now we're abducting you!" She laughed. "How romantic!"

"You and Brooke are leaving together?"

"It's not just me, Turner. Look."

Brooke was walking toward them, and with him Dr. Moratuwa, newly outfitted in saffron-colored baggy shorts and T-shirt. They were the work clothes of a Buddhist technician. "Oh, no," Turner said. He dropped his wrench with a thud.

Seria said, "Now you see why I had to leave, don't you? My family locked him up. I had to break *adat* and help Brooke set him free. It was my obligation, my *dharma!*"

"I guess that makes sense," Turner said. "But it's gonna take me a while, that's all. Couldn't you have warned me?"

"I tried to! I wrote you on the Net!" She saw he was crestfallen, and squeezed his hand. "I guess the plans broke down. Well, we can improvise."

"Good day, Mr. Choi," said Moratuwa. "It was very brave of you to cast in your lot with us. It was a gallant gesture."

"Thanks," Turner said. He took a deep breath. So they were all leaving. It was a shock, but he could deal with it. He'd just have to start over and think it through from a different angle. At least Seria was coming along.

He felt a little better now. He was starting to get it under control.

Moratuwa sighed. "And I wish it could have worked."

"Your brother's coming," Brooke told Seria gloomily. "Remember this was all my fault."

They had a good headwind, but the crown prince's helicopter came on faster, its drone growing to a roar. A Gurkha palace guard crouched on the broad orange float outside the canopy, cradling a light machine gun. His gold-braided dress uniform flapped in the chopper's downwash.

The chopper circled the boat once. "We've had it," Brooke said. "Well, at least it's not a patrol boat with those damned Exocet missiles. It's family business with the princess on board. They'll hush it all up. You can always depend on *adat*." He patted Moratuwa's shoulder. "Looks like you get a cellmate after all, old man."

Seria ignored them. She was looking up anxiously. "Poor Omar," she said. She cupped her hands to her mouth. "Brother, be careful!" she shouted.

The Prince's copilot handed the guard a loudspeaker. The guard raised it and began to shout a challenge.

The tone of the chopper's engines suddenly changed. Plumes of brown smoke billowed from the chromed exhausts. The prince veered away suddenly, fighting the controls. The guard, caught off balance, tumbled headlong into the ocean. The Dayak crew, who had been waiting for the order to reef sails, began laughing wildly.

"What in hell?" Brooke said.

The chopper pancaked down heavily into the bay, rocking in the ship's wake. Spurting caramel-colored smoke, its engines died with a hideous grinding. The ship sailed on. They watched silently as the drenched guard swam slowly up and clung to the chopper's float.

Brooke raised his eyes to heaven. "Lord Buddha, forgive my doubts. . . ."

"Sugar," Seria said sadly. "I put a bag of sugar in brother's fuel tank. I ruined his beautiful helicopter. Poor Omar, he really loves that machine."

Brooke stared at her, then burst into cackling laughter. Regally, Seria ignored him. She stared at the dwindling shore, her eyes bright. "Good-bye, Brunei. You cannot hold us now."

"Where are we going?" Turner said.

"To the West," said Moratuwa. "The Ocean Arks will

spread for many years. I must set the example by carrying the word to the greatest global center of unsustainable industry."

Brooke grinned. "He means America, man."

"We shall start in Hawaii. It is also tropical and our expertise will find ready application there."

"Wait a minute," Turner said. "I turned my back on all that! Look, I turned down a fortune so I could stay in the East."

Seria took his arm, smiling radiantly. "You're such a dreamer, darling. What a wonderful gesture. I love you, Turner."

"Look," said Brooke, "I left behind my building, my title of nobility, and all my old mates. I'm older than you, so my romantic gestures come first."

"But," Turner said, "it was all decided. I was going to help you in Brunei. I had ideas, plans. Now none of it makes any sense."

Moratuwa smiled. "The world is not built from your blueprints, young man."

"Whose, then?" Turner demanded. "Yours?"

"Nobody's, really," Brooke said. "We all just have to do our best with whatever comes up. *Bricolage*, remember?" Brooke spread his hands. "But it's a geezer's world, kid. We got your number, and we got you outnumbered. Fast cars and future shock and that hot Western trip . . . that's another century. We like slow days in the sun. We like a place to belong and gentle things around us." He smiled. "Okay, you're a little wired now, but you'll calm down by the time we reach Hawaii. There's a lot of retrofit work there. You'll be one of us!" He gestured at the satellite dish. "We'll set this up and call your banks first thing."

"It's a good world for us, Turner," Seria said urgently. "Not quite East, not quite West—like us two. It was made for us, it's what we're best at." She embraced him.

"You escaped," Turner said. No one ever said much about what happened after Sleeping Beauty woke.

"Yes, I broke free," she said, hugging him tighter. "And I'm taking you with me."

Turner stared over her shoulder at Brunei, sinking into hot green mangroves and warm mud. Slowly, he could feel the truth of it, sliding over him like some kind of ambiguous quicksand. He was going to fit right in. He could see his future laid out before him, clean and predestined, like fifty years of happy machine language.

"Maybe I wanted this," he said at last. "But it sure as hell wasn't what I planned."

Brooke laughed. "Look, you're bound for Hawaii with a princess and eight million dollars. Somehow, you'll just have to make do."

PATTERNS

PAT CADIGAN

I have this continuing fantasy of assassinating the President. Any President.

To step forward within a crowd, raising my weapon and aiming it at the President's head. Sometimes in the movie unreeling in my mind, my hand comes up holding a Luger Parabellum P08 with the ridiculously long 190mm barrel. Other times I am holding a more likely Mauser Military Pistol. Twice I have found myself clutching an Uzi with the stock detached, three or four times I held a .357 Smith & Wesson Magnum. Once—only once—I stared down the length of a crossbow at the chief executive.

In the fantasy, I am not scared or angry. I don't think about the fact that I am taking a human life—the President, after all, is not so much human as manufactured, a product made flesh by the bipartisan system and the media in accidental conjugation. Is it wrong to fire at the dot pattern on a TV screen? I feel nothing beyond a mild nervousness, the slight (very slight) stage-fright I used to experience during my acting days. That my stage-fright was never acute enough to give me the cold sweats or send me vomiting into the handiest receptacle probably contributed to my lack of success in the theatre. In a one-person show, I could have been overlooked.

I know what you're thinking. I dream of assassination as a way to become visible at last. You are wrong. There is far more power in invisibility than in fame.

In fact, my fantasy movie has never proceeded beyond the point at which I raise my weapon and train it on the President. The action freezes when the President's gaze rests on the instrument of his/her destruction. But I know the rest of it:

I brace myself and fire. The President falls backwards, face a red ruin, body jerking in every direction. He/she is caught by aides and Secret Service agents and lowered to the ground. The crowd is completely silent. They are neither frightened nor in shock, just passive as the dot pattern re-arranges itself. I lower the weapon to my side, then turn and walk away without hurry. Nobody looks at me. I walk some unmeasured distance to a car I recognize as mine, parked at an innocuous curb. I get in, twist the key waiting in the ignition and drive off.

In the days to come, there will be no mention of what happened to the President, ever, nor will there be any news about the government again. With one shot, I have obliterated not just the President but both Houses of Congress, the Supreme Court, Social Security, the National Endowment for the Arts, the Government Printing Office, the Gross National Product, the FTC, the CIA, the HEW and the Immigration and Naturalization Service, among others, as well as postponing forever the next election year. But life goes on anyway. I drive an endless highway across the United States and through the windshield I observe the permanent status quo I have visited on the American people. They don't know what has happened and they don't find it odd that they keep living in the same homes, working the same jobs, hearing the same music on the radio, watching the same dot patterns. Like me, they travel without destination. The days melt into each other with no distinguishing characteristics. The seasons come in and go out as they were meant to do in textbooks, but no one grows older. The treadmill has achieved a state of being both in motion and at rest simultaneously. Test pattern. Entropy.

All because I shot the President's dot pattern.

Seen in close-up, the dot pattern could almost be taken for a collection of organisms, very cooperative organisms which have discovered a choreography that will produce patterns pleasing to the eyes of much larger and much less cooperative organisms.

Quotation from Chairman Busby Berkeley and Miss Amy Lowell: *Christ! What are patterns for?*

I'll tell you.

The screen crackles when I put my finger on it. Static electricity; the dots warning me off their pattern. I pull my finger back and make it a pistol barrel pointing at the President, who is giving the State of the Union address. The President looks directly at "me" and hesitates. The dots at work on his pattern burble and boil and show me the red ruin that could be the result of my gun hand. Then the President's head re-forms and he goes on with his speech. We are in great need of re-form in this country, he says, but even so, the State of the Union in general is most hope-inspiring.

Now. While there's still hope.

I cover the President's face with my finger. Loud crackling, followed by a close-up which put my finger absurdly on the President's moving mouth. He doesn't bite, but there is some mild electricity running up my arm.

"It was all them cop shows," his mother said. "All that violence, they oughta get it off the tube." She said it on television, at his televised trial. Christ! What are patterns for? First-degree murder.

"Always such a good kid," my mother would say. "Never a moment's trouble. Helped around the house and never answered back, either. Good-natured, you know. And when all the other kids were hanging out on the streets or chasing each other around and getting into trouble, *my* kid was studying. *My* kid always wanted to be somebody."

How true. I could have had my own show, in fact. If the technology had been good enough in those days, I might have lived in a suburban dot pattern, walked to school to my own theme music, mouthed dialog to my own laugh track. And achieved endless childhood in syndication. I could have been syndicated; I could have been a contender. Instead of a COMMERCIAL INTERRUPT FOR STATION IDENTIFICATION. It is often necessary to amputate a frame or two for the sake of format. So sorry, apparently the program director spliced this one a little early. But since it happened anyway, you have sixty seconds to contemplate your mantra. *Now* how much would you pay?

Late at night, the patterns change and rearrange. I can't sleep. Two, three, four in the morning, the dots perform before my dry eyes. Slices, dices, juliennes. How much would you pay? Don't answer yet . . . stainless steel never needs sharpening. Now how much would you pay? Don't answer yet . . . act now and we'll throw in the fabulous Kalashnikov rifle, the most successful automatic rifle ever made! Gas operated, simultaneous bolt action and cocking, with a handy selector lever for single shot or automatic at a rate of 100 rpm, that's 100 rpm! *Isn't that amazing?* A mere 8 pounds with a folding metal stock, perfect for the murder of the head of state of your choice! Call now, operators are standing by!

I blink. When you awake, you will remember everything.

I want to call friends to ask if they have just seen this, too. Then I remember, all my friends are electric.

In living color.

A Famous Actor has shot himself. When they found him, the television in his townhouse was still on, murmuring merrily to itself as it played one of his old movies. I see it on the six o'clock news. Dot pattern of a dot pattern.

Now how much would you pay?

I have taken to dreaming in dots. Reruns. I raise my arm. I am holding a Browning GP35. I know nothing about guns. Its rate of fire is 25 rpm with a muzzle velocity of 1110 feet per second and it is going to make cheap chuck of the President's face. I know nothing about guns. The dot pattern knows. Point-blank range is that distance at which the bullet achieves its highest velocity, the distance the President is from me now. And it's on every channel, even cable.

Cable?

When I awake, I remember everything, in dot patterns, in living color.

A soap opera actress reports being assaulted in a restaurant by an irate woman wielding a Totes umbrella, shouting, "You leave that nice lady's husband alone, you slut! Hasn't that poor woman had enough trouble without you trying to steal her man?" The actress's companions manage to pull the woman away. The rest of the people in the restaurant—

diners, waiters, waitresses, busboys, maitre d'—all watch. They are neither frightened nor in shock.

And now, what will I do?

I consult the schedule. It is not time to run all the drug dealers out of Florida. Last night, the score was evened for the right-thinking on the mean streets of New York, it won't have to be done again for another week. I think I will defend my heavyweight title against the challenger in Las Vegas. I double up my fists and inspect the knuckles. Yes, these can go fifteen rounds, piece of Duncan Hines cake.

I press my knuckles against the screen. Wild crackling. The dots swarm in liquid patterns around each point of contact. Electricity is flowing up both arms, dancing through the nerve endings which sizzle into life and join the pattern.

My hands are being taped as I hold them out. I got to keep my fuckin hands up, do I hear, just keep my fuckin hands up and let him dance himself out and then jab his motherfuckin head off. The dots pulse, live from Caesar's Palace, more live than life. Fitted out with this dot pattern to wear, I could strike sparks in the moving, living air.

Now I know it can be done. The fight goes by in a swirl of dot pattern light. I keep my fuckin hands up and let him dance himself out and then jab his motherfuckin head off. The fight is not important. Now I know it can be done.

But I have to wait until the swelling goes down and the black eye fades. Never mind. You should see the other dot pattern.

More on that story from our correspondent in Washington. Dot-pattern Washington snaps under the scanning line. The White House looks a little fuzzy. So does our correspondent. I touch her microphone; the dots leap in frenzy as I reshape their pattern into a 127mm barrel version of the Gyrojet pistol and then back into a microphone. Not yet. Tonight there is a press conference.

Brought to you by, sponsored in part. The whole world is waiting and watching. Ladies and gentlemen on every channel, the President of the United States. The reception has never been so good, it must be me. The dots dance for me now and we know each other; tropism. Whenever they appear, I turn to look and my looking excites the patterns.

What are patterns for?

I'll show you. I'll ... *show* ... you. As I show myself.

The dots sparkle around my hands in the continuing fantasy shown live on every channel. I run my fingers through them like a helping of stardust and reshape the pattern. They know what I need here. The Colt Commando with telescopic butt fully extended for shoulder firing, as used by the Green Berets, who have also been on this channel. The dots remember the pattern and here it is.

I step forward in the crowd of reporters demanding to be called on. The President's dot pattern scans the room, looking for a likely questioner. Then he sees "me" and hesitates. I have raised the Colt to my shoulder. Everyone is watching.

I touch my finger to the screen. The President's head disappears in a red mist, dot patterns gone insane. The room is completely silent, neither frightened nor shocked. Behind the podium, the Great Seal, the curtains, the President's aides, and Secret Service agents begin to unravel from the hole where the President's head was.

Embarrassed, puzzled anchorman. We are sorry for the interruption in transmission. Apparently we are having technical difficulties. We'll have more information for you after this.

No, we won't. That is all the information we are ever going to have, ever.

Fade to commercial. Dogs pounce on bowls of food. I sit on the couch, nodding. It's all over now. It wasn't quite how I expected it to go but it was, after all, adapted for television.

The commercial is followed by another commercial and then the embarrassed, puzzled anchorman. Apparently we are permanently cut off from our hook-up in the nation's capital. We will try to have some news on the rest of the press conference as soon as possible.

A fast recap of the statements and questions up until the moment I murdered the President's dot pattern, when things unraveled like celluloid melting away, a promise of an update soon. They patch the foreshortened evening schedule with a made-for-TV movie. Time to go.

I leave my apartment, go down to my car parked at an innocuous curb. The key is not waiting in the ignition but in my pocket. Such a good kid, never a moment's trouble. We can live in the same homes, work at the same jobs, hear the same music on the radio, watch the same dot patterns. We travel without destination. What are patterns for?

Nothing, any more.

There used to be too much violence on TV. But not now.

DR. LUTHER'S ASSISTANT

PAUL J. MCAULEY

When Mike lost his appeal and had been sentenced and chipped, he had to get a job. That was the law in Holland, where most convicts weren't imprisoned but tagged with chip controllers and stripped of their entitlement to the universal unearned wage. After his personal counsellor explained about the monthly report Mike would have to make, and the penal chip's reflexive programming which would induce a minor epileptic fit if Mike ingested any alcohol or proscribed drug, or strayed outside Amsterdam city limits, or broke curfew, after all this, he told Mike that convicts were expected to make reparations to society.

"It is very simple, very straightforward. It is the Dutch way. What it is, you do society good and yourself good too."

This from a skinny 70-year-old geezer in baggy blue jeans, a fake Rolex, a wrinkled pop-art T-shirt, and a bowl-cut hair transplant. Mike was beginning to suspect that Holland's workfare system was run entirely by geezers and babushkas who'd grown bored with their statutory right of access to unlimited leisure. Up there on the top floor of the Nieuwe Stadhuis, an old-fashioned open-plan office that was a maze of partitions and big glossy-leaved plants and cubicles like the veal-fattening pens in the prison camp farm, there wasn't one official younger than Mike's parents.

"What convicts need to learn," the counsellor said, swivelling back and forth in his chair, "is a sense of responsibility. A job will give you that. Do you have any preferences?"

Mike shrugged. His right eye was swollen shut from where they'd put in the chip, and although he'd been off Hux for three months now, he'd still felt as if he was trapped in some low-rez virtuality with Alice-in-Wonderland rules, where you were put in jail until you were proven guilty, whereupon you were released.

The first time he'd been sent down, in England, he'd done time in one of the huge prison camps. Greenham Common, a place that had once been some kind of military base. He'd been convicted for writing bogus prescriptions to support the habit he'd acquired working as an intern. Most interns prescribed themselves something to keep going through the 120-hours on-call shifts—those few who didn't cop a habit, drop out, go crazy or die from exhaustion just had to be androids—but Mike had been caught along with about 200 others in a media-inspired sweep and been handed ten years' hard labour, no remission. His medical degree had scored him a position in the camp's infirmary, but hard was just what it had been. And his wife had divorced him, taken off for the States with his baby son, and he'd acquired a serious dependency on Hux which after his release had had him running packages back and forth across the North Sea to support it, until one day a customs officer in Schiphol Airport took an interest in his overnight bag.

Hux was bad stuff, temporary infections of fembots

which rejigged the sensory areas of the brain so that your whole nervous system became an erogenous zone, and the world was gently and irresistibly fucking you: you could come by stroking a piece of velvet, smelling the steam that lifted off fresh-boiled rice. But unlike most fembots, those self-organizing clades of machines smaller than bacteria that operated down in the dance of molecules at the femtometre scale of thousand billionths of a millimetre, Hux had disabled self-replicating facilities and a life-span measured in minutes. Strictly speaking, pseudodrug fembots like Hux weren't addictive—they caused no permanent metabolic changes—but if you liked the trip you had to have a regular supply. Which was how Mike's habit had gotten him into the courier business, which was how he'd ended up under the chip.

When he said he didn't suppose he'd be allowed to work in a hospital, the counsellor agreed that it wasn't an option and paged through his terminal with maddening slowness until he came up with what he called an 80% match.

"Which is not so bad. The position's been open quite a while. It requires someone with medical qualifications."

"Don't I get a choice in this?"

"Of course," the counsellor said, suddenly not relaxed at all. "If you don't take what's offered, you can go to the general labour pool. However, I doubt you'd like that very much, because you would work alongside dolls, heavy physical work. Just keep in mind that for troublemakers there's always the general labour pool. Do as you're told, and we will get along fine."

And that was how Mike found himself working for Dr Dieter Luther in one of Amsterdam's sex arcades.

"I've just two requirements," Dr Luther told Mike on his first day at the sex arcade. "First that you're not afraid of blood.

Second, that you can fuck with the meat all you want, but only out of hours. Given your curfew, that will allow you only 20 minutes or so after we close, but needs must, eh, young man?"

"Whatever you say, Dr Luther," Mike said, giving his best shit-eating grin. Compared to the filth and cold and brutality of Greenham, working out his sentence in a sex arcade was a dream: all he had to do was feed the sex toys and clean their cubicles at the end of each night, and once in a while assist Dr Luther in his little sideline.

Dr Luther said, "You will remain my assistant only if you do whatever I say. That is the first and last rule, young man."

Dr Luther was a tall fastidious man of about 60, with silky white hair brushed straight back from his high, liver-spotted forehead. He had a dozen silk suits of different shimmering pastel colours, and smoked foul Bulgarian cigarettes using an ancient yellow ivory holder. He held the cigarette as if he was up to his neck in water, had a way of looking around with slow preening motion, and liked to think of himself as a privileged observer of human psychology.

"I am in a very distinctive position," he told Mike.

"A sex arcade is the one place where true desire is made publicly manifest. It is the one place where honest sexual roles are played for real instead of inside the head. By honest, I mean those which are not compromised by the world, those which are true to the self's base desires. And here it is possible to gauge by sexual satisfaction the correlation between dream and actuality, between vision and performance. Sex is art, and the sex arcade is the possibility of Arcadia, of eternal return."

A lot of what Dr Luther said was simply for effect, Mike thought, like his cabinet full of medical oddities, and the shelf of brutal 20th-century pornography with titles like *Little Anal Annie* and *Piss Party*, stuff that had involved real live human women, not dolls. The customers went pathetically quiet if Dr Luther flashed them a page or two, as if granted a glimpse of the Arcadia he was always talking about.

"No imagination, Michael," Dr Luther would say afterwards. "They're born consumers, and can't think beyond what's put in front of them. Sheep to the slaughter, Michael, sheep to the slaughter."

There was always a creepy feeling in the arcade, as if Dr Luther's spirit had settled into every plush-carpeted corner, like a mist. Mike would be working away when he'd look up and see Dr Luther watching him, his cigarette holder held up by his neck. Sometimes he would make some remote, tangential remark, sometimes he would just watch while Mike creamed up one of the dolls, or sometimes he would describe in explicit detail what the doll was designed to do, how it performed, and then ask if it made Mike excited.

"Whatever you want," Mike took to saying after a while, but even that kind of harmless remark would make Dr Luther smile and he'd take out his notebook and gold pen and jot something down as if he was running an experiment with Mike as its subject. Soon, Mike was tempted to snatch notebook and pen and write down just what he thought of Dr Luther, but he restrained himself with the thought that no matter what, this had to be better than the general labour pool. The Dutch took drug-running a lot less seriously than the other European states. Mike only had to take three years of this, less with remission for good behavior. He'd still be young enough to start over, start another life, maybe another family.

Sometimes Dr Luther would tell Mike to leave off what

he was doing, they had work to do. Dr Luther had a few dozen customers with special needs that went beyond the normal parameters of the sex arcade. Mostly this involved modification of dead sex toys or worked-out straight dolls in the basement operating theatre. Delivery and disposal of what Dr Luther called his little custom jobs was arranged by a chic, hard-faced Frenchwoman who looked about 20 but was, Dr Luther said, at least 60.

What Mike did was hand the appropriate instruments and control bleeding with a diathermy pen while Dr Luther worked on the naked, nerve-blocked blue-skinned doll on a stainless steel table. The surface of the table was hatched with channels that drained blood into a plastic bucket under one corner, like a morgue slab. Dr Luther worked with quick, crude artistry, cutting new orifices and grafting pockets of mucosal epithelium and muscle to shape them, closing mostly with interrupted sutures using thick 20-day catgut because the clients liked the resulting Frankenstein effect. Mike didn't mind the butchery, and in a way it was interesting. Dr Luther was good, and sometimes held a running commentary on his procedures, as if Mike was his pupil rather than his assistant. They were at their most intimate, down there in the basement, over the sacrifice on the stainless steel table.

Sometimes Mike wondered if maybe Dr Luther didn't get off on cutting up dolls up for his special customers, not that he could ask. And besides, it wasn't even illegal. Dr Luther actually had a licence for his operations. It was on the wall of his little operating theatre, right next to the steel table. The clients were licensed, too, and what happened to the customized dolls wasn't much different to what happened to the live targets in the combat games arenas out at Rotterdam.

* * *

Dr Luther's sex arcade was in the basement and ground floor of a building with a high-peaked roof of red tile, in a cobbled side street that ran back from a narrow sleeve of water, Oude Zidjs Voorburgwal, which marked where the old medieval walls had been. This was in the Red Light District, the Walletjes, right in the heart of the oldest part of Amsterdam. Dr Luther was an oddity in the sex-business community, which was mostly run by Africans or Caribbean islanders from the old Dutch colonies, but he was well-liked and greeted everywhere he went, even by the affable cops, greetings he acknowledged with a lift of his panama hat.

"You fuck around with Dr Luther, you get fucked over pretty good yourself," Wayne Patterson told Mike. "He's been around forever, guy, used to pimp real human girls when he was younger back in the last century, moved into dolls most before anyone else. He's even supposed to have run with the liberationists one time, turning dolls into fairies."

"You believe in fairies?" Mike had never before given much thought to dolls, which to him were just there, visible yet invisible, like computers or runabouts. Something about the blue skin made doll faces blurs unless you forced yourself to look closely, and then all you saw was the same broad flat unbridged nose, the same wide lipless mouth, the weak chin, the small round brown eyes. Dolls moved slowly and carefully, as if through hedges of invisible razors, pausing between stages of each task before moving to the next. Mike couldn't picture them running free in the wild places of Europe; they'd been changed too much to become animals again, to revert to their monkey ancestry.

"Most people don't, but I do. I saw one, one time, out on the fringe. It wasn't some doll that had wandered off with a bad chip," Wayne said, with a kind of reverence. "This was something else."

"I thought the peepers had rounded up all the libera-tionists." Mike remembered that a handful had ended up in Greenham a few months before he'd been discharged, but he hadn't had anything to do with them: they were politi-cals, the active edge of a movement that wanted to give dolls the same rights as humans.

"Maybe most of them, but not all. Word is Dr Luther does business with the liberationists, and the cops let him. What you have to understand about Dr Luther is that he's like the King, guy, you can't touch him."

Wayne Patterson was originally from London, a scrawny geezer who'd been living in Amsterdam for 20 years. He'd been under the chip for more than half that time, on and off, though he was clean right now.

He told Mike, "Dr Luther's had assistants before, not one came out the other side. Maybe they tried to rip him off. I learnt one thing under the chip, it's keep your nose clean. They stop you doing the one thing you were sent down for, that's all they're allowed to stop, but it's like you're visible, you try some scam and they got you back in to reprogram your chip before you get started."

Wayne Patterson worked as a tout for the live sex clubs, standing outside the doors and giving tourists the spiel, or handing out cards in the canalside cafés. One night he had tried to give one to Mike, who'd told him, hey, excuse me, I work here too, and Wayne had said yes, wait a minute, you're Dr Luther's new assistant, and had come around the ropes and bought Mike another espresso and soon enough gotten his story out of him and was giving him advice. Wayne Patterson grooved on telling zeks what to do, was Mike's opinion, although he had to admit the scrawny old bastard knew his way around.

"What you need to establish," he told Mike, "is a rou-tine. See, you're in the slam right now, sitting here with me watching the girls go by. Some zeks can't cope with that, but you're intelligent, you'll catch on."

But routine was what Mike had in plenty. He had to spend 14 hours a day under curfew in the zek hostel, mostly sleeping or zoning out in the tattered lounge, watching soaps or sport on the big ancient television with the few zeks who like him worked nightshift. It was a relief, not to have to think about what went on in the cubicles, the insertions, the laborious exertions, the exchange of fluids.

Working in the sex arcade was beginning to make him go a little crazy about sex, wanting it and not wanting it at the same time. His counsellor said that was good, it meant he was getting over his dependency on Hux, and when Mike said he preferred the low-rez haze of cold turkey, the counsellor had added that if he couldn't handle the temptation, he could always quit and go into the general labour pool, giving Mike a mean smile because he knew Mike wouldn't.

Mike kept telling himself it could be worse. In the little window between the end of his curfew and the start of work was the best time, when he hung out in one or another of the cafés in Nieumarkt's big cobbled square, nursing an espresso, slapping at the mosquitoes that skated the night air under the strings of lights. Maybe Wayne Patterson would stop by, maybe not, but there was always a festive mood in early evening, with the lights and thumping music of the little funfair, and entire families of tourists gawking and giggling at the sampler holos hung out in front of the sex shows and arcades, and human prostitutes of all five sexes out looking for business. Parents out with their kids, a lot of the parents no older than Mike, which hurt to think about. His son would be, what, eleven? No, twelve. Twelve years old, and Mike didn't even know exactly where he was. Trying not to think about that was hard.

Still, sometimes a particularly outrageously sexy girl

walking by would get right to him. Mike couldn't help it. He was still young, just past 30, and sex with a live human girl didn't seem at all possible. He couldn't afford the prostitutes, had nowhere but the zek hostel to take any girl he picked up. His lust felt raw and unclean after Hux's pure intensity, but now it was all that he had.

He would watch the girl go by in the soft evening light, maybe in a white T-shirt cut to show the sides of her breasts, and pearl-shimmer short-shorts cut just above the curve of her ass, her long legs gleaming, and he'd say, sort of wincing, "Oh man, that sort of thing ought to be made illegal."

"That's absolutely the wrong response," Wayne Patterson said. "If you like her so much, you should ask her to sit with you, have a drink. Nice young fellow like you."

"Yeah, and in five minutes she'd know I was a zek."

"Plenty of women go for zeks, believe me," Wayne Patterson said, although the one he introduced to Mike was a raddled ex-whore weighing about 100 kilos, most of it spilling out of her tight red dress, who was savvy enough to see Mike's alarm and sweet enough not to comment on it until Wayne Patterson had gone off to take a leak, when she told Mike that Wayne was a good fellow who mostly meant well and besides, she understood that Mike worked for Dr Luther, so he must be copping freebies.

"Well, not exactly," Mike said.

Mike didn't mind handling the sex toys, but they didn't once give him a hard-on. They lay supine and uncomplaining in their two-by-two-metre cubicles on plastic-covered thick foam mattresses, blue skin black in the dull red lights, more pathetically ludicrous than arousing. They were like those breeds of dog so selected for one characteristic that they can hardly function at all. A couple had breasts so big they could hardly sit up to use their bedpans; others had huge over-complicated labia like sea anemones or insectivorous tropical blooms, which needed special creams to stop them getting infected with yeasts, or internal arrangements so strange Mike would rather put his dick in a meat grinder.

As far as Mike was concerned, dolls were just things, less than animals because they had been designed. He lusted hopelessly after the girly-girl whores that paraded the cobbled streets of the Walletjes, but he'd as soon screw a vacuum cleaner as a doll.

And then he fell in love.

The sex arcade had closed and Mike had finished hosing down the cubicles and feeding the sex toys their syrup when he found Dr Luther waiting for him by the service door, slowly and voluptuously smoking a cigarette, a little black bag at his feet.

"I have a little business meeting tonight," he said. "You'll come along, Michael. Hold still, now."

Mike jerked back, because Dr Luther had waved something towards his face. Dr Luther gripped Mike's chin, showed him what looked like a pocket torch. He held it up to Mike's right eye and there was a brief flash.

"All done," Dr Luther said, releasing Mike.

"What was that?"

"I reprogrammed your chip for tonight. Extended your curfew."

"That's not legal, is it?"

"It is not legal, but I am sure you will not mind."

"You want me to break the law, and I don't know what for?"

"I am the law, Michael, as far as you are concerned. Come now. We have a rendezvous."

They rode the trams out to a service station at a road junction near Schiphol airport. At two in the morning it was surprisingly busy: long-distance lorry drivers made noise at the bar; ordinary families ate in groups, eyes on the flickering teevee screens; a minor rock group Mike recognized from his trawling of daytime television made a lot of noise at the bar with their road crew and hangers-on. Dr Luther watched all this benevolently, as if he had created the whole scene for Mike's edification.

Mike was sort of scrunched up in one corner of the booth. His eyes were hurting. This was too like the times he had picked up his packages when he had been in the courier business. Pressure was swelling in his right eyesocket, not quite sharpening to pain.

Dr Luther nudged him and said, "See the fellow who looks like an undertaker, buying a cup of coffee? He'll go outside, and one minute later we'll follow him."

Mike looked just as the guy turned from the counter. A swarthy square face framed by a helmet of black hair, a cheap black suit and big shiny black shoes, a bootlace tie at the collar of his white shirt. He saw Mike looking at him and turned away, headed for the door.

Mike said, "Is this worth your while? I can't see that you'd make much from people like that. Whatever it is you're selling."

Dr Luther pulled out a pocket watch and flipped up its lid. "Money isn't the issue," he said. "What we are dealing with here are liberationists. They want the thyrotropic hormone that I use to bring the sex toys to rapid maturity. It's part of the process of making fairies, Michael."

Mike supposed that he was to say something, but he didn't know what to think about it at all, except that maybe Wayne Patterson hadn't been retailing as much shit as he had thought.

He drank down the last of his herbal tea and followed Dr Luther out into the hot windy night. The sharp sweet stink of gasohol. The distant roar of the motorway, which made a ribbon of orange light beyond a screen of trees. They went around the side of the service station. The kitchen door was propped open, and inside, in bright light glancing off white porcelain and stainless steel, dolls in white paper overalls worked at a rapid pace amongst the deep-fryers and griddles, bald blue heads gleaming in the harsh light.

The liberationists were waiting in the shadows by the kitchen dumpbins. There were three of them, the swarthy man who'd come into the service station, another man who looked enough like the first to be his brother, and an older woman in a ragged denim dress, her grey hair in dreadlocks. Dr Luther murmured to Mike that since the big crackdown last year, the liberationists were living wild with their creations, and that it wouldn't do to mention it.

The woman, who was clearly in charge, looked at Mike and said, "Who's the guy?" She was about 60, with a round face and a head that seemed slightly too small for her fleshy body. Mike looked away from her direct gaze.

"My assistant," Dr Luther said.

"A zek? Gee, Dieter, maybe we ought to do the deal another time."

"He's fine. You are fine, aren't you, Michael?"

"Sure," Mike said.

One of the men in black laughed. Behind them, in the dumpbin, something rustled through the waste food: rats, Mike thought, suddenly nervous. During his time at Greenham he had come to loathe rats.

"He's under a chip," the woman said, "we can give him something to get him happy that it won't register."

Dr Luther said, "Are you offering to sell after all this time? I am surprised."

"I'm offering him a freebie, Dieter. It isn't for sale. It isn't mine to sell."

"And yet you can give it away. Well, do a deal with

him if you like, but on his own time. Meanwhile, you have to pay for the hormone."

"Pretty soon we'll be able to make that ourselves, too," the woman said.

"Of course, it is not difficult. But do you have the equipment to refine it? I would advise you not to try using it otherwise; it will have unpleasant side effects on your patients." Dr Luther added, "You know, it is possible that we can trade . . ."

"Maybe I can give you a freebie, too. Turn you on, Dieter. Do you some good."

The woman was being playful, Mike saw. This was a routine she and Dr Luther had gone through many times.

"Come on," one of the men said, the one who'd come into the service station. "We get this done. We go." He had some kind of Balkan accent.

"I have thirty millilitres at 2000 units per," Dr Luther said, holding up a sealed silvery plastic baggie. "I think you know the price."

"As we agreed," the woman said, and held up a sheaf of crumpled US dollars, green bills worn thread-bare by their long use as the currency of the grey market.

Mike had been watching the exchange, and didn't notice the figure rising from the dumpbin until it vaulted to the ground and looked straight at him. A blue-skinned high-cheeked elfin face, eyes flooded with amber reflections from the kitchen's light. Beautiful, in a ragged lace dress that half-concealed, half-revealed her slim body. A changeling, a fairy.

The kitchen door clattered open, and a doll limped out, shouldering a greasy bag of waste food. Mike looked around for a moment; when he looked back, the fairy had gone.

The two men had stepped backwards into the shadows, vanishing in the same way the fairy had. The woman looked at Mike and said, "Hey, now you know why we do this. You come by some time, you can turn on like they do. Really, our stuff will get by your chip."

Mike said, "Oh yeah? What does it do?" He was acutely aware that Dr Luther was watching him.

"It'll take you on a one-way trip to fairyland, young fellow. What do you say?"

"My assistant stays clean," Dr Luther said. "If I get into trouble with the authorities, I can't answer for the consequences."

"I think your assistant's in love," the woman said, and then she turned and walked off into the darkness beyond the light that fell from the kitchen.

Dr Luther said, "You do not entertain that idea, Michael. With me you stay clean."

"Listen, I only work for you. I'm not like one of your dolls."

"Of course not. You don't want to be owned by anyone. That is quite natural. But you are mine, Michael, while you are chipped. I give back your proof of employment, your werkgeversverklaring, you go to the general labour pool. Like this poor thing here."

The doll had halted outside the kitchen door, stupidly confused by the presence of humans where no humans should be. Dr Luther caught its chin in one hand and the sack of garbage it was carrying dropped with a ripe splatter: He raised his other hand and the scalpel caught the light from the kitchen. Then he cut the doll's throat.

It stood with blood gushing dark red down the front of its paper coveralls, then collapsed face forward into the spill of chicken bones and plastic and rotten lettuce leaves and soggy half-eaten rolls.

Mike stepped back as blood pooled towards his boots. He was too shocked to speak.

"Remember that the fairies are just one step from this," Dr Luther said. He kicked the dead doll's head. "Let me tell you about dolls. They were originally gene-spliced in South Korea as a way of trying to out-compete its neighbours of the Pacific Rim, and soon every nation was using them as cheap slave labour. Kobolds, they were originally called, although no one but the Peace Police uses this term now. The liberationists cure the dolls by taking out their control chips and inserting new ones, and infect them with fembots which hardwire the chips into the dolls' cerebral cortex, then bring them to sexual maturity. Most dolls are male, did you know that?"

"Does it matter?" The talk of chips had reminded Mike of his own; his right eye itched from the inside.

"Not usually, of course. There's nothing magical about them, and nothing there for you, my dear Michael. I've been offering to distribute that drug for several years, but always I am refused."

"She said it wasn't hers to sell."

"She helped make the fairies, Michael. What do you think?"

Mike thought about that on the ride back, and on and off all the next day, speculation mixed with the glimpse he'd had of the fairy's fine-boned face, its wild fearless gaze.

"I heard talk of a place out there where it doesn't matter you're chipped," Wayne Patterson volunteered the next evening, in the café where Mike was whiling away the time before the sex arcade opened. He explained in his dogged old man's way, "The thing is, they say you can find anything out on the fringe, but when you're out there . . . You're there, that's all that matters on the fringe. You can't fall any further. Nothing at all to do with fairies."

"You said you saw a fairy?"

"The peepers killed most of them when they broke up the liberationists," Wayne said. "Maybe there are one or two left, but that's it. It's more important they're fringers than fairies."

Mike said, "Right now I've something more interesting to think about. Last night, I learnt there are still liberationists."

He explained what had gone down, and Wayne grew serious. "I tell you one thing, Mike. Don't fuck with Dr Luther. He's been around a long time. He's got all sorts of connections and immunities."

"That drug turns out to be real, there are maybe what? A million zeks, two million? Most of them wanting to be turned on. And then there are the straights."

Wayne said, "You used to be on Hux, right? Bad stuff, Mike. I think you want a taste again. I seen this before. Go talk to your therapist, he'll tell you."

"What I was into . . . I don't need a replacement for that. What I need is to get out from under the chip, away from Dr Luther and his little tricks. And I know that costs money. There are places that'll take it out easy enough, but then I need a new identity, don't want to look at tripling my sentence if I get caught. And you, Wayne, what about you?"

"What about me?" Wayne said, looking confused.

"You got to get yourself out, too. You're stuck here and you deserve better. Name a place you want to go, you can get there." He could see the idea growing in Wayne by the way the old man's eyes started to lose focus. He said, "All I need is someone who knows the fringes, someone who can find out where the liberationists are hiding."

"Those guys you were talking about," Wayne said. "They sound an awful lot like some ghosts I was staying with some time. You know, stateless people. These were from I think Albania."

Mike smiled. "I believe it's my round," he said. "What do you want, coffee or juice?"

Later, at work, Dr Luther made no mention of the last night, for which Mike was very grateful. He wasn't sure if he could hold his tongue if Dr Luther made one of his remarks. He prepped a doll for surgery, washing its stringy blue body with alcohol, giving it a shot to put it under with the pneumatic hypodermic. Dr Luther worked quickly, building a muscular orifice in the doll's abdominal wall: this was for the special customer who took to heart the old maxim about understanding death by fucking life in the gall bladder.

"You'll help with the delivery tonight," Dr Luther said, after they had rolled the doll onto the gurney and Mike was sluicing blood from the stainless steel table. Dr Luther snapped off his gloves and dropped them into the bucket of clotting blood. "Just look tough and say nothing. That's all Eve wants. You mess up, she'll tell me, but I trust you not to mess up, Michael. And don't bother coming back when you're done. This is an expensive rush job, no need to open the arcade tonight."

"I'll do my best," Mike said, nice as pie, thinking that if Dr Luther wanted him out of the way that night there were more subtle ways to go about it. Arrogance was as bad a vice as stupidity.

The delivery was in the smart neighbourhood to the west of the Damrak, on Prinsengrácht canal, a stone's throw from the Anne Frank House. Eve, the hard-faced Frenchwoman, didn't lift a finger as Mike manoeuvred the groggy doll out of the water taxi and across the cobbled street into the elevator of the tall narrow apartment building.

The special client lived in the penthouse. It was done out in retrochic: a gleaming hardwood floor; glass walls on three sides of the living room looking out across the lights of the city; leather and chrome furniture spotlit like museum pieces, which was probably what they were. An actual human butler, whom Mike at first mistook for the client, a small grave Thai in a loose black smock, helped instal the doll in a ceramic and stainless steel bathroom while Eve waited by the door. The butler handed her a fat envelope which she put in her Chanel bag.

On the way down, Mike said, "What happens to it?"

Eve gave him a hard look and said, "They do things to it, maybe fuck it, maybe not, and then kill it, slowly."

"Not my idea of sex."

"You don't have much imagination, do you, Michael? That's good. Don't ask questions, and you'll be all right."

Outside she handed him a bill before she stepped into the waiting water taxi. Ten ecus.

He stood at the edge of the quay and said, "What do I do, buy a cup of coffee?"

In the water taxi, Eve looked up. "Isn't it almost your curfew? You go home now, stay cool."

But going home was the last thing on Mike's mind; instead, he walked back to Dr Luther's sex arcade. It was shut, its frontage dark amongst the neon hustle and bustle of midnight. A black, official-looking limo was illegally parked on the corner under the big Pepsi-Cola hologram, its human driver reading by the hologram's red, white and blue light, oblivious to the colourful crowds that swirled around him while he waited for his boss to finish with his cheap thrill. In the Neiumarkt Square beyond, the lights of the funfair's big wheel slowly revolved against the purple night.

Mike got in at the back door at the bottom of a set of narrow slippery steps, using the key he'd taken on the way out. He was looking through the steel pharmacy cabinet in the basement when he heard footsteps above and then muffled voices.

Each of the cubicles had an intercom set. In the old days the girls would have used them in case the customer got rough; now they were marked for customer convenience. Mike switched them on, one by one, his heart tripping at each click, until he heard Dr Luther telling someone that it was risky, they probably wouldn't even come, with an edge to his voice Mike had never heard before.

A man's voice, heavy and slow, fluent Dutch coloured by an unidentifiable accent, said, "That's your problem. I trust for your own sake you'll find a way."

"I could tell them that the batch was contaminated. It would work as long as they haven't started to use it."

"I don't want details, Luther. Just that it's arranged."

"Well, as long as I'm not involved beyond that."

"We arrest them, leave you. My word."

"I'm losing a source of income, you know."

"Hardly a major worry for you, given your special clients. You know we can make it up to you. Tomorrow night."

Mike didn't need to hear any more. He shut off the intercom, and went through the pharmacy cabinet, then the surgical kit. That was where he found the reprogramming device. It was a slim black tube with a gridded lens at its flared end, a digital input pad and a red button set in its shaft. He prayed that the thing wasn't date specific, that what had worked yesterday would work today, and put it to his right eye and pressed the button. Then he pulled open the refrigerator and grabbed a couple of sealed bags of thyrotropic hormone, and went out the way he'd come in.

On the hot, crowded, neon-lit street, he saw the limo pull away, moving slowly over the cobbles. A moment later, Dr Luther appeared at the door of the arcade. He carefully locked it, and went off in the opposite direction. Mike ran all the way to the club where Wayne Patterson was working.

* * *

At that time of night, the trams were mostly empty. Wayne Patterson sat on one side of the aisle, Mike on the other. Mike felt a buzzing excitement, couldn't stop telling the old man what he'd heard, although all Wayne would say was that of course Dr Luther was a snitch, just about everyone on the Walletjes was, it was how they got through life, it didn't mean anything.

"But it does!" Mike said passionately. He was thinking of that sweet glimpse, the beautiful creature. He could have reached out . . . He remembered that Wayne Patterson had told him about the time he'd worked in a termination plant. They strapped the dolls in bucket seats on a kind of chain, shot them in the head with a captive bolt, and the seats carried them into the incinerator. Inspectors were supposed to make sure every doll was dead before it burned, but Wayne had said maybe one in a hundred woke up with a broken skull, started to scream and struggle, and the inspectors knew all about it, because why else would the dolls have to be strapped in . . .

It was still hot when they reached the service station at the motorway intersection, the night air close and absolutely still. Traffic made a rushing noise beyond the screen of trees. Lights twinkled out in the heath, little fires. Wayne Patterson shivered, said it was so spookily the same.

"Then you can find them."

"Look, Mike, they've a mind to it they can find you. But they don't want to—"

"The liberationists can't be that far away. Luther expects to meet up with them tomorrow. And they said they'd look out for me. They want to turn me on."

"And you're going to let them."

"Sure. I have to try the goods first, don't I?"

"The goods. Right. But that's not really why you're doing this, is it?" When Mike didn't answer, Wayne sighed and said, "Might as well get it over. Stay close to me, kid. Don't go running off no matter what you see."

A hundred metres beyond the neon orange glow of the parking lot, it was almost pitch black. The stars were bright, but there was no moon. The two men kept tripping on heather roots exposed in the sandy soil. Once, Wayne made Mike stand still for a whole minute because of shadows on a low ridge ahead, until he suddenly snorted and said, "It's okay, I think they're just bushes."

They were: dwarf willows, with an old torn sleeping bag bunched up in their shelter. "Someone was here," Wayne Patterson remarked, and Mike laughed, something relaxing in him, and told Wayne he was a dead loss as an Indian scout.

"Hold up," Wayne said. "I think I hear someone coming."

That was when they were rushed. There were two packs, coming from right and left, throwing plastic sheets over both men, knocking them down by press of numbers. Mike felt hard little fingers clutching at the baggies of hormone solution, and tried to hug them to his chest, but something bit his wrist and he howled and let go, kicking against the weights on his legs, which suddenly vanished. He sat up, convulsively threw away the plastic sheeting, called out Wayne's name.

Silence.

Mike reached out, walking his fingertips centimetre by centimetre across sandy soil until they encountered Wayne Patterson's nylon windbreaker. The old man didn't move; there was no pulse in his throat. Mike straddled him and started heart massage and mouth-to-mouth, but Wayne didn't respond and then Mike found the thin spike that had been driven into his right eye and with a sudden convulsive movement flung himself away from the corpse.

That was when he heard the music.

It came from the north, deeper in the wasteland. A faint glow showed there and Mike walked towards it, stumbling over tussocky grasses in near darkness. It was past two o'clock in the morning, and his right eye throbbed. Reprogramming had only increased the limit that the chip allowed by a few kilometres, and he cloudily wondered how much time he had before the extension on his curfew ran out.

The light came from a fire which burned in a little steep-sided hollow. There were two huts built right into the sides of the hollow like entrances to mine shafts, their walls made of crates with product names still stencilled on their sides, their steep roofs of overlapping flattened tins. A wailing music rose up from somewhere near the fire. It was a wild skirl of women's voices, a dissonant chorus that sent chills snarling at the base of Mike's spine. He'd never heard music like it.

As Mike went down the slope, his right eye suddenly swarmed with black chevrons—a warning that he'd reached his limit. He clapped his hands over his eyes and cried out, and tripped and fell, rolling down the sandy slope and coming to rest at the feet of the men who'd come around the fire to meet him.

They helped Mike up. He had to squint around the chevrons to see them. They were dressed in shabby black suits, or long dark coats over jeans and ragged pullovers. With black curly hair and a gypsy look, they all looked a little like each other, as if they were all brothers or uncles in the same family, the same family indeed as the men who had escorted the woman liberationist. They spoke what sounded like Italian, slow enough that Mike could almost understand it. One of them held up a bulky old-fashioned radio with a grey plastic grill front and twisted a dial, and the music stopped.

Mike had fallen into the middle of a gang of ghosts, part of the population of second-or third-generation refugees from the central European wars or from further still, old-style Russians who'd fled the Islamic Jihad, and Africans who'd migrated like so many birds up Italy into Europe's heartland. There were millions of them living in the wild places outside the cities and arcologies, enduring the hot summers and cold winters, the ice storms and droughts caused by the great climatic overturn. They had no money but used an elaborate system of barter; no government but that of the family or group; no law but that which the EC refugee commission imposed upon them. They took medical care from U.N. clinics, work and food where they could.

One of the men, a tall broad fellow perhaps a few years younger than Mike, said in broken French that he and his brothers were from Albania, that he would be honoured if Mike would break bread here with them while they waited for his friend, and Mike, misunderstanding, told him about Wayne, the way he had been killed.

The man said he understood, that they could do something for this Wayne if perhaps Mike had some money . . . ?

Mike discovered that the slender roll of notes he'd stashed in the key pocket of his jeans was gone: all he could offer were a few coins, silver-thin ecus and a heavy English five pound coin with milled edges. Poor enough fare for the ferryman, but the tall man jingled them in his palm, then clapped Mike on the back.

Somewhere on the other side of the fire, the radio started up with the women's chanting voices again. An unlabelled green bottle with a chipped neck was passing from hand to hand. A moment later, just as Mike was trying to explain that he couldn't drink brandy, the woman liberationist stepped out of one of the huts.

* * *

"Quite a sight you made," she said, "stumbling this way and that across the heath, like King Lear with his fool, looking for Cordelia."

Her grey dreadlocks were flattened to one side, as if she'd been sleeping, and her skin gleamed with sweat; her cotton dress, printed with a Martian scape of sand and pitted rocks, clung to the upper slopes of her loose breasts. She looked drunk, or stoned.

"Were those really children?"

"Of course they were. Fairies don't need money."

Mike wondered how she knew the kids had stolen his bankroll. He said, "I was bringing you some thyrotropic hormone. They got that when they killed my friend."

"Oh, and are you sure that's what he was?" The way she said it, Mike knew what she'd done. She added, all concern, "Is there something wrong with your eye?"

"I'm out here at my limit. I can't go any further. That hormone was all I had. And the money. Except I can tell you something—"

One of the Albanians handed the woman the bottle of brandy. She swigged deeply, wiped her mouth. "You came to see the fairies. If you still want that, you'll have to take this in your mouth. Hurry. We don't have much time."

She thrust out her hand, palm-up: a leech-like gob of live jelly curled and uncurled there. Mike stepped back, and she laughed.

"No one said it would be easy!" Then her face was in his, brandy fumes so strong it was a wonder his chip wasn't triggered. "I can show you such wonders. Do you have the courage?"

"Why I came out here—" But he couldn't explain. He

had no plan, only desire, sudden and physical as hunger. "Yes," he said. "Yes, I will. Yes."

Then her hand was over his mouth, and he could feel the thing against his lips. "Don't swallow," she said. "Don't chew. Just let it in."

Mike opened his mouth with an act of will, felt the thing squirm onto his tongue. He gagged, but it had already sunk into his mucosal membranes. A slow throbbing spread out from the soft tissue at the muscular root of his tongue, filling the cave of his mouth. A wave of nausea rolled over him and he doubled over and vomited.

The woman held his hair back as his stomach wetly clenched, forcing up chyme thin as egg white. When he was able to stand, she said, "Now you're almost ready."

Mike started to ask what she'd done to him, but suddenly there was a great beating of wings and light stabbed down, flooding the little hollow. Moments later a helicopter descended from the darkness beyond the glare, blowing out the fire and sending ashes flying up. An amplified voice said something that was lost in the helicopter's roar.

The Albanians were disappearing into one of the huts. The woman grabbed Mike's hand and dragged him into the other. "Crawl," she said, and pushed him into the dark at the back, which turned out to be an old drainage pipe.

Mike crawled, following the sounds of the woman as she turned left at a Y-junction, Warning chevrons floated before him; his right eye felt as if it was filled with mercury.

Maybe ten, maybe twenty minutes of this. At some point the chevrons faded from Mike's sight: the woman was leading him back towards Amsterdam. Mike began to appreciate how the dolls moved around. There had been kilometers and kilometres of pipes installed at the beginning of the century to drain saltwater see page, part of the now-abandoned reclamation schemes.

The pain in his eye and the chevrons came back: he felt a sudden breeze. The woman pulled him up. They were in an inspection manhole. Mike could hardly see now. He said, "I can't go any further," but the woman only said she'd see about that and started climbing. Mike followed, hand over hand up the iron staples that made a ladder up the manhole. Hot hands grasped his, pulled him up, and something, a fairy, grinned into his face. With the chevrons swarming in his sight Mike couldn't tell whether it was the one he'd seen before. It kissed him full on the mouth, and he felt the hot worm of its tongue writhe across his teeth.

The creature giggled and then it was running into the darkness towards tangles of pipes and block-houses, an abandoned chemical plant or pumping station lightless except for a single warning light flashing red on top of a tall chimney.

As Mike started after the fairy, the structure seemed to flow into itself, growing taller, turrets reaching up against a sky softly luminous and dusted with living stars as a meadow is dusted with daisies. A woman took his hand; she was tall and fair, dressed in a loose gown that swept to her feet, with a coronet thrust carelessly in her long loose hair. Her laughter was like a bell; her soft hand thrilled in Mike's own, and he turned and pulled her to him and kissed her until she pulled away, laughing again. "You have to save yourself," she said, and led him on until black light filled his eyes and spiralled into his head and took him away.

Mike came awake all at once, sweat starting from every pore. His right eye hurt like crazy, tender as when he'd been chipped. He was lying in a nest of greasy, smelly rags, head-first inside a dead-end pipe just long enough to hold him. Light flickered beyond his feet; there was the sound of people moving around. He turned himself around, pain flaring in his eye with every movement. When he stuck his head out to take a look where he was, the same fairy he'd seen that one time at the service station smiled at him from about a metre away and he remembered and managed not to scream.

He was in some kind of vault, big as a church, lit by vague shafts of light that fell through grids high above. A double row of steel girders held up a ceiling of concrete slabs. They stood either side of a central channel that was filled with black water in which grossly fat dolls wallowed on their backs like beached walruses. Naked blue-skinned fairies moved amongst the girders, going to and fro, weaving in and out, forming groups of six or eight or ten that slowly collapsed against each other, writhing and crawling and licking and stroking in languorous slow motion before flowing away in different directions.

It made mike think of the ant heaps under the flagstones of the path of his parents' house. When he'd been little he'd lever up the slabs to watch with a mixture of curiosity and revulsion the swarming secret life. He'd forgotten that emotion until now.

Every so often a fairy would step up and bend to kiss the bloated blue-skinned belly of one of the dolls that wallowed in the trough of black water—no, they were sucking at tubes which jutted from crusted ligatures and dribbled clear pink goo. Mike saw the woman, hands cupped on the shiny swollen belly of one of the dolls, cheeks hollowing as she sucked. She straightened, slowly licked her lips, then dreamily stalked up the slope. Mike hastily slid out of his hole, falling to his knees on wet gritty concrete.

The woman crouched beside him. Stuff like egg albumin glistened on her chin. "Welcome to fairyland," she said. "I can tell you're not seeing it as it is."

"Oh, I am. I am. Jesus, you live like this?"

"Once we thought only of freeing them," the woman said dreamily. "We unchained their minds, sharpened their intelligence, induced sexual maturation. We liberated them. We believed they should decide their own destiny, but we didn't realize that we weren't making them more human, but less. Did you ever read science fiction?"

"Not really." Mike found all those old movies that showed up on cable kind of disturbing, full of the violent aspirations of a bad century. They put odd thoughts in his head, fantasies of instant gratification, limitless power. Stuff like that could mess up your life, he should know.

"They always thought the aliens would come from the stars. But they're here, Mike. We made them. When the peace police came down, some of us escaped. We ran into the wilderness. The fairies found us, took us in. We'd changed them and they started to change us." She giggled. "Here we are. Isn't it wonderful?"

Mike said, "Dr Luther wants to turn you in. You go to him again, he will."

"Dr Luther told the peepers you'd lead them to us. He thinks that he can get the drug for free if he can find out where we live. There's a recording circuit in your chip. So we took it out."

"I knew it! You're crazy!"

Mike felt a wave of panicky despair. He really didn't need this. His flaky old counsellor had been clear about that one point: trying to interfere with your chip automatically tripled your sentence. He'd be an old man before he came out from under, childless, unloved. He'd be like poor dead Wayne Patterson.

He said, without hope, "Take me back."

"Mike, Mike. Don't you understand? You have so much to give. You have what they need, what they want. They're only the third stage. We were the first, the dolls the second,

fairies need for the fourth, for the fusion. Certain genes . . .
Fairies, males and females both, are sterile, but still they are
making a new generation. They learn so quickly. They strip
bowel epithelial cells to the haploid state and fuse them,
gestate the embryos in the abdominal cavities of males
when they run short of females.

"They need you, Mike. They need what you have to add
to what they have already taken, as much variety as possible, yes. Don't think you're the first or the last. And you'll
be rewarded. You came here for the drug, but you can't use
the drug without the catalyst. That's what I made you put
under your tongue. It's part of you now, has sunk its pseu-
doneurones into your limbic cortex. When it receives the
blessing, then you'll see all this as it really is!"

Mike said, "Blessing?"

The fairy's hot fingers feathered Mike's cheek. He didn't
know if he was going to throw up or come. Its beautiful
knife-blade face was centimetres from his. Its eyes were
flecked with gold, and he could see his own face, unshaven
and ripely bruised around the right eye, reflected there. Its
lips branded his own, and he felt its hot tongue slide into
his mouth, sweet and hot and wet.

And he saw.

The fairy and the woman took him by the hands and
he rose and walked down the broad sweep of soft living
marble. The woman swung a little sack of soft leather, threw
a pinch of gold dust from it into the air, then tied it around
Mike's neck, telling him it was his price, his reward.

He hardly noticed, seeing the filigreed pillars that arched
gracefully to the mother-of-pearl roof of this sumptuous
chamber, hearing the siren song of the silken-skinned creatures that bathed in the silver waters of the central pool,
joyously and generously offering their sweet intoxicating
milk to any who craved it. He saw the lambent joy in the

fairies that surrounded him, their touches waking waves of pleasure that pierced him to his core as they divested him of his clothes and pressed against him, moving together on and over and under, and Mike was taken in and he accepted and became a part of the flowing movement. Skin on skin, hotter than human. The arching press of strange, boned penises, not seeking to enter him but only flowing, tracing exquisite patterns across his skin. The woman's laughter floating somewhere, tiny bells that tripped the mechanisms of his heart. It was better than Hux, it took him all, skin and muscle, nerve and bone and blood and brain. Someone fed him clear pink milk from their mouth, and it was an explosion of delight running through his core, rising and rising, the fairies intent around him now, still moving on him as he came in wave after wave, his come arching gloriously, caught in a crystal bottle by an intent fairy, sperm flickering like stars, like phosphorescent fish schooling in a coral grotto as Mike screamed with pleasure, and fainted.

Night, warm wind stinking of halogens blowing across the coarse grass in which Mike lay. There was a plastic bag in his hand—he remembered that it had been a leather sack chock full of gold dust, but it held only a dredging of coarse sand—and then he remembered everything else, and laughed.

From a little way off, Dr. Luther said, "Well you're awake, even if you haven't come to your senses."

"Oh Christ."

Dr Luther came forward and helped Mike sit up. Amsterdam's sickly aurora, glowing at the level horizon, provided enough light for Mike to see Dr Luther's quizzical expression.

"You still have your chip," Dr Luther said.

"I do? I thought I was free . . ." What he felt was relief.

"It went off, then came back on. That's how we found you. The police are waiting, Michael, but they let me talk to you first. It is a small enough favour considering the help I gave. Where are they, Michael? They left you here. Where did they take you?"

"I don't know. Somewhere strange. Wonderful and strange. I don't know where!"

Then he cried out, because Dr Luther had grabbed hold of his hair, pulled his head back.

"The drug, Michael. Tell me about the drug. It's real, isn't it? Tell me where, Michael, and you can walk free. All the cops want are the liberationists, the people who killed Wayne Patterson, who did this to you. Be smart. I can help you. Tell me all about it."

"Wayne Patterson was working for you, wasn't he? They knew, that's why they killed him. I've been a fool."

Dr Luther wrenched at Mike's hair. "Tell me!"

It was hard to stay clam, but knowledge gave Mike strength. "Listen," he said quietly.

When Dr Luther bent closer Mike got a hand under his chin and pushed. Then they were rolling over in the dirt. Mike kicked and kicked, and Dr Luther went limp for a second, long enough for Mike to break free and stand up. He was breathing in great gulps, shaking with the rush of adrenalin.

Dr Luther slowly climbed to his feet. He brushed at the crumpled, stained trousers of his silk suit and looked sidelong at Mike with a wary expression. He suddenly looked old and frail.

Mike said, "You don't get it, do you? There are no more liberationists. The fairies don't need them any more. You told me they weren't anything, just modified dolls. You're wrong. They're as much like dolls as we are like dogs."

Lights flashed and danced in the distance: a line of figures was walking slowly across the heath towards them.

Dr Luther said, pleading now, "Time's up, Michael. The police will put you in the general labour pool if you don't tell them. Last chance."

Mike said, "You don't get it, do you? Matter of fact, you'll never get it."

He remembered, as if in double-image, the pleasure and the reality. The fairies had used him and taken his germ cells and cast him away, but he understood and forgave them. They owed their creators nothing, and even the glimpse of their world was payment enough, for he knew no matter how much he might yearn for it, he couldn't live there. They learn so quickly, the woman had said of the fairies. Learn and change, busy becoming something else, growing away from their origin. She'd given her all, and so had he, all he was able to give.

He began to laugh. His children—what would his children be like? Still laughing, free at last, he walked past the old man towards the waiting police.

BRUCE STERLING'S IDEA OF WHAT EVERY WELL-APPOINTED "CYBERPUNK SF" LIBRARY COLLECTION SHOULD POSSESS

THE CANON:

BURNING CHROME by William Gibson
Gibson's short stories.

NEUROMANCER, COUNT ZERO, MONA LISA OVERDRIVE
by William Gibson
The "Cyberspace Trilogy."

MIRRORSHADES THE CYBERPUNK ANTHOLOGY Bruce
Sterling ed.
Useful pointer to actual no-kidding Movement Cyberpunks.

MINDPLAYERS by Pat Cadigan
Her best novel. An absolute must-have.

HEATSEEKER by John Shirley
Shirley's short-stories. His most significant and influential work.

DESERTED CITIES OF THE HEART by Lewis Shiner
Shiner's best SF novel.

SLAM by Lewis Shiner
Intriguing cyberpunk mainstream non-genre novel.

SOFTWARE, WETWARE, FREEWARE by Rudy Rucker
Best-known novels of deranged math-professor/hacker/cyberpunk. This would be the inimitable Rucker's idea of a trilogy if not for the threatened appearance of "Limpware."

TRANSREAL by Rudy Rucker
Every short piece Rucker ever wrote. Enormous. Like being hit in the head with a bowling ball.

BLOOD MUSIC by Greg Bear
Bear's most c-wordish book.

CRYSTAL EXPRESS by Bruce Sterling
Sterling's short work.

SCHISMATRIX by Bruce Sterling
Posthuman space opera.

ISLANDS IN THE NET by Bruce Sterling
21st-century global information politics.

THE DIFFERENCE ENGINE by William Gibson and Bruce Sterling
19th-century cyberpunk by subgenre's foremost critics'-darlings.

OTHER USEFUL FICTION:

VIRTUAL LIGHT by William Gibson
A new, more intimate view of the future by the gomi-no-sensei.

IDORU by William Gibson
Light, graceful, and brilliantly inventive.

HALO by Tom Maddox
Remarkable SF treatment of robots and artificial intelligence. Available online in its entirety at no charge.

GLOBALHEAD by Bruce Sterling
Sterling's second story collection.

THE EXPLODED HEART John Shirley
Shirley's second story collection.

PATTERNS Pat Cadigan
Cadigan's short work. Great range of topics and treatments.

SYNNERS by Pat Cadigan
Cadigan's well-received second novel.

FOOLS by Pat Cadigan
The logical extreme.

TEA FROM AN EMPTY CUP
Cadigan drinks tea and lives in Britian

FRONTERA by Lewis Shiner
Shiner's first novel, about a mission to Mars.

LOOK INTO THE SUN by James Patrick Kelly
Interesting novel by peripheral cyberpunk.

WILDLIFE by James Patrick Kelly
This highly bizarre short-story fixup novel is a catalog of cyberpunk ontological riffs.

ARACHNE by Lisa Mason
Cyberspace robots vs. drug-addict San Francisco lawyer-careerists.
Weirdissimo.

SNOW CRASH Neal Stephenson
Fine example of second-generation cyberpunk by Seattle hacker.

THE DIAMOND AGE by Neal Stephenson
This guy may be the first native-born cyberpunk writer.

CRYPTONOMICON by Neal Stephenson
Awe-inspiring creative power

HARDWIRED by Walter Jon Williams
Williams' most successful effort.

SPACETIME DONUTS, WHITE LIGHT by Rudy Rucker
Rucker's early novels. Brilliantly deranged.

LIVE ROBOTS by Rudy Rucker
Paperback double reissue of Rucker's novels SOFTWARE
and WETWARE.

HACKER AND THE ANTS by Rudy Rucker
The indefatigable Rucker tackles artificial life issues.

INVOLUTION OCEAN, THE ARTIFICIAL KID by Bruce
Sterling
Sterling's first two novels. SF adventures.

HEAVY WEATHER by Bruce Sterling
Cyberpunk eco-disaster novel. Sterling's darkest work.

HOLY FIRE by Bruce Sterling
The European art scene in the late 21st century.

SEMIOTEXT(E) SF Rudy Rucker, Peter Lamborn Wilson,
Robert Anton Wilson, eds.
Story anthology of bad craziness. Quite likely to cause pro-
tests from scandalized parents and censors.

MAGAZINES

ARTBYTE
Cybeculture without the dotcoms.

ASIMOV'S SCIENCE FICTION.
Least reactionary of the standard American SF magazines.

INTERZONE
Foremost British SF magazine. Libraries should carry this worthy zine as a public service, since individual US subscriptions are costly.

WIRED
The first magazine of the 1990s that actually looked and acted as if it belonged in that decade.

NON-FICTION, CRITICAL STUDIES

STORMING THE REALITY STUDIO Larry McCaffery ed.
Cyberpunk's man-in-academe gives his highly postmodern take on matters in this bug-crusher anthology.

CYBERPUNK: OUTLAWS AND HACKERS ON THE COMPUTER FRONTIER by Katie Hafner and John Markoff.
The best book to date on the outlaw "computer underground."

ACROSS THE WOUNDED GALAXIES Larry McCaffery ed.
McCaffery interviews various weirdo leading-lights of pomo SF, including Gibson and Sterling.

THE HACKER CRACKDOWN, LAW AND DISORDER ON THE ELECTRONIC FRONTIER by Bruce Sterling
A flash photograph of a crucial technology in legal disarray.

TERMINAL IDENTITY by Scott Bukatman
Headlong foray across the wild terrain of postmodern technology theory.

THE HAPPY MUTANT HANDBOOK Mark Frauenfelder, Carla Sinclair, Gareth Branwyn, Will Kreth, eds
The first Boing Boing book. More weird fun per micron than normals will ever imagine.

TRANSIT LOUNGE: WAKE-UP CALLS AND TRAVELERS TALES FROM THE FUTURE Ashley Crawford and Ray Edgar, eds
Compilation of the oddest articles from the Australian cyber-arts magazine 21*C. Introduction by William Gibson.

ESCAPE VELOCITY by Mark Dery
Cyberculture: threat or menace? Round up the usual suspects: Stelarc, Moravec, Pauline, Sirius, Mu, Frauenfelder, Haraway, Orlan, Cronenberg, Dibell, Reznor, Leary, Lanier, Laurel, Barlow, Sobchack, Ross, Milhon, Kelly, Gibson, Cadigan, Shirley, etc etc—Good Lord, there's just no end to them.

ABOUT THE AUTHORS

Despite his relatively small body of work, **Alfred Bester** (1913–1987) was awarded the Nebula Grand Master award, primarily for writing the classic science fiction novels *The Demolished Man* and *The Stars, My Destination*, each combining elements of mystery with the science fiction novel and creating the first gritty, post-modern yet realistic future worlds as backdrops for his stories. His experimental approach to stories and novels helped spark the beginnings of the New Wave of the 1960s. Although he wrote three other novels, including the excellent *Golem¹⁰⁰*, his fame rests on his first two books and a number of excellent short stories, including "Adam and no Eve," Time Is the Traitor," "The Pi Man," and his most popular short story, "Fondly Fahrenheit."

Cordwainer Smith is the pseudonym under which Paul Myron Anthony Linebarger wrote science fiction between 1950 and his death in 1966. All but a handful of Smith's thirty-two published stories and the novel *Nostrilia* are part of his visionary Instrumentality of Mankind series, which he began writing when he was a teenager but which did not see professional publication until the appearance of "Scanners Live in Vain." The Instrumentality stories provide a fragmentary history spanning some fifteen thousand years of human history and galactic colonization and have been widely praised for their imaginative depictions of alien civilizations and sympathetic renderings of individuals adjusting to the rigors of a civilization in which interstellar war, immortality, faster-than-light space travel, suspended animation and telepathic combat are the norm. Smiths' complete science fiction has been collected in the definitive *The Rediscovery of Man: The Complete Short Science Fiction of Cordwainer Smith* and *Nostrilia*. Smith had also published several pseudonymous mainstream novels and a spy thriller *Atomsk*, as well as the psychology text *Psychological Warfare*.

Regarded as one of the most important writers of science fiction in the twentieth century, **Philip K. Dick** (1928–1982) built his reputation on subtly complex tales of intersecting alternate realities. His novel *The Man in the High Castle*, set in a future where Japan and Germany emerged victorious from World War II, won the Hugo Award for best novel in 1963 and is regarded as one of the best alternate history tales in science fiction. *Dr. Bloodmoney* offers a vision of American society in the aftermath of nuclear war. *The Three Stigmata of Palmer Eldritch* and *Ubik*, both set in worlds where time slips and reality shifts are the norm, crystallize the mood of paranoia and often comically chaotic instability that characterizes much of his writing. Several of his best known stories have been successfully adapted for the screen: his novel *Do Androids Dream of Electric Sheep?* was filmed as the blockbuster movie *Blade Runner* in 1982, and his short story appearing in this volume, "We Can Remember It for You Wholesale" was adapted as *Total Recall* in 1990. Revival of interest in Dick's work after his death in 1982 led to the publication of his many mainstream novels, several volumes of his collected letters, and the five volume *Collected Stories of Philip K. Dick.*

James Tiptree, Jr. was the best-known pseudonym of psychologist Alice Sheldon (1915–1987). Not surprisingly, much of the ground-breaking science fiction she began publishing in 1968 is concerned with gender roles and sexual identity. She is the author of two novels, the galaxy-spanning *Up the Walls of the World* and *Brightness Falls from the Air*, a dark meditation on the significance of death. Her short fiction, however, is her most highly-regarded work. She won the Hugo Award for the story appearing in this volume, "The Girl Who Was Plugged In" and both the Hugo and Nebula for "Houston, Houston, Do You Read?" Collections of her stories include *Ten Thousand Light Years from Home, Warm Worlds and Otherwise, Star Songs of an Old Primate, Out of the Everywhere and Other Extraordinary Visions*, and the retrospective *Her Smoke Rose Up Forever.*

Rudy Rucker has been active in all aspects of the cyberspace frontier, from his seminal novels in the subgenre, including *Software* (1982) and *Wetware* (1988), each of which won the Philip K. Dick award for best science fiction novel of that year. Other noted books by him include *Spacetime Donuts, Master of Space and Time*, and *The Hacker and the Ants*. Using his mathematical and computer teaching as springboards, he has also published several nonfiction books on mathematics, infinity, and higher dimensions. He has co-edited anthologies and the book *Mondo 2000: A User's Guide to the New Edge*. Recently he has been busy coding a new architectural game code for the Windows system, currently called Pop Framework. He most recent novels include *Spaceland*, about a Silicon Valley middle manager and his encounter with beings from the fourth dimension, and a

historical novel about the life of the Flemish painter Peter
Bruegel the Elder called *As Above So Below: A Novel of
Peter Bruegel*, both published by Tor Books.

William Gibson began publishing short fiction in 1977, but
his reputation was made with his first novel, *Neuromancer*,
which appeared in 1984 and has since earned the status of
a revolutionary work of contemporary science fiction. The
book, which won the Hugo, Nebula and Philip K. Dick
awards, became the bible of the cyberpunk movement, and
an important breakthrough novel that seeped into cultural
mainstream where the many concepts it explored—cyberspace, virtual reality, the internet, computer crime, artificial
intelligence—were fast making the transition from specula-
tive fancy to irrefutable reality. A fusion of the hardboiled
detective narrative and the cutting-edge science fiction
story, *Neuromancer* and the two follow-up novels with
which it forms a loose trilogy—*Count Zero* and *Mona Lisa
Overdrive*—blazed trails through the hitherto unexplored
frontier of computer technology and microchip-driven tel-
ecommunications. It popularized the concept of "plugging
in" to link the human brain directly with the neural network
of computer systems. The human/machine interface it en-
visioned, though built on traditional science fiction themes,
marked a conceptual shift that turned science fiction's normally outward-looking perspective inward. The complex
and often inscrutable reality it extrapolates is one where
traditional geographic and cultural boundaries have disin-
tegrated and been reshaped by the uses and abuses of computer generated data. The hacker subculture dominates the
world of these novels, and its often criminal members have
the status of outlaw heroes. The novels are also memorable
for their dazzling, kinetic styles, which update the stylistic
experimentation of the New Wave movement with contem-

porary techno-jargon and narrative cuts and splices characteristic of video and computer entertainments. The impact of computer technology has been as inescapable in the rest of Gibson's fiction as it has in the modern world. *The Difference Engine*, which he wrote in collaboration with Bruce Sterling, is a celebrated "steampunk" novel that projects the world that might have been had Charles Babbage's early work on computers taken root in Victorian England. His novels *Virtual Light, Idoru*, and *All Tomorrow's Parties* all share characters and explore a variety of computer-oriented themes, including nanotechnology, computer personality constructs, and "nodal points" or fluxes in the data stream of that are auguries of transformational events in history. Gibson's short fiction has been collected in *Burning Chrome*, which includes "Johnny Mnemonic," the basis for the Robert Longo film of the same name.

The topics of **Greg Bear**'s science fiction have ranged from nanotechnology run amok in the novel *Blood Music*, based on the Hugo and Nebula Award-winning novella in this book, to the transformation of souls into awesome energy fields in the sf-horror hybrid *Psycholone*, and future evolution in *Darwin's Radio*. He is the author of the Songs of Earth and Power heroic diptych, comprised of *The Infinity Concerto* and *The Serpent Mage*, and two collections of short fiction, *The Wind from a Burning Woman* and *Tangents*. Renowned for his hard science fiction epics, Bear has written the trilogy that includes *Legacy, Eon* and *Eternity*, which features a multiplicity of alternate worlds and timelines accessed through the interior of a hollow asteroid. Novels of equally impressive scope include the alien contact story *The Forge of God* and its sequel, *Anvil of Stars*; the nanotechnology opus *Queen of Angels*, and its follow-up *Slant*; and the Nebula Award-winning *Moving Mars*, which chronicles the fifty-year history of Earth's Mars colony and its revolt against the mother planet. Bear has also written *Dinosaur Summer*, a sequel to Sir Arthur Conan Coyle's *The Lost World*, and *Foundation and Chaos*, which builds on the concepts of Isaac Asimov's *Foundation Trilogy*.

Although **Lewis Shiner** entered the fiction world with the burgeoning cyberpunk movement of the early 1980s, he prefers not to be bound by the tropes of any one literary genre or movement, choosing instead to just write fiction that transcends these limitations. When he does write science fiction or fantasy, as in the novels *Frontera, Deserted Cities of the Heart*, and *Glimpses*, he combined realistic extrapolations of the future with sparse prose that acknowledges elements of mystery and literary fiction as well. He is also an accomplished short story writer, with more than thirty-five stories published in all fiction areas, from children's books to fantasy to horror. He has also written several non-fiction articles, including an appreciation of James P. Blaylock, and articles for *The New York Review of Science Fiction*, and edited the anthology *When the Music's Over*.

He's been called "cyberpunk's Patient Zero" by such luminaries as William Gibson, and **John Shirley** has spent most of his life living up to that sobriquet. A former punk rock singer and songwriter, he still keeps his hand in the music business, supplying bands such as Blue Oyster Cult with material for their most recent albums. Present during the beginnings and rise of the cyberpunk movement in the 80s, he transformed a decade of living on the edge into such cutting, gritty novels as *Transmaniacon, City Come a-Walkin'*, and *The Brigade*. Having never met a genre he couldn't bring howling to the ground, he has written several horror novels, including *In Darkness Waiting* and *Wetbones*.

His collection *Black Butterflies* garnered both the Bram Stoker Award and the International Fantasy Award for a single author collection. In 1996 he returned to science fiction with the release of his novel *Silicon Embrace*. He has also made a name for himself in scriptwriting, authoring several drafts of *The Crow* as well as episodes of the short-lived television series *VR5* and the more popular *Poltergeist: The Series* and *Star Trek: Deep Space Nine*. While his latest works have been more in the vein of dark fantasy and horror, with the published novellas *The View from Hell* and *Her Hunger*, it's a safe bet that no matter what comes next, it will more fiction that is not to be missed.

Michael Swanwick emerged as one of the stunning new talents of science fiction in the 1980s initially through the publication of his richly allusive, multilayered short stories which show the influence of literary postmodernism as much as the traditions of fantasy and science fiction. The best of his short stories have been collected in *Gravity's Angels* and *Tales of Old Earth*, which includes his Hugo Award-winning "The Very Pulse of the Machine." His work as a novelist is equally unconventional, ranging in its approaches from cyberpunk to heroic fantasy and focused on the interplay of new science and old social structures in their shaping of a civilization and the individual. His first novel, *In the Drift*, is set in a postapocalyptic America where nuclear catastrophe creates a fragmented society struggling to stabilize. *Vacuum Flowers, Griffin's Egg* and the Nebula Award-winning *Stations of the Tide* all are explorations of the impact of cataclysmic natural disasters and sociopolitical events on human societies established on alien worlds that have grown estranged from the mother planet's influence. Swanwick has also written *Jack Faust*, a modern variation on the Faust theme, and *The Iron Dragon's Daughter*, an epic high-tech fantasy. He is the author of several provocative and controversial essays on the craft of fantasy and science fiction, several of which have been collected in *A Geography of Unknown Lands* and *The Postmodern Archipelago*. He is also a recipient of the Theodore Sturgeon Memorial Award.

Bruce Sterling began publishing science fiction in 1976, and his first novel, the picaresque extraplanetary adventure *Involution Ocean*, was published the following year. Shortly after, he made his mark with a series of visionary short stories about bioengineering and prosthetic transformation set in his Shaper/Mechanist universe, which culminated in the novel *Schismatrix*. With the publication of *Islands in the Net* in 1988, Sterling came to be regarded as one of the most provoctive writers in the cyberpunk medium, and confirmed his roles as its leading prophet with his groundbreaking *Mirrorshades* anthology. His novels, which frequently focus on the cultural dislocation and social alienation that has come with the information age and computer revolution include *Heavy Weather, Holy Fire*, and the satirical *Distraction*. His short fiction has been collected in *Crystal Express, Globalhead*, and *A Good Old-Fashioned Future*.

Paul J. McAuley has a Ph.D in Botany and worked as a researcher in biology at various universities, including Oxford and UCLA. For six years he lectured on botany at St. Andrews University. At age 20, his first completed short story was accepted by the American magazine *Worlds of If*, but the magazine went out of business before publishing it, making him feel that he should concentrate on an academic career instead. He began writing again after a stint living in Los Angeles, and has since become a full-time writer. His first novel, *Four Hundred Billion Stars*, won the Philip K.

Dick Memorial Award, and *Fairyland* won the 1995 Arthur C. Clarke Award for best SF novel published in Britain and the 1996 John W. Campbell Award for best novel. In 1995, his short story "The Temptation of Dr Stein" won the British Fantasy Award, and his 1996 novel *Pasquale's Angel* won the Sidewise Award for Best Long Form Alternate History fiction. As well as short stories and novels, He also writes a regular review column for the British SF magazine *Interzone*, and contributes reviews to *Foundation*.